Through her marriage to Reggie Kray, Roberta Kray has a unique and authentic insight into London's East End. Roberta met Reggie in early 1996 and they married the following year; they were together until Reggie's death in 2000. Roberta is the author of many previous bestsellers including *No Mercy*, *Exposed*, *Survivor* and *Stolen*.

ROBERTA
KRAY
HUNTED

SPHERE

SPHERE

First published in Great Britain in 2022 by Sphere

1 3 5 7 9 10 8 6 4 2

A CIP catalogue record for this book
is available from the British Library.

ISBN 978-0-7515-7684-9

Typeset in Garamond by M Rules
Printed and bound in Great Britain by
Clays Ltd, Elcograf S.p.A.

Papers used by Sphere are from well-managed forests
and other responsible sources.

MIX
Paper from
responsible sources
FSC® C104740

Sphere
An imprint of
Little, Brown Book Group
Carmelite House
50 Victoria Embankment
London EC4Y 0DZ

An Hachette UK Company
www.hachette.co.uk

www.littlebrown.co.uk

HUNTED

PROLOGUE

1983

She shinned up the drainpipe with effortless grace, alternating her hands and feet in quick succession, keeping her gaze fixed firmly on her destination. The ascent was fast and agile, as smooth as a cat's. On this moonless night she was no more than a fleeting shadow, something dark, a furtive movement that might only be caught out of the corner of an eye. But one mistake, one false move and the consequences would be dire: she would hurtle to the ground, and it would greet her with the same lack of mercy it reserved for any breakable object.

When she reached the second-floor window she skilfully manoeuvred herself on to the sill, jemmied the old wooden frame and gently released the catch. Quickly she lifted the lower half of the window, slithered through the gap, stood up and listened for any sound in the house. Silence. She quietly closed the window again, just in case, God forbid, it caught the attention of a passing plod out on his rounds.

The large, detached properties in this part of Hampstead were regularly patrolled by the law just in case any light-fingered

1

lowlifes took it into their heads to try and plunder the riches that lay within. For her this danger only added to the thrill. The threat of being caught ignited nervous sparks that both scared and energised her.

She took the torch from her belt, switched it on and swept the light across the room, keeping the beam aimed low. It was a bedroom, but not the one she wanted. A week's surveillance had revealed to her that the master bedroom was directly below. The windows of that room, like all the others on the ground and first floors, were alarmed, but perhaps in the mistaken belief that the upper floors were inaccessible, the owners hadn't bothered securing them. Or perhaps they just hadn't wanted to spend the extra money. A false economy, as it turned out.

She padded out on to the landing and paused again before softly descending the stairs. She knew, courtesy of the newspaper gossip columns, that Gerald and Fiona Myers were attending a charity gala in the West End tonight. It was unlikely they'd be back much before midnight, but she wasn't going to take any chances.

The master bedroom was large and plush with a deep-pile carpet, heavy velvet curtains, a bank of wardrobes, a chest of drawers and a dressing table. It smelled of expensive perfume. The first thing she did was to cross to the window and check that everything was quiet outside. Once she'd established that her presence was still undetected, she focused her attention on the spoils.

The dressing table was her first port of call. She was not a ransacker, not the type of burglar to turn things upside down. Although she worked at speed, she created as little disturbance as possible. Everything she picked up, she put back in exactly the same place – unless she chose to keep it. All neat and tidy. The longer it took them to realise they'd been robbed, the better. And anyway, it offended her sensibilities to make a mess.

Her fine, black cotton gloves left no prints behind as she sorted through the jewellery box. Rings, necklaces, bracelets, brooches and earrings were all slipped into the pouch that hung from her waist. She gathered them eagerly, her eye for glitter as keen as a jackdaw's. Once the box was exhausted, she opened and closed drawers, searching for other valuable items. A couple of diamond-encrusted watches were rapidly added to her haul.

In one of the wardrobes, she found a row of fur coats – mink and sable – and made a fast, mental calculation of what they were worth. She wasn't going to take them, though. For one, she didn't want to be haunted by the ghosts of so many dead animals, and for two, it was damn nigh impossible to slide elegantly down a drainpipe with half a ton of fur on your back. She could have thrown them, of course, but she'd still have had to carry them down the road.

She closed the door and moved on to the next wardrobe, clearly the preserve of Mr Myers, from where she took gold cuff-links, tie pins and a Breitling watch from a row of cubbyholes at the top. Quickly she rifled through the pockets of the Savile Row suits but didn't come across any cash.

Once she'd completed her search of the bedroom, she set off back upstairs. If her dad had been here, he'd have gone in the opposite direction, down to the floor below, which might have paintings, silver or porcelain. Never look a gift horse in the mouth, he would have said. But she preferred to stick to her own methods. Jewellery was easy to carry and easy to fence – and if you had to run, it wasn't so heavy that it would weigh you down.

She had only climbed a couple of stairs when she heard a ting, slight but distinct, coming from the ground floor. Like the sound of a phone being put down. Immediately she stopped dead, her pulse starting to race. She shut off the torch. There was someone else here. She strained her ears, but everything was

3

silent again. Still she didn't move. If she had heard them, they might hear her too.

The front of the house had been in darkness when she'd arrived, the only light coming from the streetlamps. She hadn't checked the rear. And that, she was beginning to think, could have been a big mistake. What if Mr and Mrs Myers hadn't gone out after all? Perhaps they had been sitting in one of the back rooms while she was breaking in. Or, looking on the brighter side, maybe she wasn't the only cat on the premises. The noise she had heard might not have been a phone at all but just the sound of a pet carelessly roaming through its territory.

She waited, holding her breath. Ten seconds passed and then twenty. Nothing. Relief was gradually seeping into her when suddenly her worst fears were confirmed. A door opened, a throat was cleared and footsteps moved rapidly across the wood floor hallway. A man, she thought, from the heavy tread. She tensed, in two minds whether to flee upstairs or hold her ground. Before she could make the decision, the front door opened and closed and everything was quiet again.

Quiet but not naturally so. Something felt wrong. The departing man had left in his wake a singular atmosphere, an almost eerie sense of emptiness that made the hairs on the back of her neck stand on end. Had it been Mr Myers? She didn't think so. He'd have put on the light instead of walking in the dark.

She finally shifted, returned to the landing and peered over the banister. *Up*, not down, an inner voice urged. But although all her instincts were telling her to scarper, to get out as fast as she could, something drew her towards that ground-floor room. A minute, that's all it would take, to slip down there and take a look.

Before caution could get the better of her, she had switched on the torch again and was descending the stairs. She rounded the corner, moving quickly and quietly. There was a large garden room at the rear and, just before it, a room with its door ajar. Was this where the man had come from? She listened for a while but heard nothing. An odd, slightly acrid smell hung in the air. Carefully she nudged the door open and stepped inside.

From the light of the torch, she could see that she was in an office or study. She swept the beam across the room. There was a desk in disarray and a couple of filing cabinets with their drawers pulled out. Papers lay all over the floor. Myers was either the untidiest person in the world or she wasn't the only robber who had found their way into the house tonight. She sucked in a breath, grateful that her fellow intruder hadn't gone upstairs. It could have resulted in a somewhat awkward confrontation.

She took a few more steps, moving the light across the walls, until the beam illuminated a picture that had been swung back to reveal an open safe. Apart from a few stacked-up folders and several brown envelopes, it appeared to be empty. This was probably where the really good stuff had been stored, the most valuable jewellery and a decent wad of cash. Men like Gerald Myers always kept a big stash in reserve, some readies to fall back on in case of emergencies.

As she edged around the desk to take a closer look, her foot made contact with something on the floor. She flicked the beam down, gave out a yelp, slapped a hand to her mouth and instantly froze. Shock ran through her, draining the colour from her face. A man was lying sprawled on his back with his head twisted to one side. There was a hole in his chest from a fatal gunshot. His lips were twisted and his teeth bared. A pair of glassy eyes stared blindly up at her.

'Jesus,' she said hoarsely.

Panic swept over her. She had never seen a dead body before, never mind one that had met its end so violently. Horror seeped into her bones. She felt simultaneously cold and clammy and sick. Was it Gerald Myers? She thought so, thought it must be. She had only seen his picture in the paper, but it was enough for the features to seem familiar.

Hysteria was rising in her – she didn't want to look at him, couldn't stop looking at him – and she had to fight to keep herself together. A surge of adrenaline finally propelled her into action. She dropped her hand from her mouth and lurched back, trying to put some distance between her and the corpse. Her knees were shaking, her legs threatening to buckle.

She had to get out of the house. There was nothing she could do for Myers other than call the law anonymously once she was a safe distance away. She didn't have to go back upstairs. She didn't have to slide down any drainpipes. The front door would be fine. She could leave the same way the killer had. These thoughts, all perfectly logical, jumped into her head, but her body wouldn't respond. Her central nervous system refused to connect with her legs. She was rooted to the spot again.

'Come on,' she muttered. 'What the hell are you doing?'

It took pure determination, an effort of will, to get her limbs moving. Her pulse was racing as she backed out of the office and stumbled along the hall. She needed fresh air. She needed to get away from death and all its horror. One foot in front of the other, one step at a time. Salvation was in sight when disaster struck. She heard the crunch of car tyres on gravel and saw the flashing blue lights through the narrow windows flanking the front door.

Christ, what now? Instantly she could see how it would look: a burglar in the house, a dead man in the study. They would put two and two together and she'd be spending the next twenty years behind bars. Her first instinct was to run, to head for the stairs, but it was pointless. She couldn't leave through the window and hiding would only add to the appearance of guilt. Instead, she reversed into the study, switched on the light, and threw the jewellery and the jemmy on the floor, hoping it would look like they'd been accidentally dropped in the killer's hurry to leave. She staggered back into the hall as fast as her legs would allow and was standing in the shadows when the law walked in.

'Thank God you're here,' she said, her voice an octave higher than it usually was. 'It's this way. Something terrible has happened. There's been a murder.'

1

1984

Cara Kendall was escorted off the premises of HMP Leaside at eleven o'clock on Thursday morning 8 November. She walked a little way from the gates and stood on the pavement with a carrier bag hanging from her right hand. The day was grey, gloomy, with an overcast sky and rain in the air. She hunched her shoulders, shivering in her thin denim jacket. Nothing felt quite like it should. She was finally free after eighteen long months, but instead of the anticipated joy and relief, she felt only a curious flatness.

She frowned. Perhaps it was natural, she told herself, a normal reaction to having to face the world again after being behind bars. You couldn't just expect to slot back in and carry on from where it had all stopped. It would take some adjustment, a realignment, before normality could be resumed.

She looked up and down the street, hoping for a friendly face, but all she saw were strangers. If there was one thing that could be said for Jimmy, it was that he was reliably unreliable. She wasn't surprised that he hadn't shown up, but she was disappointed. What was wrong with the bloke? Why say you're going to do something if you're not going to bother? She'd hardly been expecting fireworks and a fanfare, but a lift would have been welcome.

Well, she wasn't going to wait. If he wasn't here already, he wasn't coming. He'd let her down and there was nothing new about that. He was probably still in his pit, snoring like a pig while he slept off a midweek bender. For Jimmy Lovell promises were like IOUs, easily given but rarely honoured.

Although they were no longer a couple – he'd taken up with some dumb redhead called Rochelle only weeks into her sentence – they had stayed in touch with occasional visits and letters. Even before she'd gone inside, their relationship had been on the rocks, so his infidelity hadn't come as any great shock. Jimmy wasn't the sort to let the grass grow under his feet. For all his faults, she'd still been looking forward to seeing him. She didn't want him back, but she did want some company. And perhaps she'd also been hoping to regain a little of her pride – which was why she'd made an extra effort with her appearance just to show the cheating sod what he'd be missing.

What a waste of time that had been. She ran her fingers through her cropped fair hair and rolled her artfully made-up eyes at her own stupidity. She should have guessed that he'd be a no-show. She had hardly been his priority when she'd been his girlfriend, and now they were separated she was even lower down his list of concerns.

'I'll be there, babe,' he'd said last week in the visiting room, leaning forward and giving her that rakish grin. 'You've got my word on it.'

Cara started walking towards the bus stop. The first day of the rest of her life. Wasn't that how the cliché went? She was twenty-four, young and healthy, with the world at her feet. And if being in the slammer had taught her anything, it was that she could take care of herself. She didn't need a man to run her life or tell her what to do. From now on the only person she was going to rely on was Cara Kendall.

Freedom. She breathed in deeply, inhaling the diesel-laden air. Now *that* was the smell of London. For the first time she felt a flicker of excitement. Tonight, she'd be sleeping in her own bed, and tomorrow she could get up at whatever time she liked and do whatever she wanted to do – so long as she stayed out of trouble. Going back inside was definitely not on the agenda.

She should have listened to her dad: 'Don't be a mug, love. It only ever ends badly.' But it was too late for regrets. And, of course, he'd never followed his own advice. If he had, he'd still be alive now. It was two years since he'd slipped from the roof of a house in Mayfair and been impaled on the spiked railings below. She half closed her eyes and shuddered. It had been dark, icy, dangerous. Why had he even attempted the break-in? But she knew the answer to that: Richard Kendall might have been less agile, less limber, than in his glory days, but he'd never been able to resist a challenge.

'You fool,' she muttered.

Cara had thought about him a lot while she'd been inside. He hadn't been the best of fathers, far from it, but he'd been *her* father, and it was still hard to accept that he was gone. And yes, he'd been way down the scale in the morality stakes – a thief, a gambler, a womaniser – but he'd also been the kindest, funniest person she'd ever known. And there was something else she knew for a fact: he'd have been standing outside the prison gates today had circumstances permitted it.

She hadn't seen his body after he'd died, hadn't wanted to, but now a part of her regretted it. Perhaps it would have been the start of coming to terms. Sometimes she imagined that he wasn't dead at all, that it was just a case of mistaken identity, a fateful error which he'd chosen to go along with. Always in debt to one casino or another, it would have been the perfect opportunity for him to disappear and begin a new life somewhere else.

There were, unfortunately, a couple of obstacles to this fantasy, one of them being that her mother had gone to the mortuary to identify him – despite being separated for years, they had never divorced – the other that his face was known to half the cops at West End Central. So, it was a ludicrous fantasy, but still she clung on to it, a tiny glimmer of hope being better than none.

Just as she reached the bus stop, Cara heard a vehicle slowing behind her and turned her head, sure that it was Jimmy. Her lips began to widen. Better late than never, she thought, whilst simultaneously trying to bring to mind some cutting yet witty comment about him being late for his own funeral. But her smile quickly faded. It was a car rather than a van. The driver was wearing a baseball cap and sunglasses, and he wasn't Jimmy. He stared hard at her before he put his foot on the gas and accelerated away. The episode, quickly over, left her flustered.

She gazed after the black BMW, watching it disappear into the distance. What had that been about? Just a bloke playing silly buggers, or maybe he'd mistaken her for someone else. But her instincts told her otherwise. Her instincts told her that what had just happened had been a deliberate act of intimidation, that the man had been trying to scare her. Not a good start to her first day of freedom.

Cara's heart started to pump. She'd done her time and the slate, theoretically, had been wiped clean, but theories weren't facts and people bore grudges. The family of Gerald Myers still hadn't got any answers. Whoever had killed him had got away scot-free. Maybe they reckoned she'd got off lightly too, that she knew more than she had ever told.

And then there was the law. They hadn't been convinced by her story and had tried their very best to pin an accessory to murder charge on her. That two people, completely independent of each other, had chosen to burgle the same house on the same night was a coincidence too far. *Their* take on it was that the two of them had broken in together, separated – her going upstairs, him downstairs – and that her accomplice had murdered Gerald Myers after forcing him to open the safe.

The memory of those long, relentless hours in the interview room would always be in her head, a reminder of how close she'd come to being banged up for years. 'If we were working together, why wouldn't we have left together?' she'd asked. But DI Steadman had just curled his sceptical upper lip and replied, 'Because he double-crossed you, love, took the cash and the diamonds, and scarpered.'

'If that was the case, I'd be telling you his name, right here, right now. Why would I protect him?'

'I'm sure you have your reasons. About half a million of them, I should think. Your pal got away with quite a haul.'

'There was no pal. I'm not denying that I broke in, but I was on my own. I didn't even hear the gunshot,' she'd insisted. 'Gerald Myers must have been dead before I got in the house.'

'So you keep on saying.'

'Because it's the truth.'

And on it had gone, hour after hour, with her protesting her innocence and him trying to prove otherwise. Her story, she had to admit, had sounded thin to her own ears, but she'd stuck to it. Most of it was true, and the truth was easy to remember. Her only deviation was to deny having taken any of the jewellery from upstairs, claiming instead that she'd heard a noise from the ground floor shortly after climbing through the window and crept partway down the stairs to investigate.

'That's when I heard him leave. I couldn't see him, but I heard him. He went out of the front door.'

'And then you went down to the study?'

'Yes.'

'Why did you do that?'

'Because something felt wrong. I thought the house was empty, but it wasn't and . . .' She'd shrugged, struggling to find the words to explain it. 'That's when I found Mr Myers.'

'And the jewellery on the floor? The jewellery from the bedroom upstairs?'

'The man must have dropped it.'

'That was careless of him.'

In the end, unable to prove a connection to the killer, Steadman had only done her for breaking and entering, but that hadn't stopped the judge from giving her three years. She'd served half the sentence and that had been long enough. It had been a result, she supposed, bearing in mind how things could have panned out.

Cara sighed and gazed along the street towards the last point she had seen the black BMW. She hoped it was just paranoia that was churning her guts. Shifting from one foot to the other, she found she couldn't stand still. Her mouth was suddenly dry. She wasn't looking for trouble, but what if it was looking for her?

2

The bus eventually arrived, and Cara got on, climbing up the steps to the top deck. She made her way along the aisle to an empty front seat and sat down. As a kid this was always the place she'd loved most, high above the hustle and bustle, like being on top of the world. Now she used it as a vantage point to gaze down on the streets of London, checking out what might have changed while she'd been away – not much, by the looks of it – and whether there was any sign of the BMW. She was probably making something out of nothing. But still, she felt uneasy.

Eighteen long months she'd been absent from the outside world, during which the IRA had put a bomb under the Tories, Princess Diana had given birth to her second son, Torvill and Dean had skated their way to Olympic gold and the coal miners had gone on strike. Events had happened. Life had moved on. But not for her. She was back to where she'd started, on her way home to the Mansfield estate. The place had only one thing to recommend it: was marginally better than HMP Leaside. Jimmy had claimed he'd been keeping an eye on the flat, checking the mail and making sure she didn't get any squatters in her absence, but whether this was true was questionable.

She frowned as Jimmy entered her head again, still annoyed by his failure to pick her up. He'd be full of excuses like he always was, a hundred and one reasons why he couldn't get off his backside, jump in the van and travel ten miles down the road. At the very least he owed her a drink, and she'd be straight round to claim it once she'd had a long hot shower and sloughed off the stench of prison.

Twenty minutes later the bus drew up outside Kellston station. She got off and started walking along the high street. Almost immediately it began to rain. She turned up the collar of her jacket, cursed and ducked into the Spar. Here she picked up some basic provisions – coffee, milk, bread, butter, ham, eggs – before paying at the till with the small amount of money she'd been given on leaving jail. Even this simple act, the exchange of cash for goods, felt alien to her.

It was still raining when she left the shop. She walked at a quick pace, sloshing through the puddles with the two carrier bags swinging against her legs. There was nothing unusual about rain in November, but it was just her luck that the heavens had opened the minute she'd got off the bus. Already her feet were squelching in her trainers. She felt like a drowned rat.

'Damn you, Jimmy,' she muttered.

Cara took a right into Mansfield Road and a minute later was passing through the gates to the estate. It looked the same as it always had, grey and dreary, a concrete monstrosity. Apart from a few spindly trees, it was devoid of any green. Sodden litter gathered in the gutters, and graffiti covered the lower parts of the buildings. The three high-rise towers rose up towards the sky, a blot on the landscape and visible from miles away. Two of the towers, Haslow House and Carlton House, stood next to each other, while the third – where Jimmy lived – was set apart. Temple Tower, that was called, or at least it had been when she'd gone away. The council had changed its name twice in the last twelve years.

With the rain having driven most people indoors, the estate was pretty much deserted. A few youths were lurking in the entranceways to the shadowy passages that linked the front and back of the towers, pushing their dope and their pills and whatever else the locals needed to get them through the day. The whole estate was a dumping ground, a final refuge for the poor and the desperate and the forgotten.

As she hurried along the path, she raised her gaze and peered up at the tenth floor of Haslow House, four windows from the right, but couldn't see anything to cause her concern. The flat had been her dad's for almost twenty years, and because she'd lived there on and off since childhood, he'd managed to get her on the tenancy when she was eighteen. She was grateful for this now. The Mansfield might be a dump, but at least she still had a roof over her head.

Cara shook herself like a dog as she entered the foyer, shaking off the rain. She found a lift that was working, stepped inside, wrinkled her nose at the smell and quickly pressed the button for the tenth floor. The lift juddered as it rose, making the kind of noises that threatened imminent breakdown. The very thought of it brought her out in a cold sweat. She'd had enough of confined spaces.

When the lift reached its destination and the metal doors slid open, she heaved a sigh of relief, leapt out on to the landing and made her way along the corridor. She could hear the sound of a radio floating through the walls, George Michael singing 'Careless Whisper'. When she reached her flat, she fumbled in her pocket for the key, inserted it in the lock and went inside.

The second she crossed the threshold, Cara sensed that something was wrong. She put down the carrier bags and frowned. There was someone else here; she was sure of it. She wasn't alone.

'Jimmy? Jimmy, is that you?'

As soon as she'd spoken, she wished she hadn't. If she had uninvited guests, she'd just, rather stupidly, announced her presence to them.

3

Cara held her breath, in two minds as to whether to beat a hasty retreat. Squatters, burglars, the law? Whoever it was, they shouldn't be in her home. And then there was the man in the black BMW: he could easily have got here before her, although why he should want to was another matter altogether. She felt a rush of anxiety and her heart started to thump, but before she could decide what to do next there was movement, the sound of footsteps and a moment later a stranger appeared at the living-room door.

'Who the hell are you?' he said, before she could get the very same words out of her own mouth. 'What are you doing in my flat?'

Cara stared back at him. He was slight, in his early thirties with light brown hair down to his collar. Dressed in jeans and a T-shirt, there was nothing especially threatening about him – his expression was more startled than aggressive – other than the fact he was questioning her right to be here. For a couple of surreal seconds, she wondered if maybe she was in the wrong flat. Was it possible that her key fitted another lock in the same corridor? But then she realised this was nonsense. Of course this was her flat. She could see past him into the living room, to the moss-green walls and her dad's old sofa.

'*Your* flat? I think you'll find its mine. What the hell are *you* doing here?'

The frown that had appeared between his grey eyes deepened and then suddenly cleared. He smiled, showing a row of straight white teeth. 'Oh, you're not Cara Kendall, are you?'

She nodded without returning the smile. 'Yeah, I'm Cara.'

'Jimmy said you wouldn't be back until the new year.'

'What's Jimmy got to do with all this?' But already her stomach was sinking. Anything to do with Jimmy was usually bad news.

'He rented the flat to me for six months.'

Cara's mouth fell open. 'He did what?'

'Ah, I take it he didn't run it past you first. He said he had. He told me you'd agreed.'

As it happened, Jimmy had run the idea past her when she'd first gone inside, and she'd said absolutely not. The idea of a stranger being in her home, touching her things and using her bathroom, revolted her, which was ironic, she supposed, bearing in mind her own cavalier attitude towards other people's property. Anyway, with the money her dad had left she'd had enough in her bank account to cover the rent while she was banged up. 'I told him I didn't want to let it out.'

'Looks like he lied to us both, then.'

'The little shit,' she muttered. 'He had no right.'

'So where do we go from here? I'm Will, by the way, Will Lytton.'

Cara couldn't believe this was happening. If Jimmy had been around, she'd have happily strangled him. She picked up the

20

bags, walked past Lytton, strode through the living room, and went into the kitchen. It was time to be assertive. 'Well,' she said, 'I'm sorry, but you're going to have to leave. Jimmy didn't have permission to let the place to you. And now I'm back so . . .'

Lytton leaned against the doorframe as she unpacked the groceries. 'And go where?'

'I don't know. Haven't you got any family, mates?'

'I paid up front,' he said. 'Six months in advance. I paid until the end of January.'

Cara pulled a face. 'You'll have to sort that out with Jimmy.'

'I think it's up to you to sort it out.'

'And how do you figure that out?'

Lytton shrugged. 'It's your flat.'

'Exactly, and I want it back.'

'So take it up with Jimmy. He's the one who's caused this mess, not me.'

Cara emptied the Spar carrier bag, put the bread on the counter, threw the other provisions into the fridge and slammed the door. 'I'll do that,' she said, pushing past him into the living room. She snatched up the phone and punched in the number. It rang and rang, but Jimmy didn't answer. Big surprise. No wonder he'd been a no show today; he was too much of a coward to come clean to her face. Jimmy's maths had never been all that. He probably hadn't realised, until it was too late, that Lytton wouldn't be gone before she got out of the slammer.

'No reply,' she said, hanging up. She knew Jimmy would be avoiding her, that he'd try and lie low until she'd calmed down a bit, but hell would freeze over before that happened. He'd taken six months' rent off Lytton while *she* had been paying the council. He was a thieving toerag.

'How do you even know Jimmy?' she asked.

'I don't, not really. I met him in the Fox. We got talking and

21

I mentioned I was after somewhere to live. He said he might be able to help and …' Lytton gave another shrug. 'He brought me to look at this place, said it belonged to a friend of his who was travelling.'

Cara gave a snort.

Lytton glanced back towards the kitchen, his eyes alighting on the carrier bag she had brought out of prison with her. 'I guess you travel light, huh?'

'When was the last time you saw him?' she said, ignoring the comment.

'A while ago. Three weeks, four? I bumped into him in the pub. He asked if there was any mail for you, but that was about the sum of the conversation.'

Cara scowled. So Jimmy hadn't even been round to check up on the flat, to make sure it wasn't being trashed or used as a drugs den. Typical. She made a quick survey of the living room and was almost disappointed to find that it was perfectly clean and tidy. Even the carpet had been hoovered. If she'd been hoping to evict Lytton based on his levels of hygiene she was out of luck. There was something missing, though. 'Where's the photo of my dad?'

'In the cabinet,' Lytton said. 'Sorry, but it's kind of odd living with a picture of a total stranger.'

Cara opened the cabinet, took out the photo in its gilt frame and placed it back in its usual position on the shelf above the table. She felt marginally better after she'd done it, as if she'd gone some way towards re-establishing her territory. She stared at his picture – it was the first familiar face she'd seen since they'd unlocked the gates of HMP Leaside – and wondered what *he'd* have done if he'd got home to find some random bloke occupying the flat.

'Would you like a coffee?' Lytton said. 'It's the real stuff, not instant. I've just made a pot.'

Cara couldn't think of much she wanted more than a strong cup of coffee – well, apart from a stiff Scotch – but this wasn't the time to be fraternising with the enemy. 'No thanks. Look, you can't stay here. It's not on. This is my flat and I want it back.'

'I understand that, but I've got nowhere else to go until the end of January. Like I said, I paid for six months.'

Cara said reluctantly: 'So what if I give you your money back? I mean, for the remaining time.' She didn't fancy her chances of recovering the cash from Jimmy, but if it was the only way to get rid of Lytton . . .

'It's not just the money. I haven't got time to look for another place. I've got essays to write.'

'You're a student?'

'A mature student,' he said, and then added with a wry smile, 'Obviously. I'm doing a history degree.'

'Aren't there halls you could move into?'

'No.'

'It's not even legal to sublet,' she said, trying a new tactic. 'You're not here *legally*. If I went to the council—'

'If you went to the council, you'd be in as much trouble as me. They wouldn't believe that you knew nothing about Jimmy subletting the place. Odds are they'd chuck us both out.'

Cara wasn't sure if this was true or not, but she certainly didn't want the council on her back. 'This is ridiculous.'

'Isn't there anywhere *you* could stay until January?'

'What? Me? Why should I? This is my flat, for God's sake!'

'Well, strictly speaking, it's mine at the moment.'

Cara glared at him. She opened her mouth to retort, but smartly closed it again. Arguing would get her nowhere – he'd dug in his heels and wasn't going to shift – so she might as well save her breath. She strode out of the flat, fuming.

4

Cara stormed along the corridor, went down in the lift to the ground floor, pushed through the foyer doors and set off across the estate towards Temple Tower. Bloody Jimmy! This was all his fault. All she'd wanted was a hot shower and a change of clothes and instead she'd come home to find a student cuckoo in the nest. She muttered under her breath as she walked, shaking her head in disbelief.

After a while she broke into a jog, partly to keep warm – she was still wet from earlier – but mainly because she couldn't wait to get her hands around Jimmy Lovell's neck. How could he do this to her? She'd made her feelings clear, crystal clear, when he'd come to visit her, but he hadn't taken a blind bit of notice. That was Jimmy all over. He could never resist the temptation of making a few quid on the side.

The rain had eased off into a drizzle, but the sky was still low and grey. She glanced up, hoping that she'd make it to the tower before the next downpour. At this rate she'd end up with a dose of pneumonia on top of everything else. And what was the betting that Jimmy wouldn't even be in? No, he wouldn't be so stupid as to stay in his flat. He'd have done a runner as soon as he heard the phone ringing, or probably well before. Which begged the question of why she was even bothering to do this. But she had to start somewhere. Once she was sure he was out, she'd check all his regular haunts until she tracked the weasel down.

Temple Tower was almost identical to Carlton and Haslow – same structure, same litter, same graffiti – but it had a different atmosphere to it. She always felt apprehensive when she came here, as though she was entering enemy territory. Her eyes quickly scanned the surrounding area, alert to would-be muggers or any other dangers. A woman on her own was fair game to some scumbags.

Slowing to a walk as she approached the main door, Cara noticed a group of dubious-looking lads loitering in the foyer. At best, they'd feel obliged to make a few suggestive comments, at worst to try and feel her up. She veered off to the right to avoid them, choosing to take the external staircase instead. Jimmy's flat was on the third floor, so it wasn't too much of a hardship to forego the lift.

She bounded up the concrete steps, taking them two at a time as she tried to prepare herself for both confrontation and disappointment. When she reached the right landing, she stopped, took a moment to catch her breath and then marched along the corridor. Jimmy's door had peeling blue paint and a bell that didn't work. Before she knocked, she leaned the side of her face against the door and listened. Nothing.

She rapped three times and waited. Still nothing. Immediately she crouched down, opened the letterbox and peered into the hall. There was no sign of life, but that didn't mean he wasn't hiding in the living room.

'Jimmy!' she called out. 'I know you're there. Come on. Answer the door. I'm not going anywhere until you do.'

Cara had the feeling she was talking to herself but wasn't ready to give up quite yet. The thought of having to traipse all over Kellston filled her with gloom. It could be hours before she found him. 'Don't mess about. I'll wait here all damn day if I have to.'

But Jimmy, if he was inside, wasn't persuaded by idle threats. There was no movement, no indication that he was there. She stayed crouched for a while, listening closely, straining her ears to catch the slightest sound. Then, slowly, she pulled herself upright again. Four more raps on the door. 'Jimmy!'

Cara rattled the door handle in frustration. She didn't expect the door to be unlocked, but to her surprise it was. A big grin spread across her face. The silly bugger had either forgotten to lock it when he left or not bothered to lock it when he came back. Either way she now had access to the flat. If he wasn't in, she could make herself a coffee, warm up and wait for him in relative comfort.

She quickly went inside and closed the door behind her. 'Jimmy?' There was no response. Perhaps he was still tucked up in bed. When he'd had a skinful, that man could sleep through Armageddon. She walked along the hallway and tried the bedroom first, putting her head around the door to see if he was there. The bed was empty, the rumpled covers pulled back. Pausing, she remembered all the nights she'd lain there beside him, convinced they'd be together for ever, sure that nothing would ever come between them. It had taken her longer than it should to figure out the obvious: the nearest Jimmy Lovell ever came to fidelity was drinking in the Fox every Saturday night.

Cara retraced her steps and went into the living room. The place was always untidy, always littered with beer cans, ashtrays and takeaway cartons from the Chinese. Today was no different. She sniffed and frowned. It smelled of sweaty bloke and stale tobacco and something else she couldn't quite identify. Once upon a time she'd have cleared up, sweeping the debris into a bin bag and running the hoover over the carpet, but how he chose to live wasn't her business any more. She was no longer his girlfriend, and she certainly wasn't his skivvy.

Desperate for that coffee, she crossed the room and pushed open the door to the kitchen. What she saw stopped her in her tracks. Jimmy was lying sprawled face down on the lino, one arm stretched out, the other by his side. For a few crazy seconds, she thought it was some stupid game, that he was just pretending, playing possum, that if she poked him with the toe of her shoe he'd grunt and laugh and eventually get to his feet again.

But gradually the truth dawned. She saw the blood in his hair, the stillness of his body. Her eyes widened with horror. Lurching forward, she dropped to her knees, took hold of his shoulder, and rolled him partly towards her. His face was battered, his eyes closed. She grabbed his wrist. 'Jimmy?' His skin was cold to her touch and she knew he was dead. There was nothing she could do, no help she could give. A cry rose in her throat and froze on her lips. Racked by shock and pain, she slipped her hand down into his, squeezing his fingers as if through touch she could force life into him again.

Now her pulse was starting to race. She could hear her own breathing, fast and shallow. He couldn't be gone. It wasn't possible. Not Jimmy. Jimmy was always the life and soul. Everybody liked him. Who'd do a thing like this? Why? She felt sickened and stupefied and guilty. She remembered how she'd been bad-mouthing him, cursing him for not showing up at the prison, for letting out her flat, for doing all the things she'd gladly forgive him for now.

27

Leaning over his body, she whispered his name over and over. Her insides were ice and she had started to shiver. Inwardly she was praying: *Don't let this be real, don't let this be real. Please God.* She touched his hair, his neck, his arm. A kind of panic was rising in her, something like hysteria. A groan escaped from deep within her chest. All the love she had ever felt, all the anger, the bitterness and joy crashed through her mind and collided into one mighty explosion of grief.

Cara could barely recall standing up, but she had managed it somehow. Now she was swaying on unsteady legs, looking down at Jimmy while she tried to work out what to do next. No, she knew what she had to do. She had to call the law. As soon as this thought entered her head, fear entered too. She had a flashback to finding Gerald Myers's body at the Hampstead house. Two bodies in eighteen months. What if they tried to blame her again?

Suddenly she had an impulse to run, to get away from the flat as fast as possible. No one need ever know she was here. She could slip out, go home, pretend she had never seen what she'd seen. Except she couldn't. To do that would mean leaving Jimmy lying on the cold kitchen floor. It could be hours before he was found, days even. He didn't deserve that, and she would never do it to him.

Before her fear of repercussions could overwhelm her, Cara stumbled into the living room, picked up the phone and dialled 999.

5

Cara had received a second shock when the law turned up at Jimmy's flat. Her old nemesis, DI Larry Steadman, was the investigating officer. She hadn't understood at first – this wasn't his patch – but it turned out she was behind the times. At some point during her incarceration, Steadman had been transferred. She was staring at him now across the table in an interview room at Cowan Road, wondering if that transfer had been a coincidence or if he'd specifically requested it.

Thinking about this was easier than thinking about Jimmy's murder. She was still trying to absorb that, to fight her way through the horror. Even though she'd seen him, held him, she still wasn't anywhere near coming to terms with his death. But she had to concentrate, to keep focused on what Steadman was asking. He had a hawkish, predatory look, and she had the sense of him circling around, waiting to swoop down and finish her off.

'You touched the body, then?'

Cara nodded. 'I had to, didn't I? I had to make sure ... you know, that he ... he could still have been alive.'

Steadman curled his lip as if she'd deliberately set out to destroy evidence. 'When was the last time you saw Jimmy? Before today, I mean.'

'Last week. He came to see me at Leaside.'

'And how did he seem?'

'Fine. He seemed fine. The same as always.'

'He wasn't worried about anything?'

'Not that he told me. No, I don't think he was worried. If he was, he was hiding it well. And Jimmy wasn't the sort to make enemies. Everyone liked him.'

'Well, clearly not everyone.'

Cara couldn't argue with that. She pushed her damp hair out of her eyes and wondered who the hell Jimmy had upset so much. Although he moved in criminal circles, he'd never been more than a minor villain himself. She couldn't see why anyone in that world would want to do this to him. His killer, she thought, was more likely to be an angry husband or boyfriend.

'Were you two a couple?' Steadman asked.

'Not for a while.'

'But he came to visit?'

'Occasionally. We were still mates, kind of.'

'Kind of?'

Cara shrugged. 'We were together for years, on and off. You don't just stop caring about someone.'

'Even if they cheat on you? I've heard Jimmy was something of a ladies' man.'

Cara knew he was trying to rile her. She kept her mouth shut.

Steadman kept his cold eyes on her. 'What were you doing at his flat?'

'He was supposed to pick me up from Leaside this morning, but he didn't show. I went round to see what had happened to him.'

30

'You can't have been happy.'

'Not especially,' she said. 'But as it turns out, he had a good excuse.'

'What time did you get there?'

'I'm not sure. Just before twelve, I think. Yes, it must have been. I called you lot about five minutes later.'

Steadman had an irritating habit of raising his eyebrows at everything she said, as if he didn't believe a word. 'And the front door was open?'

'It was unlocked, if that's what you mean. It wasn't open.' Cara wondered if anyone had witnessed her rapping on the door and peering through the letterbox. Would the neighbours mention it to Steadman? Usually, the Mansfield residents were tight lipped when it came to talking to the law, but there were always exceptions. She felt sick about it now, guilty and ashamed for yelling at Jimmy while he was lying dead in the kitchen. 'I knocked for a while, but he didn't answer so I tried the door and ... that's when I went in and found him.'

'That's two bodies you've discovered now.'

'Thanks for reminding me.'

'Bad luck just seems to follow you around.' Steadman smirked. 'If it is just bad luck.'

Cara glared at him. 'If you think I had anything to do with Jimmy's death, you're wrong. Jesus, that's ridiculous. He was twice the size of me. And anyway, why would I want to kill him?'

'Hell hath no fury ... isn't that what they say? You've been inside for eighteen months, and he's been ... well, I don't suppose he's been sitting home of an evening, embroidering cushions while he patiently waited for your release.'

'I've already told you. We weren't together any more. What he did was none of my business.' Cara had one of those déjà vu

31

feelings, like she'd been through all this before. Or maybe she was just reminded of her previous encounter with Steadman. He'd been trying to stitch her up then as well, using every dirty trick he could to pin an accessory to murder charge on her. He'd failed when it came to Gerald Myers – galling for him, she was sure – and was probably hoping for more success with Jimmy. She felt a brief flurry of panic, imagining being arrested and thrown into a cell again. Quickly, trying to keep the alarm from her voice, she asked, 'When did Jimmy die?'

'We don't know exactly. We're waiting on the pathologist.'

'But you've got a rough idea. You must have.' Cara glanced towards the other cop whose name she had been told but had immediately forgotten. He was about fifteen years younger than Steadman, in his late twenties, and hadn't said a word since they'd all sat down. Either he'd been told to keep his mouth shut or he was just the quiet type. 'Today? Yesterday?'

It was Steadman who answered. 'Hard to say at this point.'

This didn't help Cara much, but she thought it took a while for a body to cool, several hours at least – and Jimmy had been cold. 'It wasn't me. I didn't kill him.'

'No one's accusing you.'

'Really? Only it's beginning to sound like that.'

Steadman put his elbows on the table and steepled his fingers. 'Although that doesn't mean you couldn't have paid someone else to do it for you.'

'Yeah, right, and then the first thing I do on getting out of jail is to swing round to his flat, discover the body and make myself the prime suspect.'

'Perhaps you wanted to make sure you'd got your money's worth.'

Cara gave a hollow laugh. 'You're crazy. Jimmy had his faults, but I never wanted him dead.'

'Just beaten up, then. Was that it? Did it go too far? Is that what happened?'

'Don't try and pin this on me. I had nothing to do with it.'

'I hope not, Cara, because if you did, I will find out.'

'Can I go now?' she said tightly. 'I've told you everything I know.'

Steadman nodded, looking pleased with himself. 'Don't leave Kellston. I'm sure I'll need to talk to you again.'

6

The black BMW was parked in Cowan Road, near enough for its occupants to be able to keep an eye on the entrance to the police station, but far enough away to not stand out in the long row of cars that lined the road. Rain spattered the windscreen. Terry Street wound down his window and lit a cigarette. He gazed pensively towards the low red-brick building before turning his head to look at his companion.

'I want to know everything she does, everywhere she goes, everyone she meets.'

'Why don't I just have a little chat with her, save us all some time?'

'Yeah, 'cause that really worked a treat with Jimmy Lovell. She's no bloody use to us down the morgue.'

'It won't come to that.'

'It weren't supposed to come to that with Lovell.'

Boyle leaned forward and placed his hefty forearms on the steering wheel. 'I told you, boss, I barely—'

'Yeah, yeah, you said. Still singing with the angels though, ain't he?'

Boyle shook his head and heaved out a breath. 'Give me a chance with her. She'll tell me everything. Just give me five minutes. You've seen the size of the tart. She's hardly going to put up a fight.'

'Are you even listening to me? Just follow her, okay? She knows where Jimmy stashed the goods and she'll want to get her hands on them as soon as. Once she has them, that's when we make the move.'

'What about the others? What if they get there first?'

'They won't, not if you do your fuckin' job properly.' Terry pulled on the cigarette, annoyed at how a simple deal had so quickly gone down the pan. Now the law would be sniffing around, making trouble where trouble wasn't needed. 'Look, here she is. Follow her and keep your distance. You can drop me off on the corner.'

Boyle started the engine and pulled away from the kerb. 'She don't look too happy.'

'Anyone would think she was having a bad day.'

7

Cara walked quickly away from Cowan Road, relieved that the interview was over, but afraid that Steadman wasn't finished with her yet. It was only now that she realised he hadn't asked the obvious questions – if she'd seen anyone in the vicinity of the flat, if she had passed anyone on the stairs – which made her think that he already had a fair idea of when Jimmy had died. What she couldn't figure out, however, was if he really believed she might have had something to do with it or if he was just whistling in the wind. Maybe he'd simply grabbed the opportunity to give her a hard time.

As if it all wasn't terrible enough. While she'd been with Steadman, she'd forced herself to keep her emotions in check. Crying in front of her old adversary hadn't been an option but now tears were starting to stream down her face. She wiped them away with the back of her hand. That Jimmy was dead, gone for ever, seemed impossible even though she'd witnessed it with her own eyes.

Cara walked past the off-licence on the high street, stopped and doubled back. She went in, searched the shelves for cheap wine and bought a bottle of red. Now wasn't the time to be in a state of sobriety. She should have been celebrating her freedom but instead she was mourning the loss of Jimmy. Getting drunk seemed the only sensible thing to do. Oblivion was what she craved, a fast escape from reality.

She strode on to the Mansfield, indifferent now to whatever dangers might be lurking there. Nothing could be worse than what she'd already experienced. She looked towards Temple Tower and saw that two panda cars were parked outside the entrance. The law would be going door to door, making enquiries, asking the residents questions they'd be unlikely to answer. Keeping your mouth shut was rule number one on an estate like this.

At Haslow House she crossed the foyer and stepped into the lift. As she travelled up, she wondered if she should have mentioned the man in the black BMW to Steadman. She couldn't see that it had any bearing on Jimmy's murder, but something about it had been off. And what about Will Lytton? She hadn't mentioned him, either, but that had probably been a good thing. Steadman was nasty enough to tip off the council about the sublet. Anyway, unwelcome as he was, she couldn't see Lytton as a murderer: whoever had done for Jimmy had been powerful, vicious and out of control.

She still had her money on it being an angry husband or boyfriend. A jealous, possessive beating that had gone too far. Jimmy always had liked playing with fire. This time he had taken up with the wrong woman, overstepped the line and made the kind of mistake from which there was no coming back. She wondered who he'd been seeing – Rochelle, she suspected, had fallen by the wayside long ago – and whether Steadman would be able to track her down.

Cara opened the door to her flat and went inside. Lytton put down the book he'd been reading and stood up as she entered the living room, looking first at her and then over her shoulder.

'No Jimmy? Couldn't you find him?'

'Jimmy's dead,' she said bluntly, walking straight past.

Lytton laughed, thinking she was joking. He followed her into the kitchen. 'Remind me never to get on the wrong side of you.'

Cara took the wine out of the carrier bag and put it on the counter. She rummaged in a drawer for the corkscrew, grabbed it and started peeling the foil off the bottle. Glancing up at him, she said: 'I'm not kidding. I found him at his flat. I've just spent the last half hour down Cowan Road.'

Lytton's face visibly paled. 'What? Jesus, what happened?'

'Someone gave him a beating, a bad one. I don't know when. The law wouldn't tell me.'

'Christ, that's awful. I can't believe it. Poor guy. Shit. Are you all right?'

Cara managed to dislodge the foil. She wound in the corkscrew and pulled out the cork before she replied. 'No, I'm not all right. I'm about as far from all right as I could possibly be.' She reached behind her, opened the cupboard and took out a glass. Then, because even in this time of crisis it felt ill-mannered not to offer him a drink, she held up the bottle and said, 'Want one?'

Lytton shook his head. 'No, thanks. Is there someone I can call?'

'What?'

'You shouldn't be alone at a time like this.'

Cara could have pointed out that she wasn't alone – *he* was there – but couldn't be bothered to state the obvious. 'No, no one.'

'A friend? A relative? It's no problem.'

'No,' she said again. Friends had never figured much in her life, at least not close ones. From the age of eleven she had been shifted from school to school, never being in any place long enough to forge the kind of bonds that would be lasting. Even now most of the people she would loosely classify as friends were actually Jimmy's mates rather than her own. 'I don't want to see anyone.'

Lytton gave her a sceptical look.

Cara picked up the bottle and glass and took them through to the living room where she placed them on the coffee table. She took off her damp denim jacket and threw it over the back of the sofa. Then she sat down, poured herself a large drink, lifted the glass to her mouth and took two fast gulps. The wine had a sharp, sour taste but she knew she wouldn't care after a glass or two. You got what you paid for.

Lytton perched on the arm of the easy chair and said: 'What about your mum? Is she still around?'

'On the south coast. She's in rep, an actress; she tours for most of the year. Anyway, she never cared much for Jimmy. She thought he was a bad influence.'

'And was he?'

'Perhaps. Or maybe it was the other way around. Who's to say?'

But Lytton seemed intent on procuring some emotional support. 'You could call her, let her know what's happened.'

'What for?' Cara had no desire to call. She didn't hate her mother but had learned to live without her. Shelagh Kendall had always put her career – such as it was – before any maternal obligations. As a baby and then an infant, Cara had been dragged from theatre to theatre while her mum pursued the elusive goal of stardom. And later, when Cara was older, she'd been dumped with various relatives until she could be packed off to boarding school. 'She wouldn't be any help even if she was here.'

'Are you sure? Only—'

'Haven't you got essays you should be writing?'

'They can wait. Unless you want me to go. I can make myself scarce if I'm in the way.'

Cara shrugged. 'Please yourself. But I don't need babysitting.'

'Okay,' Lytton said, getting the message and rising to his feet. 'If you're sure.'

'Before you go, could I ask you something?'

'Ask away.'

'The last time you saw Jimmy, was he with anyone? A girl?'

Lytton hesitated, but then shook his head. 'I don't think so.'

Cara stared at him. 'You don't need to spare my feelings. We used to be a couple, but we split up after . . . Anyway, we haven't been together for a while. I'm only asking because he could have stepped on someone's toes. You know, a jealous husband or boyfriend. If I can find out who he was seeing, it might give me a clue as to who did that to him.'

'I don't think he was with a girl, but I can't be sure. The Fox was crowded.'

'Okay,' Cara said, disappointed.

Lytton leaned down and picked up his book from the coffee table – a paperback about Victorian London – and as he straightened up, he said: 'He was talking to some blokes at the bar for a while, though. Terry Street and a couple of others.'

'You know Terry Street?'

'Only by sight,' Lytton said. 'Doesn't everyone round here?'

Cara frowned, wondering if this encounter meant anything. Jimmy hadn't been in the same league as Street and his cronies. Normally they wouldn't have given him the time of day. 'Friendly talking or . . . less friendly?'

'I couldn't tell you. Not for sure.' Lytton paused and gazed into the middle distance, as if he was trying to recreate the

40

scene in his head. 'No, I really don't know. Do you think it's important?'

Cara, unwilling to share her thoughts with a man she'd only met this morning, kept her suspicions to herself. 'I shouldn't think so.'

'Right, I'll be off then. Look, I'll ask around, see if anyone's got a spare room going. The last thing you need at the moment is all this trouble with the flat.'

'Really?' Cara said, surprised.

'None of this is your fault.'

'Not yours either,' she said, 'but I appreciate it.'

He nodded and walked out of the living room.

Cara took another drink and then a few more while she considered this development. It was a relief to think she might soon be getting her home to herself again. She listened as Lytton moved about in the hall, presumably putting his jacket on, and didn't really relax until she'd heard the front door open and close. Then she sat back and released her breath, unaware that she'd even been holding it.

8

The flat felt very quiet and still. Jimmy's murder filled her mind. Why? When? Cara remembered the coldness of his skin, his closed eyes, his battered face. It was real, final, beyond terrible but, like with the death of her dad, a part of her was still in denial. She could be asleep, having a nightmare, one of those long, convoluted dreams that would eventually end. She closed her eyes, prayed and opened them again. No, this was no bad dream.

Cara gazed blankly into her glass for a while. Then she turned her head to look at her dad's photograph. 'And where are you when I need you?' she murmured. In truth, when it came to parenting, her father had been no better than her mother, happy to send her away rather than take on the burden of looking after her himself. But at least he had tried to make up for it later, allowing her to live here with him after she'd finally rebelled and walked out of school on her seventeenth birthday.

'What's the point of spending all that money,' she'd argued, 'when I can't bear the place?'

'You're not there to enjoy yourself, hon. You're there to learn, to pass your exams, to have a better start in life.'

'What's better about being miserable? I don't get it.'

'You'll thank me for it one day.'

But eventually, after much persuasion, he had given in, although only on the proviso that she got herself a job within three months. Which was how she'd ended up working in Connolly's, the caff on the high street, waiting on tables and washing up pots. It had hardly been the best job in the world, but preferable to sitting at a school desk all day.

Cara had hated all the schools she'd been banished to, with their cold, draughty corridors, authoritarian teachers and endless loneliness. The other girls, daughters of minor diplomats, lawyers and middle-class businessmen, had quickly seen her for what she was: an imposter. She had never fitted in, never belonged. How could she when her father usually paid the school fees by relieving families like theirs of their hard-earned cash and valuables? A fair redistribution of wealth was what he'd called it, although numerous judges had begged to differ.

Cara leapt up from the sofa and strode over to the window. For God's sake, why was she thinking about all this? Because it was easier than thinking about Jimmy. Anything was easier than that. She folded her arms across her chest and looked down. Her gaze roamed across the depressing expanse of concrete, before lifting to take in the better view that lay beyond. From here you could see the dome of St Paul's on a clear day. Today, with the rain, she could only make out a misty outline.

She returned her gaze to the estate, following the progress of an elderly woman who was braving the rain to take her pooch for a walk. The woman moved slowly, as if every step was an effort. The dog, a miniature dachshund, pulled on the lead and waddled eagerly ahead. As the two of them passed through the gates, Cara noticed a black car parked a little way up Mansfield Road. Instantly her heart missed a beat. The BMW? She couldn't say for sure at this distance, but there was definitely someone in it.

She pressed her face against the glass, trying to get a better look. She screwed up her eyes and stared intently at the car. What was the driver doing? Waiting for someone? Waiting for *her*? No, she couldn't start jumping to conclusions like that. There were millions of black cars in the world and nothing to say that this was the same one she'd seen earlier. She stared and stared, but it didn't get her anywhere. From this distance she couldn't even tell if it was a man or a woman inside.

Frustrated, Cara left the window, refilled her glass and drank the wine while she went into the kitchen, retrieved her prison carrier bag and wandered into the hall. With the toe of her foot, she pushed open the door of her father's old bedroom and looked inside. This was where Lytton was sleeping. It was all neat and tidy with his clothes put away and just a few books on the bedside table. Nothing to complain about other than his actual presence. She stood on the threshold, tempted to go in and poke around – what did she really know about him? – but instead moved on to her own bedroom.

Cara chucked the bag on the bed and did a quick survey. At first sight the room looked exactly as she'd left it, but the closer she looked the more certain she was that it had been disturbed. One of the drawers in the dressing table hadn't been closed properly, and the suitcase that she kept stored on top of her wardrobe was now lying slightly to the right rather than being perfectly centred. Someone had been in here. Jimmy or Lytton? One of them, or maybe both, had been going through her stuff.

She put down the glass, went over to the wardrobe, opened the door and got down on her knees. Anxiety fluttered in her throat. Her shoes had been moved. She was sure of it. They might still be in pairs, but they weren't lined up as she'd left them. Quickly she pulled them all out and stared at the smooth oblong of wood that was left. It was here, under this fake shallow base, that she kept her secret stash.

She ran her fingers over its surface, found that one of the corner screws wasn't flush and instantly knew that her hiding place had been discovered. Swearing softly, she stood up, retrieved the tiny screwdriver from the dressing table drawer, knelt down by the wardrobe again, unscrewed the four corners of the base and gently lifted it up. She prepared herself for the worst, expecting to see nothing but empty space, but there, exactly where she'd left it, was the roll of five-pound notes. Relief mingled with confusion. How could they have missed it? They couldn't. It didn't make any sense. She snatched it up, did a quick count – two hundred quid, all present and correct – peeled off ten of the notes and put the rest back.

Once the base was securely screwed in again, Cara neatly lined up all the shoes, got to her feet and closed the wardrobe door. It had been her dad's tip to always keep some cash in reserve, a useful fund for emergencies. She had never told Jimmy about it, but he might have guessed that there'd be money somewhere on the premises. Or Lytton. She hadn't entirely ruled him out, either. What she couldn't understand was why it hadn't been taken. Or had it been borrowed and put back? She had no answers at the moment.

Cara put the fivers in her purse, returned to the living room and checked on the black car. It was still there. Now its presence was starting to feel more suspicious. There was nothing to hang around for in Mansfield Road, unless there was a drugs deal going down. But even that didn't seem likely, not after all this time.

If she hadn't already drunk half the bottle of wine, she might have been more cautious, but it suddenly seemed like an excellent idea to go down and investigate. She didn't intend to confront the driver, just to walk past the car and see what happened. There was no harm in that, was there? Before her brain could convince her otherwise, she grabbed her jacket and hurried out of the flat.

9

Anger was dogging Cara's footsteps as she strode along the path towards the open gates. Gradually the reality of Jimmy's death was sinking in, bringing with it not just grief but a stinging rage, too. How could anyone do that to him? She pushed her hands into her pockets, screwed up her face and tried to blink away that foul final image of his body lying on the kitchen floor. She didn't want to remember him like that. It was the happy, laughing Jimmy she wanted to hold on to, the man she'd fallen in love with all those years ago.

Cara didn't look directly at the car as she approached. She stayed on the other side of Mansfield Road, keeping it in her peripheral vision until she drew level. Only then did she sneak a glance in the driver's direction. It was a bloke all right, and she was pretty sure it was the same one from earlier – he was still wearing the stupid baseball cap and shades.

The man turned his head and looked the other way as she passed by. That wasn't a normal thing to do, especially when there wasn't anything or anyone else to look at. Just trying to hide his face, she reckoned. She kept on walking. Her intention was to skirt around the estate and see if he followed her. And what if he did? Well, she'd cross that bridge when she came to it.

By the time Cara had covered another ten yards, she was starting to think she'd got it wrong. Then suddenly she heard it – the distinctive sound of a car door being closed. Yes! Now she just had to find out why the man was on her tail. And there was only one way of doing that: she would take him by surprise, catch him on the back foot and demand some answers. This, to her somewhat addled brain, felt like a perfectly good plan of action.

She slowed down, giving him the chance to get closer. She could hear his footsteps behind her. Although he was keeping to the other side of the road, she knew he had her in his sights. She could feel his eyes on her, feel the prickle on the back of her neck and had to fight hard to resist the temptation to glance over her shoulder. Now the idea of *not* confronting him seemed ludicrous. How else was she going to find out what his game was? A niggling voice in the back of her mind told her she was playing with fire, but she ignored it. The booze had made her brave . . . and reckless.

The only question now was when. No time like the present, she thought. Then, just as she was girding herself to turn around, quickly cross over and take him by surprise, the door to the pool hall opened and three girls tumbled out. They were swaying and swearing, one of them, a redhead, swinging a bottle of vodka from her hand. There wasn't enough room for them all on the pavement and the trio, either oblivious to her presence or just unwilling to give any ground, jostled her into the road.

'Oi!' Cara protested. 'Watch where you're going!'

'Watch where you're going yourself,' the redhead retorted.

She was dressed in fishnets, a black leather miniskirt and a lacy top. The girl glared hard at Cara, as if she was itching for a fight. 'Who do you think you're talking to? You don't own the bleedin' pavement.'

Cara rolled her eyes and began to walk off – she had more important things to do than trade insults with a boozed-up, third-rate Madonna – but the redhead pursued her, took hold of her elbow, and jerked her around.

'Hey, I know who you are.'

'Good for you. Now would you mind letting go of me?'

'You're Jimmy's ex. You're Cara Kendall. You're the one who found him this morning.'

The efficiency of the Kellston grapevine never failed to amaze. It was impossible to even set foot in Cowan Road nick without everyone knowing the details five minutes later. Cara couldn't deny any of it and so she just said: 'And?'

'And you found Jimmy at his flat.'

Cara shifted her elbow and managed to extricate herself from the girl's grip. 'Yeah, which means I'm having a bad enough day as it is. Please don't make it any worse.'

Her words had an unexpected effect. Suddenly the aggression slipped from the redhead's face and her lower lip began to quiver. 'God, it's too fuckin' awful. Is it true that he was beaten to death? That's what they're saying. Is it true?'

Cara didn't want to be having this conversation. The girl was even drunker than she was. She glanced across the road and noticed that her tail had caught up with her. He was a big bloke, far taller than she'd realised and twice as wide, a real heavyweight goon. He ambled on past, his hands in his pockets, as if he had no interest at all in what was going on outside the pool hall. What would he do now? Wait for her further along, she presumed. 'That's how it looked.'

'Come on, Rochelle,' one of the other girls, a blonde, said. 'We're going to be late. We've got to go.'

Cara flinched at the name. There couldn't be that many Rochelles in the neighbourhood. Jesus, was this the girl Jimmy had cheated on her with when she'd first gone to prison? She felt a familiar spasm of hurt, of anger. There was no point in recriminations, not now, but the bitterness still lingered.

'Stop buggering about. We're going to be late,' the blonde said again.

'Fuck off, then.' Rochelle retorted. She walked to the kerb, sat down, took a swig from the bottle of vodka, placed the bottle on the pavement and covered her face with her hands.

Her pals, if they could be called that, stared at her for a moment and then just shrugged their shoulders and walked away.

Cara gazed after them, hoping they'd change their minds and come back. They didn't. She transferred her attention to Rochelle. The girl was sobbing now, weeping into her hands, a wretched, snorting noise that sounded like a pig in pain. She was tempted to walk away herself – Rochelle was hardly her responsibility – but didn't have the heart to do it.

Instead, she crouched down beside her and waited for the crying to stop. She looked along the road, wondering if her tail was still in the vicinity. Having seen his size, she was starting to think that it might not have been the best idea in the world to confront him. Perhaps Rochelle had inadvertently done her a favour.

With nothing else to do, Cara examined the girl more closely. Rochelle was probably in her early twenties. She was slender but curvy, with long legs and big permed hair. There was a jagged rip in her fishnets, just below the knee, but it was impossible to tell if this was accidental or an ill-advised fashion statement. Jimmy's type? God, any female had been Jimmy's type if he was

50

in the mood. She sighed as all of this went through her mind, still trying to process his death, to make some sense of it.

Eventually the crying subsided to an ugly snivelling. Rochelle wiped her snotty nose on the back of her hand, took another swig of vodka and turned her face to Cara. 'He were a right laugh, Jimmy.'

As epitaphs went, Cara reckoned it wasn't such a bad one. For all his faults, Jimmy had always been good company. 'Were you two, you know, still together, then?'

'Not really. Not for a year or so. We was still mates, though. Why would anyone do that to him? Why would they?'

'I don't know. I've been asking myself the same thing. When was the last time you saw him?'

Rochelle's eyes filled with suspicion and her voice took on a defensive edge. 'What's that got to do with it? It didn't have nothin' to do with me.'

'I didn't say it did. I'm just trying to understand. Jimmy wasn't normally the type to upset people. Whoever did it must have had a reason.'

'I ain't seen him around for a day or two.'

'What about girls? Do you know who he was dating?'

'How would I?' Rochelle's mouth became sulky. 'He wouldn't tell me, would he?'

Cara, whose knees were beginning to ache, tried a different tack. 'Have you seen him with anyone dodgy recently? Blokes, I mean.'

Rochelle took another slug of vodka while she thought about it. 'All Jimmy's mates are dodgy.'

Cara couldn't argue with that. 'Dodgier than usual, then. You know, like someone you wouldn't expect to see him with.'

'Nah.'

While Rochelle made further inroads into the vodka, Cara

decided she'd better try and get the girl up while she could still stand. 'Do you live on the Mansfield?'

'Temple,' Rochelle said. 'Same as Jimmy.'

'How long have you been there?'

'A while. Like . . . I don't know . . . a few years.'

Cara had never noticed her before but there were a lot of people living on the estate. And she had been away for the past eighteen months. 'Come on, then,' she said, standing up and hoping that Rochelle would follow suit. 'Let's make a move before it pisses down again.'

For a moment it looked like Rochelle was going to stay where she was, but then she slowly rose to her feet. 'You and Jimmy wasn't together when we hooked up,' she said abruptly, as if Cara had accused her of stealing her man. 'You'd split. He told me you'd split up.'

Cara could have told her that this wasn't strictly true – she hadn't written the letter until after she'd heard about Rochelle – but there didn't seem much point. 'Sure. We'd broken up by then.' She had a sudden yearning to know what else Jimmy had said about her, but instead she asked, 'How did you know I was Jimmy's ex?'

'He's got a picture of you in the flat, ain't he? The two of you.'

As they started walking, Rochelle linked her free arm through Cara's, although this was clearly more a technique for helping her walk in a straight line than any gesture of sisterly affection. The girl was still swigging from the bottle of vodka, and her voice suddenly became belligerent again. 'What was you doing at Jimmy's this morning?'

'He was supposed to pick me up from Leaside, but he didn't show. I went round to give him a mouthful.'

'So how did you get in?'

Rochelle was talking like a possessive girlfriend, even though she and Jimmy hadn't been a couple for a good while. Cara kept her voice calm and neutral. 'The front door was unlocked.'

'Not broken in or nothin'?'

'No.'

Rochelle seemed to be considering this, but then all she said was, 'You got a fag?'

'I don't smoke.'

Cara noticed that the black car was still parked in the same place, but there was no sign of the driver. She glanced over her shoulder – he wasn't behind them – and was tempted to cross over and take a peek inside, except that would have meant dragging Rochelle with her. Instead, she said, 'Do you know who that bloke was, the one who walked past us at the pool hall?'

'What bloke?'

'The big one, tall. He was wearing a baseball cap and shades. A few minutes ago. He was on the other side of the road.'

'I didn't see any bloke. Why? What's he got to do with anything?'

'I don't know. Nothing, probably.'

They were at the entrance to the Mansfield now. The rain had started coming down again, but Rochelle appeared oblivious. The girl walked slowly, tottering on her high heels, more interested in the bottle she was holding than the fact they were both getting soaked. Cara took the path that led towards Temple Tower. 'Did Jimmy say anything to you about being in trouble? Did he owe money to anyone?'

Rochelle didn't answer her query. Instead, she announced bluntly: 'Jimmy could be a fuckin' shit. Don't you think? Don't you think he could be a fuckin' shit?'

Cara didn't want to badmouth Jimmy – she'd done enough of that earlier – but she understood that Rochelle was only deflecting grief with anger. It was a way of coping with the shock of it all. She felt it in herself, too, a kind of bubbling resentment towards him, a simmering rage that he had managed to get himself murdered. 'He had his moments.'

Rochelle sniffed hard, wiped her face again and said tearfully, 'We was good together, me and him.'

Cara didn't want to hear about how good they'd been together. Although she suspected that she wasn't going to get anywhere with her questions – Rochelle was too drunk to focus – she still persisted. 'Try and think. Did Jimmy ever mention being in trouble? He must have crossed *someone*. This didn't just happen out of the blue.'

'He didn't say nothin'.'

'What about Terry Street?'

'What about him?'

'You ever see the two of them together? In the Fox, maybe.'

'What would Jimmy be doing with Terry Street?'

Cara shook her head, silently praying that the killer, whoever it was, would be found soon. Then she thought of something else to ask. 'Did Jimmy ever mention a bloke called Will Lytton to you?'

'Why do you keep asking me this stuff? You're giving me a fuckin' headache.'

'I'm just trying to—'

'Where are we going?'

'You said you lived in Temple.'

Rochelle stopped dead and stared at the tower. A couple of panda cars were still parked outside. Cara stared, too. Up in Jimmy's flat, the scene-of-crime officers were probably still collecting evidence. Or had they finished by now? She had no idea how long these things took.

'Come on,' she urged, trying to pull Rochelle forward.

But Rochelle wasn't having any of it. 'What are we doing

here? I don't want to be here.' She yanked her arm away from Cara's, turned around and headed back towards the gates.

'Where are you going?' Cara called out.

Rochelle ignored her.

Cara was in two minds whether to follow, but she was cold and wet and sick to the stomach. Jimmy was cold too, cold and dead. She shivered at the horror of it all. Nothing was ever going to be the same again. She'd had enough. It was time to go home.

10

DI Larry Steadman sat in the incident room flicking through the file on Jimmy Lovell. The dead man, thirty-four, had worked as an electrician, held a few convictions for burglary and handling, and was what could only be described as a small-time villain. There was no history of violence. Other than the dramatic way he'd met his end, there was little of interest about him, except for one outstanding fact: he had been in a relationship, on and off, with Cara Kendall.

This wasn't news to Larry. After the murder of Gerald Myers, he had looked into the Lovell connection. Could he have been the killer? A moment of panic, an uncharacteristic act of brutality? But as it turned out, Lovell had been drinking in the Fox that night with plenty of witnesses to corroborate the story. Kendall had refused to say who her accomplice was, maintaining through numerous interviews that she had broken in alone, heard another intruder in the house and simply had the misfortune to stumble on a body.

Larry didn't believe a word of it. It frustrated him that he'd never been able to solve the crime and he still had sleepless nights trying to slot the pieces together. He didn't like being lied to, being outmanoeuvred, being made to look like a bloody fool. In his mind he had built up an alternative scenario to the one Cara Kendall had provided, one where her partner had forced Myers to open the safe, shot him, taken all the valuables and scarpered before Kendall, still upstairs, discovered what he'd done – leaving her to face the music when the cops arrived.

Some of this theory was still fuzzy around the edges. Surely, when Myers had unexpectedly appeared and confronted the intruder, she would have heard the commotion, heard the gunshot even if a silencer had been used? But maybe there hadn't been a commotion. Maybe Myers had been forced to keep quiet. Or maybe she had decided to keep out of the way so that Myers wouldn't know there were two of them. Only later, after she'd heard the shot being fired, after she'd heard her partner leaving, had she ventured downstairs and discovered what he'd done.

So why hadn't she grassed him up? He'd taken off with the contents of the safe and even called 999 from the house to tip them off about the body. It was because of this that she'd been caught red-handed on the premises. Another few minutes and she'd have been gone, too. He'd done the dirty on her, but she'd still refused to give his name.

Larry had come up with several possible reasons for this, including fear, misplaced loyalty, greed – she might have reckoned that there was still a chance of claiming her part of the haul – or the desire to exact revenge without the assistance of the law. He had tried to scare her with the threat of an accessory to murder charge, but she hadn't caved.

And now she was out of jail, and Lovell was dead. Killed last night, sometime between ten and twelve according to the pathologist. They would get the details later. Cara and Jimmy had shared a bed and probably a whole lot more. Like secrets, for example. Like the truth about what had really happened that night in Hampstead.

'You're becoming obsessed by that girl,' Gaynor had said, back at the time of the Myers investigation. 'You never stop talking about her.'

His wife had hit a sore point. He would not have attached the word obsessed to his feelings – it seemed too intense, too close to something unhealthy – and yet Cara had preoccupied his thoughts as much as a new lover might. Her blue-green eyes, the blondeness of her hair, the curve of her neck, the small scar on the back of her right hand: all of these things he had kept carefully stored away, like a secret buried hoard only to be dug up and examined in private. 'By the case, perhaps,' he'd retorted defensively, 'not Kendall. A man died, remember? She knows who murdered him, but she refuses to say.'

Larry already knew that he wouldn't tell Gaynor about Cara Kendall's release from jail, just as he hadn't told her his real reason for requesting a transfer to Cowan Road. A better chance of promotion, he'd claimed, smiling even as he spoke the lie. The truth was too complicated. It ran something along the lines of keeping your friends close and your enemies closer, but she would have misunderstood. She would have mistaken his desire for justice for a different kind of longing. She would have gazed at him through suspicious eyes.

What Larry felt for Cara had nothing to do with lust. He constantly told himself this, and would admit, at most, to an intense fascination. Would he have cared so much if she'd been stupid or ugly? That was a question he preferred not to answer.

DC Ray Tierney came into the incident room, slipped off his raincoat and hung it over the back of a chair. The smell of damp permeated the air. Steadman looked up at him, raising his eyebrows.

58

'Anything?'

'Nothing useful,' Tierney said. 'You know what that lot on the Mansfield are like. They'd rather pull out their own teeth than talk to the law. The neighbours claim they didn't hear any disturbance last night or see anyone go into Lovell's flat. They wouldn't even admit to seeing Cara Kendall there this morning.'

'There's a surprise.'

'We had any joy with next of kin?'

'His parents are dead, but we've tracked down a younger brother living in Surrey. I've put a call in to the local plod.'

Tierney sat down and gazed across the desk at his boss. 'You really think she's lying?'

'I wouldn't rule it out. The truth and Cara Kendall are strangers to each other.'

'She seemed upset, though. I mean, she was trying not to show it, but . . .'

'Perhaps he knew too much.'

Tierney frowned. 'Even so. You'd have to be a cold-hearted bitch to organise a hit and then nip round to see the result.'

Larry shrugged. He was not sure yet what he thought about Ray Tierney. The two of them hadn't been working together for long, only four months, and there hadn't been enough time to get used to each other's personalities or idiosyncrasies. Tierney was from Yorkshire, but Larry didn't hold that against him. What mattered more was whether he could be trusted, whether he'd have Larry's back in a tight spot. The jury was still out on that one. He gazed across the desk at his colleague.

'Don't make yourself comfortable. We're going down the Fox. That was Jimmy's usual drinking hole. Let's see if we can find out what he's been up to recently.'

11

In the bathroom Cara stripped off her damp clothes and stepped into the shower. For the next few minutes, she stood motionless, letting the hot water stream over her. She wanted to clear her mind, to think of nothing. Everything bad was jumbled up inside her head. Eventually she picked up the shampoo and washed her hair. Then she grabbed the soap and a sponge and set to work vigorously cleaning herself from head to toe. If she could have sloughed off the pain of Jimmy's death, she would have, but no amount of scrubbing was going to purge the ache inside her.

When she was done, she turned off the water, padded over to the cupboard and opened it. On the shelves inside were two blue towels she didn't recognise. Lytton's. For a moment, with everything else that had been going on, she had almost forgotten about him. It occurred to her that the bar of soap she'd just used had probably been his, too. She wrinkled her nose at the thought of it having travelled across his body just as it had travelled across hers.

Cara chose one of her own white towels and wrapped it around her. She bent and retrieved her clothes from the floor, carried them through to the kitchen and dumped them in the washing machine. A memory came back to her of Jimmy and her dad lugging the machine into the flat a few years ago, the two of them huffing and puffing from the weight of it. She'd been happy that day, smiling and laughing, delighted by the prospect of no more wasted hours down the launderette. That joy over something so trivial seemed regrettable now, as if happiness was rationed and she had wasted part of her quota on an inanimate object.

On her way to the bedroom, she stopped at the window and looked down and across to Mansfield Road. The black BMW was gone. She checked the surrounding area, but it was nowhere to be seen. Her shoulders relaxed a little. Still convinced that the man had been following her, his absence felt like a reprieve. And then she felt guilty for worrying about herself when Jimmy was dead. *He* was the one she should be thinking about. Except she couldn't, not properly. She was too scared of being overwhelmed.

Cara went into her bedroom, dropped the towel and got dressed in a fresh pair of jeans and a cream sweater. She combed her hair while she stared at her reflection in the mirror. What now? She felt cut away, adrift. It had been the same after her dad had died. All you could do was carry on, but that was easier said than done. One day at a time, one week, one month, one year, until eventually the grief would settle into something that, if not painless, was at least bearable.

The doorbell rang, cutting through her thoughts. She stood very still, the comb poised above her head, while she wondered who it was. No one she wanted to see, that was for sure. Could it be the law? DI Steadman, perhaps, come to give her another grilling. Well, he could go whistle. She'd already told him everything she knew.

The bell went again, three insistent rings. Her determination not to answer wavered. What if it was something urgent? What if Steadman had got a lead, a clue that could lead him to Jimmy's killer? What if there was a piece to that clue that only she could provide? None of this seemed very likely, but she couldn't take the chance.

Cara flung down the comb, left the room and walked barefoot along the hall. As soon as she opened the door, she wished she hadn't. Rochelle was standing there, looking wet and bedraggled and very, very drunk. The bottle of vodka, almost empty now, hung from her left arm while her right was attached to Jimmy's best mate, Murch.

'Hey,' he said. 'We wondered how you were doing.'

'Yeah,' Rochelle added unnecessarily, 'how ya doin', hon? How are ya doin'?' Her words were slurred, and her eyes narrowed as though she was trying to get Cara into focus.

Before Cara could think up an excuse as to why she couldn't invite them in, Rochelle had lurched forward, dragging Murch with her. The two of them stumbled into the living room and took possession of the sofa.

Cara closed the front door and followed them through. Quickly she snatched up the wine and the glass from the table, took them into the kitchen and placed them on the counter. From the doorway she asked her uninvited guests, 'You want coffee?'

'Ta,' Murch said.

'You got a fag?' Rochelle asked, as if Cara might have taken up smoking during the limited amount of time they'd spent apart.

'No.'

Cara turned away, put the kettle on and got three mugs out

of the cupboard. God, this was all she needed. Hopefully, once they'd drunk the coffee, she could get rid of them. She didn't want company; all she wanted was to be alone. Why had she answered that damn door? She was an idiot, a fool. When she turned around again, Murch was coming into the kitchen.

'Sorry, she's a bit out of it. I didn't want to leave her down the pub.'

'That's all right,' Cara said, even though she'd had enough of Rochelle for one day.

Murch leaned against the counter and scratched his neck. 'I still can't get my head around it. Shit. Jimmy gone like that. Why would . . . I mean, it doesn't make any fuckin' sense. Did the law say anything? Do they know who did it?'

'If they do, they're not telling me. He was beaten up. That's all I know.'

'When? Do you know when it happened?'

Cara shrugged. 'Last night? This morning? They wouldn't tell me that, either.'

'Did they give you a hard time?'

'What do you think?'

'Shit,' he said again.

Cara stared at him. Murch was a small squat man with over-developed muscles and a moonlike face. Today he was dressed in one of his trademark shell suits, purple and lime green. The colours made her eyes ache. She had never liked him much – he was shifty and a letch – but she could tell that Jimmy's death had hit him hard. 'Did you see him last night?'

'He was in the Fox for an hour or so. Early. About six o'clock. But he didn't stay.'

'Did he tell you where he was going?'

'Things to do, he said.'

'What sort of things? A woman?'

Murch lifted and dropped his heavy shoulders, his gaze sliding away from her.

The kettle boiled and clicked off. Cara busied herself with the mugs and the coffee. While she was making the drinks, she tried to remember what Murch's actual name was. She knew that Murch was short for Murchison but couldn't recall his Christian name. Had she ever known it? Jimmy had probably told her, but it had gone in one ear and out the other.

Cara pushed a mug across the counter. 'Help yourself to sugar.'

Murch put in three heaped teaspoonfuls and gave the coffee a stir.

Cara's gaze slid down to his knuckles – even friends fell out from time to time – but there were no marks on his hands. She felt bad, then, for even suspecting him. It had been a fleeting thought, based purely on personal dislike. 'Was Jimmy seeing anyone?' she asked. 'Anyone in particular?'

Murch shook his head. 'No one he told me about.'

Cara couldn't tell if he was lying or not. 'Only if he was messing about with someone's wife, then maybe—'

'I never saw him with no one. Maybe he was robbed. Did the law find his wallet?'

'I've no idea. There wasn't a break-in, though. No one forced their way into the flat. Did he even have any money? You know what Jimmy was like: get it one day and spend it the next. He was always broke. Unless . . .' She hesitated. 'Unless he'd been up to something. Had he? Did he mention anything to you?'

'No, he didn't say nothin'.'

Cara sighed, unsure as to whether she was being stonewalled or if Murch was as much in the dark as she was.

When they went back into the living room, Rochelle had fallen asleep, her head lolling, her arm hanging over the side of the sofa. The bottle of vodka was tucked in beside her. Cara carefully removed it and put it on the coffee table. The girl stirred but didn't wake.

Murch sat down beside Rochelle and Cara took the armchair. There was an awkward silence during which Cara wondered which of her guests had suggested coming round to see her. She and Murch had never been close, and Rochelle was a virtual stranger. *What are you doing here?* she felt like asking. *What do you want from me?* But she swallowed down the questions, thinking that maybe Murch just needed to be with someone Jimmy had known well, someone who'd understood him like he had. Men weren't always good at expressing their emotions.

'Someone told me they'd seen Jimmy with Terry Street,' she said. 'A few weeks back, in the Fox.'

Murch, who'd been examining the carpet, looked up sharply. 'Who said that?'

'Did you ever see the two of them together? Did Jimmy mention anything?'

'Nah, Jimmy never hung out with Terry. Out of his league, weren't he? Terry, I mean. Whoever told you that got it wrong.' Murch held her gaze with the intensity of a liar, of someone determined to make her believe he was telling the truth. 'What business would he have with Terry Street?'

'I don't know – the kind that got him murdered, perhaps.'

'Christ, Cara, you don't want to go throwing around accusations like that. You need to keep your mouth shut. If Terry gets to hear about it, you'll be right in the shit. He didn't have nothin' to do with this. Why would he?'

Cara kept her eyes on him. Was he protesting too much? Trying to cover up something? It was hard to tell. He always looked shifty at the best of times. 'You can't be sure of that.'

'Sure enough,' he said.

Small whispery snores escaped from Rochelle as she slept on. Cara envied her the oblivion. She thought of the half bottle of wine sitting on the kitchen counter and wished her guests would leave her in peace. Well, perhaps peace wasn't exactly the right word, but alone at least.

'I always reckoned you and Jimmy would end up together,' Murch said, changing the subject. 'I told Jimmy that, told him he was lucky to have you.'

Cara doubted this was true and questioned his motives in saying it. To make her feel better? Or himself? To try and make her trust him? Shifting in the chair, she sipped her coffee and gazed at him through watchful eyes. She felt a surge of resentment and knew that this was because, deep down, a part of her had always believed that she and Jimmy *would* eventually get back together. Despite their rows, their splits, their apparently irreconcilable differences, there had been a bond between them, a rare connection.

'He was gutted over that Hampstead business.'

'Not as gutted as I was,' Cara said.

'Yeah, you got a rough deal.' Murch paused and then asked, with unconvincing casualness, 'So what made you go ahead after Jimmy pulled out?'

Cara frowned, wondering where he was going with this and why he wanted to know. In truth, she had asked herself the same question a thousand times. Everything had been ready, all the surveillance done on the house, when Jimmy had suddenly announced that he was cancelling the job. *I've got a bad feeling about it*, he'd said. When pressed, he hadn't been able to explain exactly what he meant or what the feeling was based on or give any sort of rational reason as to why they should call the whole thing off. 'I still don't understand why he did that.'

'I reckon sometimes you just have a hunch that something's not quite right, you know? If it smells bad, it probably is bad.'

Cara had another explanation, but it wasn't one she was going to share with Murch. What she'd suspected back then was that Jimmy didn't think she was up to it, that he reckoned she'd bottle it because of what had happened to her dad. His unilateral decision hadn't gone down well with her, which was why, she supposed, she'd decided to go it alone. Her pride was at stake and her independence. If he had no faith in her, that was fine, but it didn't mean she had to pull out. She had wanted, she knew, to prove a point. That hadn't worked out so well. Eighteen months of not so well, in fact.

'He made his choice and I made mine,' she said.

'Yeah, but he still felt bad about it. Like he'd let you down.'

'There was nothing he could have done even if he had been there. It wouldn't have made any difference. It wouldn't have changed anything.'

'Who's to say?' Murch's gaze roamed the room, but eventually came back to settle on her again. His tongue slid across his thick upper lip. 'It was risky that, going in alone.'

'Tell me about it.'

'You must have got the fright of your bloody life when you realised someone else was there.'

Cara sensed he was probing, that this was more than idle curiosity. 'I'd rather not think about it, to be honest.'

Murch persisted. 'There were plenty of rumours doing the rounds.'

'What sort of rumours?'

'You know what Kellston is like. You can't move for bleedin' gossip.'

'What sort of rumours?' she repeated.

'Oh, you know, the usual sort of crap; that you'd teamed

up with someone else after Jimmy backed out, that the two of you went into the house together, that you knew who killed Gerald Myers.'

Cara glared at him. 'Now you're sounding like the law.'

Murch held up his hands, palms out, in a gesture of defence. 'Hey, don't shoot the messenger, love. I'm just repeating what I heard. Jimmy put them straight. We both did. I mean, you were just unlucky, weren't you? There weren't nothin' dodgy about it. Wrong place, wrong time and all that.'

'I didn't even see the bloke, never mind know him. All I heard was the footsteps.' Cara stopped. Why was she even bothering to explain? He'd been in the courtroom with Jimmy, had sat through the whole case and was already aware of her version of events. But still she felt the need to proclaim her innocence. 'It's rubbish. Jesus, why do people talk such crap?'

'Yeah, but . . .'

Cara never got to hear what was coming next as Rochelle chose that moment to wake up. The girl peered at the table, at the cooling mug of coffee, before reaching for the vodka.

'You've had enough,' Murch said, his voice edged with irritation.

'Since when did you become my keeper?' Rochelle retorted. She took a swig from the bottle and giggled. 'We should put some music on. It's too fuckin' quiet in here.'

Cara had reached the limits of her patience. Before Rochelle could start rooting through her dad's expansive (and expensive) record collection, she rose quickly to her feet and said: 'Look, thank you both for coming, I really appreciate it, but I have to go out soon. I've got things to do.'

'What things?' Rochelle asked sulkily.

Cara wasn't going to debate the matter. Even if she had been able to think of something – which she couldn't – it was none of Rochelle's business. She strode out of the room, hoping the two of them would follow, and opened the front door. But then found herself standing alone, gazing out into the empty corridor. There was a rapid and whispered exchange going on in the living room. She strained her ears but couldn't catch what they were saying. 'Come on,' she muttered under her breath, desperate to get rid of them.

It felt like an eternity before her guests finally unglued themselves from the sofa and joined her in the hall.

'You know where I am, love,' Murch said. 'You need anything, just ask.'

Cara forced a smile and nodded. 'Thank you.'

Rochelle glared at her as if her hospitality left a lot to be desired, and then rudely pushed past without so much as a goodbye.

Cara closed the door and leaned against it for a moment. She could hear their footsteps gradually receding on the tiled floor, and then Rochelle's strident voice floating through the quiet.

'I said she was a bitch, right? She don't give a damn about poor Jimmy.'

12

Cara walked back into the living room with Rochelle's words ringing in her ears. Anger rose in her, but she quickly pushed it aside. What did she care? Just some drunken ex sounding off, a girl who had only known Jimmy for five minutes and whose opinions weren't worth a second thought. It still stung, though, as all false accusations did.

Although it was only five past three, the day was drawing in, a greyness descending over the city. She collected up the mugs and took them through to the kitchen where she rinsed them out and left them on the drainer. While she dried her hands on a tea towel, she replayed the conversation with Murch in her head. Had he been fishing for information or just making conversation? She couldn't decide. Did it matter? She couldn't decide that, either.

A dull headache was nagging at her temples, a result of the wine she'd drunk earlier. She gazed at the bottle, tempted to finish it, but her desire to get plastered had passed. Instead, she made herself a ham sandwich, put it on a plate and carried it through to the living room. She ate standing up, looking out of the window. Spots of rain spattered the glass. She stared blankly at the outside world, unable to comprehend how things went on as normal, how the earth was still spinning for everyone else when for her it had stopped dead.

She'd longed to see the back of Murch and Rochelle, but now they were gone the flat felt eerily quiet. She turned on the stereo, flicked through some records and chose Joni Mitchell's 'Blue'. As Joni's plaintive tones filled the room, she tried to draw Jimmy closer to her, but already an abyss had opened up between them. He was there – wherever *there* was – and she was here.

She switched on the lamp and lay down on the sofa. Almost immediately she sat up and wrapped her arms round her knees. The music floated into her, piercing her soul. She closed her eyes, trying to blank out reality, to remove herself from the present, to go someplace where she wasn't so utterly alone. First her dad and now Jimmy: she had lost the only two men she cared about and didn't have a clue how to deal with it.

The record came to an end, and she didn't bother getting up to put another one on. She let the silence envelop her, let the past leak into her mind. She'd been fourteen when she'd first set eyes on Jimmy. A warm summer's evening. Dad had taken her to a wake at a local pub on the south side of Kellston where the mourners had spilled out into the courtyard and were standing under hanging baskets full of geraniums, petunias and ivy. The dead man, an old acquaintance of her father's, had been called Albert North.

'We'll only stay ten minutes,' he'd said. 'I just want to pay my respects.'

But ten minutes had stretched into fifteen and then twenty. Her father, it seemed, knew almost everyone there and felt obliged to have a word with them all. While he circulated, she sat on a bench, drinking Coke through a straw. She'd been starting to get bored when Jimmy – she had not known his name then – had stopped to chat to a small group of blokes standing near her. With nothing better to do, she had surreptitiously watched and listened.

The initial conversation had been nothing extraordinary, the normal exchanges between twenty-something males – football, beer, cars – the kind of stuff usually guaranteed to send her into a coma. But not on this occasion. She could not explain, not to this day, why the presence of Jimmy Lovell had affected her so much. She had felt a sudden shifting inside her, a constriction in her chest, a shortening of breath. It had been more than his good looks, more than his smile. She'd had the weird sensation of already knowing him, of coming face to face with her future, of gently falling through time and space. Was there such a thing as love at first sight? The sensible, rational part of her had scoffed at the idea, but she could find no other explanation.

'It's a good turnout,' one of the blokes had said.

'Old Albert was a legend.'

'The best cat burglar in London.'

'In the country, mate. There was no one to touch the geezer. Some of the jobs he pulled off . . . Jesus, do you remember that hotel in Cannes? He got away with a bloody fortune.'

'And spent it all, too, in less than a month.'

They laughed, throwing back their heads.

All of this had been slightly more interesting to Cara, who'd had no inkling, until this point, of the colourful life of Albert North. But then she'd received her second shock of the day. As the group were recounting more of Albert's exploits, one of them had said: 'And then there was that toff's house. Suffolk, Sussex, was it? Somewhere like that. He got a massive haul from that place – paintings, tom, the whole shebang. Half a million they reckoned at the time, and we're talking over twenty years ago. Him and Paul Duffy cleared the place out.'

'No, that wasn't Duffy, it was Richard Kendall.'

Cara had almost choked on her Coke, turning her face to one side to splutter out the fizzy brown liquid. Quickly she'd wiped her mouth with the back of her hand. Her dad? They couldn't be talking about her dad. It must be some other Richard Kendall. Her dad was an art dealer, not an art stealer. But no sooner had these thoughts swung through her mind than all doubt was obliterated.

'He's here, isn't he? I'm sure I saw him earlier.'

'Yeah, he was talking to Albert's old lady.'

'He and Albert were quite a team.'

'The best.'

Cara's emotions, already in tumult, had dissolved into confusion and bewilderment. How had she reached the age of fourteen without knowing the real way her father made his living? She had been so stupid, so naïve. But then why wouldn't you believe what your parents told you? And suddenly all those times when her dad had been 'abroad', when she couldn't see him during the school holidays, made a different kind of sense. He hadn't been in Paris or Florence or the deepest depths of South America, but behind bars at Her Majesty's pleasure.

When her father had eventually come to collect her, she hadn't mentioned what she'd overheard. It still hadn't sunk in properly and she hadn't known what to feel – proud that he was one of the best cat burglars in the business or shame that he was a thief? There was so much she'd wanted to ask, but it would be another couple of years before she got up the courage to have *that* conversation.

In retrospect, Cara couldn't say which of the two events, discovering her father's secret or seeing Jimmy for the first time, had had the greatest impact on her. It was, perhaps, the powerful combination of them both that ensured the evening was forever imprinted on her mind. Of course, Jimmy hadn't even noticed her back then. Why would he? She was just a teenage girl, small for her age and about as interesting as an empty crisp packet. But he had left a lasting impression. And when she was nineteen, when they finally met again, she had felt the same tumultuous emotions as on the first occasion.

And now? Cara lowered her chin on to her knees. Their relationship had always been stormy, passionate, a battle of wills – but full of love, too. Somehow, no matter how many times they had parted, they had always found a way back to each other. There had been a rightness about it, an inevitability. It seemed impossible, unbearable, to imagine a future without him.

Cara's thoughts were disturbed by the thin clatter of the letterbox. She didn't immediately get up. Late post, she assumed, and probably a bill. Nothing to hurry for. It was a couple of minutes before she dragged herself up off the sofa and padded to the front door. Leaning down, she picked up a white envelope and flicked it over.

Her name had been handwritten across the front but there was no address or stamp. She tore it open as she walked back into the living room. A single sheet of paper was inside. She unfolded it and looked down at the words. Shock ran through her, a gasp escaping from her lips. Printed in block capitals across the middle of the page was the threat:

GIVE IT BACK OR YOU'LL BE NEXT.

13

Cara slumped on to the sofa, still tightly grasping the note. Give it back? Give *what* back? She stared at the words, trying to work out what they meant. Her mouth had gone dry, and her heart was pounding. Then, as if the note was burning her fingers, she flung it on the coffee table along with the envelope. It lay there like a hot threat while she grappled for some understanding.

She wondered if Murch or Rochelle had written it. Why Murch would do such a thing was beyond her, but she wouldn't put it past Rochelle. Some kind of sick joke, perhaps. Except the more she considered it, the less likely it became. Somehow, she couldn't see the girl lurching home, putting pen to paper, and then staggering back to Haslow House. It didn't seem her style. So, who?

The man in the black BMW, the goon who had followed her, had to be top of the list of suspects. Another attempt to intimidate her. And it had worked. The very wording of the note suggested that whoever had killed Jimmy now had her in their sights. Ice slivered down her spine. She took a couple of deep breaths, trying to calm herself. Don't jump to hasty conclusions. It was also possible that someone was taking advantage of Jimmy's murder as a way to put the screws on.

In frustration, Cara banged her fists on her knees. Damn it! If she hadn't waited so long after hearing the letterbox go, she might have caught the perpetrator in the act. She sprang up and went over to the window even though she knew it was too late. Quickly she examined the scene below. There wasn't much to see: a couple of middle-aged women chatting by the gate from beneath bright umbrellas, a kid circling on a bike and a group of teenagers, still in their school uniforms, kicking a ball around.

Cara was tempted to leg it downstairs, to interrogate them all as to whether they'd seen anyone leave the building recently, but instantly dismissed the idea. People came and went all the time. She would end up looking like a crazy woman. And anyway, the guilty party would probably have left by a different exit to the main front door. They could have slipped out the back or gone down to the underground car park.

Glancing over towards Mansfield Road, she saw that the black BMW hadn't returned. She stayed by the window on the lookout for possible suspects but couldn't spot anyone worth serious consideration. Too late, she thought again. Maybe she should go to Cowan Road and report the note. But that was like inviting Steadman to take even more interest in her. She pulled a face. What could the law do anyway? Sod all.

Give it back. Cara wrapped her arms around her chest while she tried to work out what it meant. Something Jimmy had taken. Money? A package of drugs? She didn't think it would be the latter. Jimmy used to duck and dive, but he'd never been involved in anything heavy. Her original thought, that he'd slipped between the sheets with some dodgy bird, could be disregarded, too. Whatever it was, this person knew Jimmy couldn't have given it to her – she hadn't seen him alive since she'd got out of jail – so they must think she'd taken it from his flat. Or, if it wasn't there, that he'd told her on his visit to HMP Leaside where he'd hidden it.

Cara frowned, wondering why the killer hadn't ransacked Jimmy's flat when they'd had the opportunity. Panic when the beating had gone too far? Or perhaps they had searched the place – it was hard to tell with Jimmy's general untidiness – and come up with nothing. So now they were turning their attention to her.

Her throat tightened. She thought back to last week when Jimmy had visited. He'd been his usual cheerful self, happy and upbeat, without a care in the world. She would have known if he was worried. Something must have happened between then and now, something so serious it had cost him his life. She would have to talk to Murch again. If anyone knew what Jimmy had been up to, it would be him.

Terry Street's name jumped into her head. This whole thing had the smell of gangland about it. Cold and nasty and brutal. She stiffened, knowing she could be next in the line of fire, that if she didn't watch out, she would meet the same fate as Jimmy. But she couldn't give back what she didn't have.

Cara's fingers dug into her sides. A simmering fury rose in her, mingling with the fear and grief. No matter what the cost, she wouldn't let Jimmy's killer get away with it. Sooner or later, they would have to show their face. Eventually, however long it took, she would make them pay for what they'd done.

14

DI Larry Steadman raised the pint to his lips and surveyed the Fox from where he stood at the bar. It was his second visit to the pub today. During the first he and Tierney had made a sweep of the lunchtime drinkers but had been met, on the whole, by a wall of silence. If anyone knew what Jimmy Lovell had been up to, they weren't saying. Of the few who were prepared to speak, it was only to sing his praises. If they were to be believed – and they weren't – Jimmy was whiter than white and had never put a foot wrong in his life.

Larry gave a quiet snort. He examined the customers to his right and left and, without turning, even the ones behind him. A wide, gleaming mirror ran the length of the back of the counter. Reflected in the glass, behind the bottles and optics, were the many faces of Kellston: the young, old and middle aged, the law-abiding and the less so, the sensible and the reckless, even a few local toms. Everyone was welcome in the Fox so long as they behaved themselves.

To the naïve or uninitiated, it may have looked like he was

just having a drink at the end of a long, hard day. But Larry was still working, checking who was there and perhaps, more interestingly, who wasn't. There was no sign of Terry Street or any of his firm. Still, it was early yet. His absence didn't necessarily mean he'd had anything to do with the attack on Jimmy Lovell, although when it came to acts of violence the most serious could usually be traced back to his door.

Terry Street's power and influence lay under Larry's skin like a bad itch he couldn't scratch. The man had the law in his pocket. It was common knowledge that he greased the palms of numerous cops – and that they, in return, turned a blind eye to his activities, gave him free rein to run his girls, deal his drugs and generally get away with breaking every rule in the book. Kellston was his patch, and he ran it as smoothly as a well-oiled machine.

It was a pleasurable thought to imagine ending his career, but an unrealistic one. Larry knew that the alternative to letting Street rule the manor was anarchy. Taking him down would leave a vacuum that would be fought over by every two-bit firm in the surrounding areas. They'd descend on Kellston like a pack of wolves, tear each other apart and create enough collateral damage to occupy every waking hour of every cop at Cowan Road.

And who needed that? Better the devil you know, Larry supposed, even though it didn't sit easily with him. Sometimes you had to accept the lesser of two evils. It wasn't what he'd signed up for, but it was what he was stuck with. At least for now. Once he'd nailed Cara Kendall he'd put in for another transfer and try for a move to somewhere less appallingly bleak and depressing.

The Fox was a small oasis in the midst of all the dreary greyness. It didn't play loud music or have its walls lined with slot machines. It was old-fashioned but in a good way, with comfortable seats, excellent beer and a convivial atmosphere. A roaring log fire welcomed the clientele with a blast of much-needed warmth as they walked in. Every time the door swung open Larry glanced in the mirror. He was hoping that Cara Kendall would show up, but suspected she'd keep her head down for a few days.

The pub, despite being moderately busy, was more subdued than usual. Even in a dive like Kellston, murder could still shake people up. Jimmy Lovell had been well liked and his death had shocked the community. Whether this shock would translate into any useful leads was another matter altogether. He was hoping that one of his snouts might hear a whisper before too long.

Ray Tierney came back from the gents, took out a tissue, blew his nose, stared at the result, scowled, screwed up the tissue and put it back in his pocket. 'I still can't get rid of the stink of that bloody morgue.'

'It has a tendency to linger,' Larry said. 'The trick is not to breathe too deeply.'

'I wouldn't mind, but we didn't learn anything we didn't already know.'

It was true that there had been no surprises from the pathologist. Jimmy Lovell had been badly beaten up – broken ribs, a ruptured spleen – and the final blow had resulted in his skull making violent contact with the edge of the kitchen sink. It was this injury that had finished him off, causing a fatal bleed on the brain.

'Someone didn't like him,' Tierney said. 'Or wanted to shut him up. You still think Cara Kendall had something to do with it?'

'I'm not ruling it out.'

'So what do we know about her? Apart from the fact she fancies herself as Spiderwoman.'

Larry, who had gathered every detail he could on Cara's life, pretended to think about it while he decided how much to share. 'Various public schools, left at seventeen, then she worked in Connolly's for several years. No criminal record until the Hampstead fiasco, although I doubt that was her first job.'

'There aren't many round here with a private education.'

'For all the good it's done her. Her mother's an actress – no one famous – and her late father was Richard Kendall, renowned cat burglar and keen acquirer of furs, diamonds, paintings and anything else that their rightful owners hadn't screwed to the ground.'

'Like father, like daughter.'

'Yeah, you can't beat family tradition. And he made a bloody fortune if all the rumours are true.'

'So how come Cara ended up on the Mansfield?'

'Because her old man spent his cash as fast as he made it. Gambling, cars, women, fancy restaurants ... Money burned a hole in his pocket. He was the type who lived for today and sod tomorrow.'

'What happened to him, then?'

Larry, knowing that Tierney was still green about the gills from his visit to the mortuary, took some pleasure in recounting the gruesome details of Richard Kendall's death. By the time he'd finished, Tierney's lunch looked in imminent danger of making an unwanted reappearance.

'Christ,' Tierney murmured, his eyes glazing slightly and his left hand moving towards his guts. A thin hissing sound escaped from his lips. 'That's beyond gross.'

'Yeah, not a pleasant way to go. You'd have thought it would have put her off climbing through high windows for life, but it seemed to have the opposite effect.'

'Maybe eighteen months inside will have given her a new perspective.'

'I wouldn't count on it.'

Tierney's hand lingered on his stomach for a moment before dropping back to his side. 'She seemed pretty cut up about Lovell this morning.'

'Believe me, she's not as innocent as she looks. She thinks she can wrap us all around her little finger, that she's smarter than the rest of us, but she'll screw up eventually. I'll see her behind bars again if it's the last thing I do.'

Perhaps Tierney identified something more personal than professional in his tone, because he threw him an odd look, opened his mouth, thought better of whatever he was going to say and smartly closed it again.

Larry downed what was left of his pint. 'Let's head over to Temple and see if we can find Mr Murchison.'

15

Cara didn't know where all the time had gone. It only felt like minutes since she'd taken to the sofa and wrapped her arms around her knees, and now the clock claimed it was seven-fifteen. Outside, it was pitch black. She blinked and rubbed her eyes. She hadn't been asleep, but rather in some odd state of suspended animation, as if a part of her had closed down and she'd only been functioning on a very basic level of breathing in and out.

She swung her legs round and put her feet back on the floor. Looking around the room, she felt at a loss as to what to do next. Should she go to Temple or the Fox and see if she could find Murch? She wanted to talk to him again, but not in the presence of Rochelle. Better to wait, she decided, until she could catch him alone. Anyway, he'd probably been on the booze for most of the afternoon.

Beside the coffee table was a bamboo magazine rack. She leaned over and flicked through the publications: old copies of *Tatler*, *Country Life*, *Golf Monthly*, as well as some art magazines. They'd belonged to her dad, and she hadn't had the heart to throw them away. He'd subscribed to them as a means of keeping abreast of the activities of the rich: where they lived, how much they were worth, when they holidayed and the events they'd be attending. The social calendars of the wealthy had provided him with numerous tips as to who would be where and when – useful information for a cat burglar.

She lifted her head and glanced at his photograph. Her father's attitude towards the affluent had been deep and ingrained, containing a resentment that she'd never fully understood. He'd come from thoroughly middle-class roots and had never suffered deprivation. Yet his compulsion to steal hadn't just been about envy or greed, but a desire to equal things out a little, to rob the rich of what he felt they didn't need. Excessive wealth had always been anathema to him. Not that he was any kind of Robin Hood: although generous to a fault when he had money in his pocket, most of what he stole he squandered.

Cara knew that he'd been kicked out of the family at the age of fifteen, spent some time in borstal and eventually found his way to Kellston. But even after his stretches inside – or maybe because of them – he'd never been able to go straight. Instead, he'd honed his skills, becoming ever more proficient in the art of breaking and entering, until he'd gained that reputation of which he'd been so proud. Anyone could be a common thief, but he'd decided to become an extraordinary one.

The phone began ringing, and Cara jumped. She couldn't decide whether to answer it or not. What if it was the law wanting to grill her again? Or a follow-up to the note, some menacing, faceless voice issuing her with more threats, demanding that she give back what she didn't have? She dithered for so long that eventually the caller rang off.

A minute later, the phone started up again. This time she rose to her feet, strode across the room, snatched up the receiver, put it to her ear, but didn't speak. There was the sound of pips going, a crackling on the other end of the line and then the light sound of breathing. Cara maintained her silence, as did the caller. Eventually the impasse was broken by her mother's dulcet tones.

'Cara? Cara? Is that you, darling?'

'Yes, it's me.'

'What's wrong with this line? Can you hear me?'

'Yeah, I can hear you, Mum.'

'Oh, good. Only I wasn't sure I'd got the right number. I rang you just before but—'

'I was in the bathroom,' Cara lied, not wanting to explain her reasons for not answering the first time. 'Sorry.'

'I was only calling to see how you are. Glad to be home, I bet. I'm so relieved you're out of that place. Anything could have happened. I mean, you hear all these stories, don't you? Some of those women are so . . . Still, it's over now. You can put it behind you and start again.'

'Yeah.'

'No point in dwelling on it, is there? We all make mistakes. We just have to learn from them. To be honest, I'm surprised you're in. I thought you'd be down the pub celebrating. I'd have rung earlier only I've not had a minute all day.'

'How is work?' Cara asked quickly, in two minds as to whether she should break the news about Jimmy or not. She would have to tell her eventually but wasn't sure if she could deal with all the questions right now. Or the expressions of shock. Or the sympathy. Her mum had never cared much for Jimmy, thinking him too old for her, too reckless, too unreliable. All perfectly reasonable objections, but not ones she wanted to dwell on.

'Endless rehearsals, darling. And the director's a complete

ass. You'd think we were doing *King Lear* instead of bloody *Cinderella*.'

Cara nodded even though she couldn't be seen. In the past, her mother had often been cast in the leading role in the Christmas pantomime, but age had caught up with her. Now, much to her chagrin, she'd been cast as one of the ugly sisters. 'It's a job, at least.'

'He's a moron. The guy's barely out of short pants and he's telling *me* how to walk across a stage. I've forgotten more than he's ever going to know about acting. If he says to me once more—'

'Mum, I have to tell you something,' Cara interrupted, before she was forced to listen to what was likely to be a long and tedious list of complaints. 'I've got bad news.'

There was a brief silence on the other end of the line. 'Christ, you're not in *more* trouble are you, Cara? Please tell me you're not. You've only been out of jail for five minutes.'

'Jimmy's dead,' she blurted out.

'What?' Her mother gave an odd half laugh, as if Cara might be joking. 'How? What? Lord, no. He can't be. Are you serious?'

'Of course I'm serious.'

'Was it some kind of accident?'

'He was beaten up at his flat. He died last night or this morning.'

Her mother sucked in an audible breath. 'God! That's awful, darling. That's . . . Are you all right? I mean, I know you're not, you can't be, but . . . God, poor Jimmy.'

'The police don't know who did it yet.'

'Why would *anyone* do it? Was it a robbery?'

'It might have been,' Cara said, not wanting to share her own suspicions, or to reveal that she'd been the one to find him. 'They're not sure.'

'You should get off that estate. How many times have I told you? You shouldn't be living in a place like that. Look, do you want me to try and get a few days off? I could come to London and—'

'No,' Cara said quickly. 'Thanks, but you don't have to.' She wondered why people always thought you needed company when you were grieving. 'To be honest, I'd rather be on my own.'

'But you shouldn't be. It's not right. You need family at a time like this.'

Cara's fingers tightened around the receiver. Before her mother could deliver any further homilies on the importance of family – it had never previously been high on her list of priorities – she started to wind up the conversation. 'I'm all right, really I am. You don't have to worry. I've got friends here. I'll be fine. I'll give you a call in a day or two. Are you still at the same B&B?'

'Yes, yes, I'll be here until the season's over. But—'

'Okay, I'll let you know if I get any more news. We'll speak soon.' Cara reiterated that she was all right, said a fast goodbye and hung up.

For a moment she stood with her hand still on the phone, as if it might suddenly spring into life again. She hoped she'd done enough to deter her mother from coming but wasn't certain of it. Shelagh Kendall loved drama on and off the stage and might well take it into her head to come flying to the rescue.

Cara sighed. Being economical with the truth had become a habit in her dealings with her mother. Their relationship worked best at a distance, where old resentments could be safely kept at bay. She was still musing on this when she heard the sound of the front door opening.

16

Fright was the first thing Cara felt, all rational thought being replaced as adrenaline coursed through her veins. She stood by the table, momentarily convinced that an intruder was in the flat. Her eyes frantically searched the room, looking for a weapon, a way to defend herself. It took a few seconds for the truth to penetrate, for her to calm down and realise it was only Will Lytton.

'For God's sake,' she murmured, irritated by her own stupidity.

By the time Lytton came into the living room she had resumed her position on the sofa. He said hello and gave her a long interrogative look, as if trying to assess how drunk she might be.

'Any news?'

Cara shook her head. 'Nothing. One of Jimmy's mates came round, but he doesn't know any more than I do.'

'Nothing from the police?'

'No.'

'I guess it's still early days.' He held up the carrier bag he was holding and said, 'Fancy a beer?'

Cara hesitated, not wanting to get too friendly with him, but then realising that this was exactly what she *should* be doing. How else was she going to find out whether he was who he said he was, and whether she could trust him or not? 'Sure. Thanks.'

Lytton went into the kitchen. She heard the rustle of the bag, the sound of the fridge door opening and closing, and then the clicks as he popped the caps off a couple of bottles. He brought the beers back into the living room, handed her one and sat down in the chair.

'Ta,' she said.

'I don't suppose it's really sunk in yet. It must be hard for you. It takes a while when someone dies suddenly.'

'Yeah, it still doesn't feel quite real.' Cara took a swig of beer, watching him closely whilst she pretended not to. She didn't want his empathy or his sympathy, but she did want to go over his story again. 'I've been thinking about what you said, about seeing Jimmy with Terry Street in the Fox. That just seems so odd.'

Lytton shrugged. 'I wouldn't place too much importance on it. People chat while they're waiting to be served.'

'Do you think that's what it was, then, just a bit of banter?'

'Could have been.'

Cara felt he was downplaying it, that this morning he had made it sound different. 'Even that's odd, though. I've been in the Fox lots of times with Jimmy, lots of times when Terry Street was there, and they've never exchanged a single word.'

'Well, that was before,' Lytton said.

'Before?'

'Before you went ... travelling. Maybe things changed while you were away.'

'That's what I'm worried about,' Cara said.

Lytton drank some beer, leaned forward and put the bottle on the coffee table. His gaze fell on the note and he stared at it, frowning. 'What's this?'

'It came this afternoon. Someone put it through the door.'

Lytton reached for the note, but then drew his hand back, wary perhaps of not depositing his fingerprints on it. 'Christ. Have you shown it to the police?'

'Not yet.'

'But you're going to?'

'I shouldn't think so. What's the point?'

'It's a threat.'

Cara smiled thinly. 'I know what it is. I can read.'

'So what are you going to do about it?'

'There's nothing I can do.'

'You can go to the police. Jesus, Cara, a man's been murdered and now you're being threatened. This is serious.'

'The law can't do anything. It's just a note. There won't be any prints. No one's *that* stupid. What are they going to do? Give me a twenty-four-hour guard?'

Lytton shook his head. 'It's a clue to who killed Jimmy, though, isn't it? Or rather, it's a clue as to why. What do they mean by "Give it back?"'

'I've no idea.' Cara clocked his sceptical look and scowled at him. 'I don't. I swear it. If Jimmy was involved in something dodgy, he never told me. And he certainly didn't give me anything. How could he have? I didn't take anything from his flat, either.'

'Someone thinks otherwise.'

'You think I *wouldn't* give it back – whatever it is – if I could?'

'It wouldn't do any harm to report it.'

It had crossed Cara's mind while they were talking that Lytton could have written the note, posted it through the door and cleared off for a few hours. An attempt to scare her into returning the mystery item. But return it to whom? And why suggest going to the law? A double bluff, perhaps, a ruse to make her trust him.

'I'll sleep on it,' she said. 'Can we change the subject now?'

For the next few hours, although they talked at length, little of any substance was revealed. They interrogated each other like a pair of would-be lovers, each trying to find out as much as they could. Most of his answers were vague. He glossed over his past, providing little detail, claiming only that he'd worked for a number of years in shipping.

'It was tedious,' he said. 'Too much paper pushing. I'd had enough. That's why I decided to go to college.'

'Why history?' she asked.

'I'm interested in what makes things happen.'

Cara sensed his reply had undertones, a meaning that went beyond his decision to take a degree. 'Like cause and effect?'

'Something like that.'

Was his reticence part of his personality or was he being deliberately evasive? Every time she tried to probe deeper, he volleyed back with another question of his own, something about her childhood or her parents or what her plans were for the future. Her answers were as insubstantial as his, flimsy as gossamer. Despite the beers – they were on their second now – her tongue hadn't been loosened. She remained as careful as she would talking to the law.

The room, lit only by the single lamp, was shadowy. She studied Lytton as well as she could, his angular face and cool grey eyes. Everything about him was calm, pleasant, natural, but she knew it might all be an act. At the same time, she couldn't see what connection he could have to the goon who had followed her. The two of them seemed incompatible, loose pieces of a jigsaw that wouldn't fit together.

Cara saw Lytton's gaze stray to the wall directly in front of him, and linger on the large, framed print that hung there. She stared at it too. The picture, called *Farm at Watendlath*, portrayed two female figures, probably a mother and daughter, dressed in white and standing hand in hand in front of a farmhouse overlooked by a large green hill. The colours, although soft, were vibrant, too. 'It's by Dora Carrington,' she said. 'It was my dad's. Do you like it?'

'I don't know much about art,' he replied noncommittally.

Cara had always loved the picture. She had imagined, or maybe just hoped, that it reminded her dad of family, of the daughter he had, of the time – brief as it was – when he had loved her mother. 'But you know what you like, surely?'

Lytton's gaze returned to her.

Cara was suddenly aware of the words she had spoken and of how they sounded – provocative, almost flirtatious. She frowned and to cover her discomfort quickly added, 'I think the original is in the Tate.'

A faint smile played around Lytton's lips. He left a brief pause before he spoke again. 'So, were you and Jimmy together for long?'

The change of subject caught her off balance. She drank some beer before she answered. He guessed, perhaps, that she wanted to talk about Jimmy. People often did want to talk when they'd lost someone close – a way of holding on, of bringing them back to life for a while – but she remained suspicious of Lytton's motives. There was a lot she could have told him, but caution held her back. 'Five years, on and off.'

'He seemed a decent bloke.'

'He was, on the whole. He was no saint, but there was more to him than ...' She didn't elaborate. Instead, she turned the focus back on Lytton. 'What made you want to live in Kellston?'

'I wasn't bothered where I lived, so long as it was near to college.'

'Lucky, then, you meeting Jimmy like that.'

'Lucky for me. Not so great for you. So how did you two first meet?'

'In Connolly's,' she said. 'The caff on the high street. I worked there for a while.'

The talk, the cat and mouse, the game – if it was a game – went on. She supposed she was glad of the distraction. It prevented her from sinking down into a quagmire of grief. His questions meant she had to stay alert and pay attention. She couldn't afford to let down her guard.

It was getting late when Lytton said: 'Look, I meant to tell you: a mate of mine has a room available, but it's not free until after Christmas. Would you mind if I stayed here till then? I know it's not ideal, but I won't be in your way. I'm in college most days.'

Cara considered the suggestion. This morning, before the arrival of the note, her answer would have been an unequivocal no, but now she was not so adamant. It was only six or seven weeks and perhaps it would be useful to have someone else around. He might act as a deterrent if the goon decided to come to the flat. Not that Lytton would be much use if things turned nasty – he was too slight, too placid – but at least he would be a witness. On the other hand, if Lytton was somehow mixed up in all this, she'd be agreeing to live with the enemy.

When she didn't answer immediately, Lytton said: 'I'll understand if you'd rather not have me here. I can keep looking if you want.'

Cara decided not to make an instant decision. 'I'll sleep on it,' she said, for the second time that night.

17

In the morning Cara was woken by the distinctive sound of water gurgling in the pipes. For a moment she was disoriented, thinking she was back in Leaside, before reality caught up with her. Lytton must be taking a shower. She squinted through the dark at the alarm clock by her bed – seven-forty – surprised by having slept through the night. She had expected hours of wakefulness but had dropped off the moment her head had hit the pillow. A combination, perhaps, of exhaustion, beer and her mind's desire for oblivion.

She would not get up until after Lytton had left. Small talk over breakfast was the last thing she wanted. But she had to keep busy once she was up and about. If she didn't start moving, and *keep* moving, the awfulness of Jimmy's death would drag her down into a dark pit of despair. What she needed was a plan for the day.

She lay on her back, gazing up at the ceiling. Should she take the threatening note to the law? Although she felt reluctant to set foot in Cowan Road again, the idea that the note might contain some clue to the murder made her think twice. Perhaps Lytton was right. And if she was going to do it, better sooner than later. She didn't relish the thought of seeing Steadman, but perhaps it was the lesser of two evils.

A visit to Kellston cemetery – something she would have done yesterday if yesterday hadn't been such a diabolical nightmare – was on the cards, too. She would buy flowers and tidy up her dad's grave. And then there was Murch. Would he be at work today? If he wasn't, she might be able to catch him at home. Hopefully, the delightful Rochelle would have made herself scarce by now.

So, that was three things to do, enough to keep her occupied for at least part of the day. She would have to start looking for a job soon as well. Connolly's wouldn't want her back, not with a prison record, but she was sick of waitressing anyway. She heard Lytton leave the bathroom, return to his bedroom and then walk quietly through to the living room. She hoped he wasn't the type who idled over breakfast.

While she waited, Cara's thoughts inevitably turned to Jimmy again. She remembered the letter she had written to him from Leaside. Gossip had been rife in the jail, relayed on visits by mothers and sisters and friends of the inmates, and it hadn't taken her long to hear rumours about his infidelity. With eighteen long months stretching ahead, she had suspected she'd go mad thinking about what he might be doing – and with whom. If they weren't together, she couldn't feel cheated on. It was as simple as that. Pride had been her main motivation for ending the relationship, but she'd known – or thought she'd known – that they'd already reached the end of the road.

They'd wanted different things, that was the trouble. Jimmy had always been content to drift through life, to never look back, and never look forward, either. After five years she'd wanted something more. Not a wedding ring, necessarily, but something that at least came close to a commitment. Had she hoped that the separation would focus his mind? That he'd realise she was the one he really wanted? Why was she even thinking about it? None of it mattered any more.

Eventually she heard the front door opening and closing. She got out of bed, pulled on her dressing gown and went through to the kitchen. It was clean and tidy with a plate and a mug washed up and left to dry on the drainer. There was the smell of toast in the air. She looked out of the window and checked the weather – grey and rainy – before she made a strong cup of coffee and took it back to the bedroom where she quickly got dressed in jeans, T-shirt, a navy-blue sweater and trainers.

While she perched on the end of her bed, sipping the hot coffee, she went over last night's conversation with Lytton. He hadn't given much away. Had anything he'd said been true? If she was going to let him stay then the first thing she should do, she decided, was to take a look in his room. It was doubtful he'd leave anything incriminating in there, but it wasn't impossible. Everyone made mistakes.

Cara stood up, put her coffee down on the dressing table, went out into the hallway and pulled the bolt across on the front door. It was unlikely that Lytton would come back, but better safe than sorry. She didn't want to get caught in the unpleasant act of snooping. Gently she depressed the handle to his room and pushed the door open. She didn't immediately go in, but stood on the threshold for a moment, as wary as if the inside might be booby trapped.

Slowly she advanced, her eyes doing the initial search. His bed was made, his clothes all put away apart from a light grey T-shirt lying across one of the pillows. The room, once her dad's, was typically male, unfussy and practical with none of the softer touches she had made to her own. Lytton, she noted, hadn't imposed any of his own personality on to it, but that wasn't so surprising; he had known he would only be here for six months.

She went over to the bedside table and opened the drawer. Inside was a paperback copy of an *A–Z*, a tube of antiseptic cream and an opened pack of biros. Nothing interesting like a chequebook or personal letters. The cupboard below contained three unused spiral notepads.

The wardrobe was next on the list. A few shirts were hanging inside, along with a tie and a summer jacket. She recalled the comment he'd made yesterday morning about her travelling light and thought the same could be said of him. Too light for someone of his age. At the bottom a squash racket was propped up against the side, and a large black sports holdall had been pushed towards the back. She noted exactly where the holdall was positioned before pulling it out, kneeling down and undoing the zipper. The only items inside were a pair of balled-up white socks and a white wristband. She checked the pockets – empty – zipped it up again and put it back exactly where it had been. This wardrobe hadn't had a false base when her dad had been living here, but she checked it anyway, just in case Lytton had decided to install one.

While she was on her knees, Cara peered under the bed. Nothing. Not even dust. She felt around the edges of the mattress for any lumps or bumps and ran her hands over the pillows. Then she got to her feet again, closed the wardrobe door and walked over to the chest of drawers. There were socks and underwear in the top drawer, T-shirts and a pair of jeans in the lower. She carefully felt around and under the clothes. She checked the top and bottom of the drawers in case anything was taped to them but came up with zilch. With a sigh, she closed the drawers and stepped back.

Cara stood for a while, hands on her hips, looking around. She stared at the carpet but couldn't see any obvious place it had been disturbed. Her eyes surveyed the room again. She felt frustrated by the failure of her search, as if Lytton had outwitted her. Clearly, he didn't keep anything of importance in the flat, not even his passport, if he had one. And that was odd, wasn't it? But it didn't prove that he wasn't who he said it was, or that he had any ulterior motives in being here. Perhaps her suspicions were all in her head.

Defeated, she left the room, closing the door softly behind her. She put on her raincoat and went to the kitchen where she plucked a carrier bag, a cloth and an empty plastic bottle from under the sink. She filled the bottle with cold water – she would use it for her dad's flowers – and screwed on the lid. In the living room she put the note back into its envelope and stuffed it into her coat pocket. Then, with a tightness in her guts, she set off to face Steadman.

18

Cara changed her mind numerous times on the way to Cowan Road. Should she? Shouldn't she? Was she doing the right thing? It might be better to wait a few days and see if the law actually caught the bastard who'd killed Jimmy. But she knew she was only looking for excuses. The longer she waited, the less use the note might be. If there was a chance, any chance at all, that it might help the investigation, she had to hand it in.

Anxiety gripped her as she walked through the glass doors of the police station. The thought of providing Steadman with yet more ammunition – he was bound to believe that she *had* taken something – made her feel almost queasy. It would give him the perfect excuse to put the screws on again. Still, looking on the bright side, there wasn't a whole lot he could do to make her life more miserable than it already was.

It was still early, and the foyer was quiet. Knowing how popular grasses were on the Mansfield, Cara expelled a sigh of relief. It wasn't wise to voluntarily enter the station, not without good reason, although she could always claim, if challenged, that she'd been called in to go over the events of yesterday.

The desk sergeant looked up as she approached the counter. 'Good morning.'

Cara kept her voice low even though there was no one else around to overhear the conversation. 'Hi. Is Inspector Steadman available?'

'He's not here yet, miss. Can I help?'

'Do you know what time he'll be in?'

'Hard to say, to be honest. Later this morning, perhaps.'

This, to Cara, felt like a sign – it wasn't meant to be – and also a blessed reprieve. She could take off now without feeling guilty. 'I'll come back later, then,' she said, unsure as to whether she actually would.

'Would you like to leave a message?'

'No, thanks. It's all right.'

Cara turned around and was on her way out when the young cop, Steadman's silent sidekick, came through the main door. She put her head down, hoping to escape his attention, but he stopped straight in front of her. Sadly, today, he wasn't quite so taciturn.

'Hello. It's Cara, isn't it? Are you here to see the inspector?'

She smiled weakly. Briefly her gaze sought the sanctuary of outside before returning to the constable. 'I was just ... just wondering if there was any news about Jimmy.'

'No arrests as yet,' he said. 'Would you like to come through?'

'What for?'

He gave her a patient if slightly pained look. 'So you can tell me what's really on your mind.'

'There isn't ...' Cara started saying, but then had a change of heart. If she had to hand over the note, wasn't it better to do it now than to face Steadman later on? 'Okay, well, there might be something.'

'This way,' he said, heading towards the internal doors that led to a long corridor beyond.

Cara followed him to a small room, a different one to yesterday, but much the same when it came to general decor: magnolia paintwork, a table and four chairs, scuffed lino on the floor. A window was set up high in one of the walls. He switched on the light, a neon tube, and it flickered and fizzed for a moment before finally coming to life.

'Grab a seat,' he said, as he walked around the table. 'How can I help?'

Cara pulled out the chair opposite to his and sat down, placing the carrier bag in her lap. 'I'm sorry, I don't remember your name.'

'Tierney,' he said. 'DC Ray Tierney.'

Cara nodded. She didn't trust him any more than she trusted Steadman, but at least he seemed less obviously hostile. He was in his late twenties, she estimated, a tall-ish, broad-shouldered man with a square jaw and pale face. Straw-coloured hair flopped over his forehead. He gazed at her through brown eyes, a look of avid curiosity. She knew there was no going back, but still she hesitated. Then, aware that the longer she took, the longer she would be there, she quickly reached into her pocket, took out the envelope and slid it across the table.

'This came yesterday. About three o'clock, just after three.'

Tierney took the note out of the envelope and his eyebrows shifted up. 'Nice,' he murmured. He glanced at her. 'You've handled it, I suppose?'

'I didn't know what was inside until I opened it.'

'Has anyone else touched it?'

Cara thought about last night, about Lytton, but he hadn't picked up the note. She shook her head. 'No, no one. But I don't imagine there'll be any prints other than mine.'

'And now mine,' Tierney said, laying the note down carefully on the table. '*Give it back.* What does that mean?'

'I don't know what it means. I've got no idea. You won't believe that, but it's true. What *could* I have?'

'Why wouldn't I believe it?'

Cara stared across the table at him. 'I've just got out of Leaside. Why are you going to believe anything I say?'

Tierney didn't reply to this. Instead, he said, 'Any guesses as to who might have written it?'

Cara shrugged. She could have thrown Terry Street's name into the ring, but that didn't seem a smart thing to do, especially when she didn't have any evidence. And if it got back to him – Cowan Road was full of double-dealing cops – she could find herself on a collision course with a major East End gangster. 'Whoever killed him, I presume. Unless it's some kind of sick joke.'

'Who'd make a joke like that?'

'If I knew, I wouldn't be here.'

'Jimmy didn't say anything to you? I mean, when he came to visit. He didn't say anything about being in trouble?'

'No,' she said. 'And before you ask, I didn't take anything from his flat. I don't have a clue what this is all about.'

Tierney gazed down at the note again. 'Did Jimmy have any enemies that you know of, anyone he might have fallen out with?'

'Twenty-four hours ago, I've have sworn he hadn't – he always got on with everyone – but obviously . . . well, someone had a problem. Have you had the results back from the post-mortem yet?'

'It was pretty much as we thought.' Tierney paused, as if in two minds as to how much to tell. 'He was badly beaten up, but it was a blow to the back of his head – a fall against the edge of the sink – that actually killed him.'

Cara felt her throat tighten. The thought of him lying there, alone and dying, made her want to weep. Her voice trembled a little as she spoke. 'Was it quick, do you think?'

'Yes, I'm sure it was.'

Cara didn't know if this was true, or if Tierney was just saying it to console her, but she wanted to believe him. It was a small mercy, but it was something. 'And do you know when?'

'Late Wednesday night, probably.'

On Wednesday night Cara had been counting off the hours until she'd be free again, lying in her bunk, yearning for freedom. Why hadn't she felt anything? All those years they'd been together, the connection they'd had, and yet she hadn't had a clue that anything was wrong. Suddenly the walls seemed to be closing in on her. She took a few deep breaths, grabbed hold of the carrier bag, pushed back her chair and stood up. 'Right, I'll leave it with you. I just thought you should see the note, in case ... I don't know. It must mean something, I suppose.'

'Why did you wait before bringing it in?'

'I'd had enough of you lot for one day. No offence.'

'None taken.'

Tierney escorted her back to the foyer. 'If anything else happens, if you get any more notes or ... You'll let us know, yeah?'

'Sure.'

'Okay. Take care of yourself.'

Cara could have retorted that she'd have to – clearly no one else was going to do it for her – but didn't want to come across as self-pitying or belligerent. She already had one

103

enemy at Cowan Road, there was no point in encouraging another. Instead, she forced a smile, nodded and said: 'I will. Thank you.'

She felt his eyes on her as she headed for the door. Although her legs wanted to run, she made them walk, not too fast, not too slow, just the right pace for someone who was completely innocent. And that was the strange thing: she *was* innocent. It was just this damn place that made her feel like she wasn't.

19

Cara was halfway down the high street, on her way to the cemetery, when she got the disturbing feeling that she was being followed again. A tremor ran through her. She could feel someone's gaze on the back of her neck, could sense it. Quickly she swung round, but the only people behind her, at least the only ones in her line of sight, were women with prams, a couple of youths and some OAPs peering into the window of the butcher's shop. She quickly surveyed the street, up and down, but there was no black BMW.

Was she imagining it? No, she was certain she wasn't. Suddenly everyone seemed suspicious, even the old ladies with their tired faces and stooped bodies. She looked a little closer at the two youths, but neither of them was taking any interest in her. They appeared to be behaving normally, leaning against the wall, smoking while they chatted to each other. She stared at them for a while before shifting her gaze again.

The goon, she thought, was too big, too noticeable, to be able to hide himself in a hurry. Perhaps they had put someone else on to her, someone with more guile. They could be using a different car, too. Except they wouldn't be using a car, would they? It would be too difficult to follow her that way, impossible without holding up the traffic.

She swallowed hard while her gaze darted to the left and to the right. Whoever it was would have to show themselves eventually. Now people were being forced to walk around her because she was blocking the pavement. Dirty looks were being thrown. Muttered tutting reached her ears. She didn't care. She would stand there for ever if she had to.

The flaw to this plan soon became apparent: her tail, if it wasn't the goon, could walk straight past without her knowing. Or disappear into one of the shops or alleyways. And what was she going to do if a likely suspect did appear? She could hardly start accusing strangers in the street. Then she began to doubt herself again. Perhaps she was just being paranoid. A minute ago, she would have sworn that she was being followed, but now that certainty was beginning to waiver.

She turned and started walking again. It was not impossible that her brain was frazzled, her senses off kilter after everything that had happened. Murder, especially the murder of a loved one, didn't do much for rational thinking. Could her instincts be trusted? Well, maybe they could and maybe they couldn't, but she wasn't going to risk going straight to the cemetery if there *was* a tail on her. It was too quiet there, too lonely.

However, Cara wasn't prepared to abandon her plans. It was over eighteen months since she'd last visited the grave and apart from the pure practicalities of cleaning the headstone and tidying up, she felt a deep and urgent need to go there. It was the only place she could feel close to her dad, and she wanted that feeling more than anything.

She had to think. She had to figure out a way. Her gaze took in the shops as she passed them – the newsagent, the grocer, the barber – until it came to rest on the Kellston Record Shack. Its door was open and the sound of Bob Marley drifted out on to the street. She gave a mental nod as an idea took root in her head.

Inside, the Shack was busy, its main aisle packed with teen-agers. The younger ones were bunking off school, the older ones on the dole. There was high unemployment in the country, but it was especially bad in areas like this. With little else to do, the kids gravitated towards somewhere they could listen to music for free and browse without being pressured to buy.

Cara had been here often and knew the layout well. The shop was in an upside-down L-shape, a long central room with a smaller one going off to the right. It was towards this smaller space which housed the blues, jazz and American soul imports, and where she couldn't be seen from the street, that she was ultimately headed. But not too quickly. She didn't want to give the game away.

She spent the next ten minutes flicking through the records on display, drifting slowly from row to row and lifting out the occasional LP to look at the outer sleeve more closely. Resisting the temptation to glance towards the shop window, she pretended to be absorbed in the latest offerings from the Eurythmics, Madonna and Stevie Wonder. She knew she hadn't been followed in – no one had entered the shop since she had – which meant, if everything went to plan, that she should be able to disappear before too long.

Mavin, the owner of the Shack, was behind the counter at the far end. He had a customer and she waited until he'd finished serving before wandering over. To anyone watching, it would hopefully look like she was just enquiring about some record or another.

'Hey, babe,' he said, smiling when he saw her. 'You okay? Haven't seen you in a while.'

'No, I've been away.'

Mavin had the good grace not to pursue the subject. Away could mean a number of things, but round here it usually meant doing bird. 'Good to have you back.'

'Good to be back. How's business?'

'It's been better.'

'Busy at least,' she said, looking over her shoulder.

'Yeah, lots of busy, but not so much buying.'

Suddenly Cara caught a glimpse of a man outside the shop. It was a fleeting glimpse, a blur of features, a vague impression of dark clothes and dark hair before the bloke moved swiftly to the side and out of sight. If he hadn't moved so quickly, she probably wouldn't have clocked him. It was that fast, evasive action that gave him away. And now her faith in her instincts had been restored.

'I still miss your old man,' Mavin said. 'And not just because of all the dough he used to spend in here. These kids don't know nothin' about music. All they want to listen to is what they're told they should be listening to.'

Cara smiled. Her dad used to spend entire afternoons chatting to Mavin while he perused the new stock, record by record. She leaned forward and lowered her voice. 'Could you do me a favour? Could you let me slip out the back way? There's someone I'm trying to avoid.'

Mavin, fortunately, was the type who didn't ask too many questions. He didn't even glance at the customers to try and spot who she might be talking about. Instead, he simply gestured towards his left. 'Help yourself, babe. You know the way.'

'You're a star,' she said. 'Thanks.'

'Don't be a stranger.'

Cara smiled again. She strolled casually into the smaller area and then, the moment she was out of sight from the street, hurried through the door marked STAFF ONLY. This led to Mavin's office, a tiny room with a couple of filing cabinets, shelving lined with yet more LPs and a table stacked with boxes. It wasn't the first time she'd left this way; she'd done it once before with her dad when he'd had to make a quick escape from some thug of a debt collector who'd followed him to the shop.

Quickly she unbolted the back door and stepped out, pulling the door shut behind her. She crossed the short yard that contained nothing other than hardy weeds pushing through the concrete, opened the gate and peered up and down the alley. Empty. Thank God. She didn't hang about but wrapped her fingers tightly around the carrier bag and took off like a rocket, sprinting as fast she could.

20

When she got to Station Road, Cara cautiously looked towards the corner where the road met the high street – no sign of the dark-haired man – before turning left and crossing over at the first opportunity. Then she took a right and zigzagged through a maze of alleyways until she came out a short distance from a little-used side entrance to the cemetery.

By now she was certain she was alone. With luck it would be a good ten minutes before her tail even realised that she'd given him the slip and by then he'd have no idea where she'd gone. He could waste a good hour searching before returning to the Mansfield and waiting for her there.

There was a florist nearby and she went in and bought a bunch of lilies. As she left the shop, she had another good look around and then strode quickly to the cemetery. Once inside, she relaxed a little, but not too much. It wasn't smart to be overconfident. Although she felt a certain level of smugness at having outfoxed her shadow, she couldn't be a hundred per cent sure that he wouldn't search for her here. Unlikely, but not impossible.

The side entrance led into the older, neglected part of the cemetery where the grass was long and the graves, many of them over a hundred years old, were in a state of cracked abandonment. She passed large ostentatious memorials and crumbling mausoleums covered in ivy. Smaller, more modest resting places had headstones with inscriptions that were barely legible. Grey stone angels raised their faces to heaven and clasped their hands in prayer.

Cara's level of vigilance increased as she left behind the older part of the cemetery and advanced into the relatively more modern section. This was closer to the main thoroughfare, and she kept her eyes peeled, constantly looking around. So far as she could see there wasn't another living soul in the place, but then nine-thirty on a Friday morning probably wasn't the most popular time for people to visit.

Her father's final resting place was tucked away along a narrow path. She walked with her shoulders hunched, keeping herself as small as possible. The ground was soft, and the smell of wet earth hung in the air, mingling with the heady scent of the lilies. As soon as she got to the grave, she immediately crouched down, her fingers reaching out to touch the white marble headstone.

'Well, here I am.'

Cara sighed as she took in the state of the grave. No one had been here since she'd been sent down, and the weather had taken its toll. The headstone was dulled and dirty, and the wind had blown all kinds of debris on to the plot. Litter, leaves and twigs had gathered in the oblong kerb in front of the stone, a soggy tangle that lay under and between the white quartz crystal chips.

'I suppose you've heard about Jimmy,' she said, as she began to tidy up. 'If you see him, tell him he's left a right old mess behind.'

She removed the rotten remains of the previous flowers she had left, laid them on the grass and poured out the stagnant water from the urn. Then she emptied the carrier bag. She poured water on to one side of the cloth, wiped down the headstone and the edges of the kerb, then dried and polished them with the other side. She sat back on her heels to view the effect. Better, she thought.

'And now I've got some dirtbag following me around – maybe more than one – and I don't know what he wants. No, I do know what he wants – he "wants it back", but as I don't have a clue as to what *it* is, it makes it kind of tricky.'

She raised her eyes and scoured the surrounding area, just to make sure she had no unwanted company. Everything was quiet. The only sound she could hear was the wind rustling through the trees and the very distant hum of traffic. She went back to work gathering up the leaves and the other rubbish, poking between the quartz to release all the twiggy pieces and the sycamore keys. She shoved her haul into the carrier bag, intending to dump it in the bin on her way out.

'Mum called yesterday. She's okay. Well, she's got the hump with some ass of a director, but that's nothing new. I told her about Jimmy.' Cara's voice wavered and she took a moment before continuing. 'What was he playing at, Dad? I know he was never whiter than white, but this is something else. I don't understand what's going on. I mean, why would anyone want to do that to him? He must have got involved in something completely bloody stupid. And I bet Murch knows more than he's saying. Those two were always thick as thieves.'

Cara took the cellophane off the lilies and broke the stems so they were short enough to prevent the flowers from toppling over. She put fresh water in the urn, arranged the lilies and placed them in front of the headstone. 'I've got Steadman on my back, of course. Just my luck that he's working in Kellston now. I'm telling you, that man has got it in for me. If he could bang me up tomorrow and throw away the key, he would.'

She shoved the cellophane and the broken-off bits of stem in the carrier bag along with the rest of the rubbish. 'Listen to me, moaning for Britain. You don't have to worry. I'm okay. I *will* be okay. It's just shaken me up, you know. I feel . . . I feel like . . .' Cara couldn't put it into words. 'Oh, I'll be all right. It's just the damn shock of it all.'

She sat crouched for a while, staring at the grave. It still seemed impossible that she had lost the two people she cared about most and in such a short space of time. How was anyone supposed to deal with that? There was a chasm in her life, and she didn't have a clue how to fill it.

The sky was growing dark, storm clouds gathering above. A few drops of rain fell on her head. Cara got to her feet and pulled up the hood of her raincoat. She picked up the carrier bag with her left hand, put the fingertips of her right hand to her lips and then gently transferred the kiss to the top edge of the headstone. 'See you soon, Dad. Take care of Jimmy, won't you?'

It was at that very moment that she became aware of it – a slight shifting of the air, a movement, a presence. Horror sliced through her, cold as a knife. *Someone was standing behind.* She whirled around, fear sweeping through her body, her heart almost leaping out of her chest. Even as she turned, she was bracing, preparing to defend herself against the oversized goon or the dark-haired man.

'Sorry, love. I didn't mean to give you a fright.'

There, standing only a few feet away, was an elderly woman wearing a tatty mac and holding a small pink rose in a pot.

Cara stared at her, open mouthed. There was no threat here, not unless the old dear was hiding a gun in her pocket. Gradually the adrenaline started to subside. 'It's okay,' she finally managed to mumble. 'I-I just didn't realise you were there.'

'You've gone white as a sheet.'

'Have I?' Cara said, raising a hand to her face.

'It's a quiet place, ain't it? Enough to give anyone the jitters. Still, this lot won't give you any bother.' The old woman gestured towards the surrounding graves. 'Good as gold, they are. All nicely tucked up and sleeping soundly.'

They're not the ones I'm worried about, Cara might have said, glancing quickly round the cemetery, but instead she simply smiled and nodded. She wondered if the woman was all there or if she just had an odd sense of humour.

'I'm here to see my Gordon. Every Friday I come, regular as clockwork.'

'That's nice.'

'It's something to do, love. It breaks up the day.'

The more Cara looked at her, the more familiar she became. The wizened face was topped with a fringe of white hair and framed by a bright yellow headscarf. She had to be at least eighty, probably more, and was small but upright with skinny legs and fragile bony wrists. Yes, she lived on the Mansfield. She'd lived there for years. Alma something. Cara racked her brains. Alma Todd, that was it.

Alma's pale eyes fell on Richard Kendall's headstone. 'He was a right gent, your dad. Always had time for a chat.'

Cara, who wasn't in the mood for company and had been planning on slowly edging away, now felt too guilty to go through with it. 'You knew him, then?'

'He was one of a kind. Must have broken your heart losing him like that.'

114

'I still miss him.'

Alma's lips parted, showing a row of creamy white dentures. 'Oh, you never stop missing them, dear. That's just the way it is.' She sighed. 'I heard about Jimmy Lovell. Dreadful business that. In his own home, too. None of us are safe these days.'

Cara's fingers tightened around the carrier bag. 'I just hope they find who did it.'

'You and me both, love. There was never no harm in the lad, not like some I could mention.'

'No, there was never any harm.'

Alma inclined her bird-like head as if expecting or hoping for additional comment, but when none was forthcoming, she carried on regardless. 'Make the most of life while you're young, that's what I say. You never know what's around the corner. You get to my age and suddenly you're invisible. Nobody notices the old ones. Ghosts, that's what we are. We hear plenty, see plenty, but we may as well be deaf and dumb.'

Cara was spared the difficulty of thinking up a suitable reply. Alma glanced at the sky and said, 'Right, I'd best be off before the heavens open. Gordon's going to worry if I'm late.' She reached out and patted Cara's arm. 'You take care of yourself, love.'

'You too.'

Cara watched her walk away. The old woman was sprightly for her age, her feet moving quickly and silently across the damp November earth. She wondered how long Alma had been coming here, how many Friday mornings she had visited the cemetery, how many small pots of roses she had placed on Gordon's grave. Life was lonely for those who were left behind.

Loneliness. Cara rolled the word around, feeling it gradually seep down into her. A dull pain settled in her chest. Quickly she shook herself. It was all right to feel sorry for someone else, but she couldn't afford a descent into self-pity. For now, at least, she had to be strong, had to be tough, had to keep her wits about her. Jimmy's killer was out there somewhere and that somewhere might not be too far away.

21

Larry Steadman parked in front of Temple, switched off the engine, but didn't immediately get out of the car. Instead, he turned to Tierney and said: '"Give it back"? Sounds like Cara Kendall knows more than she's been telling us.'

'She says not. She claims she doesn't know what it means.'

'And you believe her?'

Tierney shrugged. 'You think she's playing us?'

'It wouldn't be the first time.' Larry was peeved that he'd missed her at the station, that he'd missed the opportunity to see her again face to face. Tierney couldn't read her like he could; he wouldn't have been able to tell if she was lying or not. 'She'll have an angle. You can count on that.'

'She didn't ever get to see Jimmy, though, did she? Not alive, I mean. He couldn't have given her anything.'

'She could have helped herself while she was at the flat.'

'But if it was at the flat why didn't the killer take it? Why didn't he even look for it? The place was untidy, but it hadn't been turned over.'

Larry shifted his gaze and stared out through the windscreen. He was still trying to work out what it all meant, to bring it into sharper focus in his mind. 'Maybe there wasn't anything to find. Maybe he went there to do a job he'd been paid for, did it and left.'

'You still think she was involved? But what about the note?'

'What about it? For all we know she could have written it herself. There's nothing like making yourself look the victim when you're up to your neck in it.' Larry paused, aware that he was juggling two contradictory ideas at the same time – the note was real/the note was a red herring – and not sure which of them he currently favoured. 'Okay, say the note is genuine, we've only got her word as to when she found Jimmy. She could have taken "it", stashed it at her own flat or somewhere else, then gone back to his and made the 999 call.'

Tierney looked sceptical. 'Bit risky, all that coming and going. What if one of the neighbours had seen her?'

'What if they had? I doubt they'd share the bloody information with us.'

'True, but she couldn't have been certain of that.'

Larry made a dismissive-sounding noise. 'She's a risk taker. We're talking about a girl who climbs up drainpipes and clambers over roofs for a living. A bit of toing and froing from a flat isn't going to faze her.'

'But why bother going back at all? She could have left Jimmy to be found by someone else. Putting herself at the scene is just asking for trouble.'

'Maybe she likes trouble. Or maybe she reckoned it would put her in the clear as regards whatever's gone missing. If she was taken straight down the station and interviewed as a possible suspect, she could claim that she didn't have the opportunity to remove anything.' Larry rolled this theory around his mind

118

for a moment, found nothing much wrong with it, and nodded. 'Yeah, that's a possibility. If whoever killed Jimmy comes after her, she can shrug her shoulders and plead innocence.'

'Unless it was small,' Tierney said. 'She could have been carrying something small and we'd never have known about it.'

Larry glanced at his watch. 'Let's see if Mr Murchison can shed any light on the affair.'

The two of them got out of the car and walked towards Temple. The greyness of the day merged into the concrete greyness of the tower. As Larry's gaze travelled upwards it took in the drab façade, the endless rows of windows and the rusting balconies. Everything about the place screamed misery. It was beyond depressing, but at least he didn't have to live here.

They went through the door into the litter-strewn foyer and got into a lift that smelled of dope and urine. Larry pressed the button for the seventh floor.

'What's the score on Murchison?' Tierney asked as the lift began its juddering ascent.

'Nothing much. A few misdemeanours in his youth, but he's been clean since then. He's an electrician, works for his dad in the family business. Colin and Jimmy went to school together and they've stayed tight. Best buddies by all accounts. If anyone knows what Jimmy was up to, it'll be him.'

'And do you think he's likely to share that information?'

Larry grinned. 'Not with any enthusiasm.'

They exited the lift and walked along the corridor to Murchison's flat. Larry knocked and after a short wait the door was opened.

Colin Murchison looked them up and down and scowled. He was a short, stocky man who wore the same half surly, half wary expression that was common to most of the males on the Mansfield estate. Dressed in blue workman's overalls, there was a white logo on his right breast pocket with the words 'Murchison Electricals' printed underneath. Resentment coloured his voice. 'You're the law, right? You're early.'

Larry, after trying to track him down all day yesterday, had finally managed to get in touch early this morning and arrange a meet for ten o'clock. He looked at his watch again – it was a quarter to ten – and said drily, 'You want us to come back in fifteen minutes?'

'Not much point, is there? You may as well come in now you're here.'

Larry and Tierney followed him through to a living room that was only marginally tidier than Lovell's. Murchison sat down at the table and flapped a hand towards the sofa. 'You got news on Jimmy?'

Larry shook his head. 'Not yet, I'm afraid. It might help if we knew what he was involved in.'

'Involved? What's that supposed to mean?'

'Well, he got on the wrong side of someone, Mr Murchison. You any idea of who that someone might be?'

Murchison's round face flushed red, and his eyes grew narrow, a reaction that could have been down to genuine indignation or, just as likely, a sign that he was about to start lying. 'Jimmy weren't involved in nothin'. I'd have known if he were. What are you trying to say – that it was his own fault he got wasted?'

'No one's saying that.'

'Sounds like it to me.'

'So why do you think Jimmy was killed?'

Murchison shifted in his chair and scowled some more. 'A robbery, weren't it? Maybe someone followed him home.'

'Why would anyone think he was worth robbing?'

'Thinking ain't got nothin' to do with it, not round here. Those junkie lowlifes would batter their own mothers for a fix.'

Larry wasn't buying it. He decided to change tack. 'When was the last time you saw Jimmy?'

'Wednesday night, about six. He came into the Fox for a pint, but he didn't stay long. An hour or so.'

'And how did he seem?'

'Seem?' Murchison echoed.

Larry was used to evasions and all the playing-for-time techniques from people who pretended not to understand the question while they tried to decide how much to tell. 'Happy, sad, worried? Angry, quiet, confused?'

'The same as always. Just normal.'

'Which was?'

Murchison shrugged. 'Shit, I don't know. He was just Jimmy.'

'Nothing on his mind?'

'Nothin' he told me about.'

'What *did* you talk about?'

'Football, work, I dunno. Then he said he had things to do, got up and left.'

Larry persisted. 'What sort of things?'

'How would I know? I'm not his bleedin' keeper. Could have been anything, a bit of skirt, maybe.'

'Was Jimmy seeing anyone, anyone in particular?'

Murchison's shoulders shifted up again. 'Nah. I dunno. No one special, far as I know.'

'Come on, Colin,' Larry said, using Murchison's Christian name for the first time. 'Help us out here. You want us to catch the bastard who killed him, don't you? Did Jimmy have any enemies, anyone he'd fallen out with recently?'

'Jimmy wasn't the falling out sort. He got along with people.'

Larry changed direction again. 'Did you see Cara Kendall yesterday?'

Murchison hesitated before answering, as if suspecting a trap in the question. His boots did a brief dance on the floor. 'Yeah, I went to see her in the afternoon. I just wanted to make sure she was okay.'

'And was she?'

'What do you think?'

'I've no idea. That's why I'm asking.'

Murchison's mouth drooped at the corners. 'She weren't exactly dancing on the table, if that's what you mean. Poor cow found him, didn't she? She didn't say much. I reckon she was still in shock. Anyway, I didn't hang about. I don't think she was in the mood for company.'

Larry wondered if that was any company or just Murchison's in particular. He sat back and asked casually, 'I've always thought it odd that Jimmy wasn't with Cara on the Hampstead job.' He was aware of a quick interrogative glance from Tierney, a what-the-hell-has-that-to-do-with-anything sort of glance, but carried on regardless. 'Do you know why he didn't go with her?'

'You'd need to ask her that.'

'I'm asking you. You were Jimmy's mate. He must have said something to you.'

'Look, those two were always falling out. On one minute, off the next. That's how it is with some couples. Far as I'm aware, he didn't know nothin' about Hampstead.'

Larry doubted this. 'So do you know who she *was* with that night?'

'She wasn't with no one. She went in there on her own.' Murchison briefly pressed his lips together. 'What's going on here? Why are you asking about this stuff? It ain't got nothin' to do with Jimmy.'

'Just background, that's all.'

'It's old news. I don't get why you're bringing it all up again.'

Murchison rose to his feet. 'Are we finished here? I've got work to go to.'

In the lift, going down, Tierney looked at Larry and said, 'Well, that was a waste of time. What was with the Hampstead questions? You reckon there's a connection between the murders of Myers and Lovell?'

Larry still wasn't sure what he thought. 'Can't rule it out,' he said. Although he wasn't entirely sure if he could rule it in, either.

22

Cara followed the same route she had come, taking her time despite the rain. She dumped the carrier bag full of leaves and debris in a bin and then tramped slowly through the long grass, not meeting another living soul along the way. When she got to the gate she stopped, looked left and right along the road and felt a sudden reluctance to go on. Once she was back on the streets, her tail might pick her up again.

Still, she could hardly spend the whole day in the cemetery. Despite her misgivings she set off, glancing frequently over her shoulder as she walked back through the twisting alleys and eventually, a few minutes later, came out on Station Road. Here she paused again and peered intently all around her. She was only minutes away from the Record Shack. The fastest way home was straight up the high street, but the high street was where she was most likely to be spotted.

Unwilling to give up her freedom quite yet, Cara went to the café by the station and stared in through the window. Once she'd established the absence of any dodgy characters – there were only two customers and both were women with shopping at their feet – she went inside and ordered a coffee.

She chose a table away from the window and sat down. What next? Murch, perhaps. A frown settled on her forehead. Although she had to talk to him, she didn't relish the prospect. Anyway, he was probably at work. Tonight would be better. Yes, she'd call him about six, and if he wasn't in she'd try the Fox.

While she drank her coffee, her gaze flicked constantly towards Station Road. She examined the passers-by, quickly dismissing most of them, her eyes only lingering on the men with dark hair. Were any of them acting suspiciously? She couldn't decide if she was being followed purely as a means of intimidation – like the goon slowing down at the bus stop – or to establish exactly where she was going and who she was seeing. Both, perhaps. Except she was hardly likely to reveal anything useful if she was aware of being tailed. This contradiction confused her.

Cara's thoughts ran on to Steadman. Her face darkened. She couldn't trust him to properly investigate Jimmy's death. He was too fixated on the idea that she was involved, and for as long as he believed that, he'd be travelling down blind alleys and looking in all the wrong places. Damn the man! He was stupid and vindictive. And while he was preoccupied with her, he'd never find the real killer.

Her gaze roamed across the street to a row of old Victorian houses. Most of these were B&Bs or divided and subdivided into flats and bedsits, but a few were commercial premises, offices for solicitors and accountants and chiropractors. She focused on one of the shabbier buildings, its peeling paintwork in need of attention. She must have walked past the place hundreds of times, barely registering the names that were listed on metal plaques to the side of the door, but now one of them suddenly came to her.

Cara had an idea. She couldn't swear it was a good one, but it might not be her worst. She gulped down the rest of the coffee, made another quick survey of the outside world and left the café before she could change her mind. The rain was still coming down, gathering in the gutters and creating puddles on the pavement. She pulled up her hood and jaywalked across the street with one eye on the cars and taxis, the other on her fellow pedestrians.

She might have hesitated, taken a little longer to think about it, if it hadn't been for the possibility of her tail still being around. Instead, she tried the door – it was open – and swiftly stepped inside. The interior of the building had as little to recommend it as the exterior. It smelled musty and damp like an old cellar. Dim lighting, dark green walls and a threadbare carpet only added to the general atmosphere of gloom.

As she ascended the stairs, Cara could hear the regular clacking of a typewriter coming from high above. The man she wanted was on the first floor. Her right hand slid along a banister worn and blackened through age. Now she was starting to have serious doubts. Could anyone who worked here be any good? The air of seedy dilapidation didn't fill her with confidence.

But it was this or the waiting game. And she was too impatient to sit it out and see what happened. She had to try and get some control over the situation. On reaching the landing, she followed the sign, turned right and soon found herself at the office she was after. The top half of the door was opaque glass and bore the inscription 'Glen Douglas, Private Investigator'.

She knocked lightly but got no response. Then she tried the

handle. The door opened, emitting a tinging sound to announce her presence. She walked into what appeared to be a waiting room, a small drab space with magnolia walls, a few plastic chairs and a coffee table heaped with dusty magazines. If her heart had already been sinking, it now began to plummet. The place was a dive.

Cara might have turned on her heel and walked out again if the door to the inner office hadn't abruptly swung open to reveal a middle-aged, rather portly man with shrewd eyes and thinning salt-and-pepper hair. He wore a slightly startled expression, as if he wasn't used to finding people actually waiting in the waiting room.

'Mr Douglas?' she asked.

'That's me.'

'I'm Cara Kendall. I need . . .' She hesitated, debating whether this was really such a smart idea, wondering if she should make her excuses and go and look instead for a private eye who appeared less likely to have a heart attack if he ran for a bus. But having made it this far she decided she may as well carry on. 'I need some help.'

'You'd better come through, then.'

Douglas's office wasn't much of an improvement on the outer room. There was a desk, a phone, a fax machine, a couple of chairs, three filing cabinets, and a drooping plant on the windowsill. He walked around the desk, sat down and nodded towards the other chair. 'So, what's the problem?'

Cara sat down too, gathered her thoughts, took a deep breath and then launched into it. 'I'm being followed. Since yesterday, yesterday morning.' She went on to quickly explain about leaving prison, the goons in the car, finding Jimmy's body and the threatening note that had been posted through her letterbox. 'I don't know what they think I have, but I haven't got it. And

I reckon if I can find out who's following me, I'll be one step closer to finding out who killed Jimmy.'

'You've had an eventful twenty-four hours.' Douglas looked neither surprised nor alarmed by her story, as though it was perfectly normal for random females to walk in off the street and regale him with tales of murder and mayhem. 'Have you been to the police about the man who's tailing you?'

'I've told them about the note, not about the tail.'

'Why not?'

'Because I wasn't sure about it until I went to the cemetery this morning. And anyway, I don't think they'd take me seriously. In fact, I'm sure of it. Steadman, that's DI Steadman, isn't my biggest fan. He's off on some wild goose chase, trying to prove I had something to do with Jimmy's murder.' She leaned forward and held Douglas's gaze. 'I didn't, though. I swear. We weren't together, but I still cared about him.'

'You don't think you might be better off leaving this to the police?'

'No,' Cara insisted, frowning in frustration. 'Are you not listening to me? By the time the law realise they've got it all wrong, it's going to be too late. Whoever killed Jimmy will have crawled back under whatever stone he came from and that'll be that. And I need to know who wrote that note. Until then, I'm completely in the dark as to what's actually going on.'

'Okay, say I do find out who your tail is. What are you going to do then?'

'I suppose it depends on who it is.' Cara didn't want to mention Terry Street in case Douglas didn't fancy getting on the wrong side of the local hoods. 'Maybe I *will* go to the law once I know who's behind it all.'

Douglas gazed at her. His face was impassive, and it was hard to read what he was thinking: that she was crazy, perhaps, some attention-seeking fantasist. Still, business was business. He opened a drawer, took out an oblong of laminated card and slid it across the desk. 'These are my rates.'

Cara inwardly winced at the hourly rate, doing a fast, mental calculation as to her current financial situation – not great – whilst trying not to look too dismayed. 'That's fine. But something like this won't take long, will it? I mean, it's pretty straightforward. All we have to do is arrange a time for me to leave the flat and you can be there waiting. I'll go to the shops or whatever and that way you'll see who's following me, job done.'

'It might not be quite as simple as that.'

'Why not?'

Douglas gave her a patient smile. 'We could get lucky. If the man's got a car, I should be able to get a trace on it, get a name. But that won't necessarily provide you with the information you need. Whoever's following you is probably working for someone else. I'll have to follow them to find out who. It could all take a bit of time.'

Cara hadn't considered these complications. 'How much time?'

'A few days, perhaps. Don't forget your tail could be watching you for hours, all day even, before he gets relieved or decides to head back to base. I can only go as fast as he does.' Douglas placed his hands on the desk and gave her another brief smile. 'Look, why don't you go home and think about it? Give me a call if you want to go ahead.'

'I don't have to think about it. Can you start right away?'

'I'll need a retainer,' he said. 'Forty should cover it.'

Cara reached into her bag and took out her purse, hoping she wasn't about to make a serious mistake. Before she relinquished the cash, she asked: 'So have you been in this business for long?'

'Over twenty years.'

'And you work on your own?'

'I prefer it that way. I've got people I can call on if I need them. There's a lot to be said for being your own boss, for not having to answer to anyone.'

Well, she could relate to that, Cara thought, as she handed over eight fivers. And if he'd managed to stay afloat for twenty years, he had to be competent at least. Although the state of his office, and the worn look to his suit, suggested business wasn't exactly thriving.

Douglas wrote out a receipt and gave it to her.

'So what happens now?' she asked.

'Were you followed here?'

Cara shook her head. 'No, I gave him the slip on the high street. About an hour ago.'

'Are you sure?'

'I used the alleys to get to the cemetery. He couldn't have tailed me without my noticing.'

'You got a description?'

'No, I only caught a glimpse. I'm sure it wasn't the same guy who I saw yesterday, though.'

'Yeah, there's likely to be more than one of them. They'll be doing shifts.' Douglas pushed a sheet of paper across the desk. 'Write down your address and phone number. You do have a phone, don't you?'

'Yes.'

'Good. It's better that we talk that way rather than you coming here. We'll get started tomorrow morning.'

'Why not today, this afternoon?'

'Because I'm busy this afternoon. In the morning, leave the flat at around half eleven, go buy your pint of milk or whatever and then go straight home. Don't look around for me or for them. Just try and act as naturally as possible. Hopefully, they'll be doing a shift change round about lunchtime and I'll be able to follow our off-duty guy.'

'And then?'

'And then you wait to hear from me. I'll be in touch as soon as I know anything.'

Cara finished writing down her details and passed back the sheet of paper. 'I'll be using the Mansfield Road entrance. That's where the black BMW was parked yesterday.'

'Right,' Douglas said, standing up. 'Be careful when you leave. You don't want to be spotted coming out of here.'

As they walked through the waiting room Cara looked again at the less than salubrious decor. 'Have you ever thought about doing this place up? Giving it a lick of paint, perhaps?'

'What for?'

'It's not exactly welcoming.'

'No one comes here,' Douglas said. 'I do most of my business by phone.'

'I came here.'

'So what's your point? You still employed me.'

'It was touch and go,' Cara said.

23

Cara peered cautiously around the front door before stepping outside, hurrying along the short path and turning right along Station Road. With her purse forty pounds lighter, she hoped she hadn't been fleeced and that Douglas would do what she'd paid him to do. What were the odds? With his shabby suit and casual manner, he didn't exactly inspire confidence, but maybe he was smarter than he looked.

At the traffic lights on the corner, she paused, unsure as to where to go next. She didn't really want to go home. The flat was empty – Lytton, presumably, was still at college – and without any distractions, she was afraid of sinking down again, of becoming incapacitated by pain and misery. The temptation to visit the off-licence, to buy more booze and get blind drunk, was something she had to resist. Sober thoughts were bad enough, drunken ones were likely to tip her over the edge.

She had to keep busy, keep moving. It wasn't exactly walking weather, but she didn't care. She'd had enough of confined spaces. After eighteen months of staring at the world through bars, she might as well make the most of her freedom. It was still raining, but getting wet was preferable to being trapped indoors with only her memories for company.

When the lights turned to green, she quickly crossed the road and headed south, in the opposite direction to the Mansfield. It was possible that her tail had gone back for the car and was cruising around looking for her. Or would he have given up by now? Perhaps he'd assume she'd caught a train or a bus and was miles away. Still, it would be wise to keep off the main street just in case.

Cara took the first side road she came to and began to explore. This end had always been the better part of Kellston – once, way back in time, it had even been fashionable – and the further away you got from the railway, the bigger the houses were. Within ten minutes she was starting to come across large, detached properties with generous gardens. Most of these had been converted into flats but a few still appeared to be single residences.

To take her mind off things, she tried to choose which of them she'd break into if she really *had* to. As she walked casually past, she noted the state of the upper windows, the side access, any alarms or signs of occupancy. Although it was just a game she was playing, she felt that sudden rush of adrenaline, the kick that always accompanied her bad intentions.

It had been an act of perversity, she knew, to break into the Hampstead house after what had happened to her dad. His gruesome death should have been a lesson to her, a warning to stay on the straight and narrow, but instead it had had the opposite effect. She had reacted to his loss by trying to emulate what he had once done so well. In the process she had felt like she was kicking back at society, at all the rules that said the rich should get richer and the poor should stay where they'd been put. Not to mention putting two fingers up at all those vile disdainful girls who had scorned her at school and made her life a misery.

Cara's hands clenched in her pockets. She was aware that none of this reflected well on her, that she had a twisted sense of right and wrong, but she didn't care. And now that Jimmy was gone, she cared even less. Everything seemed pointless. What was the purpose of toeing the line when the line didn't give a damn about you? She thought of the future, of the years stretching ahead, and felt consumed with emptiness.

Indifferent to where she was going, she trudged on, taking left and right turns at random. Eventually, in Weld Road, she came upon a grand, imposing house with high walls and a pair of fancy wrought-iron gates. A dark red Mercedes was parked in the drive. Everything about the building screamed money, from the state of the roof – not a tile out of place – to the vine-covered exterior and immaculate paintwork. Her gaze flicked to the sash windows on the second and third floors, and the sturdy-looking drainpipe that was just asking to be climbed. Yes, if she had to choose, this would be the one.

Cara stood for a while, peering through the gates. Had she been intending to break in, she wouldn't have lingered, but imaginary thieving didn't require caution. Already she could envisage the inside, the generous rooms with their plush carpets and Persian rugs, the paintings hanging on the walls, the upstairs bedrooms with their wardrobes full of tailored clothes and drawers full of treasure.

She moved off, smiling faintly. Fantasies were all very well, but Steadman would have her in the frame as soon as the 999 call went in. In fact, he would probably try to pin any local burglaries on her, no matter what the method. Which didn't bode well for a happy future in Kellston. She wondered what, if anything, would get Steadman off her back. Him finding out who'd killed Gerald Myers, perhaps, and getting them put away. But what were the chances of that? Pretty slim after all this time.

Cara often wondered who'd been in the house with her that night. Maybe if she'd been more alert to the atmosphere, she could have got out of the place before the flashing blue lights turned up on the doorstep. She should never have gone downstairs. She should have got the hell out while she still had the chance. But no matter how many times she went over it in her head, it wasn't going to change the outcome.

She plodded on, alert to any cars that passed by. It was quiet in these backstreets and, on the whole, she only had her thoughts for company. Now that she'd employed Glen Douglas, all she could do was wait. But inactivity drove her mad. How was she going to get through the next twenty-four hours? And that was probably the earliest he would be in touch with her. It could be closer to two days before she finally learned the identity of her tail.

Cara considered heading back to the railway station, catching a bus and going up West. There she could roam about freely without having to constantly be on her guard. She could go to the National Gallery and look at the paintings, walk through St James's Park, merge with the crowd and do some window shopping. But none of it appealed to her. Not today. She was too jumpy and anxious, too preoccupied by Jimmy's murder.

Wet and hungry, she turned for home. Although it didn't really matter if her tail picked her up now, she saw no reason to make it easy for him and so chose the least direct route back to the Mansfield. Instead of the high street she took the narrow roads running parallel and then circled round the back of the estate and went in through the entrance closest to Temple.

She looked around for her tail – no sign – and then checked the concrete forecourt for Murch's white van. Sometimes, if he had a job close by, he came back for lunch, but he must be working further afield today. His absence wasn't unexpected, but it was still disappointing. She had convinced herself that Murch knew something, *had* to know something, and having to wait before she could question him again filled her with frustration.

Cara strode quickly past Temple and had almost reached Haslow House when she became aware of footsteps behind her. She spun round, her heart in her mouth, but was relieved to see that it was only Rochelle. The relief didn't last long. The girl, dressed in a miniskirt and puffa jacket, stared at her with an expression that could hardly be called friendly. Her mouth was sulky, her eyes cold with indignation.

'I've been looking for you. I've been all over, to the flat and everything. Where have you been?'

Cara couldn't see that it was any of her business. 'What do you want?'

'What do you think? I want to know who killed Jimmy.'

'You and me both. Why are you asking me? I don't know any more than I knew yesterday.'

Rochelle pushed out her lower lip, like a petulant child. 'Did you tell the pigs about me?'

'Tell them what?'

'About me and Jimmy.'

'I didn't think there was anything to tell.' Cara stared back at her. The smell of alcohol wafted off the girl, although whether that was down to yesterday's excesses or a morning top-up was impossible to discern. She wasn't blind drunk, but she didn't seem entirely sober, either. 'You said you hadn't seen him for a few days.'

'I hadn't. I don't want to talk to them, though.'

'Yeah, well, nobody wants to do that.'

Rochelle continued to pout. 'I don't know fuckin' nothin' so why should I talk to them?'

'No one's saying you should.'

'So why are you looking at me like that?'

'I'm not looking at you *like that*. Jesus, Rochelle, why do you have to take everything the wrong way?' In truth, it couldn't fail to cross Cara's mind that there could be something more to the girl's disinclination to speak to the law than a general loathing of the boys in blue, but she didn't think Rochelle had anything to do with Jimmy's death: her show of emotion yesterday had been too raw, too real. More likely she had other reasons for wanting to avoid them, like an outstanding warrant or unpaid fines. 'I'm not going to mention you if that's what you're worried about.'

Rochelle didn't say thanks – it probably wasn't in her vocabulary – but she moderated her tone a little. 'They were at Murch's this morning.'

This didn't surprise Cara. The law would be working their way through Jimmy's friends, starting with the closest. Murch would want the killer found, but he'd still be cautious about offering up information, especially if he thought that Terry Street had been involved. The desire for retribution would be tempered by the even greater desire for self-preservation. 'What did he tell them?'

'I dunno. I weren't there. I saw them go in, though. They didn't stay long. Only five minutes, ten.'

'Do you reckon Murch knows anything?'

Rochelle shook her head. 'He wouldn't hurt Jimmy.'

'That's not what I'm asking. What I mean is, does he know . . . does he have any idea *why* anyone would want to kill him? There has to be a reason.'

'Maybe Jimmy knew too much.'

'Too much about what?'

'I dunno. Whatever they killed him for.'

Cara sighed. Rochelle, she was certain, knew nothing of importance. She could feel the rain seeping into her shoes and started edging away, as if she had things to do, places to be. 'Okay, then. I'll see you around.'

'Where are you going?'

Cara heard the sharpness in her voice again, the barely disguised hostility. She thought there was something unhinged about the girl, something that was less to do with grief and more to do with a kind of mania. Rochelle could change in an instant, flip from sulky to angry, from placid to aggressive, in the blink of an eye. 'I'm going home.' And then, in case Rochelle decided to tag along, she quickly added, 'The law said they'd probably want to speak to me again.'

'That's no reason to rush off.'

Cara made a show of looking around, as if she expected Steadman to arrive at any moment. 'I'd rather get it over and done with.'

Rochelle took a step forward and leaned in, her face sly. 'Jimmy had secrets.'

This stopped Cara in her tracks. What was Rochelle up to now? It could just be a ploy to keep her there, to keep her talking, but then again, she might actually have some information. 'Doesn't everyone?' she answered casually.

'He told me things.'

'What sort of things?'

Rochelle suddenly grew coy. 'He wouldn't like it if I told you.'

'What's the point of mentioning it, then?'

'He told me why you were in the slammer.'

Cara wondered why she had even bothered to stop. 'That's hardly hot news. I was the one banged up, remember?'

'He told me more than that.'

'If you've got something to say, just say it.'

Rochelle twisted a strand of hair around a finger, inclined her head and gazed at Cara. The gesture was oddly childlike, but the twisted smile held a hint of mockery.

'Come on, Rochelle. Don't mess about. I haven't got time for these games.'

'He said you'd be a rich woman when you came out.'

Cara laughed. 'Rich? Yeah, right. As you can see, I'm rolling in it. Queen of Kellston, that's me.' She saw a pink flush spread across Rochelle's face and quickly added: 'He was just having you on. You know what he was like. He was winding you up.'

'Jimmy wouldn't do that.'

'Maybe you misunderstood.'

'Stinking rich, he reckoned. He made me swear not to tell no one.'

Cara shrugged. 'Well, what can I say? I wish it was true, but it isn't.'

Rochelle hesitated, as if she was weighing up how much more to reveal. She lowered her gaze, stared at the ground and only slowly raised her eyes again. 'Maybe . . . maybe it was to do with that house you broke into.'

'What do you mean?' Cara was starting to feel uneasy now, less certain that Rochelle was spouting nonsense. 'The Myerses' house? Is that what he said?'

'Not exactly.'

'So what *exactly* did he say?'

Rochelle, suspecting that Cara was rattled, produced that weird smile again. 'He said that the cat got the cream, but no one knows about it.'

'What?'

'The cat got the—'

'Yeah, I heard you. I just don't get why he'd say that. I don't understand. What else did he say?'

'Nothin'. Just that I wasn't to tell no one.'

Cara felt simultaneously spooked and sceptical. 'And have you?'

'Course not. It's a secret, ain't it?'

This didn't fill Cara with confidence. It was an odd thing to make up, but Rochelle *was* odd. God alone knew what went on in that head of hers. And yet, somehow, worryingly, she could almost imagine Jimmy speaking those words. 'What made you think it was to do with the house?'

''Cause we were talking about it, what you'd done and the like. Jimmy was going on about how you could climb anything, get into anywhere and how smart you were. I said that you couldn't be that smart or you'd never have got caught.' Rochelle sniggered, pausing as if expecting a retort. When Cara didn't rise to the bait, she looked disappointed. 'Anyway, that's when he said the cat thing. Then he got all antsy about it and told me I had to keep my mouth shut.'

'Do you think he told anyone else?'

'How would I know?'

Cara wondered how many other people in Kellston thought she was loaded, how many others had listened to some crazy tale of Jimmy's and believed it. She knew what he was like . . . *had* been like. He'd sucked up attention like a sponge, and although he'd never been a fabricator, he hadn't been beyond stretching the truth if it made for a good story. 'For God's sake,' she muttered.

'I don't get what you're so pissed off about. What does it matter if everyone thinks you're filthy rich?'

'What matters is how they think I *became* filthy rich.'

Rochelle stared blankly back at her.

Cara could have explained, could have said that it made it look like she'd lied about what had happened that night in Hampstead, maybe even colluded in the murder of Gerald Myers. It suggested that her mystery partner-in-crime would be handing over half the proceeds once she got out of jail. Or had maybe left her share somewhere. Which would account for why she was being followed – someone hoping, probably, that she would lead them to a secret stash. She could have told Rochelle all this but had neither the energy nor the inclination. 'Forget it. I have to go.'

24

Ray Tierney found a parking space without any trouble. He pulled the car in and switched off the engine. His gaze quickly took in the surrounding area as he checked to make sure he hadn't been followed. Then he wound down the window, sat back and lit a cigarette. This was their usual spot, open and quiet and away from prying eyes. She would be here soon. Holly was always reliable.

While he waited, he thought about the letter from his mother. A knot formed in his stomach. Things were bad in Yorkshire. With his father and two brothers still on strike, money was tight and life was a struggle. He sent what he could every month, but he knew it barely scratched the surface. Ray was glad he'd made the move down south before everything had spiralled out of control – to be a copper now was to be the enemy – but he no longer took any pride or pleasure in his job. The miners and the police were at war, and he found himself in the unenviable position of being stuck in the middle.

Although Ray was relieved to have put some distance between

himself and all the complications of home, he no longer felt comfortable in his own skin. His sympathies lay with the strikers, with the miners whose livelihoods were being taken away, but this wasn't something he could openly express. Every day he went to work, every day he remained silent as his colleagues crowed and gloated over brutal victories achieved up north, he felt more like a traitor. He was bitter and disillusioned. He had thought about jacking it in but knew better than to make any hasty decisions. Jobs weren't easy to come by.

Ray glanced in the rear-view mirror and saw Holly Abbott walking towards the car. She was a slim brunette, nineteen, with wiggling hips and the kind of curves that guaranteed good tips from her job as a barmaid. Holly was one of his better informants, a girl who kept her eyes and ears open and who had the nous to know what was fact and what was merely gossip. There were plenty of villains who frequented the Fox and most of them, particularly after a skinful, couldn't resist shooting their mouths off about what job they'd done, who they'd done it with and how much they'd made. Bragging was in their blood, an irresistible urge, and Holly exploited this weakness to the full.

Why she did it was anyone's guess, and Ray knew better than to ask. Every snout had their own motivation – money, revenge, control – and that was their business, not his. Good informants were invaluable, and he would never risk conflict by openly delving into the psychology of their willingness to grass. Some stones were best left unturned.

'Afternoon,' Holly said as she climbed into the car, bringing with her the smell of musky perfume. 'You got a spare fag?'

Ray offered up his pack even though he was sure she already had one in her handbag. Holly didn't believe in smoking her own if she could smoke someone else's. After the cigarette was lit and she'd taken her first puff, she sat back, stared at him, and said, 'What's with the face?'

Unaware that his face was any different to how it usually was, Ray frowned. 'Huh?'

'You look like the world just kicked you in the balls.'

Ray frowned some more, wondering if Holly was unusually perceptive or if anyone could read him like a book. He made a mental note to adjust his features before going back to Cowan Road. 'It's been one of those days.'

'I take it you wanted to see me about Jimmy Lovell.'

'Yeah,' Ray said. 'You heard anything?'

Holly shook her head. 'A lot of talk, but that's all it is.'

'What kind of talk?'

'Oh, that it was a robbery, that some woman's husband took offence at him screwing his wife, that he got on the wrong side of a drugs deal, that it was a hit, that it was a case of mistaken identity . . . Take your pick. Do you want me to go on?'

'Why do you think he was killed?'

'How would I know?'

'Because you know bleedin' everything,' Ray said.

Holly grinned at that. 'Could be any of them, couldn't it? Or none. People are just talking, the way they always do, making it up as they go along, pretending they're in the know, even though they know sod all.'

'Anyone in particular with a strong opinion?'

'They've all got strong opinions even when they're talking out of their arses.'

'He was a regular, wasn't he? How well did you know him?'

'Not that well,' she said. 'He was nice enough, funny, a bit of a flirt, but he never crossed the line. I didn't have any problems with him.'

'Did you have anything else with him?'

'Behave yourself!' she said, adjusting the neck of her blouse and pretending to be offended. 'He was old enough to be my dad.'

Ray didn't think thirty-four was that old, but perhaps it was when you were nineteen. 'Okay, I was just checking.'

'It's a shame,' she said. 'Nice bloke like that. You never know what's round the corner, do you?'

'What about girlfriends? Did he bring anyone into the Fox?'

'I can't say I noticed, but it gets pretty busy. Wasn't he with that Cara girl, the one who went down?'

'On and off, apparently. But I don't imagine he was living the life of a monk while she was banged up.' He gave Holly a wink. 'While the cat's away and all that . . .'

Holly pulled a face. 'That's men for you. You're all the same: when it comes to women, you're only ever after one thing.'

Ray could have begged to differ – chasing women had never been on his list of favoured pastimes – but he wasn't about to open that can of worms. He lived in constant fear of his colleagues finding out he was queer. It might not be illegal, but it certainly wasn't acceptable. In order to avoid suspicion, and although he despised himself for it, he had learnt to play the game and to adopt the necessary lustful looks and an air of casual sexism. 'That's a bit harsh, sweetheart. We can't help the way we're made.'

'You could work on it.'

Ray made a point of glancing towards her cleavage. 'And where's the fun in that?'

Holly wound down the window and flicked off the ash from her cigarette. 'I take it you're not getting very far with finding the killer.'

'Give us time. It's only been twenty-four hours. What about Cara Kendall? Have you heard anything about her?'

'Only that she's out of jail,' Holly said. 'And that she was the one who found Jimmy.'

'Was she in the Fox last night? I mean, did she come in after we'd left?'

'I wouldn't know. I've never seen her before. She got sent down before I started working there.'

'She's small, about five foot two, pretty, blonde.'

Holly thought about it, but then shook her head. 'I don't think so. Someone would have said something, wouldn't they? She'd have been the centre of attention if she had come in.'

'And Terry Street? Did he show his face last night?'

'Terry? No, I didn't see him.' Her hazel eyes grew inquisitive. 'You don't think he's connected, do you?'

'I've got an open mind.'

'First time a copper ever had,' she said. 'Is it true that Cara's a cat burglar? I heard she broke into a house and found a body.'

'What else have you heard?'

'Only that you lot tried to pin a murder charge on her.'

'Not me,' Ray said. 'I wasn't around back then.'

'You don't get many women in that line of work,' Holly said with admiration in her voice, as though Cara Kendall was responsible for smashing through one of those glass ceilings the feminists were always banging on about.

'She got caught. It was hardly the most promising start to a career.'

'Maybe not.' Holly laughed, chucked her fag end out of the window and said: 'I'll keep my ear to the ground about Jimmy Lovell. I hope you catch the shit who did it.'

'You and me both. Can I drop you off anywhere?'

'No, ta. I'm fine. I've got a pal who lives near here.'

Ray watched as she got out of the car, keeping his gaze on her until she turned the corner and was out of sight. He'd been hoping for more – a lead, a hint, a clue as to who'd killed Jimmy – but it had always been a long shot. Villains might get loose tongued when it came to a spot of robbery or shifting some dodgy gear, but murder was another matter altogether. Still, it was early days. The rumour mill had yet to get going properly. Over the next week or so, Jimmy Lovell would be the name on everyone's lips.

He started the engine and set off back towards Kellston. It couldn't do any harm, he decided, to call in on Cara and see how she was doing. The note, if it was genuine, was an interesting development. It indicated that the killer was still around, still in the vicinity, and that could only be a good thing. Well, a good thing for the police, but not so good, perhaps, for Cara Kendall.

25

Terry Street wasn't unduly worried, but it wasn't smart to be too blasé. Overconfidence was a dangerous state of mind. He'd been around the block often enough to have learnt some very useful lessons: keep one step ahead and always cover your back. The law would, no doubt, be looking in his direction at some point.

He leaned his elbow on the open car window and sniffed the damp afternoon air. It would be wise, perhaps, to remove himself from the situation, but it seemed a shame to look a gift horse in the mouth. Lovell's death would have shaken up Cara Kendall and it wouldn't take much to break her down completely. She hadn't yet got the goods in her possession – he was pretty sure of that – but she was bound to try and collect soon. She'd want to grab what was hers and get out of Kellston as fast as she could.

If Boyle hadn't screwed up, it would all be done and dusted by now. Trouble was, the fool didn't know his own strength. 'Just rough him up a bit,' was what Terry had said, but Boyle had taken it too far. And Lovell, he suspected, had put up more of a fight than expected. Still, there was nothing that could be done about that.

Boyle was like one of those overly loyal dogs, desperate to please, moist eyed and panting, perpetually demanding his master's attention. He had plenty of muscle, but nothing much in the brain department. The trick was to keep things simple and uncomplicated, to give him small rewards and tell him as little as possible: the less he knew, the better. Not that he would ever deliberately grass, but a few clever questions could easily floor him.

Terry chose the men he worked with carefully. It was the ambitious ones you had to watch, the ones who got ideas above their station and couldn't wait to stab you in the back. He knew this because he'd been one of those men. When he was twenty-three, he'd wasted Joe Quinn and had been looking over his shoulder ever since. Taking over Kellston had been relatively easy, keeping it less so. For the last ten years he'd been fending off the new pretenders – not just from rival firms, but from his own inner circle, too.

Terry had learnt from his mistakes – some of them bloody ones – and grown wily in the process. He had 'friends' in high places, greased the right palms and ran his manor like a well-oiled machine. He was not like Joe, who'd ruled entirely through violence. To be successful you needed more than brute force: cunning, diplomacy and intuition had their place, too. And it didn't do any harm to sleep with your eyes open.

A girl came around the corner and Terry grinned. He appreciated a pretty face and a decent pair of pins. An eight out of ten, he reckoned. Yeah, he wouldn't kick her out of bed. He watched as she grew closer. When she was adjacent to the car, he leaned over and opened the passenger door.

Holly Abbott got in, swept her long brown hair off her face and smiled. 'Mission accomplished,' she said.

'Well done, babe. Did he ask about me?'

'Only in passing. He wanted to know if you were in the Fox last night, but that was all. He didn't go on about it. Mainly he just asked about Jimmy and what he was like, and whether I'd heard any rumours about the murder.'

'And what did you tell him?'

'That I'd heard plenty, but they were all shit. I said I'd keep my ears open, though.'

'Anything else?'

'He asked about Cara Kendall, whether she'd been in, too. I told him I didn't know what she looked like. Oh, and he asked whether Jimmy had brought any other girls to the Fox. To be honest, I don't think they've got a clue.' Holly smiled, but her eyes were cold and calculating. 'Did I do all right, Terry?'

'You did fine,' he said, taking out his wallet and peeling off a few notes.

Holly slipped the notes in her bag and opened the car door. 'I'll give you a bell if anything comes up.'

Terry almost suggested a drink – there was something he wouldn't mind coming up this afternoon – but quickly stamped on the idea. It was a mistake to mix business with pleasure, no matter what the temptation. 'See you, sweetheart,' he said. 'Mind how you go.'

'See you.'

He studied her arse as she wiggled along the street, knowing he'd done the right thing, but still regretting it. Women couldn't be trusted once you brought sex into the equation: one quick tango between the sheets and they reckoned they had a claim on you. That's when it got messy. Holly was useful to him, very useful, and he couldn't afford to screw that up.

Terry liked to perpetuate the myth of grassing being the ultimate sin. It made people think twice about spilling their guts to the law. Personally, he had no qualms about informing on the competition or on anyone else who wasn't towing the line – just so long as it couldn't be traced back to him. And that's where Holly came in. He could send her off to DC Tierney with information on any fool who'd crossed him, taking them out of the game with no repercussions to himself.

Tierney didn't know he was being played, didn't suspect it for a minute. And maybe he wouldn't care even if he did know. Holly's tip-offs got the riffraff off the streets and kept arrest levels up. And she had a good deal, too, being paid by the law and by Terry. Double bubble was nothing to complain about. Could he trust her? He didn't need to. She had as much to lose as him if the truth ever came out.

26

As she hurried along the corridor, unlocked the door to her flat and went inside, Cara's head was full of what Rochelle had said. *The cat got the cream.* What? If Jimmy had told Rochelle that, who else had he shared it with? She had no idea what he'd meant but could see how it would have sounded: somehow, she was going to profit from what had happened in Hampstead.

She hung up her damp raincoat, went through to the kitchen, made a mug of coffee and took it back to the living room. Her thoughts were still racing as she stood by the window and looked down on the estate. Somewhere out there, not far away, her tail would have resumed his surveillance. And he wouldn't be happy that she'd given him the slip earlier. From now on he'd be watching her like a hawk.

She tried to apply logic to the Hampstead situation, a dose of sensible reasoning. Perhaps someone thought she'd managed to remove an item of value from the house before the law arrived or had thrown it from a window to a waiting accomplice. Or chucked it in a neighbour's garden for Jimmy to pick up later.

But she couldn't see why one item should be more significant than any of the other things that had been taken. Or did they think that the killer of Gerald Myers had given her something – something he had left with Jimmy – a generous reward for not revealing his identity? She sighed and rubbed her temples. Maybe she was on the wrong track entirely and what Jimmy had said had absolutely nothing to do with Hampstead at all.

This, she decided, was as likely as anything else. Rochelle was hardly a reliable witness and could easily have got hold of the wrong end of the stick. Yes, perhaps she was overcomplicating the matter. Jimmy had nicked something or found something or been holding something, refused to give it back and now the owner believed it was in her possession. But even if this was true, how was she going to persuade them that it wasn't the case?

The phone rang, cutting across her deliberations. She walked over to the table, picked up the receiver and put it to her ear. The pips went – a call from a phone box – and she waited for the line to clear before saying, 'Hello?' First there was just silence and for a moment she thought it was her mum again, another of those tricky connections from the south coast, but then the heavy breathing started – slow and deliberate and menacing. She felt the hairs on the back of her neck stand on end.

She slammed the phone down and stared at it. Almost immediately it began to ring again. This time she didn't answer. Although she knew it was just an attempt to intimidate her, there was something deeply disturbing about that disembodied breathing. She waited until the ringing had stopped before taking the receiver off the hook and laying it on the table.

'Pathetic,' she said, trying to sound braver than she felt.

Cara strode back to the window. There was a phone box near the gates and she wondered if that was where the call had been made from. It was empty now. She peered along Mansfield Road but couldn't see the goon or anyone else who looked particularly suspicious. Was this going to be her life from now on? Constant harassment, constant aggro? She couldn't see an end to it, or at least not an end that didn't end badly.

Jumpy and anxious, Cara went into the kitchen, grabbed a cloth and wiped down the counter even though it was perfectly clean. Germs weren't her enemy, but inactivity was. She had to keep busy or she'd go crazy. Next, she scrubbed the sink and taps, and after that the front of the cupboards. She was about to start on the fridge when the doorbell went. Her heart missed a beat. Was it *him*? The enemy? Having established that she was home, he could have decided to pay her a face-to-face visit. She stood very still as if even the slightest of movements might resonate through the living room, across the tiny hall and through the front door.

The bell went again. He couldn't make her answer. He couldn't force her to do anything. All she had to do was stay put and there was nothing he could do about it. Well, not unless he broke down the door. God, he wouldn't do that, would he? She prayed that he wouldn't go that far. She glanced around the kitchen, aware she was surrounded by potential weapons – pots and pans, a drawer full of knives, a rolling pin. If the worst came to the worst she could at least try and defend herself.

It was after the third ring that she thought about the spyhole. It could be worth taking a gander just to see what her tormentor looked like close up. She slipped a short, sharp knife into her back pocket before taking off her trainers and walking in her stockinged feet across the living room and into the hall. Here she stopped and listened – she could hear a faint shuffling – before putting her eye to the tiny glass circle in the door.

Cara was just in time to see DC Ray Tierney turn his face away and move out of view. His heavy footsteps echoed in the corridor outside. Relief flooded through her. She was tempted to leave it, to let him go, but then she thought about Jimmy. What if there was news? Quickly she opened the door and called after him, 'Sorry, I was in the kitchen.'

Tierney stopped and retraced his steps. 'Do you have a minute?'

'Has something happened?'

'I just wanted to check up, make sure you were all right. You know, with the note and everything. I didn't want you to think we weren't taking it seriously.'

Cara stepped aside and let him in. They went through to the living room where Tierney stood by the table. She saw his gaze alight on the phone with its receiver removed from the cradle.

'Dodgy call,' she said. 'Someone with an asthma problem.'

'That's unpleasant.'

'From a phone box. Beep, beep, beep, and then the heavy breathing. I guess someone's trying to scare me.'

'Do you live here on your own?'

Cara hesitated, unsure as to whether she wanted to bring Lytton into this. It had been a straight question, however, and if she lied, Tierney might easily find out about it. 'No, I've got a flatmate,' she said. 'Just until January. He's a student called Will Lytton. He's not here much; he spends most of his time at college.'

Tierney nodded, as though he was thinking about that hesitation. 'At least there's someone around at night.'

'We're not a couple or anything,' Cara said sharply, reacting to his reply and wondering if he was putting two and two together and making five. Flatmates, that's all.' She was about to carry on but decided against it. Too many denials might only increase his suspicions.

'Will Lytton,' he repeated, as if fixing the name in his mind.

Cara nodded. It wouldn't do any harm, she supposed, if the police *did* look into Lytton. At least that way she'd know if there was anything dodgy about him. She would just have to take her chances as regards the council finding out about the illegal sublet. 'A history student,' she said. 'He's at Kellston Poly.'

Tierney's gaze roamed around the room. Cara didn't ask him to sit down or offer him a brew. Now that she knew there was no fresh information on Jimmy, she preferred to keep the conversation as short as possible.

Tierney, however, seemed to have other ideas. 'Have you had any more thoughts on what the note might mean?'

'No, I've no idea. I mean, obviously someone thinks I've got something that belongs to them, but I haven't got a clue as to what it is – or who they are.'

'It must be worrying for you, being targeted like this.'

Cara examined his face – he looked sincere enough – but she still wasn't sure how genuine his concern was. Was this one of those good cop/bad cop routines where Tierney pretended to believe in her innocence after Steadman had made it clear that he didn't? 'It's confusing,' she said, unwilling to confess to the fear she actually felt. 'I think I was followed this morning after I left Cowan Road. A dark-haired bloke, but I didn't get a good look at him.'

'Are you certain?'

Cara nodded. 'Pretty sure.' She considered telling him what Rochelle had told her, about how Jimmy had said she was going to be rich, but then he'd want to know who'd said it, and annoying as the girl was, she didn't want to put the law on to her. Plus, it could well be nonsense, in which case it would hinder rather than help the investigation.

'If Jimmy had got hold of something, have you any idea at all where he might hide it? Did he have a key to this flat?'

'It isn't here if that's what you're thinking. It can't be. There really isn't anywhere to hide anything, and I don't reckon he'd have taken the risk of Will coming across it. I don't suppose he'd keep it in his own flat, either. That's the first place they'd look, isn't it?'

'So where else?'

Cara shrugged. She was suddenly thinking about the base of the wardrobe and how it had been disturbed. Was it possible that someone other than Jimmy or Lytton had been here? That someone, whoever they were, could have left her stash where it was either because they didn't want her to know they'd been there or because it was small change compared to what they were really looking for?

'What is it?'

'I don't know. I can't be a hundred per cent sure, but I think someone might have been through my room. It was just a feeling when I walked in there for the first time, like things weren't exactly how I'd left them. I can't swear to it, though. I mean, it's been eighteen months.'

'But nothing's missing?'

'No, not that I've noticed.'

Tierney kept his eyes on her. 'Are you certain Jimmy didn't say anything to you when he visited?'

'I've been over it a hundred times in my head, but I can't think of anything, nothing out of the ordinary. And he wasn't acting any different to usual. None of this makes any sense. Jimmy wasn't stupid. He might not have been the most upright citizen in the world, but he wasn't some big-time villain. He wouldn't get involved in anything heavy. He wouldn't risk his life for money.'

'Doesn't it depend on how life-changing that money might be?'

Cara supposed he had a point, but it still didn't sound like Jimmy to her. 'He was easy come, easy go. That was his nature. He might have been a bit of a chancer, but that was as far as it went.'

'But you haven't been around for eighteen months. Maybe . . . I don't know, maybe he'd fallen into bad company.'

'Someone like Terry Street, you mean?'

'What makes you say that?'

Cara gave him a pained smile. 'Because when it comes to bad company, he's top of the list in Kellston, isn't he?' She remembered what Lytton had said about seeing Jimmy and Terry Street talking in the Fox but didn't share this information with Tierney. A chat at the bar was meaningless without something solid to back it up, and she didn't want to be the one pointing the finger. She was happy, however, for the law to make their own enquiries. 'Jimmy never mentioned him, but . . . well, I don't suppose he would, not to me.'

'You wouldn't have approved?'

'What do you think?'

Tierney folded his arms and then unfolded them again. 'Okay, I'll leave you in peace. Just ring the station if you're concerned about anything. We're here to help.'

'Try telling your boss that,' Cara said as she walked him to the door.

'What is it with you and DI Steadman?'

'He hates my guts.'

Tierney didn't bother to deny it. 'He's just doing his job.'

Cara gave a snort. 'Is that what you call it? He's convinced I had something to do with Jimmy's death and for as long as he carries on believing that you're never going to catch who really did it.'

'Thanks for the tip,' Tierney said drily.

Cara opened the door. 'I'm serious. He's off on some wild goose chase while the real murderer is out there laughing his socks off.'

'Take care of yourself. And don't forget what I said: call if you're worried about anything.'

Cara watched as he walked away, wondering why she'd wasted her breath. Tierney wasn't any different to Steadman. Cops always stuck together, no matter what. If she was relying on them to watch her back, she'd be making a major mistake. She looked up and down the corridor, alert to any sign of her tail. Nothing. No one. She closed the door and pulled the bolt across.

She was about to return to the living room when she remembered the knife. Taking it from her back pocket, she held up the short, sharp blade and stared at it. It would be enough to cause some damage if she was ever in dire straits. She slipped it into her coat pocket, just in case.

27

Cara went through to the living room and put the phone back on the hook. Hopefully, by now, her heavy breather would have given up. Then she embarked on a methodical search of the flat, starting with the kitchen. She didn't really think Jimmy had hidden anything here, but better to be safe than sorry. She'd kick herself later if she'd overlooked the obvious.

Cara emptied out the cupboards and poked around in cereal and pasta, in sugar and teabags. She knew it was futile – Jimmy would never have left anything valuable where Lytton might accidentally stumble across it – but carried on regardless. She cleaned the inside surfaces of the cupboards and made sure nothing was taped to the upper side. Then she put everything back neatly, noticing there were a good many more dried herbs and spices than when she'd left. Lytton, it appeared, was a more adventurous cook than herself.

Next, she got down on her hands and knees and checked under the sink. She pulled out bottles of bleach, washing powder and a bucket full of old cloths. Feeling around the pipes, she searched for anything that shouldn't be there, but only came up with a few rusty nails and a coil of copper wire. Dust and cobwebs smeared her fingers. A spider scuttled across her hand, making her jump. It all needed a good clean, but she didn't fancy taking on the wildlife.

She put everything back and closed the door. Then she stood up, looked around and headed for the fridge. Inside were the groceries she'd bought yesterday and a couple of beers. Two red peppers loitered in the corner. There was nothing in the ice box but a tray of ice cubes. She gave up on the fridge and quickly moved on, checking the cutlery drawer and the one underneath full of bits and bobs, then the pots and pans on the shelves and finally the gaps along the sides of the oven.

Once she'd exhausted the possibilities of the kitchen, Cara shifted her attention to the living room. She removed the cushions from the sofa and felt down the sides, retrieving a small ball of fluff and a pound coin. She grinned and slipped the coin into her pocket. Finders keepers. She pushed the sofa on to its back and peered at the underneath, looking for any signs of an incision or any suspicious lumps and bumps, and then went through the same routine with the armchair.

Once the furniture was restored to its normal position, she took the Dora Carrington print off the wall and flipped it over to see if the brown tape on the back had been disturbed. It hadn't. She put it back where it belonged. She checked her father's photograph but found nothing to suggest that it had been tampered with, either. It would help, she thought, if she had some idea of the size of the thing she was looking for. This was like searching for a needle in a haystack. She flicked through the record collection in case anything had been slipped between the album covers but came up with zilch. It was the same with the books.

Cara was en route to the bathroom when the phone started ringing again. She stopped, thought about it but then continued along the hallway. If it was her mother or the law, they'd call back. If it was her heavy breather, he could go to hell.

The bathroom wasn't big, and the number of hiding places was limited. She checked the toilet cistern – nothing – and then carefully levered out the side panel on the bath. Even while she was doing these things, she knew it was a waste of time. Jimmy might not have had the greatest imagination in the world, but he wouldn't have been so stupid as to use any of the obvious places. She rooted around in the bathroom cabinet amongst the usual paraphernalia, pushing aside bottles of shampoo, a can of shaving foam, razors and aspirins.

Cara didn't bother with Lytton's room. Jimmy definitely wouldn't have left anything there. Instead, she went straight to her own and began with the drawers, pulling them out completely to make sure nothing had been attached to any of the surfaces. She rummaged through sweaters and T-shirts, through underwear and socks and tights, but the search was fruitless. She tried the wardrobe, checking the pockets of all the clothes that hung there. She crouched down on the floor and put a hand down into both pairs of her winter boots, feeling around for any foreign objects.

She decided not to unscrew the base of the wardrobe again but pondered on the possibility of Jimmy having stashed the mystery item there before retrieving it at some later date. It would explain the disturbance, although other things would too. She sat back on her heels and sighed. If 'it' was in the flat, it was so well hidden that even she couldn't find it. But on balance, she thought, it probably wasn't here.

'Where have you put it, Jimmy?' she murmured.

If it wasn't in his flat and not in hers, where else could it be?

God, the possibilities were endless. She presumed the police had searched his van, but he could have put it in a bank deposit box or buried it under a tree in Epping Forest. What she didn't understand was why he hadn't revealed the truth when he was being beaten to a pulp. She couldn't think of anything so valuable that it was worth dying for.

28

By five o'clock Cara was sitting at the living-room table looking down on the estate. From here she could see the gates through which Murch would eventually drive in. She was keeping her eyes peeled for his white van and at the same time surveying the area for her tail. The black BMW wasn't parked in Mansfield Road, but that didn't mean anything. The goon, or whoever else was following her now, could easily have changed his car or simply be on foot.

The phone had rung three more times since she'd ended her search of the flat, but she'd resisted the temptation to pick up. An answer machine would be useful. With one of those she could filter out any unwanted calls and not miss anything important. But she couldn't afford to splash out right now; what little money she had she would need until she found herself a job. Tomorrow, when she went out to buy the pint of milk, she would pick up a local paper and see if there was anything promising.

Cara could not imagine what 'promising' meant. Everything

she was qualified for, which was very little, was dull and predictable and usually meant spending hours on her feet for a minimum wage and a few lousy tips. She inwardly groaned and then berated herself for it. At least she still had choices, which was more than Jimmy had.

She thought of the house she had passed in Kellston this morning and wondered how big a haul she might get from it. Maybe, if nothing improved, she could do one last job and hot foot it out of London for ever. By the time Steadman came knocking on the door, she'd be well gone. She could hop across the Channel, go to Paris or Rome, flog the gear there and start a new life. Quite what this new life would consist of, she couldn't imagine, but it had to be better than what she had here.

Cara smiled. It was only a fantasy, but a little voice still whispered in her ear, 'Why not?' There was nothing to keep her in Kellston, other than memories.

It was getting on for six and dark already when Murch finally made an appearance. She followed the van with her eyes until it drew up near Temple where he got out, removed his tools from the back and strode towards the entrance of the tower.

Cara stood up and went into the hall. She put on her raincoat, unbolted the door and left the flat. It was chilly outside and raining. She pulled up the hood of her coat as she hurried along the path, knowing that she was probably being followed again but resisting the impulse to glance over her shoulder. There were plenty of people around, most of them just coming back from work, and this gave her a feeling of relative safety. No one was likely to try anything with so many would-be witnesses.

Murch's flat was on the seventh floor, and she shared the lift with three other residents. No one spoke. Everyone avoided each other's gaze. The only sound was the juddering noise of the lift and the soft breath of four human beings. Cara sneaked a glance at her lift mates, just to reassure herself that her tail wasn't closer than she thought, but none of them were likely candidates.

When the doors slid open on the seventh floor, she almost leapt out, glad to be free of the claustrophobic metal box. No one followed her. She made her way round to Murch's flat and knocked on the door. When he opened it, his face fell as if he wasn't exactly overjoyed to see her.

'I need to talk to you,' she said. 'Can I come in?'

Murch, as if suspecting unwanted and unwelcome questions, hesitated. 'I was just about to take a shower.'

'This won't take long,' she said, stepping forward so that he was forced to stand aside. Having waited all afternoon, she wasn't about to take no for an answer.

'You want a brew?' Murch asked grudgingly when they were in the living room.

'No, ta.' Cara sat down on the sofa, moving a copy of *The Sun* to one side. 'Have the law been to see you?'

'This morning. That Steadman came here with his sidekick.'

'Tierney,' she said.

'Yeah, that's the one.' Then, as if he'd just remembered his manners, he said: 'How are you doing? You okay?'

Cara lifted and dropped her shoulders in response. 'Aren't you going to sit down?'

Murch perched on the arm of an easy chair and glanced at his watch.

'What did they say to you?' she asked. 'The law.'

'They asked me when I last saw Jimmy, how he seemed, what time he left, if he was seeing anyone new, that sort of thing. They wanted to know if I had any idea who'd killed him.'

'And do you?' Cara asked bluntly.

'Shit, you think I wouldn't tell if I did?' Murch leaned

166

forward and placed his hands, thick fingers splayed, on his thighs. 'Jimmy never said nothin' to me. I've already told you: if he was involved in anythin' dodgy, he kept it to himself.'

Cara sensed he was lying, just like he'd been lying yesterday. How could she get the truth out of him? Chipping at a man's self-esteem wasn't something she'd normally consider, but right now she felt she had no other option. 'So he confided in Rochelle, some girl he had a fling with, but not you? That seems odd. I thought you and Jimmy were tight.'

The dig hit home. No one likes to think they're lower down the pecking order than some casual squeeze. Murch glared at her, a red flush staining his cheeks. 'What's the stupid bitch been saying?'

Cara didn't answer. She held his gaze, letting the silence grow between them, knowing he'd be the first to break it.

'You can't believe a word she says. She's got a screw loose. She's not right in the head. That girl's a . . .' Murch scrabbled around in his head for the right words. 'She's a bleedin' attention seeker.'

'Well, she certainly got my attention.'

'What are you listening to her for?'

'Because no one else is talking. Why did Jimmy tell her I'd be a rich woman when I came out of the slammer?'

'He didn't.'

'How do you know?'

'She's just making it up.'

'Why would she?'

Murch raised his hands and dropped them again. 'Why the fuck does she do anythin'? To make herself feel important, probably.'

'Why do you hang out with Rochelle if she's so crazy?'

'Have you ever tried getting rid of her?'

Cara couldn't argue with that. Rochelle was tough to shift once she'd attached herself.

'Did the law ask you about Hampstead?'

The sudden change of subject caught Murch off guard. 'Hampstead?'

'Yes, did they ask you about it?'

'Yeah. They asked why Jimmy didn't go with you.'

'And what did you tell them?'

Murch's hands rose briefly into the air again before slapping down on his thighs. 'That I didn't know. What the fuck else would I say?'

Cara could see the agitation growing in him. He was starting to look like a cornered man, but she wasn't sure how to take advantage of this. She tried a shot in the dark. 'Jimmy said the same thing to Terry Street, didn't he? That I was going to be a rich woman.'

Murch's eyes slid away from her. 'What? No.'

'For God's sake, Murch. I've got some thug on my back, some goon following me around and making intimidating phone calls. I've had a note through the door demanding that I "give it back", even though I don't know what "it" is. I'm in deep trouble so please stop stonewalling and give me some bloody information.'

'Fuck,' he said.

'Do you know what it means – *Give it back*?'

Murch shook his head. 'I dunno. I swear.'

Did Cara believe him? Not for a moment. 'But Jimmy did speak to Terry Street, didn't he? Come on, Murch, I need some help here.'

For a moment it seemed that Murch was going to carry on denying it, but then a thin stream of breath escaped from his lips. 'He may have done, but it was weeks back. It didn't mean nothin'. You know what Jimmy was like.'

Cara's heart sank. 'What did he say?'

'He got chatting to them at the bar – Terry and a couple of his pals – and Hampstead came up. I don't remember what he said exactly, we'd all had a few, but it were something along the lines of them not knowing the half of it.'

'And?'

'That they shouldn't believe everything they read in the papers.'

Cara could imagine it: Jimmy trying to impress the biggest villain in the East End. And once he'd caught his attention, he wouldn't have wanted to give it up. 'And that stuff about me being rich when I came out?'

Murch looked away, as if unwilling to admit that he'd been lying earlier. 'I dunno. He may have.'

'But why? I mean, why would he say that?'

'He was pissed.'

'Yeah, I get that, but even so. What was he getting at? That I'd taken something valuable from the house, that I knew who killed Gerald Myers? I don't understand where he was going with it.'

'He weren't going nowhere. He was just ... I dunno, just making out that he knew more than they did.'

'There must have been more to it than that,' Cara persisted. 'He's dead, for Christ's sake. And the note I got: someone thinks I've got something worth having. Try and think. What else did Jimmy say that night?'

'You don't know it's connected.'

'I don't know that it isn't, either.'

'I don't remember nothin' else.' Murch's mouth set in a stubborn line, and he glanced at his watch again. 'I'd tell you if I did, but I don't.'

Cara could see that she'd got as much out of him as she was

going to. At least for today. She stood up and said, 'Look, if you think of anything else, you'll let me know, yeah?'

'There ain't nothin' else.'

'It might come back to you.' When she got to the front door, she turned to him again, deciding to leave him with something to reflect on. 'You should be careful, Murch. Once they're sure I haven't got what they want, you could be next on the list.'

Cara thought his face might have paled, but she couldn't be sure. The light was dim in the hallway with just a bare low-watt bulb hanging from the ceiling.

'Why the fuck would they come after me?'

'Because you were his best mate, and if I haven't got it, someone else must have.'

29

As she went down in the lift, Cara pondered on the expression that had been on Murch's face: guilty, scared, bewildered, shifty? Well, he always looked shifty so she couldn't read much into that. She didn't regret her final words because she knew he was holding out on her. Perhaps, given time to think it over, he might eventually come clean.

She walked through the foyer, out of the doors and into the damp evening air. The rain was just a drizzle now, a fine sparkle in the orange streetlamps that were scattered across the estate. She glanced back at the tower, looking up towards the seventh floor, but there was no sign of Murch. As her gaze dropped, however, she caught sight of someone else.

Alma Todd was sitting at the window of her first-floor flat, watching the world go by, or at least as much of the world as the Mansfield estate offered. Still, it was some activity and probably made a change from the TV. Cara waved and the old lady waved back. She should call round one day, she thought, take some flowers or a cake or a small bottle of Scotch. It must be lonely for her on her own. Cara knew what it was like to be lonely but knew too that it must be ten times worse when you were knocking on ninety.

She strode on towards Haslow, pushing her hands deep into her pockets. Her right hand made contact with the handle of the small kitchen knife, and she felt reassured. If her tail decided to make a move, she'd be ready for him. Not that she thought he would. It was a little quieter now, but still busy enough for her to feel safe.

A part of Cara still couldn't accept Jimmy's death – she was in that denial stage of grief – even though she had seen his body herself. She kept thinking, hoping, that time would slide back to that moment when she'd walked out of the gates of HMP Leaside and that he would be standing there waiting for her. Five years of her life had been invested in him, one way or another, and the future felt impossibly empty. She had left him so many times, but he had always drawn her back. Now there would be no more reconciliations, no more second chances, no more anything.

At Haslow, she got into an empty lift, snivelling, and pushed the button for the tenth floor. She could feel the emotion well up in her and had to force it back down. She couldn't afford to give in to it, not yet. There was a murderer on the loose. She had to keep her wits about her. In fact, there were two murderers if she included the killer of Gerald Myers. Or were they one and the same?

Cara was still contemplating this as she got out of the lift and walked towards the flat. What if Jimmy had said something to suggest that he knew the identity of the man who'd murdered Myers? That would be reason enough to kill him. But it didn't explain the note business. God, the more she tried to put the pieces together, the less sense they made.

She glanced along the corridor before unlocking the door, wondering as usual how far away her tail was. Waiting near the gates or somewhere much closer? She had no idea whether she'd been followed to Murch's. That sixth sense, that pricking on the back of her neck, had deserted her, or maybe her tail had. She hoped not. His attention was needed tomorrow. She was paying Glen Douglas good money to find out who he was.

Cara took off her coat, went through to the kitchen and put the kettle on. No sooner had she taken a mug off the drainer than the doorbell went. She had a sudden thought that it was Murch, that her parting shot had hit home, and he'd come straight over to talk to her. She dashed through to the hall and without even bothering to check the spyhole flung open the door. Instantly her jaw dropped and the blood drained from her face. An audible gasp escaped from her lips. Jimmy was standing right in front of her.

30

It took Cara a moment to recover herself. Of course it wasn't Jimmy. It was a slightly younger version of him, but with the same eyes and mouth and square stubborn jaw. Only the hair was different. And the voice. Neil was speaking now while she tried to regulate her breathing and pretend that she hadn't mistaken him for his brother.

'Sorry, we didn't mean to ... DI Steadman gave us your address. I hope you don't mind.'

'No, no, of course not,' Cara said, extending her forced and somewhat trembling smile to include the woman who was standing beside him. Jennifer, Neil's wife, was tall and slender, one of those fair-haired, fine-boned, English roses who were always immaculately dressed and always, if not always genuinely, polite. 'It's good to see you both. Come in, come in.'

Jennifer placed a hand lightly on Cara's shoulder, leaned forward and kissed some indeterminate piece of air to the right of her face. 'It's all so shocking. Terrible. We couldn't believe it when we heard.'

Neil's lips came a little closer to Cara's cheek but didn't quite touch. 'How are you?'

'Oh, you know,' Cara said, because there wasn't anything else to say.

They went into the living room and Cara gestured towards the sofa. 'Do sit down. Would you like a tea or a coffee?'

Neil looked like he was going to say yes, but Jennifer intervened before he got the opportunity. 'Thank you so much, but we can't stay long. We have to get home tonight. There's a train at half seven so … We just wanted to call in and make sure you're all right.'

'It's still sinking in,' Cara said.

Neil nodded as he sat down. 'The police don't seem to know much. Or if they do, they're not sharing the information. Still making enquiries, he said. I tried to push him, but he wasn't giving anything away. I can't believe this has happened. I know Jimmy wasn't always … but this? Who'd want to kill him, for Christ's sake?'

'I don't know,' Cara said. 'They're not telling me anything, either. It was Steadman, then, that you saw?'

'Yes, DI Steadman.'

'Not me,' Jennifer said. 'Neil made me stay in that disgusting waiting room.'

'It wasn't disgusting, darling. And I didn't *make* you do anything. I just suggested that it might be for the best.' He looked at Cara. 'I wasn't sure what Steadman was going to say. Murder's not pleasant at the best of times, but when you're faced with the gory details … Well, once you've heard something, you can't forget it, can you?'

Jennifer hesitated before joining her husband on the sofa, examining the old corduroy as if she feared contamination. Cara mentally rolled her eyes. If an old sofa offended her, God alone knew what she'd made of the estate. The three dismal towers with their grime and graffiti must have threatened the very fabric of her immune system.

Neil raked his fingers through his hair. 'It's hard to know what to do, isn't it? I mean, there isn't really anything we can do, other than wait and hope they catch whoever did it, but it makes me feel so . . . There must be *some* clues though. You'd think with all those forensics and everything . . .'

'Yes,' Cara said. 'You'd think so.'

Finally, Jennifer sat down, perching on the edge of the sofa. She sat very upright with her shoulders back and her hands neatly folded in her lap. Cara had only met her a few times before but didn't need to know her well to recognise who and what she was. She'd come across dozens of girls like her at school, girls with cut-glass accents, perfect posture and a sense of entitlement as big as Nelson's Column. These weren't the reasons Cara disliked her – or at least not the only ones – but they still got under her skin. No, what really irked her was that Jennifer had always looked down on Jimmy, her disdain barely covered by a thin veneer of Home Counties civility.

'What do you think happened, Cara?' Neil said. 'What's your take on it all? The police suggested it could have been a robbery that went wrong, but I have the feeling they don't really believe that.'

Cara wondered if Steadman had been whispering in his ear, suggesting she knew more than she was letting on. She wouldn't put it past him. Perhaps that was why he was here now, hoping she might let something slip. 'I don't have a clue. I really don't. I've been away. I only got home yesterday.'

Both Neil and Jennifer knew what 'away' meant – not travelling for work or a pleasant break on the Algarve, but eighteen months spent at Her Majesty's pleasure. However, neither of them was impolite enough to allude to it.

'The DI said you found him,' Neil said.

Cara nodded, not wanting to think about that horrifying moment.

'How awful for you,' Jennifer said. 'Sickening. I can't imagine how terrible that was. I'd faint, I think. I'm not good with blood. I couldn't cope with anything like that.'

While Jennifer talked, Cara couldn't keep her eyes off Neil. So long as he kept his mouth shut it was almost like having Jimmy back again. His voice was different because the two brothers had been separated when they were kids. After their mother died, they had gone into care, and Neil had been adopted by the affluent Hopcroft family nine months later. At six years old he'd still been young enough to be moulded, to be made into a mini-Hopcroft. Jimmy hadn't been so fortunate. He'd been knocking on ten by then, streetwise, wary and East End through and through. If it had ever crossed their minds to take on both brothers, the Hopcrofts had probably decided that Jimmy was a project too far.

'We'll need to organise the funeral, of course,' Jennifer was saying. 'Once the body is released. Although that might not be for a while. He wasn't religious though, was he? I don't suppose he'd have wanted a church service.'

Cara wondered if Neil ever felt guilty about the advantages he'd had – a loving, comfortable home, holidays abroad and a university education – while Jimmy had been left to make the best of what Kellston social services had to offer, and that, let's face it, had been absolutely bugger all. She supposed Neil couldn't be blamed for that and yet a part of her did blame him, at least for what had happened later. *You could have tried harder*, she wanted to say. *You could have made more of an effort to stay in touch.* Because the older Neil had got, the wider the rift had grown, until it had seemed that all he and Jimmy had in common was an accident of birth.

'Cara?'

Cara switched her attention back to Jennifer. 'Sorry?'

'I was just saying that Jimmy never struck me as being very religious. He wouldn't have wanted a church service, would he?'

Jennifer was probably right, but as a matter of principle – the principle being that she didn't like Jimmy's sister-in-law – she felt inclined to disagree. 'I'm not sure. He might have. I haven't really thought about it.'

'Of course you haven't,' Neil said. 'There's no need for any decisions to be made right now.'

Cara wondered if Jimmy had told him they'd split up. They must have been in touch sometime during the last eighteen months. As his ex-girlfriend she probably wasn't entitled to a say in anything, and yet she wanted a say. It suddenly felt important.

'No, no,' Jennifer said. 'But I'm sure he wouldn't have wanted a fuss.'

Which showed, Cara thought, just how little she had known him. Or was Jennifer simply thinking about the cost? The truth was that Jimmy would have wanted a bloody big fuss, a send-off to end all send-offs, a rip-roaring party to celebrate the years he'd spent on this earth. Jennifer, on the other hand, was more likely to be leaning towards the fastest, cheapest way to dispose of an embarrassing problem. To her, Jimmy getting himself murdered was just another example of his utter disregard for the social graces. In Jennifer's world, where everything was shiny and bright and respectable, violent death was about as welcome as a turd on the doorstep.

Cara pulled herself up short. Was she being unfair? She

178

caught Jennifer gazing with pursed lips at a worn patch in the carpet and decided, on balance, that she wasn't.

Neil spoke again. 'DI Steadman said you saw Jimmy last week. How did he seem to you? Was he ... I don't know, concerned, worried about something?'

'If he was, he didn't show it. He seemed fine.'

'So he didn't mention anything?'

'Like what?'

'God knows,' Neil said, twisting his hands together and then apart, as if in a vain attempt to unravel what was, at the moment, beyond comprehension. 'Don't you think something must have been going on?'

'Of course something was going on,' Jennifer said. 'You don't get murdered for nothing.'

Cara could have begged to differ, especially in a place like Kellston, but she held her tongue. Anyway, odds-on Jennifer was right on this occasion. Jimmy's death hadn't been down to some random act of violence. He'd got involved in something nasty, and that something, whatever it was, had cost him his life. 'When was the last time you saw him, Neil?'

'Oh, it's been a while.'

'No, it hasn't,' Jennifer said. 'You saw him a few days ago. You saw him on Monday.'

Neil shot her a look, one of those husband-to-wife looks that roughly translated as *Please, shut the fuck up*.

Jennifer, who either didn't understand the message or was deliberately ignoring it, stared at him. 'But you did. You met him for a drink after work.'

Cara was hanging on every word. Goosebumps had formed on her arms. What was going on here? She gazed at Neil, waiting for him to explain. When no explanation was forthcoming, she took the direct approach. 'So did you see him or not?'

Neil rubbed his forehead and his hands started dancing again. He sighed, glanced around the room, stared briefly at the floor, and then raised his head. 'I was supposed to. We arranged to meet in the Princess Louise in Holborn, only he didn't show up.'

Jennifer's frown was growing deeper by the second. 'But—'

'Yes, I know what I told you, Jennifer. I said I'd seen him, but I hadn't. I knew you'd go on about how unreliable he was, that it was typical of him, that I should have learned my lesson by now and all the rest of it. So I decided to lie. I shouldn't have, but I did. It just seemed . . . I don't know, easier, that's all.'

Cara, who was watching him closely, still reckoned he was lying. There was something off about his body language. But if he had seen Jimmy, why was he denying it? She could have confronted him, but knew he'd stick to the story while he was in the presence of his wife.

Jennifer's face was tight, her expression unhappy. Well, her husband had strung her a line (according to him), so she had every reason to be put out. Cara couldn't tell, however, what had annoyed her most: Neil lying to her or that lie being exposed in front of a third party. Probably a torrid combination of both. She'd have things to say about it, but not in front of Cara.

'I had a couple of pints, waited for an hour and then called it a night,' Neil continued. 'To be honest, I wasn't that surprised. You know what he was like. I thought he'd just forgotten.' He sighed again. 'I suppose I should have told the police all this, but I didn't. I couldn't see that it was significant. Jimmy rang the next day and apologised. He said he'd been delayed, that he had turned up but by then I was gone.'

'And you didn't arrange to meet again?' Cara asked.

'No, nothing definite. I was still a bit peeved, so I said I'd give him a call when work was less busy.'

Cara saw Neil's face fall, as if he was just realising that he'd never see Jimmy again. 'Who suggested the meet in the first place? Was it you or him?'

'He did,' Neil replied. 'I don't think it was about anything in particular. Just a catch-up, he said. We hadn't seen each other in a while.'

Cara was about to probe further – Neil wasn't savvy like Jimmy, and she felt confident that she could, eventually, prise a bit more of the truth from him – when there was the sound of the front door opening and closing and, shortly after, Lytton walked in.

Jennifer's mouth dropped open. Neil looked confused. A silence fell over the room.

Lytton was carrying a brown takeaway bag, and the smell of Indian spices instantly filled the air. He stopped when he saw everyone and said, 'Oh, I'm sorry. I didn't mean to interrupt.'

'This is Neil, Jimmy's brother,' Cara said quickly, 'and this is Neil's wife, Jennifer.' She waved a hand towards Lytton. 'This is Will Lytton, my flatmate.'

Cara saw Jennifer's eyebrows shift up a fraction and could guess what she was thinking: *Well, she didn't waste any time. Jimmy barely cold and she's already moved on to the next one.*

Lytton smiled and said hello, that it was good to meet them, and he was sorry for their loss. Then he disappeared into the kitchen, shutting the door behind him and turning on the radio as if to prove he wasn't earwigging.

'He seems nice,' Jennifer said, somewhat pointedly.

'I don't know him very well,' Cara replied. 'We only met yesterday. Jimmy rented out the flat to him while I was . . . while I was away.' She wondered why she felt the need to justify Lytton's presence. It was none of their business and yet she didn't want them to think that she had shifted her affections so rapidly. Was that very middle class of her?

Lytton's arrival had clearly come as a relief to Neil. It gave him the excuse he needed to beat a hasty retreat. He was already getting to his feet, smoothing down the tops of his trouser legs and preparing to leave. 'We'd better make a move. It was good to see you again, Cara. It's a shame it wasn't in happier circumstances.'

Jennifer's gaze was fixed on the kitchen door as she stood up. 'Yes, do take care of yourself.'

Cara walked them to the hall where they went through the whole air-kissing charade again. 'Do you have a number I can reach you on?' she asked Neil. 'Just in case there are any developments.'

Neil took a business card from his wallet and gave it to her. 'Call me any time.'

'Thanks.' Cara took the card and tucked it into the back pocket of her jeans. Neil, although he didn't know it yet, would be hearing from her sooner than he thought.

31

Cara went through to the kitchen where Lytton had laid the takeaway foil containers on the kitchen counter and was in the process of opening them.

'Sorry,' he said. 'Did I show up at a bad time?'

'No.'

'Only I got the impression there was a rather awkward silence when I walked in.'

'Was there? Well, that's probably because Jennifer thinks we're shacked up together. It was written all over her face.'

'Oh.'

'Don't worry about it. I'm not.' This wasn't strictly true, but she preferred to give the impression of being the sort of girl who didn't give a damn about what the likes of Jennifer Hopcroft thought. 'I don't think her opinion of me could get any lower, anyway. It'll give her something to gossip about on the way home.'

'Always a silver lining,' he said. 'Are you hungry? There's more than enough for two.'

Cara hadn't realised until now just how hungry she was. She hadn't eaten since breakfast and seeing and smelling the food set off a low rumble in her stomach. 'Starving. Can I give you something towards it?'

'View it as a thank you for letting me stay. And a spot of bribery in case you're thinking of changing your mind.'

'Bribery,' she repeated.' Okay, I can live with that. Thanks.'

Lytton got another plate out of the cupboard and passed it to her. 'Were they close, Jimmy and Neil?'

'Not really. They were when they were kids, but then … I suppose their lives just took different directions. They were in care but then Neil got adopted and went to live in Surrey. There were visits, of course, but not as many as Jimmy would have liked.'

'It must have been tough on him being the one left behind.'

Cara spooned some rice on to her plate, before adding chicken masala and a helping of aloo gobi. She picked up a naan bread and nibbled on the corner. 'Yeah, he'd always been the big brother and then suddenly there was no one to look out for any more. And no one to care about him. I wonder sometimes if . . .'

She stopped, and Lytton looked at her. 'If?'

'I don't know, if that's why he turned out like he did, perhaps. Always looking for attention, for some kind of affirmation that he was wanted, needed, desirable?' She thought of his numerous affairs and winced. 'Or am I just making excuses for him? He wasn't what you'd call the most faithful of boyfriends.'

Lytton took a couple of beers out of the fridge and flipped off the lids. 'It's that whole nature/nurture thing, I suppose. Are we born the way we'll always be or are we altered by what we learn as we grow up? I've always thought that it's probably a bit of both.'

'But what if the stuff you're born with isn't good stuff?'

Lytton stared at her, wondering perhaps if she was referring to herself or Jimmy.

'Oh, don't answer that,' she said quickly. 'I don't want to know.'

They took the food and went to sit at the table in the living room. If Jennifer could see us now, Cara thought: a cosy dinner for two with the lights turned down low. All they needed was Sade playing on the stereo and the picture, false as it was, would be complete.

Lytton took a swig of beer. 'Would you mind if I asked you something?'

'Probably but ask away.'

'If you knew Jimmy was unfaithful, why did you stay with him?'

Cara had asked herself the same thing often enough and never really come up with a satisfactory answer. Something to do with the triumph of hope over experience, perhaps. She took so long to answer that Lytton thought she wasn't going to.

'Sorry, none of my business, right?'

'No, it's not that. I was just trying to think of what to say. He wasn't all bad, you know. Jimmy at his best *was* the best. He was funny and kind and considerate. I couldn't have asked for anything more.' She gave a wry smile. 'It's just that he wasn't his best very often.'

'But you stuck with him.'

'No one can ever accuse me of being a quitter.' She ate some curry and rice – delicious – and put her fork down. 'Although, come to think of it, I did quit in the end, didn't I?'

'You gave it a good shot. Five years isn't a flash in the pan.'

Cara shrugged.

Lytton drank some more beer. 'Did you take the note to the police?'

'I did. I took it this morning. I'm sure they'll have arrested the culprit by now.'

'What did they say?'

'Nothing much, although Tierney – he's Steadman's side-kick – came round this afternoon. He was doing the caring cop thing, making sure I was all right, or so he said. I think he was just fishing.'

'I take it they haven't made any progress then?'

'Nothing he was willing to tell me about. Oh, and I got a phone call too, one of the heavy breathing sort, so I guess the mystery note writer hasn't given up yet. It's not much to go on, but at least we can safely say he's a man of limited imagination.'

'Not much of a conversationalist, either, from the sound of it. Can you be sure it's a man?'

'Whoever killed Jimmy was a man – he must have been, mustn't he? – and I'm presuming the note and the phone calls are connected, so . . .'

'Yeah,' Lytton said. 'I guess that makes sense.'

A silence descended on the room, broken only by the thin scrape of forks against plates.

'What's on your mind?' Lytton said, after a while. 'Apart from the obvious, I mean.'

Cara still wasn't sure how much she could trust him. For all she knew he could be the enemy within. Although she didn't really think he was, it was probably best to be cautious and not to give too much away. She wouldn't tell him about Glen Douglas, for example, or her chat with Murch, but could see no obvious harm in sharing her suspicions about Neil.

'Neil said something odd while he was here. He claimed he and Jimmy arranged to meet in a pub on Monday, only Jimmy didn't show.'

'And that's odd because?'

'Because Jennifer says Neil told her they *did* meet up. Why would he do that if it wasn't true?'

'It wouldn't be the first time a man's lied to his wife.'

Cara knew what he was suggesting. 'What, you think he may have been seeing another woman?' She considered this, but then dismissed it. 'I don't think so. They've only been married a couple of years, and he's a partner in her father's business. He's got too much to lose from messing around.'

'That doesn't stop some men. I believe it's called living dangerously.'

'Okay, say you're right, why would he then change his story and admit in front of Jennifer that he'd told her a bare-faced lie? That's just asking for trouble. I mean, I wouldn't like to be in his shoes right now. That's going to be one uncomfortable train journey home.'

'So what's your take on it?'

'That he's more afraid of someone else – maybe the law, maybe not – than he is of Jennifer. He'd been to see Steadman before coming here and probably told him that he hadn't seen Jimmy for ages. And then, when I asked, he had to tell me the same thing too. He couldn't take the risk of two different stories being out there. I think he's scared of something coming out, something that happened or was said or agreed at that meeting with Jimmy. And that something's probably connected to whatever "it" is that someone's so eager to get back.'

'That's quite a theory.'

'It's got some holes in it, granted, but I think the main structure could be sound.'

Lytton looked sceptical. 'Why didn't he just tell Steadman that he'd met Jimmy, had a few beers, had a chat and then gone home? It's hardly a crime.'

'I don't know. Maybe he panicked when he was asked the

question. Maybe he's got a guilty conscience. Maybe he saw himself being dragged into a murder inquiry and thought it was easier to lie.'

'That's a lot of maybes. What if he was telling the truth to the law and only lied to Jennifer because he didn't want to admit that Jimmy had been a no show? He could have been embarrassed or annoyed and decided to keep it to himself.'

This was pretty much what Neil had said, but Cara still wasn't buying it. 'I'm not saying that's impossible, only that I don't think it's true.'

'Women's intuition?' Lytton said with the hint of a smile.

'Call it what you like. That man's lying and I'm going to prove it.'

32

Larry Steadman got in his car, intending to drive straight home. It had been a long day, a six o'clock start, and now it was almost nine. How much progress had they made? Not much, if the truth be told. No useful forensics, no real leads, nothing to propel the investigation forward. He considered the note that had been put through Cara Kendall's door. He was still of the opinion that she could have written it herself, a false clue to send them bounding off in the wrong direction. He wouldn't put it past her.

Larry drove off the station forecourt and into Cowan Road. His hands gripped the wheel. His head was full of the case, his thoughts twisting and turning. Although she might not have wanted Jimmy Lovell killed, he still held on to the suspicion that she could have arranged for a beating to take place and then, on her release, gone over to the flat to view the result. He liked this theory, it suited him, even if there wasn't a shred of evidence to back it up.

A phone call to HMP Leaside had proved to be a waste of

time. She had not consorted, to their knowledge, with anyone likely to provide her with the necessary connections to arrange such a beating. But what did that mean? Sod all. There were plenty of women in that place who'd offer up their boyfriend's/ brother's/father's services if the price was right, and the staff couldn't watch everyone twenty-four hours a day. Her only visitors had been Lovell (intermittent) and her mother, Shelagh Kendall (once). She had written occasionally to them both, but to no one else.

The heavens had opened again, and the road was slick with rain. Larry needed to go home, to eat and sleep and recharge his batteries, but on impulse he turned right and drove to the Mansfield estate where he parked near the gates and gazed up at Haslow House. He didn't turn off the engine but peered between the windscreen wipers, their rhythmic toing and froing having an almost hypnotic effect. Was she there? What was she doing now? There must be a chance, albeit a slim one, that her thoughts were as firmly fixed on him as his were on her.

He ran through the day, frowning. First there had been Murchison, Lovell's best mate, playing dumb. Larry had got the impression he knew more than he was saying. The bloke had seemed overly defensive when Hampstead was mentioned, but he could just be the type to take offence at the law asking him anything. Was it worth bringing him into the station, making it more official? He'd give it some thought. A small, cramped, stale-smelling interview room sometimes had the effect of focusing the mind and reminding the interviewee that he was only a step away from the bare discomfort of a prison cell.

Then there was the brother, Neil Hopcroft, who had turned up this afternoon. Chalk and cheese, he thought. Other than in their physical appearance, the two brothers couldn't have been more dissimilar. Hopcroft, well spoken and well heeled, had certainly been flustered, but that was only to be expected. Murder had a tendency to disturb one's equilibrium. Anything there of interest? He didn't think so. A meeting arranged for last Monday, but a no-show from Lovell, or at least a show only after Hopcroft had given up and left.

The rain continued to fall. The wipers swished, back and forth, back and forth. Larry had managed to get hold of Lovell's phone records, but they had not proved useful. Over the past few weeks there had been several calls to Murchison, one to HMP Leaside – presumably to book the visit to see Cara – and two to Hopcroft's office, one to arrange the meeting, the other to apologise for not turning up on time.

Larry knew, however, that if Lovell had been up to something, he'd have been smart enough not to leave an obvious trail, and this included any calls that could link him to a crime. There were phone boxes for that kind of thing, places where conversations could be carried out in private.

Lovell's bank statements had revealed no unusual payments in or out, only money for work, some from Murchison Electricals and the rest from various freelance jobs he had done around the area. They hadn't been able to trace any savings accounts and there had been no large amounts of cash found in the flat. Money could have been taken by his attacker, but that didn't tally with the note. *Give it back*. But was the note genuine? The more he thought about it, the less he understood.

Hampstead. That's what he kept coming back to. What if Lovell had been putting the screws on the killer of Gerald Myers? Demanding money, perhaps, to keep his mouth shut about his identity. Cara would have told him what had really happened that night. Perhaps the two of them had been making plans for her release. Perhaps the two of them had never split up. Perhaps they *had* split up and Lovell had double-crossed her.

Then there was that other piece of information Tierney had acquired this afternoon: Cara was currently living with a student called Will Lytton. Just flatmates according to her, but nothing that came out of her mouth could be believed. Larry had run his name through the system and come up with a big fat zero. It could be worth following up though. Was Lytton even his real name?

Larry looked at his watch. Gaynor would start to worry if he was too late back. But still he didn't move. Every cop hated an unsolved murder, and the failure of Hampstead lay heavily on him. He knew he had to be careful. Cara Kendall had been inside his head before, had coiled up there like a ravenous parasite, and eaten away at his reason. He couldn't afford to let her in again, but how could he prevent it? Already he was thinking of her all the time.

When had it started, this preoccupation? Where had the line been crossed between investigating officer and suspect? He remembered those hours spent in the Hampstead interview room with her, the battle between them, how she'd resisted all his attempts to break her down. Gradually, he had got to know every angle of her face, every expression, every gesture. He had been determined to win, but his victory – a three-year sentence – had been a small one. She had got the better of him and he knew it. But he wasn't going to let it rest. One way or another, he would bring her to justice.

It took an effort of will for him to finally drive away from the estate. As he headed along Mansfield Road, he noticed a man in a dark-coloured car, waiting for someone. He didn't think anything of it. His thoughts were miles away.

33

Cara woke up on Saturday morning to the sound of rain thrashing against the window. She laid a hand on her chest, aware of the rapid beating of her heart. She'd been dreaming of Jimmy, or rather of searching for Jimmy, rushing manically from room to room in a crowded, sprawling building she'd never been in before. It was essential that she found him, but everyone she asked had shaken their heads, said they'd seen him earlier, said he might have gone.

She lifted her head from the pillow and checked the alarm clock. It was almost eight, but barely light outside. The dream still clung to her, she couldn't shake it off, and she knew no matter how hard she looked, she would never see Jimmy again. *Never.* There was a hollow sick feeling in the pit of her stomach.

Getting out of bed, she padded over to the window and drew aside the edge of a curtain. The sky was low and dark and grey. Heavy rain obscured her view of the world outside. It was going to be one of those days where it never got truly light, but passed from dawn to dusk in a wet, murky gloom. She let the curtain drop and began to get dressed.

While she was pulling on her jeans, Cara heard the front door opening and closing. She listened, not sure at first if it was Lytton coming in or going out. When there was no further sound, no footsteps, she knew that it was out. Where was he going at this time of the morning? College would be closed, and the library too. The Spar? Except there was tea and coffee in the cupboard, bread in the bread bin and milk in the fridge. She couldn't think of what else he would need urgently.

Well, it was none of her business where he went. Or was it? Although they'd talked till late last night, she had found out no new information about him. He had a way of deflecting personal questions or of skilfully sidestepping them, so that before you knew it, he'd moved on to a completely different subject. She couldn't work out if he was simply private, one of those people who preferred not to talk about themselves, or if he had something to hide.

It was possible, of course, that Lytton was exactly who he claimed to be – a man in his thirties, reassessing his life, looking for a new direction – but she couldn't be certain. Until she was, she would have to be careful. Trusting no one was rapidly becoming her default position. Better safe than sorry.

Cara finished dressing, went to the kitchen and made herself a coffee. She had three hours to kill before her prearranged trip out at eleven. The walk to the Spar and back would, with luck, be enough for Glen Douglas to latch on to her tail. And then what? Then she would have to wait for him to make the identification. Monday or Tuesday, probably. And then what? At the very least she would know who had her in their sights.

Lytton didn't come back, and Cara spent the next few hours alone. She wandered around the flat, stared out of the window, sat down, flicked through some magazines, stood up and began her restless pacing again. No matter how hard she tried she couldn't stay still. Her head was full of Jimmy, of Murch, of Neil, of everything she didn't understand. Time passed slowly. The hands on her watch had lead weights attached to them.

Finally, after what felt like an eternity, it was five to eleven. She grabbed her raincoat and headed out, giving herself a pep talk as she went down in the lift: act normal, don't walk too fast or too slow, don't look over your shoulder.

It felt exhilarating to be out of the flat, to be doing something again. But as she sloshed through the puddles she was suddenly assailed by doubt. What if her tail didn't recognise her with her hood up? What if he was hunkered down in his car and failed to notice her as she passed through the gates? Douglas would probably still charge her, simply for turning up. She would be out of pocket and none the wiser. Would she have to pay again for him to try again? Damn the weather!

All these thoughts were tumbling through her mind as she approached the exit, trying to keep her gaze focused straight ahead, trying to be nonchalant or at least to act as if she wasn't a person expecting to be followed. She pushed back her hood a little in order to show her face clearly.

Cara walked along Mansfield Road and then swung left on to the high street. Despite the rain, there were plenty of shoppers around. People needed to eat, to buy food, and the cold and the wet wasn't going to stop them. She dodged between umbrellas, keeping a steady pace. The Spar wasn't far away now. It was hard to resist the temptation to look back, to try and spot Douglas, but she knew it would be a big mistake. If her tail realised he was being followed she could blow the whole thing.

Cara went into the Spar, trotted down to the fridges at the far end and picked up a pint of milk. She should buy something for dinner tonight. Should she buy enough for two? She didn't know when Lytton would be back, but she owed him a meal, although she didn't really as his curry had been a thank you for letting him stay. It would be awkward, though, if he came home just as she was about to eat and she had nothing to offer him.

She considered all this and decided on a casserole as the best way forward. It would give her something to do this afternoon, and if Lytton didn't come back it wouldn't matter as the rest could be eaten tomorrow. After collecting a basket, she gathered chicken, leeks, mushrooms and carrots. She felt ludicrously domesticated, as if she was living a normal sort of life and doing normal kinds of things. Nothing, of course, could be further from the truth. Her ex had just been murdered, she was the target of threats, she was being followed and she was, in all probability, under investigation by the law.

Cara gave a small shake of her head as she added a couple of bread rolls to the basket. This time last week she'd been desperate to get out of jail and now she almost wished she was back there with nothing more to worry about than whether her clothes would get shrunk in the laundry or scouse Julie would kick off at lunchtime. The latter had always been a messy affair, with plastic cutlery and baked beans flying randomly through the air.

She queued up and paid, keeping her gaze fixed on the cashier and away from the front window. Then, without rushing, she left the wet coat smell of the store and began retracing her steps towards the estate. Were there eyes on her, footsteps dogging her own? She couldn't say for sure. She prayed that Douglas was in the vicinity and was doing what she'd paid him for.

As she turned on to Mansfield Road again, Cara allowed herself a surreptitious glance along the line of parked cars. No black BMW so far as she could see. A blue van with tinted windows was parked near the gates, a suspicious vehicle if ever she'd seen one. She gave it a wide berth, scared that if she got too close the side door might suddenly open and she'd be dragged inside. Could such a thing happen in broad daylight? Anything could happen in Kellston.

The phone was ringing as she opened the door to the flat. Cara hesitated, unwilling to submit herself to any more heavy breathing, but then she wondered if it could be Douglas calling to say that his mission had been successful – or otherwise. Either way, she wanted to know.

Dropping the carrier bag, Cara hurried into the living room and snatched up the phone. 'Hello?'

There was a silence, during which she almost hung up, but then a voice she recognised came on the line.

'Cara?'

'Yeah, it's me.'

'It's Murch,' he said unnecessarily. 'I need to see you. Can you be in the Fox at a quarter past twelve?'

'What's it about?'

Murch sounded flustered, his voice pitched an octave higher than usual. 'I'll explain. I'll tell you when I see you. Can you come?'

'Sure, I'll be there.'

Murch rang off and Cara slowly replaced the receiver. Was she finally getting somewhere? Her parting words yesterday must have had the desired effect. He was about to come clean. She was certain of it. She could barely wait.

34

The Fox had only been open for fifteen minutes, and although it would soon fill up, for now there was just a handful of customers. Cara had no difficulty in locating Murch, who was sitting near the back of the main room, hunched over a pint with an anxious expression on his face. He looked up as she approached and gave a tight strained smile.

'I got you a drink.'

'Ta,' Cara said, choosing a seat from where she could see the door. If anyone was going to follow her in, she wanted to know about it. She put her bag on the table, and then shrugged off her wet coat and draped it over the back of the chair. 'What's going on?'

Murch was wearing one of his trademark shell suits, this one in lime green and white, and his left leg was doing a nervous jig, bouncing as if it had a life of its own. He glanced around, checking there was no one within earwigging distance. As all the surrounding tables were empty this was hardly necessary, but he was clearly on edge. He leaned forward, speaking softly, 'I've been thinking, you know, about what you said yesterday.'

Cara waited, but no further information was forthcoming. 'And?'

Murch picked up his pint, took two large gulps as if he needed Dutch courage and put the glass back down on the table. 'You got me worried.'

'You're right to be worried. Jimmy's dead, for God's sake.'

The door to the pub opened and two girls came in, chatting and laughing as they went over to the bar. Cara instantly dismissed them as possible tails and then wondered if she was being sexist. Why shouldn't she be being followed by a couple of females? Just because she'd originally spotted a man, two men if you counted the goon, didn't mean there hadn't been a change in personnel. Douglas had said they would be doing shifts.

Murch lit a cigarette and took a couple of puffs before he spoke again. 'I don't know what Jimmy was up to. He didn't tell me nothin'.'

'But you do know something,' she said. 'Isn't that why I'm here?'

'I don't want anything to do with it.'

'Join the club,' she said, 'but I don't seem to have a choice.'

Now there was a steady trickle of customers coming in, the door to the pub opening and closing with increasing regularity. An elderly man, white-haired and stooped, approached the bar. Cara studied him for a moment, decided he wasn't in some kind of excellent disguise and turned her attention to the others: a girl in her early twenties, a middle-aged couple, and two blokes in paint-spattered overalls. The latter were possibles. She couldn't rule them out.

'What did you mean by being followed?'

'Exactly that,' she said. 'Someone's trying to intimidate me, trying to force me into giving back what I don't have.'

'Jesus,' Murch muttered, his gaze flying round the pub. 'Have you been followed here?'

'Probably, but unless they've got the whole place bugged, they're not going to hear anything.'

'They're still going to see me with you, though, aren't they?'

Cara could see the fear in his eyes, the panic, and quickly tried to calm him down. 'So what if they do? You're Jimmy's best mate and I was his girlfriend. There's nothing suspicious about the two of us meeting up for a drink. In fact, it would be weird if we didn't. That's what people do, isn't it, when they've lost someone close?'

Murch nodded, although he didn't look convinced.

'Come on, Murch, you said you wanted to see me and now you're just giving me the runaround.'

Murch attacked his cigarette again, taking a few fast puffs before he met her gaze. 'Okay, okay.' He took another gulp of his pint. Then he leaned across the table until his face was close enough for her to smell his beery breath. 'It's in the ladies,' he whispered.

'Huh?'

'What Jimmy gave me, it's in the ladies. The last cubicle. It's in the cistern.'

Cara stared at him. 'What is it?'

'I don't want nothin' more to do with the fuckin' thing. Go get it if you want it, otherwise it's staying there.'

Cara sat back, drank some of her bitter and then stood up in what she hoped was a casual manner. 'I'm just going to the loo,' she said, waving a hand in the general direction of the toilets in case anyone was watching. She picked up her bag from the table, put it over her shoulder and headed for the ladies.

200

As she walked along the narrow corridor, Cara's heart was thrashing. What was she going to find? Drugs, money, jewellery, a key? There was one advantage to this hiding place in that her tail – if he was male – couldn't follow her in there. If it was a woman, however ...

The ladies was empty. Cara strode over to the last cubicle, went in and pulled the bolt across. She waited for a moment, listening in case anyone came in behind her. Everything stayed quiet. She looked up. The toilet was the old-fashioned kind with the cistern set high on the wall, but that wasn't going to stop her. She put the seat down and, holding on to the pipe at the back, hoisted herself up, taking care to keep her feet apart and towards the edge in case the seat cracked under her weight.

Carefully she lifted the lid off the cistern – it was heavy – and manoeuvred it down to the floor. Then she climbed back up on the toilet. Even standing on her toes, she couldn't quite see inside and could only feel around with her hands. The cold water ran through her fingers as she foraged between the jumble of parts, inwardly cursing her lack of height. Where was the damn thing? She didn't even know what size it was. Something tiny, like a key, could be a nightmare to find, especially if it had got lodged under the mechanism.

Cara was starting to get frustrated when her fingers finally made contact with a small hard oblong, covered in plastic and tucked into the back corner. Although she wasn't an expert on the inner workings of toilet cisterns, she was pretty sure that this particular item didn't belong there. Cautiously she prised it out, shaking the water from the black plastic bag as she clambered down. She was excited now, and afraid too. What was it?

Although desperate to see what was inside, Cara laid the object on the floor while she carefully replaced the lid on the cistern. Then she sat down on the loo, picked up her prize and with shaky fingers pulled off the elastic bands, unwrapped the black plastic bag and delved inside.

What she pulled out was an antique silver box, about five inches in length and two inches deep, with the lid and sides enamelled in a flower pattern. Quickly she flipped open the lid and found . . . nothing. It was empty. A sigh of disappointment escaped from her lips. *Give it back.* What was so significant about this box, that someone had been prepared to kill for it? She turned it over and could see hallmarks on the bottom, but they were too small to decipher. She stared at it for a while. It was pretty enough, probably even worth a few bob, but she already suspected that it wasn't the box that mattered but what had once been inside it.

Aware of time passing by, she chucked the plastic bag in the bin and slipped the box into her bag. Murch had some questions to answer.

35

The pub had filled up considerably since Cara had excused herself. The first person she noticed as she glanced casually around was a dark-haired man at the bar. He didn't look at her, didn't even lift his head from the newspaper he was reading, but something about him set off alarm bells in her head. She sat down opposite Murch, picked up her glass and drank some bitter. Although desperate to talk to him about the box, she wasn't going to rush. She didn't want anyone making a connection between her trip to the loo and what she had taken from there. There were people sitting at the tables to either side of them now and, when it came to her tail, she couldn't rule out any of them as possible suspects.

'So how have you been?' she asked.

Murch, expecting a different question, simultaneously frowned and shrugged.

Cara carried on, undeterred. Normal conversation, nothing that could arouse suspicion, just the usual sort of talk between two grieving people. 'Jimmy's brother turned up yesterday, with his wife.'

'Oh, yeah? And what did he have to say for himself?'

'Not much. I suppose he was pretty shaken up. He'd been to see Steadman, but ... well, he didn't learn anything new. If Steadman does know anything, he's keeping it to himself. Jennifer was talking about the funeral.'

Murch gave a snarl. 'She'd probably dig the bloody hole herself if she could. That cow never liked Jimmy. She always looked down her snotty nose at him.'

'Yes, she was never his biggest fan.'

They continued in this vein for a few minutes more until Cara was certain that the people either side were preoccupied with their own conversations. Then she put her elbows on the table, leaned forward and said softly, 'Tell me about the box.'

Murch did precisely what she hadn't wanted him to do, glancing swiftly to his left and right and then all round the pub. Everything about him, from his posture to the scared expression on his face, screamed anxiety and guilt.

'Stop it,' she hissed. 'Look at *me*.'

Murch did as he was told, leaning forward at the same time. He talked quickly as if the sooner he got it out, the sooner his problems would be over. 'Jimmy gave it to me a couple of weeks ago and asked me to get rid. And don't ask me where he got it 'cause I don't know.'

'Why couldn't he get rid of it himself?'

'He reckoned someone was after him, that he couldn't risk getting caught with it.'

'Who? What someone?'

'I told you, I don't know nothin' else. That's all he said. When I asked, he said it was better I didn't know. Just get rid, he said, dump it somewhere.'

'So why didn't you?'

'I meant to, only ... I was busy. I didn't get around to it.'

Cara knew the real reason why. Even with his limited knowledge of antiques, Murch would have guessed it was worth a few quid. So he'd held on to it, hoping the dust would settle and eventually he'd be able to flog it to some dodgy pawnbroker who wasn't going to ask too many questions. 'Was there anything inside?'

'Nothin', I swear. It was empty.'

Cara believed him. Jimmy had removed the contents and put them somewhere else, but it was anyone's guess as to where that was. 'Okay.'

'What are you going to do with it?'

'I don't know yet.'

Murch kept glancing up at the clock on the wall. His pint was almost finished and he was eager to get away. 'Just keep me out of it, yeah? I don't want nothin' more to do with the damn thing.'

'I hear you,' she said. 'Loud and clear.'

Murch, relieved to have offloaded what had turned out to be a liability, pushed back his chair and stood up. 'I've got to get off. I'll see you around.'

'Just one more thing. Did Jimmy say anything to you about meeting up with Neil last Monday?'

'Nah, he never mentioned it.'

'Are you sure?'

'I just said, didn't I?' And with that he walked away, leaving in his wake the distinctive and not altogether pleasing smell of Hai Karate. Murch's choice of aftershave, like so much else about him, left a lot to be desired.

It was only after he'd gone that the fear really began to grow in Cara. She was now in possession of something highly dangerous, something that could directly link her to whatever Jimmy had taken. She took a few sips of beer while she thought about it. And the more she thought about it, the more scared she became.

36

Cara tried to figure out her next move. What she needed was a plan, but all she had was an increasing sense of panic ... and a niggling regret that she'd manoeuvred Murch into relinquishing the box. What was she going to do with it? At the moment it was lying in her bag like a bomb about to go off. Perhaps it would be safer to put it back where she'd found it, but another trip to the loo, only ten minutes after the first, might arouse suspicion in her tail.

She glanced towards the bar. Her number-one suspect, if he was still there, was obscured by a group of lads waiting to be served. She wasn't going to stare. *Stay calm*, she ordered herself. But trying to act naturally wasn't easy, especially when your heart was banging like a drum. The best thing, she decided, was to go straight home and lie low for a while, at least until she heard from Douglas.

An attractive girl with long dark brown hair was going from table to table, clearing glasses and emptying ashtrays. When she got to Cara, she picked up Murch's empty glass and asked, 'Is this done with?'

Cara nodded. 'Yeah, you can take it.'

'Thanks.' The girl nodded and smiled and was about to move on when she paused and said, 'I hope you don't mind me asking, but you're not Cara Kendall, are you?'

'That's me,' Cara said warily.

'I'm Holly. I work here.' She glanced at the glasses she was holding and gave a light laugh. 'Well, obviously. I'm not just doing this for fun. I don't mean to intrude, but I wanted to say that I was sorry to hear about Jimmy. It was terrible what happened to him. I didn't know him well, but he always seemed like a really nice guy.'

'Thanks. How did you know who I was?'

'Oh, I just presumed, with you being with Murch and that. He didn't look too good. Is he okay?'

'Just trying to keep busy, I think.'

'Yeah, they were always together, those two. It must be tough for him.' Holly sighed. 'I still can't get my head around it. It's the shock, I suppose. I know Kellston isn't exactly the most upmarket part of London, but you still don't expect ... And how are you doing? Sorry, hon, I haven't even asked.'

Cara, who wasn't sure if Holly was simply the friendly chatty sort or if she had some kind of agenda, was cautious in her reply. 'Oh, you know, just taking it a day at a time.'

'Yeah, what else can you do?' Holly laid a hand briefly on Cara's shoulder. 'Well, you take care of yourself.'

'Thanks. I will.'

Holly moved off, took a few steps and then came back to the table. She leaned in a little and kept her voice low. 'There's something else. I wasn't sure if I should say anything, only ... don't look now, but there's a bloke at the bar who's had his eye on you. It's probably nothing. He might just be some chancer, thinking about making a move, but I thought I ought to tell you.'

None of this came as any surprise to Cara. She kept her gaze on Holly. 'Do you know him? Is he a regular?'

'No, I've never seen him before. I don't think he's local.'

'Okay, thanks for letting me know.'

'That's all right. We girls have to stick together, don't we?'

Cara waited until Holly had moved off again before glancing casually towards the dark-haired man. In his early forties, smartly dressed, black overcoat. He was staring straight ahead as if studying the optics. Except there was a mirror behind the bar, running the entire length, and in that mirror he could see every move that Cara made. She looked away, not wanting him to realise that she'd clocked him.

She finished her drink while she thought about her tail. Not a regular, apparently, so not one of Terry Street's henchmen. Which blew her original theory out of the water. Or did it? Street could be using someone who wasn't part of the firm, maybe even a professional like Douglas. No, she couldn't rule out anything.

Cara got to her feet, put on her coat and slung her bag over her shoulder. Time to go. She could feel the weight of the box as she walked towards the door. Not too fast. She didn't want it to look like she was in a hurry. Just a normal exit after a quick drink with a friend. Too quick, perhaps. Would that have aroused suspicion? Her tail might already be pondering on the real purpose of the meeting. But there was no point trying to second guess what he was thinking: it would only make her heart beat twice as fast. Better to get out of here before he came to any troublesome conclusions.

Cara took a few deep breaths as she pushed open the door and left the pub. The rain was still coming down. She pulled up her hood. Then, erring on the side of caution, she slipped the strap of the bag over her head so it lay crosswise over her chest:

this way it would be harder to snatch. Now all she had to do was get safely home.

She considered taking a cab from outside the station, but immediately dismissed the idea. The Mansfield was only up the road. It would be like signalling that she was carrying precious cargo. Instead, she walked to the traffic lights, waited for them to turn red and then crossed over. The rain might have thinned out the Saturday shoppers a little, but there were still plenty of people around. Safety in numbers, she hoped.

While she walked up the high street, the questions tumbled through her head. Where had Jimmy got the box? What had been inside it? What was she going to do next? What were *they* going to do next? The answer to the second question was obvious: something small. The box wasn't big enough to hold anything like drugs. Well, not enough drugs. So that probably meant jewellery or diamonds or even letters – maybe the kind of letters that incriminated someone. Unless she was barking up the wrong tree entirely. Perhaps the box itself was valuable, rare, one of a kind, some Fabergé type of thing. But if that was the case, she didn't think Jimmy would have dumped it on Murch. He'd have squirrelled it away until the heat was off, until it was safe to try and flog it.

However, none of this tallied with what Jimmy had said about her being rich when she came out. Rich by association because *he* would be rich? That didn't make any sense. They hadn't even been together then. Although Jimmy might have thought that this breakup, like all the others, wouldn't last for long. A dull ache began to throb inside her. This breakup was as final as it got.

Cara knew that her tail would be skulking behind her, and she upped the pace a little, eager to be home. She went past the Spar and the pawnbrokers and the bank. She reached Cowan

Road and glanced along its length towards the police station. Steadman was probably inside there right now, plotting new ways to try and stitch her up. If he could pin Jimmy's murder on her, he would. And if that failed, he'd think of something else to get her back behind bars again.

All in all, her situation wasn't a good one. With the police advancing on one side and God knows who on the other, she was in a precarious position. How long before she was cornered? She could only hope that they'd both wait a little while before doing anything too drastic. Time was what she needed, time for Glen Douglas to get information on her tail, something, anything, that would point her in the right direction.

Cara was almost at the gates to the Mansfield now. The van was still there, and she instinctively moved closer to the wall. Was there anyone watching from behind those tinted windows? No sooner had this thought entered her head than she became aware of a presence behind her, of someone moving quickly. A split second was all it took for the man to clamp his hand across her mouth, yank up her left arm behind her back and start forcing her forward towards the van. Simultaneously the side door of the van slid back, and eager hands reached out to drag her in.

Panic swept through her. She tried to root her feet to the ground, but the man was too strong. Pain and terror jerked at every nerve. She could feel his hot breath on her neck, hear a soft urgent grunting emanating from the back of his throat. Voices, foreign voices, uttered words she didn't understand: they cut through the air, harsh and insistent, and her assailant responded, pushing her harder. It felt like he was going to break her arm. *Do something.* A couple of feet was all that lay between her and the van, between her and those grasping hands. *Do something.*

Everything was happening too fast. She couldn't think

straight and yet it was all vividly clear. Adrenaline coursed through her. She strained and twisted, trying to break free, but her struggles were in vain. He was too strong. She was too weak. The battle would be over almost as soon as it had begun. Dread pumped into her heart and turned her blood cold.

Cara's right hand was still lodged in her coat pocket. Her fingers curled around the short handle of the kitchen knife, and she didn't think twice. Using every last ounce of her strength, she pulled out the knife and slashed wildly at the man's hand and wrist, slicing into the soft flesh, feeling the jerk of his body as he recoiled in shock. She heard the gasp from his mouth, the guttural curses. That moment, that loosening of his hold, was all she needed. She slid free of his grip, launched herself sideways and sprinted through the gates, running faster than she'd ever run, running because her life depended on it.

All she could hear now was the slap of her trainers against the concrete and her panting breath. She didn't look back until she reached the entrance to Haslow House. There was no one behind her. The van had gone. She slumped against the door, relief streaming through her. She had got away . . . for now.

37

Cara walked unsteadily across the foyer, chose the first available lift and stumbled into it. Her body was shaking, and her breathing was fast and shallow like some small, wounded animal's. She jabbed at the button and waited for what felt like an eternity before the doors finally closed. Even as the lift ascended, she was assailed by fresh terror: what if someone was waiting for her on the tenth floor? A back-up in case she'd managed to evade them at the gates? What if this wasn't over yet. What if . . .

Cara's fingers tightened around the handle of the knife. She looked down, faintly surprised to find herself still holding it. The blade was smeared with blood. *His* blood. Bile rose in her throat. She shuddered at the thought of him and of how close she had come to being forced into the back of the van. And what then? No, she couldn't go there right now. The fear would paralyse her. She put her arm behind her back, keeping the knife out of sight but still firmly in her grasp. If anyone was waiting, she'd be ready for them.

The lift doors opened. She glanced anxiously to the left and right before stepping out. All clear. She strode quickly along the corridor, at the same time delving into her bag to pull out the key with her left hand. Only when she was at the flat did she slip the knife back into her pocket. She unlocked the door, went inside, smartly closed the door behind her and pulled the bolt across.

Such was her state of agitation that Cara almost jumped out of her skin when she walked into the living room and found a man sitting on the sofa. She stifled a gasp, only half successfully, and raised a hand to her chest. As fast as her body had stiffened, it relaxed again. 'Oh, it's you.'

Lytton's surprise was no less evident. He leapt up, staring at her. 'Christ, what's happened?'

Cara was bemused. Did she really look *that* bad? Then she realised he was staring at her coat. She lowered her eyes and saw the bloodstains, scattered splatters, bright as poppies against the cream-coloured fabric. 'Shit,' she murmured.

'You're bleeding.'

She shook her head as she put her bag on the table and slipped out of the coat. 'It's not mine. I'm not hurt.' This wasn't strictly true as her arm was still aching from where the man had yanked it up, but that was hardly life threatening. 'Some bastard grabbed me by the gates and tried to get me into a van.'

'What? You're kidding! That's . . . Are you sure you're all right?'

'I stabbed him,' she said. Then, as Lytton's eyes widened, she quickly added, 'Not seriously. Not anything he's going to bleed to death from. Just his hand. He had it over my mouth and . . . Anyway, that's where the blood came from.'

'Jesus, Cara!'

She went into the kitchen, laid the coat on the counter, took the knife out of the pocket and ran it under the hot water, watching as the water turned pink, revolved gently and disappeared down the plughole.

Lytton had followed her in. 'What are you doing?'

'Disposing of the evidence,' she said.

'You need to ring the police.'

Cara looked over her shoulder. 'What for?'

'Someone just attacked you, for God's sake. You have to report it. You have to let them know.'

'And what are they going to do about it? Arrest me, probably. I'm the one who did the stabbing, remember.'

'Only in self-defence.'

'They won't see it that way.' Cara turned off the tap, dried the knife on a tea towel and put it in the drawer. 'I think there'll be a few difficult questions about why I was carrying a knife in the first place.'

'And why were you?'

'Why do you think? They weren't going to stop at sending notes or making a few dodgy phone calls. I've a right to defend myself. Not that the law will agree. Steadman's just waiting for a chance to lock me up again; I'm not going to hand it to him on a plate.'

'But you're the victim here.'

Cara shrugged and picked up the coat. 'Do you know how I can get the blood out of this?'

'I'm not sure. Cold water? Soap? Look, I can see that your attacker isn't going to go running to the police, but what if someone else reports it? It's broad daylight. Someone must have seen.'

Cara frowned while she thought about it. Everything had happened so quickly. She hadn't had time to take in anything but the moment, the terror-stricken struggle, the fight for survival. The world around her had shrunk only to that small piece of pavement and the open door of the van. 'I don't remember seeing anyone else.' Then a small hazy memory came back to her. 'I'm not sure. Maybe some kids after I'd got away, some boys kicking a ball around when I was running towards Haslow. But I don't know if they saw the attack or not.'

She took the coat over to the sink, turned on the cold water and soaked the part of the coat that was stained. While she scrubbed at it with soap she said: 'Even if they did see, they wouldn't do anything about it. Tell their mates, perhaps, or their parents, but I don't think they'd rush to dial 999.'

'This place is a bloody jungle,' Lytton said. 'Did you get a look at him, the man who attacked you?'

'No, he came up behind, but I think it might have been the same bloke who was in the pub. I was in the Fox earlier, and I had the feeling a man was watching me. Dark-haired bloke in his forties. I couldn't swear to it, though. And there were others, two or three, in the van. He wasn't on his own.'

'Do you remember anything about them?'

'Only that they weren't speaking English. I couldn't tell you what they *were* speaking, though.'

'Are you sure you don't want to ring the police, Cara? I can do it if you like. I mean, this is serious stuff.'

'Positive.' Cara examined the coat. Even after all the scrubbing, there were still marks there. Not bright red, but still visible. 'This isn't going to come out. Damn! I'm going to have to chuck it.' Although why would she want to wear it again anyway? The stain of that man's blood, whether visible or not, would always be there. She wrung out the wet part and flung the coat on the counter.

'What are you going to do?' Lytton asked.

'Buy a new one.'

'I don't mean the coat. You got away today, but they're not going to give up. You might not be so lucky next time.'

'Luck had nothing to do with it.' Cara had never deliberately

215

hurt anyone before in her entire life, but she had no regrets about what she'd done. 'He could have been the man who killed Jimmy. If he was, he deserved everything he got.'

'I'm not arguing with that, but these people are dangerous. You can't carry a knife for the rest of your life.'

'Who said anything about the rest of my life?' Cara gave him a grim smile. 'But if that's what it takes ...'

38

Rochelle wasn't sure of the time. Somewhere around six, she thought, although it could be later. It was dark and wet and cold. She was sitting, shoulders hunched, on the low wall by the gates to the estate. A half bottle of vodka and a pack of cigarettes were keeping her company. What more did she need? Jimmy, she thought, and the pain rolled through her. He might not have loved her, but at least he'd cared. There was no one to watch over her now. Well, there was *him*, but he didn't count. She didn't want his kind of watching. He could go to hell.

She took a swig from the bottle, feeling the burn as the vodka slipped down her throat. Later, when she was drunk enough, she'd go to the Fox and find a random bloke, some mug who would buy her drinks until closing time. Deep down, men were all the same. Takers, every single one of them. Only after one thing. They'd tell you any old lie to get you in the sack.

Behind her the towers were lit up like Christmas trees. She turned her head, focused on Temple and counted up the floors until she came to the black, blank windows of Jimmy's flat. No one home. No more Jimmy. There were people behind the rows of bright squares, men and women getting ready to go out or preparing for an evening in front of the TV. Did any of them care that he was dead? Did they give him a second thought as they changed into their party clothes or put the kettle on to make a brew? Her fingers tightened around the bottle. She felt the urge to throw it, to hurl it down onto the pavement and watch it smash into a thousand pieces – but that would have been a waste of good voddie.

She shifted her gaze to Haslow House. That's where Cara Kendall lived. Her eyes narrowed into slits. Jimmy had spoken too much about her, although to be fair this was mainly because she'd always been asking questions. She had wanted to know everything: when they'd first met, what made her tick, what she liked and didn't like, why he couldn't let her go. And once Jimmy had a few beers inside him, he'd happily oblige. To hear him talk, you'd have thought the girl was something special, but Rochelle couldn't see it herself. Who cared if the stupid bitch could shin up a drainpipe or climb across a roof? It hadn't got her anywhere but behind bars. But still she'd kept asking, kept probing, even though everything he'd said had been like another stab to the heart.

Rochelle turned back, puffed on her fag and gazed at the pavement. She had imagined killing Cara, pulling out a gun and shooting her straight between the eyes. Bang! A pretty little hole in the middle of her pretty little face. No one would have known who'd done it. She could have consoled Jimmy then, given him a shoulder to cry on and eventually he'd have come to realise that *she* was the one he wanted.

But none of that was going to happen now. Rochelle studied her left knee, her hand scratching at an itch that wouldn't go away. Her bare leg looked orangey pale in the light from the streetlamp. She wondered why everything always went wrong. She was cursed, that was the problem; from the moment she'd been born, foulness had been wrapped around her, a blanket of pure evil. It wasn't her fault if she did bad things. She couldn't be blamed for the rottenness inside her.

She took another swig of vodka, surprised to find so little left in the bottle. Her mind was starting to jump around now, erratic thoughts exploding in her head like popcorn in a pan. No sooner had one idea surfaced than another instantly replaced it. She couldn't focus. There were no straight lines any more. Everything was jagged and broken.

Rochelle dropped the butt of her cigarette and watched the red end glow for a while before grinding it out with the heel of her shoe. What time was it now? She started singing: 'Wake me up before you go-go . . .' She laughed and stopped laughing. The moon slid out from behind a grey cloud, full and round. She could still kill Cara if she wanted to. What was that on the pavement? Dark stains like blood. The Fox would be busy tonight. It was Saturday, wasn't it? Sometimes the days ran into each other. She thought about changing her name. She was tired of Rochelle, tired of everything about her. There was no point in being Rochelle now that Jimmy was gone. Those marks on the pavement definitely looked like blood.

39

Ray Tierney was careful about the pubs and bars he chose to frequent. Being caught drinking in an overtly gay establishment would pretty much mean the end of his career. It wasn't a criminal offence, but it may as well have been, at least to his colleagues. Once he was outed as a bender, a queer, a fuckin' poof – these and other words were frequently bandied about – he'd be shunned by every man jack of them. It was bad enough being a northerner, but throw homosexuality into the mix and his working life would be intolerable.

His favourite watering hole was the French House in Soho, which had an interesting, partly bohemian clientele. Artists, actors and writers mingled with those of a less creative disposition. It was an easy-going, friendly sort of pub where it was possible to fall into conversation with a like-minded person and, on a good night, maybe fall into bed with them too. This wasn't going to be one of those nights. He had finished work too late to bother making the journey into the West End. Instead, he stood by the bar in the Fox, finishing his pint, while his gaze idly roamed over the other customers.

It was the loneliness that got to him. Somehow it was worse in a big city like London where everyone always seemed to have somewhere to go and someone to go there with. He hadn't made any real friends since he'd got here. Although he occasionally went drinking with his colleagues, it was hard work. Football, beer and shagging was what they mainly talked about. In order to fit in he had to assume a mask, to mimic what they said and how they said it, to hide his true self in a layer of lies.

Holly Abbott was behind the bar, along with a couple of male staff. Saturday night was always busy. He watched as she pulled pints, served shorts and pushed packets of crisps across the counter. To see her working you wouldn't think she was doing anything other than her job. A friendly smile for everyone, a bit of banter, no indication at all that she was indulging in her own particular brand of espionage. By now, getting close to last orders, there were plenty who had had one too many and whose mouths were starting to run away with them. She would be listening to everything while her watchful eyes swept the pub.

Ray wondered why she'd chosen him. Why not Steadman or one of the others? Just chance, perhaps. Or maybe it was because they were both, to some degree, outsiders. She wasn't from London, and he wasn't either. Was that enough of a reason? He considered it for a while but didn't dwell on it. Her information was always sound and that was all that mattered.

He caught Holly's eye and raised his empty glass. She nodded and as soon as she was free came over to serve him. As she was refilling his pint, she asked casually, 'Any progress with Jimmy Lovell?'

'We're following up some leads.'

Holly raised her eyebrows. 'That's a no, then.' She gestured with her head and said softly, 'You see that girl at the other end of the bar? The redhead? She's called Rochelle and she used to hang out with him sometimes. If you buy her a drink, she might talk to you.'

Ray looked over at the girl. She was young, no more than nineteen or twenty, he reckoned, dressed in a sparkly top and a miniskirt. A halo of red hair framed a thin, freckled face. Sober she certainly wasn't – she was leaning heavily against the bar – and her clumsy attempts to chat up any male in the vicinity weren't meeting with much success. Her eyes had a glazed, desperate look. Strictly speaking he was off-duty and seeing the state of her he doubted the usefulness of any kind of exchange, but he nodded at Holly and said: 'Go on. What the hell, get her whatever's she's drinking.'

Holly passed over his pint and took the money for both drinks. She put a shot of vodka into a glass, poured in a bottle of tonic water, walked down to the other end of the bar and placed the glass in front of Holly. Ray couldn't hear what Holly said, but Rochelle looked over, smiled at him, pushed herself off the bar and tottered over on high heels to introduce herself.

'Hey, hon,' she said. 'Ta for the drink. I'm Rochelle. What's your name?'

'DC Ray Tierney,' he said. 'Nice to meet you. I was hoping we could have a chat about Jimmy.'

Instantly Rochelle drew back, her smile vanishing. 'I don't talk to the filth.'

'But you do let them buy you a drink.'

Rochelle's hand tightened around the glass as if he might try and snatch it off her. 'I didn't know who you were, did I?'

'Well, now you do. Look, I'm not talking anything official here. Off the record, yeah?' A table had become free behind Ray, and he moved towards it. 'Come on, let's sit down. Where's the harm? You want to catch the bastard who killed him, don't you?'

222

Rochelle hesitated, torn probably between her loathing of the police and the possibility of squeezing another drink out of him. It was the latter that eventually won out and, somewhat grudgingly, she followed. At the table she sat down, took a large gulp of her vodka and tonic and then folded her arms across her chest. 'I don't know nothin' about what happened.'

A pungent, almost nauseating smell of perfume floated into Ray's nostrils. 'I didn't say you did. But you two were mates, yeah?'

'Who told you that?'

'I heard you used to drink with him in here.'

'No law against it, is there?'

Ray ploughed on despite her defensiveness. 'Course not. But tell me about Jimmy. What was he like?'

'What does that matter?'

'When you're investigating a case like this, it helps to get a feel for the victim, to understand what made them tick.'

'So why ain't you asking that Cara girl? She was his girlfriend – when it suited her.'

Ray didn't need to be an expert to recognise animosity when he heard it. 'You don't like her?'

'What's to like?'

'Jimmy must have found something. He was with her for long enough.'

Rochelle pulled a face, shrugged and reached for her glass again. 'Yeah, well, I reckon he just felt sorry for her. He were a right gent, Jimmy, one of the good guys. Heart of gold. Everyone liked him.'

'Someone didn't.'

'That's a fuckin' horrible thing to say.'

'It's the truth, though, isn't it? Poor Jimmy didn't die peacefully in his sleep.'

Rochelle scowled. 'If it hadn't been for her, he'd still be alive.'

'What do you mean by that?'

'Nothin'.'

'You wouldn't have said it if it was nothing.'

But Rochelle's attention had been distracted by a minor fracas at the bar where two blokes were squaring up to each other over something they wouldn't remember in the morning. She grinned like she was enjoying the show, frowning when their mates stepped in to put a stop to it.

'Rochelle?'

Eventually she looked at him again. 'Huh?'

'You were saying about how it was Cara's fault.'

'Why would it be her fault?'

'I don't know. That's why I'm asking.'

Rochelle considered this for a moment, her addled brain trying to make the necessary connections. 'You got a fag?'

It seemed to Ray that people were constantly poncing cigarettes off him, like he was some kind of free vending machine. But he dug into his pocket, got out the pack, gave her one and lit it for her. Then he prompted, 'You said if it hadn't been for Cara, Jimmy would still be alive.'

Rochelle leaned forward and said conspiratorially, 'I reckon those women are right.'

'What women are those?'

'You know, that Greenham Common lot. Them protestors. I saw them on the telly. We're all going to get blown to pieces when the bomb drops so there's not much point in nothin', is there?'

Ray sighed, wondering why he bothered. 'About Cara Kendall,' he said patiently.

'What about her?'

'Her and Jimmy,' he said, trying to pose the question in a

different way. 'You seem to think she was responsible in some way for his death.'

Rochelle's mouth grew sulky. 'I didn't say that.'

'You said he'd still be here if it wasn't for her.'

'So?' Rochelle necked more vodka, watching him over the rim of her glass. Her eyes became sly. She put the glass down and stared at him. 'Maybe he would. Maybe he wouldn't. Maybe if she'd never gone climbing into other people's houses, he wouldn't have got dragged into it all.'

Ray was interested but didn't show it. 'Dragged in? Hampstead, you mean?'

Rochelle puffed on the cigarette. Her expression changed. Suddenly she seemed almost scared, as if she might have said too much. 'I don't know about Hampstead. He never said a word. Me and Jimmy just hung out sometimes. He didn't tell me nothin'.'

'But you just said—'

'We was just mates.'

'Exactly. You and Jimmy were mates. And you're a smart girl, I can see that. If he was involved in something, you'd have sussed it out.'

'Don't give me that shit. I know what you lot are like, always playing fuckin' games, always twisting everything.' Rochelle drained her glass, rose unsteadily to her feet and glared down at him. 'I'm going for a piss, and don't bother waiting 'cause I'm not coming back.'

Ray watched her totter away from the table, barging through other customers as she headed for the ladies. He'd touched a nerve, that was for sure, but did it mean anything? Perhaps Steadman had been right about the Hampstead connection. Or perhaps she'd just had the hots for Jimmy and was looking for someone to blame for his death. He wasn't sure what to make of it all. The girl was drunk, and drunks said all sorts of crazy things.

He finished his beer, not expecting her to come back – and she didn't. A few minutes later he saw her at the bar just as the bell for last orders was ringing. She was hanging off the arm of some middle-aged bloke and laughing too loud at everything he said. It was depressing to watch, and he quickly looked away. What now? Go home, make himself a mug of cocoa and listen to the Smiths. He needed something to cheer him up.

40

It was after eleven before Lytton said goodnight and Cara waited until he'd been to the bathroom and the door to his bedroom had closed before rising from the sofa, turning off the TV and going over to the bookshelves. She pulled out a couple of her dad's books on antiques and placed them on the table. Next, she switched on the lamp. Then she sat down, pulled her bag into her lap, unzipped it and reached inside for the silver box.

Even as she took it out, she felt her fingers shaking slightly. If those thugs had been successful this afternoon, if they'd managed to drag her into the van, she'd have been facing a desperate situation. She could have ended up like Jimmy. A sound slipped from her throat, low and anguished, quickly silenced. Dead like Jimmy. Whatever they wanted was connected to this box.

Cara gazed at it for a while and then examined it more closely, looking at it from every angle, tilting it this way and that in search of clues. Where had it come from? Who did it belong to? She was struck once again by its prettiness, by the artistry in its design, by the skilful engraving and beautifully enamelled flowers. But none of that got her any closer to understanding its importance.

There was a stamp and hallmarks on the base of the box, symbols too small to identify with the naked eye. She stood up again, retrieved her dad's little magnifying glass from the sideboard and returned to the table. It took her fifteen minutes of searching through the books, of comparing, checking and double checking, to establish that the maker had been based in St Petersburg, that it was good-quality silver and that the date of production was 1890.

Establishing these facts did nothing to ease Cara's troubled state of mind. She thought of the thug's breath on the back of her neck, of the other men's arms reaching out for her, and shivered. Was it Russian they'd been speaking? She'd heard stories about the Russian mafia, of how they'd infiltrated London's crime scene, and the dread grew inside her. You didn't mess with people like that, not if you wanted to wake up in the morning.

Cara returned to the books, flicking through the pages to try and discover the worth of the box. A part of her was still hoping that it was something rare, something so valuable that its owner would be prepared to go to any lengths to get it back. If that was the case, she might be able to negotiate its return and bring this nightmare to an end. But she was quickly disappointed. There was nothing to suggest that the box was anything special. The maker, although skilled, was not a famous name and similar boxes had sold for between one and two hundred quid. Not a price to be sneered at, but not high enough to kill for, either. No, her original idea had been right: it was what had been in the box that was the prize, not the box itself.

Cara's left hand tapped out a nervous dance on the tabletop. Her eyes fell on the inch-long scar that ran from the base of her thumb towards her wrist. She had done that on the very first job she and Jimmy had been on together: a jewellery shop in the West End with a dodgy roof and scaffolding erected in front of the building. Like an open invitation to climb on up and help themselves from the second-floor storeroom.

Except it hadn't worked out quite as they'd imagined. Cara's lips curled into a rueful smile. She had cut herself on the glass when the window had shattered as she'd tried to jemmy it open. Then an alarm had gone off and they'd decided to scarper. So, not so much a job as an unmitigated disaster, but it hadn't put her off. If nothing else, she'd learned that she had a head for heights.

Cara's smile faded as another memory slid into her head: the way Steadman had stared at her hand during those long, tortuous interrogations after the murder of Gerald Myers. It was as if he believed that the scar meant something, as if he was racking his brains to work out what. Steadman's intensity had scared her then and it still did today. His grudge was as permanent as the scar itself.

This wasn't getting her anywhere. She turned her attention back to the box, knowing that she had to get rid of it. Jimmy had realised that, which was why he'd passed it on to Murch. She thought of all the bins he could have dumped it in and sighed. No, he'd had to keep the damn thing, and now she was in possession of the hottest item in London.

Cara leaned forward and switched off the lamp. She put the silver box back in her bag, slung the bag over her shoulder and went out into the hall. She checked the front door, making sure it was securely bolted, took a look through the spyhole at an empty piece of corridor, and then headed off for bed. Would she sleep? It seemed unlikely.

41

Terry Street didn't like it when people took liberties, especially when those liberties were taken on his own manor. Ivan Azarov had overstepped the mark. Still, that was foreigners for you. They couldn't be trusted. They didn't know how to stick to a deal, even when it had been shaken on.

Boyle's account of events – following Cara Kendall from the Fox, the waiting van, the attempted abduction – was only made palatable by the fact the Russians had screwed up. Kendall had fought back, blood had been drawn and she'd managed to get away. That she hadn't called the law told Terry everything he needed to know.

'What are you going to do, boss?'

'Teach the fuckers a lesson.' A swift retaliation was in order before word got around that Terry Street was a pushover, that any Tom, Dick or Vladimir could come on to his patch and behave exactly as they liked. It didn't work like that in Kellston. He had a reputation to uphold.

'The van ain't here,' Boyle said, looking up and down Mansfield Road.

Terry gazed through the windscreen at the midnight sky. 'I reckon they'll be back.'

'So we just wait for them?'

'I'm not in a patient sort of mood.'

Boyle grinned like a kid who'd just been promised an ice cream. 'We going to go to them?'

'Why not? Let's go up West and give one of those bastards a nice little surprise. That commie shit needs to learn that he can't fuck me over.'

'I hear you, boss.'

Terry sat back and gave an almost mournful shake of his head. If Azarov had stuck to his side of the bargain there wouldn't have been any need for unpleasantness. Terry had promised to retrieve the goods, the Russian to give him a generous reward. That should have been that, but instead Azarov had decided to cut him out and take matters into his own hands. Perhaps that was the way they did things in Russia, but it didn't wash here. A double cross, that's what it was, and no one did the dirty on Terry Street and got away with it.

42

By Monday Cara was going stir crazy. It wasn't that she had anywhere particular to go, but the knowledge that she couldn't go anywhere made her feel like she was back in prison. Yesterday had been a long day. She had spent it in a state of nervous anxiety, knowing that her pursuers were out there somewhere and probably not far away. And they wouldn't be happy, especially the one she'd slashed with the knife. Revenge would be at the forefront of *his* mind. She had taken him by surprise, but he wouldn't make the same mistake again.

The only fresh air she'd got was when she'd stepped out onto the narrow balcony to look down on the estate and see if she could spot anyone lying in wait. It had almost made it worse that she couldn't identify any obvious suspects or any likely vehicles. Just because she couldn't see them, didn't mean they weren't there. Not for a minute did she imagine that they'd given up.

She checked her watch. It was five past nine, only a quarter of an hour since she'd managed to eject Lytton from the flat, persuading him to go to college, insisting that nothing would be achieved by him staying with her.

'You don't have to worry. I'm not going out, and I won't answer the door if anyone rings the bell. I'll put the bolt on. No one's going to break it down in a hurry and I'll ring the law if anyone tries. I'm perfectly safe.'

'But what are you going to do? You can't stay locked up here for ever.'

'I don't intend to. I just need a day or two to work out what to do.'

Now that Lytton had gone, Cara felt both relief and anxiety. She didn't want him feeling responsible for her but being completely on her own made her realise how vulnerable she was. The day stretched ahead, all those empty hours, and she knew she had to do something, anything, to keep her imagination in check. The more she thought about those men, the more terrified she became.

She picked up the phone and rang Glen Douglas, the second time she'd tried this morning, but the phone went to answer machine again. She'd already left a message asking him to call her, so this time she just hung up. Next, she called Neil and had to go through a screening process with the office receptionist – what her name was, what it was in connection with, whether she was important enough to talk to a senior executive – before eventually being put through.

'Cara, it's nice to hear from you. How are things?'

Cara thought she heard a note of fake sincerity in his voice. 'I'm all right, thanks. Sorry to disturb you at work, but something's come up and I was hoping we could meet. Would that be possible?'

There was a long hesitation on the other end of the line. 'You can't just tell me about it now?'

'I'd rather not,' Cara said. 'It's a bit, erm ... sensitive. I mean, it's nothing to worry about. I'd just like to get your take on it.'

'Trouble is, I'm a bit tied up at work today.'

'Oh, that's okay. I didn't mean today. How about later in the week? Wednesday lunchtime, perhaps? Or early evening. Would that suit you?'

'Let me check my diary. Hold on.'

Cara wondered if he was playing for time, trying to think up excuses as to why they couldn't meet, but when he picked up the phone again, he said, 'How about tomorrow? I've got a five o'clock appointment with a retailer in Shoreditch. That's not far from you. I should be done by half five. I could meet you in that pub by Kellston station. The Fox, is it? Say about six?'

Now it was Cara's turn to hesitate. She'd been hoping for a couple of days to work out a foolproof method of getting off the estate without being spotted but guessed that if she wanted to see Neil she'd have to fit in with his schedule. 'That's fine. Thanks. Tomorrow, then.'

Neil gave a low, rather nervous laugh. 'This is all very mysterious.'

'Oh, no,' Cara said quickly, concerned that he might back out if he thought she was going to put him on the spot. 'It's nothing mysterious. It's just ... no, there are just a few things I want to run by you.'

'I'll take your word for it.'

Cara said a fast goodbye and ended the call. She stood for a moment, pleased that he'd agreed to meet her, but still unsure as to how she could get safely to the Fox and back. A minicab? That would solve the problem of leaving the estate – she could get it to pick her up from outside the main doors of Haslow – but it wouldn't stop them from following her. Even if she got another cab home, they could lie in wait for her in the foyer or up on the tenth floor.

She went over to the window and looked out at a dark threatening sky. The more she thought about it, the less she liked the cab idea. It was too risky. She threw a few more ideas around before coming up with one that seemed feasible. If she took the lift down to the underground car park, it was possible to exit from there round the back of the tower. She could then walk through the tunnel to Carlton House and go over the wall by the bins. Would that work? She thought so. Unless her pursuers had people scattered all over the estate, she stood a chance of getting out unseen.

Cara was about to address another problem – what to do with the silver box – when the phone started ringing.

'Hello?'

'It's Glen Douglas. I just picked up your message.'

'Thanks for calling back. I need to talk to you. Something happened at the weekend. I was—'

'I think we should talk face to face,' Douglas said, interrupting her. 'I'll come round to your flat if that's all right. I've got a few more calls to make so shall we say twenty minutes?'

'Okay, if you think that—'

'See you in twenty.'

Cara put the phone down. She supposed it didn't matter if her tail saw Douglas: he could be coming to any of the flats in Haslow. There would be no reason to believe it was hers. She went into the kitchen, took the percolator off the shelf and put the kettle on so she could make coffee before he arrived. Then, because she always hated waiting, she grabbed a cloth and started wiping down the counter.

While she was cleaning an already clean surface, some bad thoughts crept into her head. What if Douglas had been got at? Maybe someone had made him an offer he couldn't refuse. Or threatened him. But how would they even know that he was working for her? He could have gone behind her back and approached the Russians – if that's what they were – direct. She had a sudden dreadful image of opening the door and the enemy piling in.

Cara briefly shut her eyes, shuddering at the thought of it. Then she gave herself a mental shake. This was ridiculous. If she wasn't careful, she'd send herself mad. She had to trust someone, and it may as well be Glen Douglas as anybody else.

43

It was half an hour before the doorbell went, thirty minutes that Cara had spent impatiently pacing from room to room. Despite her resolve to trust Glen Douglas, she still peered through the spyhole at his face for a while, trying to establish if he looked duplicitous or on edge. Unable to come to any firm conclusion – he didn't look any different to when she'd first met him on Friday – she took a deep breath, unbolted the door and opened it.

Douglas nodded. 'Morning.'

Cara glanced quickly along the corridor, left and right, before standing back and inviting him in. As soon as he was in the hall-way, she shut the door and immediately pulled the bolt across again. If Douglas thought the security measures a tad extreme, he was polite enough not to mention it.

'I've made coffee,' she said. 'Come on through.'

'Sorry I'm late. I've been chasing up some leads.'

'And have you found out anything?'

Douglas followed her through to the kitchen. 'Plenty. What would you like first, the good news or the bad?'

Cara picked up the percolator and poured coffee into the mugs. 'Let's start with the bad. At least then I'll have something to look forward to. Do you take milk, sugar?'

'Black,' he said. 'Two sugars. Ta.'

She added the sugar, gave the coffee a stir and passed the mug over to him. 'Okay, I'm ready.'

Douglas perched on a stool and took a moment, like a doctor preparing to tell his patient that their days were numbered. 'You were right about the tail, except you don't just have one, you've got two.'

'Working together, you mean?'

Douglas shook his head. 'Separately,' he said.

'What? How can there be two? Why? Are you sure?'

'It would appear you're a popular woman.'

Cara frowned. This wasn't the kind of popularity anyone wanted. 'I don't get it. I don't understand. Who are they?'

'Have you heard of a man called Terry Street?'

Cara stiffened, her heart sinking. 'Of course I have. He's the local big shot, a gangster. He runs Kellston and half the East End. Damn it! I heard Jimmy had been talking to him in the Fox a few weeks back.'

'And you didn't think to mention this before?'

'I should have done. I'm sorry. I didn't think there was anything in it. Jimmy never usually mixed with that lot. He wasn't into the heavy stuff. He wasn't stupid. You get involved with those people and next thing you know you're looking at a life sentence with no parole.'

'Or worse.'

'Or worse,' Cara echoed softly.

'Do you know what Jimmy was discussing with Street?'

'I don't think they were discussing, exactly. Murch said he was drunk – Jimmy, I mean – and talking about how I'd be a rich woman when I came out, that no one knew the half of it. I

238

presumed he was just showing off, trying to impress, pretending he knew stuff they didn't.'

'It seems an odd thing to say.'

'It isn't true, in case you're wondering. I don't know why Jimmy said that.'

'Okay, well, Street's had one of his men tailing you, a piece of muscle called Boyle. There have probably been others, but he was the one on duty on Saturday.'

'And the other tail? Do you know who that is?'

'Now that's trickier. I've got a name – Pavel Kuzmin – and I've tracked him to the West End, but I can't say for sure who he's working for yet. If he's reporting to his boss, he's doing it by phone. I've got a few leads, though. Give me a day or two and I should know more.'

'Kuzmin. That sounds Russian, don't you think?'

'It could be.'

Cara gave him a quick summary of Saturday's events from meeting Murch in the Fox to the attempted abduction outside the Mansfield. Douglas's expression remained neutral throughout, although his eyebrows shifted up a notch when she talked about the knife and how she'd got away from the men. 'I know I shouldn't have been carrying it, but if I hadn't, I'd probably be in the morgue by now.'

'Are you sure they were speaking Russian?'

'No, not definitely. But it wasn't a language I recognised, not French or Spanish or anything like that. Let me show you the box.'

Cara went into the living room and got her bag, came back and laid the silver box on the counter. 'This is it.'

Douglas picked it up and examined it closely, even lifting it to his nose to smell the inside. 'And it was empty when this Murch bloke passed it on to you?'

'Yes. I'm pretty sure he didn't know what had been in it. Jimmy didn't tell him that: he just asked him to get rid. The box is Russian, though, late nineteenth century. It's good quality, maybe worth a couple of hundred on a good day.'

'You know about this stuff, then?'

'Not much, but my dad was keen on antiques. He had some books and I looked up the hallmarks and the rest. I could be wrong, but I don't think so.' Cara released a long sigh. 'No one's going to kill for a couple of hundred, are they? It's what was in the box that's important, not the box itself.'

'And you've never seen it before?'

'Never.'

'Are you sure?'

Cara heard a hint of scepticism in his voice. 'Completely sure. I'd remember if I had.' She leaned against the counter and sipped her coffee. 'What are you getting at?'

'Is there any chance it could have come from the Myers house?'

Cara gave a start. Although she'd told Douglas about being in prison, she hadn't told him the details of how she'd ended up there. 'What? How do you know about Myers?'

'Because I make it my business to know about my clients. I find it helps in the long run to get a little background detail. Saves any unpleasant surprises. You don't mind, do you?'

Cara wasn't sure if she should mind or not – she hadn't hired him to go poking around in *her* life – but seeing as it was all public knowledge anyway, she decided not to get too antsy about it. 'None of that has anything to do with this.'

'Are you certain?'

Cara hesitated. 'No, but how could it? I didn't take the box. I didn't take anything from the house. And Jimmy wasn't even there, so how could he have got hold of it?'

240

'Perhaps the killer took it. If the papers are to be believed, he got away with quite a haul.'

'So how would Jimmy end up with it?'

'The killer could have given it to him to pass on to you. The price for keeping your mouth shut about his identity.'

'I don't know his bloody identity!' Cara snapped back. 'It was dark. I didn't see him. All I heard were footsteps in the hall. Jesus, you're starting to sound like Steadman. I didn't . . .'

Douglas put down his mug and raised his hands in a placatory gesture. 'Okay, keep your hair on. I'm not accusing you of anything. I'm just trying to look at it like someone else might. You can see it, can't you? Jimmy sounding off about you being a rich woman does kind of suggest that a reward is coming your way. You keep your mouth shut to the police and at the trial, do your time, and in return you get a nice little gift. Or maybe not so little.'

'But . . .' Cara stopped and thought about it. 'All right, I can just about buy that, I suppose. I mean, I can see how it might look. Only it isn't true, and it doesn't explain why Jimmy said it in the first place.'

'Is it possible that he was approached by the killer or some kind of go-between after you were arrested, and that he made a deal without telling you about it?'

'No! No way! Jimmy wouldn't have done that.'

Douglas gave a thin smile as if inwardly wondering at a woman's capacity for self-delusion. 'Are you sure? At that point the killer couldn't have been certain you hadn't seen him. What if Jimmy encouraged him to think that you knew more, had seen more, than you actually did? There was an opportunity there, a chance to make a few quid. Maybe he thought he was doing you a favour. This way you'd have some money to come out to.'

Cara could see there was logic to the argument, but she still

241

didn't want to believe it. She drank some coffee, weighing up the possibility. Then she shook her head. 'There's only one flaw in that theory. It was eighteen months ago. If Jimmy had been handed a fortune, he'd have spent it by now.'

'Perhaps he didn't get the box until recently. He could have been given a down payment, something to keep you both sweet, with the rest to come shortly before you came out of prison.'

Cara was thinking about what Rochelle had said, about Jimmy having secrets.

'It would explain Terry Street's interest,' Douglas continued. 'He reckons Jimmy's in possession of something valuable and decides he'd like it for himself.'

'You think Street killed him?'

'Who's to say? If he did, it was probably an accident. Jimmy wasn't much use to him dead. Not if he was the only one who knew where the goods were.' Douglas reached out and flipped open the lid of the box. 'What do you think then? What was in here?'

'If we're talking small and valuable, then it has to be gold, diamonds, rubies, something like that.'

'A box full of treasure,' Douglas said. 'Any idea where Jimmy could have hidden the contents?'

'No.'

'Have a think about it.'

'I have thought about it and the answer's still the same. It could be anywhere.' Cara rubbed her face and said, 'I don't understand what any of this has to do with the Russians.'

'The note,' Douglas said. '*Give it back*. Terry Street wouldn't have written that, would he? Not if he'd never had it in the first place. What Jimmy said suggests a direct connection to Hampstead. If the killer gave him the box, he's not going to ask for it back, so who else might be keen to see it again?'

242

The penny dropped with Cara. 'You think the Russians are working for Fiona Myers?'

'It's a possibility.'

'But why? It doesn't add up. Why would she be so desperate to have it back? She can't be short of money. She would have claimed on the insurance for everything that was stolen.'

'Perhaps she couldn't. Perhaps these particular valuables were never insured.'

'Dodgy, you mean? Stolen?'

'Or not entirely legal for some reason. Perhaps the killer realised they were too hot to handle and decided to pass them on to Jimmy. That way he solved two problems in one go: he paid you off and got rid of something that he knew was dangerous.' Douglas raised and dropped his heavy shoulders. 'I don't know. All this is just conjecture, but I think it's worth taking a closer look at Mrs Myers.'

Cara remembered Fiona Myers from the trial, dressed in black and sitting very upright. The widow had never taken her eyes off her. Afraid of appearing guilty, Cara had forced herself to meet her gaze, seeing nothing but anger and hate. Fiona had listened to her testimony with a sneer on her face: her husband was dead, murdered, and all she was hearing was lies. It was warm in the kitchen, but Cara still shivered. When you lost someone you loved, and in such a brutal fashion, what was foremost in your mind was revenge.

'What if those Russians haven't just been hired to get back the box?' she said. 'No one's ever been caught for her husband's murder. Perhaps she's decided to take matters into her own hands.'

'Does she think you're guilty?'

'Not of killing him. I don't think so. But of knowing who did and covering up for them. Which is almost as bad, isn't it? I could go and see her. Do you think I should?'

'Yeah, that's a good idea ... if you want to go straight back in the slammer. She'll be on the phone to the police, accusing you of harassment and threatening behaviour and God knows what else. You need to keep your distance.'

Cara knew that he was right. There was nothing she could say, at least at the moment, to convince Fiona Myers of her innocence. 'Okay, I see your point. I'll stay away. I won't do anything stupid.'

As if the stupidity boat may have already sailed, Douglas eyed her dubiously. 'Don't you think you should tell the police about the attack on Saturday?'

'No. Steadman won't believe a word I say. He's just looking for an excuse to throw the book at me.'

'But you're the victim here.'

'I was carrying a knife. How am I supposed to explain that? He'll have me down the station for hours, trying to think of ways to stitch me up.'

'Yeah, well, you could be safer there than here.'

Cara shook her head. 'I just want a few days. I'm seeing Jimmy's brother tomorrow and I've got the feeling he knows something.'

'What sort of something?'

'I think the two of them met up last Monday. Neil says they didn't, that Jimmy didn't show, but I don't believe him.'

'Why would he lie about it?'

'That's what I want to find out.' Cara suddenly remembered what Douglas had said earlier. 'What's the good news, then? You told me there was good and bad.'

'Ah, yes,' he said, settling his elbows on the counter. 'The good news is that both your tails appear to have stepped down. There's no one on the gates, no one watching Haslow ... for now.'

Cara, although relieved to hear it, didn't rush to celebrate. 'For now?'

'They could be worried that you called the police, that there might be a reception committee waiting for them next time they turn up. After what happened on Saturday, they're probably going to lie low for a while, at least for a day or two.'

'That's something, I suppose,' Cara said, thinking that it would make it easier to see Neil tomorrow.

'Although I wouldn't take anything for granted.'

'I won't.'

Douglas was quiet while he finished his coffee. Cara studied his face – his brow was furrowed, his jaw set – and she wondered whether he was having second thoughts about getting involved. Who could blame him? It was all growing nastier by the minute. 'You don't have to carry on with this if you don't want to. I only hired you to find out who was following me.'

Douglas glanced up. 'What's brought this on?'

'You just look . . . a bit pissed off.'

Douglas barked out a laugh. 'That's how I always look, love. You'd better get used to it.'

Cara, glad that she wasn't about to be deserted, picked up the silver box and offered it to him. 'Could you keep this somewhere safe? I don't want it in the flat.'

44

DI Larry Steadman strode into the incident room and waved a sheet of paper in front of Tierney's nose. 'Did you know about this?'

'About what?'

'The desk sergeant got an anonymous call on Saturday afternoon, a report of some bloke trying to force a girl into a van.'

'No, I hadn't heard.' Tierney took the paper, laid it on the desk and started reading. 'Says here she got away and ran onto the Mansfield. A squad car was sent over to check it out, but everything was quiet by the time it arrived. Some blood on the pavement, though.'

'I know what it says. What's the betting it was Cara Kendall?'

'If it was her, why didn't she report it herself?'

Larry sat down heavily in a chair. 'If it was anyone else, they *would* have. Any normal girl would have been straight on the blower dialling 999. They'd want the beggar caught and put away, wouldn't they?'

'Could have been a domestic, just a row on the street that

got out of hand. You know what it's like on that estate. Did the caller give a description of either of them?'

'Dark-haired bloke, tallish. Nothing much on the girl. She was wearing a cream coat with the hood up.'

'It's not much to go on.'

'It's enough.'

'You going to give her a tug, guv?'

Larry wanted to see her, longed to, but he knew that it wasn't a good idea. Cara wouldn't tell him anything. So far as she was concerned, he was the enemy, and that was never going to change. 'Not me. You. She doesn't trust me.'

'She doesn't trust any of us.'

'So use your charm. And don't bring her in. We don't need some harassment claim from her solicitor. Just call round at the flat, keep it friendly and see what you can find out.'

'Okay.'

When Tierney didn't move, Larry raised his eyebrows and said, 'Now would be a good time.'

'Yes, guv.' Tierney got to his feet and lifted his jacket off the back of the chair. 'I'm on my way.'

Larry turned his attention back to Jimmy Lovell's murder. A few calls had come in, putting Terry Street's name in the frame, but there was nothing surprising about that. Most of the bad shit that happened in Kellston could be traced back to him. Street wasn't a fool, though: he wouldn't have beaten up Lovell himself. One of his heavies would have done the dirty work for him. And Street would have a solid alibi for the night in question, one that was watertight, unbreakable.

Over the past couple of years security cameras had been tried on the Mansfield, but they had never lasted long. Wherever they were put, however high, however inaccessible, they were always vandalised within a matter of hours. There were too many residents on the estate who valued their privacy – along with their right to deal, meet up and knock seven bells out of each other, without the law bearing witness to it.

Larry was still convinced that the attack on Lovell was ultimately connected to Hampstead: it was too much of a coincidence that it had taken place the night before Cara Kendall had come out of jail. *Give it back*. It was interesting that none of the property stolen had ever come to light. Either the goods had been effectively disposed of – the jewellery melted down, the cash laundered – or stashed somewhere.

Thinking about Hampstead got him thinking about Fiona Myers. He hadn't seen her since the trial. This could be a good day to pay a visit. Perhaps, with the passing of time, something had come back to her. Cara Kendall had always claimed that the burglary had been unplanned, a spur-of-the-moment thing when she'd walked past and noticed that all the lights were off in the house, but no one, and especially not the judge, had ever believed that.

Larry checked that Mrs Myers was still at the same address, strolled through to the lobby to let the desk sergeant know he'd be out for an hour or two, and then left the station. It was another grey depressing day and he drove to the rhythmic whoosh of the windscreen wipers and the sounds of Radio One. Once he'd cleared the East End the traffic improved and it wasn't long before he hit the leafier surroundings of his old stomping ground.

Strictly speaking, Hampstead was outside his jurisdiction. For the sake of courtesy, he could, perhaps even should, call in at his old nick and inform them of his intended visit and the reason for it. But that would mean a fifteen-minute delay and he was too impatient to be bothered.

The road was exactly as he remembered: quiet, tree-lined and stinking of money. Expensive cars sat on the driveways. The houses were all built to a different design, all large and detached and set apart from their neighbours with high walls and generous back gardens. A safe place, or so you'd think, to rest your weary bones after a hard day in the City.

Larry parked opposite the Myerses' house, on the other side of the road, and sat for a while staring at it. He was surprised that she had chosen to stay here, but perhaps properties were hard to shift when someone had been murdered in them. He lit a cigarette while he gathered his thoughts. Inevitably that night came back to him, not in one long stream but in a series of episodes, a jerky yet still vivid recollection of everything that had happened.

There had been something surreal about it all: the man lying dead in the study, shot through the chest; the fair-haired girl who admitted to having broken in; the open safe; the jewellery from upstairs scattered in the corner. It had reminded him of some bizarre game of Cluedo: Miss Scarlet killing Colonel Mustard with a revolver in the study. Except Miss Scarlet had denied any knowledge of the murder, expecting him to believe there had been two intruders on the same night, working independently of each other.

Larry pulled on his cigarette and scowled. He had recently started having the dream again, the one where Cara stood over the body of Myers, glanced over at Larry and laughed. 'You'll never prove it.' Of course she had never done such a thing, but the dream was so startlingly real, the mockery so cutting, that it felt like an actual event. He had always sensed in his gut that she was guilty – not of pulling the trigger, but of knowing who had – and the knowledge ate away at him.

Anger rippled through his body as he stubbed out the cigarette with unnecessary force and got out of the car. As he crossed the road it occurred to him that it would have been polite to have called first, and quickly prepared an excuse for this oversight. Manners mattered to the likes of Fiona Myers. He glanced towards the drainpipe as he walked up the path and imagined Cara's ascent, one hand in front of the other, as she climbed up towards the bedroom window.

He rang the bell and waited. No one came. He studied the three stained-glass panels at the top of the door, hoping that he hadn't had a wasted journey. Fiona Myers was probably the sort of woman who lunched with well-heeled friends, sat on committees and supported endless good causes. He pressed the bell again. This time there was a distinct movement from inside and, shortly afterwards, the door opened.

The first thing he noticed was that Mrs Myers didn't look quite the same as when he'd last seen her eighteen months ago. For a woman in her fifties, she was still attractive, but she was thinner and more angular, too thin perhaps. As if the full horror of her husband's murder had taken root, her face had acquired a tight, haunted quality.

There were a few seconds during which she clearly couldn't place him, couldn't quite recall who he was. Her brown eyes gazed enquiringly. He was familiar but . . . And then it came to her, and she briefly relaxed before suddenly stiffening.

'Inspector,' she said. 'Is there news?'

'I'm afraid not,' he replied quickly, 'at least not the kind we want. But I do have something to tell you if you can spare five minutes.'

She invited him in and, as he followed her along the hall, he said: 'I'm sorry to just drop by like this, but I was in the area and thought I'd take a chance. I hope you don't mind.'

Mrs Myers made a vague gesture with her right hand, the sort of gesture that could have meant anything. It was the only reply he got. Larry found her faintly intimidating, although he'd have never admitted to it to anyone but himself.

She led him past the drawing room and then the study – the door firmly closed – and into the back. This room, overlooking the garden, was airy, spacious and filled with greenery. Even on a grey day like this it managed to pull in what little light there was and spread it into every corner.

'Do take a seat, inspector. Would you care for a coffee?'

Larry would have cared for one but suspected she had only asked to be polite. 'Thanks, but I can't stay long.'

Mrs Myers looked relieved. They sat down on opposite sides of a low table adorned by a silver cigarette box and a bowl of white roses. She crossed her legs and inclined her head slightly. 'So, you have something to tell me.'

'Yes, I thought you should know that Cara Kendall was released last week. She's back in Kellston. I don't suppose your paths are likely to cross, but it seemed only right to make you aware of it.'

'Thank you,' she said, and then after a short pause, added, 'I'm presuming she hasn't said anything more?'

Larry shook his head. 'But please don't think we're giving up on the case. We're not. The killer will make a mistake one day, or she will, and then we'll finally get some justice.'

Mrs Myers smiled wanly, as if she had already given up on the possibility and resigned herself to a life of not knowing. 'It's an encouraging thought,' she said, but not with any conviction.

Larry was about to say that there had been developments – the targeting of Jimmy Lovell had to be connected to what had happened here – but held back at the last moment. He didn't want to give her false hope. Until he had something more con-crete, he'd keep it to himself. 'I don't suppose you've had any more thoughts about that night? I know it's been a while, but sometimes things come back to us.'

'No, I'm afraid not.' A sigh escaped from her pale coral lips. 'Gerald shouldn't even have been here. It was pure chance that he was. If he hadn't felt under the weather and decided to stay home, he'd still be alive today.'

Larry nodded, keeping his eyes on her. Most murders were committed by someone known to the victim and there had always been the faint possibility that she had hired a hitman, or even someone less professional, to dispose of an unwanted husband. However, there had been no evidence to back this up. She had money of her own and the marriage, her second, had seemed happy and stable. There were two grown-up children, one from her first marriage, one from her second – both of whom had flown the nest.

'You can't think, looking back, of anyone he might have fallen out with?'

Mrs Myers frowned, appearing perplexed. 'No, nobody. Why are you asking that? Surely Gerald was murdered because he interrupted a robbery. No one could have *known* he was going to be here that night.'

'No, it seems unlikely.' Larry was sorry now that he'd even asked the question. It made it look as if he was grasping at straws.

'They shouldn't have let that girl out until she told the truth.'

'I wish it worked that way,' Larry said. 'Unfortunately—'

'Cara Kendall is a bare-faced liar. And now she's free to carry on her life as if nothing happened.' A flush of pink rose into Mrs Myers's cheeks. 'Is that fair? She should be made to take proper responsibility for what she did. Eighteen months is nothing, a drop in the ocean. My husband is never coming back, inspector. Tell me where the justice is in that.'

Larry, hearing the vehemence in her voice, had a sudden fear that she might decide to take matters into her own hands. Did she know where Cara Kendall lived? What if she decided to go and confront her, or do something even more drastic? It would all be his fault for coming here in the first place. Quickly he said: 'It isn't justice. I completely understand. But I can assure you that we'll be keeping an eye on her. You have my word on that.'

There was a short brittle silence.

'Well, it was good of you to call by,' she said, her gaze drifting towards the clock on the wall. 'I appreciate it.'

Larry took the hint and rose to his feet. He hadn't expected to learn anything new and in this he hadn't been disappointed. He wasn't entirely sure why he'd come, but he had an inkling. Perhaps, just for a while, he had wanted to be in the company of someone who loathed Cara Kendall as much as he did.

45

Cara froze when the doorbell went. Her first frightened thought was that her attackers had decided to try again, and she almost expected to hear a shoulder against the door, or even something more powerful like a battering ram. Her eyes darted towards the phone. But then, when nothing further happened, she wondered if it could be Douglas and hurried into the hall to check out her visitor through the spyhole. She had a moment's hesitation before using it, suddenly recalling a film she had once seen where a sharp, lethal weapon had been pushed through the tiny circle just as the victim had put his eye to it. Spying had its downfalls.

Cara leaned in tentatively and saw DC Tierney standing outside. She felt some relief – at least it wasn't the Russians – but this was quickly replaced by a fresh kind of anxiety. What did he want? Visits from the police were rarely happy events. She considered ignoring him and retreating quietly to the living room but knew that she would spend the rest of the afternoon wondering what he'd come for.

Cara unbolted the door and opened it. 'Hello,' she said, and then added pointedly, 'again.'

Tierney nodded. 'Sorry to disturb you. Do you mind if I come in?'

Naturally Cara did mind but she could hardly say so. Instead, she stood back and then followed him into the living room. Tierney took up a position by the window, his expression neutral, his hands in his jacket pockets. She could have invited him to sit down but she didn't: she didn't want him making himself too comfortable.

'So, to what do I owe the pleasure?'

Tierney got straight down to business. 'We had a report on Saturday afternoon of a girl being attacked by the Mansfield Road entrance to the estate.'

Cara's pulse began to race. She made an effort to keep her voice natural. 'Really? That's awful.' She frowned. 'But that was two days ago. Aren't you a little late in responding to it?'

'A squad car attended, but it was all over by the time they got here.'

'Oh, okay. Well, I'm afraid I didn't see anything if that's what you're asking.'

'You weren't the girl, then?' Tierney asked bluntly.

Cara feigned surprise. 'Me? What on earth makes you think that?'

'We have a description. It sounds very like you.'

Cara's mind was working quickly now – a description wasn't the same as a name. Whoever had witnessed the attack hadn't known who she was. The kids playing football, perhaps? Or someone watching from a window? No, Tierney didn't know anything for sure. He was just whistling in the wind. 'Well, sorry to disappoint, but it wasn't me.'

'Are you sure?'

'I'm pretty certain I'd remember something like that.'

'Just a coincidence, then?'

Cara frowned again. 'What do you mean, a coincidence?'

'All you've been going through recently: Jimmy's death, the threatening note. Look, Cara, we can't help you if you're not honest with us.'

Cara had to refrain from giving a snort. What did the law know about honesty? Steadman would have been more than happy to bang her up and throw away the key for something she hadn't done. 'I'd tell you if it was me. Why wouldn't I? Nobody wants a bloke like that roaming the streets.'

'Do you own a cream raincoat?' Tierney asked.

Cara hesitated while she tried to remember what she'd been wearing when she'd taken the note to Cowan Road: her denim jacket or the raincoat? The latter, she thought. Yes, definitely the raincoat. She wondered if Tierney would remember – most men didn't notice what you wore – but decided it was too much of a risk to lie. 'Yes,' she said, 'along with half the other women on this estate.'

'There was blood on the ground. It appears someone was hurt.'

'Well, it wasn't me, because I wasn't there.' She prayed Tierney wouldn't ask to see the coat. Those ruddy bloodstains! She should have got rid of the coat while she had the chance, dumped it in the bins or found some other way to dispose of it. Trying to get him off the subject, she asked, 'I don't suppose you've made any progress with finding Jimmy's killer?'

'We're following up several lines of enquiry.'

'And are those lines getting you anywhere?'

Tierney gave a shrug and glanced out of the window for a moment before returning his gaze to her. 'It doesn't help when you've only got half the story.'

'Half the story,' she repeated. 'What does that mean?'

'It means it would help if we knew what Jimmy was involved in. I don't think this was a random killing or a robbery that went wrong. If you have any idea, Cara, you have to say. You want them caught, don't you?'

'You think I wouldn't tell if I knew something? I'm as much in the dark as you are.'

'Are you sure Jimmy didn't mention anything when he came to visit?'

'We've been through this,' she said. 'Why would he? We weren't even together any more.'

'But you were still friendly enough for him to come and see you, and to offer you a lift home when you came out.'

'So what? It's a big leap from that to confiding in me, to telling me what he'd been up to. I know as much as you do. All I can gather – and that's only from the note – is that he took something or was holding on to something for someone else. Why he wouldn't give it back is beyond me.'

'Presumably because it was worth holding on to.'

'Well, that didn't work out too well, did it?'

'Do you know a girl called Rochelle?'

The sudden change of tack caught Cara unawares. It was better not to lie, she thought, in case they'd been seen together. 'The redhead, yeah? I wouldn't say I know her, exactly. She used to hang about with Jimmy. I think they went out for a while.'

'And how did you feel about that?'

Cara couldn't see how that was any of his business, and she wasn't going to give him the pleasure of revealing her true emotions. 'I didn't feel anything. Like I said, we weren't together. Who he saw was up to him.'

'A bit galling, though, when you're locked up and he's out sowing his oats.'

'Now that's just the kind of thing DI Steadman would say.'

257

Tierney grinned and then straightened his face again. 'Rochelle seems to think that Jimmy's death was connected to Hampstead.'

'She told you that?'

'Not in so many words. But she said if you hadn't gone climbing through windows, he might still be here now.'

'She doesn't know what she's talking about. That girl is permanently pissed.'

'You're ruling it out, then?'

'That's your job, not mine.'

'But you must have an opinion.'

Cara thought about the theory Douglas had put forward, a theory which could possibly hold water although nothing had been proved yet. 'I don't know,' she said. 'To be honest, I can't see how it *could* be connected. That was eighteen months ago. Jimmy wasn't even there.'

Tierney kept his gaze fixed on her. 'I wonder why Rochelle would think that. It's kind of odd, isn't it?'

'Everything's kind of odd about Rochelle. I've got no idea what goes on in her head.'

'You wouldn't put much bearing on what she said, then?'

'How sober was she when you spoke to her?'

'Not very.'

'Well, there's your answer.' Cara, not wanting to dwell on the subject, decided to move the conversation in a different direction. 'Do you like being a cop?'

Tierney's lips curled into the semblance of a smile. 'What's not to like? Getting lied to, sworn at, assaulted, thrown up over and generally despised by all and sundry ... let's face it, it's a dream job.'

'Why do it, then?'

'Someone has to.'

'That doesn't mean it has to be you.' Cara paused and said, 'You're not from round here, are you?'

'Yorkshire,' he said.

'You're a long way from home.'

'Home is where the heart is.'

'I shouldn't think anyone's heart is in Kellston,' Cara said. 'It's a hard place to love.'

'I'm working on it.' Tierney moved away from the window and began to walk across the living room. 'Anyway, thanks for your time. If you hear anything about that assault – or anything else – you'll get in touch, won't you?'

'Of course,' she said, following him out into the hall, and ordering herself not to relax in case he suddenly did a Columbo, turned and said *Just one more thing*, and asked if he could see the coat. What would she say then? That she'd left it somewhere, lost it? God, then he really would know she was lying.

Perhaps Tierney picked up on her anxiety because after he'd opened the door and gone out into the corridor, he didn't leave straight away but stood and stared at her for a moment. 'Are you sure everything is okay?'

'No,' she said. 'Nothing is okay, but thanks for asking.'

Tierney looked as if he might say something else because his mouth opened slightly, but then he simply raised his hand and strode off towards the lifts.

Cara went back inside, closed the door and pulled the bolt across. She wondered if she'd made a mistake in lying about Saturday. There was something about Tierney that made you want to tell the truth, that made you feel you could trust him. But her doubts didn't last for long. If she had come clean, she'd have only ended up down the station again, being interrogated by Steadman and having to explain why she was walking around with a knife in her pocket.

As she went into the living room, it occurred to her that it was peculiar that Steadman hadn't come to the flat himself. Why had he left it to Tierney? The inspector wouldn't normally pass over an opportunity to ask a few difficult questions and generally give her a hard time. It made her suspicious, like he was up to something.

46

Cara waited by the window until she saw Tierney emerge from the tower, get into his car and drive away. Then she went to the kitchen and took the rubbish bag out of the bin. The raincoat, still damp from where she'd attempted to get the bloodstains out, was lying in a ball under the sink. She pulled it out, squashed it down the side of the rubbish and tied up the bag.

On her way out, Cara grabbed her keys. She locked up behind her and took the lift down to the ground floor. As the doors opened, she checked out the foyer and then strode towards the rear exit where the communal bins were kept. From there she couldn't be seen by anyone waiting near the gates. If Douglas was right, she was no longer being watched, but how long was that going to last? They could be back soon. They could, for all she knew, be back already. Her fingers instinctively tightened around the keys.

The bins were due to be emptied tomorrow and the malodorous smell of rotting food hung in the air. Cara had to lift a few lids before she found some space. She chucked the bag in and hoped that would be the last she saw of the raincoat. It would need to be replaced at some point, and sooner rather than later. Tierney hadn't asked to see it, but Steadman might be more thorough.

Thinking of Steadman put her even more on edge. She was like unfinished business to him, the one who had got away. And what if Douglas was right, and Jimmy had made some kind of deal with Gerald Myers's killer? The inspector was never going to believe that she hadn't known about it or, even worse, actively encouraged it. And then he would have her for concealing or aiding and abetting or whatever else he could throw at her. She would be going straight back to jail before she'd barely tasted freedom.

Cara retraced her steps, went back inside and headed for the lifts. The afternoon was closing in, the thick greyness of an early dusk creeping over the estate. From the safety of the foyer, she looked towards Mansfield Road. The kids had just started to come back from school, filtering through the gate in twos and threes, their bags slung over their shoulders. For a moment she envied them their freedom from responsibility, their happy-go-lucky existence, but then remembered all the angst of her own childhood and knew that life when you were young was rarely free of worry.

She peered between them, searching for suspicious characters. Terry Street's henchmen had probably retreated for the same reason as the Russians – nobody wanted the law interfering in their business – but it was hopelessly optimistic to imagine they had gone for good. They would be busy making new plans, nasty plans, the kind of plans that were bad for her health.

Cara felt a churning in her stomach. She was about to turn away when she noticed Lytton coming through the gate. He was back early from college and she wondered if he'd bunked off some lectures in order to check up on her. Two emotions simultaneously rose to the surface: annoyance that he felt she couldn't take care of herself, and a sneaking delight that someone cared enough to look out for her.

She leaned against the wall, waiting for him. The lift had become a source of anxiety and she worried that someone (a vicious someone) would intercept the journey part way, getting on at another floor and joining her in the small metal box from which there was no escape. Or that someone would be there to greet her when the doors slid open. With these dangers constantly lurking in the back of her mind, she was glad to have a companion to travel up with.

Cara watched Will Lytton as he walked along the path, his hands in his jacket pockets. Perhaps Jimmy had, after all, done her a favour renting out the flat to him. There had been nothing – well, nothing more than his lack of worldly possessions – to suggest anything shady. She wasn't about to trust him implicitly, but perhaps it was time to give him the benefit of the doubt.

She was still contemplating this when a girl suddenly appeared, racing across the concrete and pushing through the kids. Cara instantly recognised the distinctive red hair. Rochelle. Grabbing hold of Lytton's elbow, she forced him to stop and began jabbering into his face. Lytton yanked his arm free, took a step back, shook his head and then shook it again.

Cara hurried over to the door and opened it, but she was too far away to hear anything. She could see Rochelle's face though, twisted and angry, her red lips giving Lytton a mouthful. What was going on? How did those two know each other? Rochelle poked at his chest, but he didn't retaliate. He leaned in and said something to her. She stamped her foot like a five-year-old. The kids were staring as they went past.

It was all over in less than a minute. Lytton walked around her and began heading towards Haslow. Rochelle pursued him for a few yards but then gave up, staring angrily at his departing figure with her hands on her hips.

Cara rapidly retreated to the lifts. She was standing beside them when Lytton came in. He was clearly agitated but smiled when he saw her.

'Hey, what are you doing here? I thought you were lying low today.'

'I only came to put the rubbish out.'

'I could have done that.'

'I was going stir crazy up there. I needed some fresh air.'

'You could have opened a window.'

'I wanted to stretch my legs.' Cara stepped into the lift with him and pressed the button for the tenth floor. As the doors closed, she asked, 'What did that girl want?'

'Huh?'

'Just now. That girl who was having a go at you.'

'Oh, *her*,' he said, rolling his eyes. 'Money, of course. For some reason she thought I wouldn't object to parting with a few quid. She wasn't best pleased when I declined the invitation.'

'No, she didn't look very happy. Do you know her?'

'Well, I don't know her name or anything, but I've seen her around.'

Cara was watching him closely while she pretended not to, a less than easy task in the confines of the lift. 'I wonder why she picked on you.'

'Perhaps she thought I looked the generous type. Or a mug. Probably the latter.'

Cara considered his reply. Was he lying? She just couldn't tell. Granted there weren't that many adults around, other than a few mums accompanying the younger kids, but Rochelle had

264

picked him out like a heat-seeking missile. Something didn't smell right.

'Has everything been okay today? No trouble?' Lytton said.

'Nothing serious. DC Tierney dropped by again to see if I knew anything about an assault on Saturday.'

'So they know, then?'

'They don't *know* anything. They're just guessing.'

'I presume you denied you were the victim?'

The lift shuddered to a halt and they both got out. 'You presume right.'

Lytton frowned. 'Are you sure you shouldn't tell them? I mean, Jesus, those bastards weren't messing about.'

'I will. When I'm ready. Just not right now.'

As they walked along the corridor Cara's mind was still on the incident she'd just witnessed. And then, because she couldn't leave it alone, she said: 'I think that girl's called Rochelle. She used to hang around with Jimmy.'

'Did she?'

'It's odd how she went straight for you.'

Lytton shrugged. 'I dare say she works on the law of averages. If you ask enough people, someone will eventually put their hand in their pocket.'

'I suppose. She just seemed kind of . . . aggressive towards you.'

'Maybe that explains it.'

'What explains it?'

'Why she was acting so crazy. Jimmy's murder. Perhaps she's struggling to deal with it all. Some people don't cope well with sudden death.'

Cara wondered why Lytton was making excuses for Rochelle. He was either an extremely tolerant person or he was trying to throw her off the scent. 'I don't think anyone copes *well*, do they? They just . . . I don't know, try and deal with it the best they can. They don't go around demanding money from strangers.'

Lytton unlocked the door to the flat and they went inside. 'Everyone's different, I guess.'

The cogs in Cara's brain were still whirring. Something was wrong here. She felt unnerved, suspicious. Had Rochelle really been asking for money, or had she been accusing him of something? Cara's thoughts jumped on. What if Lytton was connected to the Russians or Terry Street? But then why was he encouraging her to speak to the law about Saturday? That didn't make sense. Unless, God forbid, he *was* the law, an undercover cop planted by Steadman, reporting back on everything she said and did. No, Christ, now she really was letting her imagination run riot. Even Steadman wouldn't go that far – would he?

'Are you all right?' Lytton asked.

Cara put her keys on the living-room table and nodded. 'Are you?'

'Why shouldn't I be?'

'I wouldn't be so calm if some crazy girl had been shooting her mouth off at me.'

Lytton gave a soft laugh and said: 'It's the Mansfield estate. I wouldn't expect anything else.'

47

It had come as no great surprise to Larry Steadman that Cara was denying all knowledge of the incident that had taken place on Saturday afternoon. Cooperation was the last thing he expected. Whatever had happened, she was keeping her mouth shut and this, in his mind, only proved that she had something to hide. What innocent girl wouldn't report it? What innocent girl wouldn't be glad to receive help from the police?

Tierney had seen no visible sign of injury, but that didn't mean anything. At this time of year, with everyone wrapped up in winter clothes, there wasn't much flesh on display. She could have been cut on the arm or the leg and he wouldn't have been any the wiser. Someone – whoever wanted 'it' back – was upping the ante, pumping up the pressure and turning threats into action.

Larry had the Gerald Myers file open in front of him. He was going through the case again, reviewing every angle and trying to put the pieces together in a different way. It was, he suspected, a fruitless quest, but still he persevered, doggedly ploughing on with his teeth gritted.

There was a virtual dossier pertaining to Cara Kendall, including a thick wad of pages recording the numerous interviews conducted with her. He was scrutinising these line by line, looking for anything he might not have picked up on eighteen months ago. But she had kept her story simple, repeating it without hesitation or contradiction. He had pushed and pushed to no avail. He hadn't been able to break her.

Larry emptied the ashtray into the bin and lit another cigarette. Who had she been working with? Sadly, Jimmy Lovell's alibi seemed unbreakable. There had been not just one but many witnesses, including the bar staff, who could place him in the Fox at the relevant time. There was no way he could have got to Hampstead and back without his absence being noticed. This bugged Larry. If Jimmy hadn't been there, who had?

He would have put her father, Richard Kendall, firmly in the frame if the man hadn't been stone cold dead by then. The manner of his death – Larry winced even as he thought about it – should have been enough to deter Cara from following in his footsteps, but it hadn't. Instead, in what appeared to be an act of perversity, she had carried on regardless, like some demented high-wire acrobat determined to defy the odds.

Cara's barrister had used her bereavement as an excuse for her 'out of character' behaviour that night. The break-in had been a one-off, he'd claimed, a reckless, thoughtless impulse that had never happened before and would never happen again. Larry gave a snort. As if anyone with half a brain was going to believe that! He had the feeling that Cara hadn't entirely approved of this line of defence and had only gone along with it in the hope of receiving a lighter sentence.

Larry had to know who'd killed Gerald Myers, and wouldn't rest until he'd found out, hauled him to court and made him pay. There was always the Lytton bloke. A student, Tierney had said, and it had been confirmed that he *was* registered at Kellston Polytechnic. A call to the poly hadn't yielded much information, other than that he was in his first year. This meant, of course, that he had moved to Kellston several months before the start of term. Was there anything suspicious about that? Not necessarily, but it was too soon to write him off completely.

If Lytton was the killer of Myers then he and Cara were taking an enormous risk shacking up together. Or were they so arrogant that they thought the police wouldn't see what was right in front of their noses? No, he didn't reckon she would be that reckless. Whatever game she was playing, it was a long one. She'd spent eighteen months in jail for a prize that must be worth the sacrifice. *Give it back.* Cara clearly had no intention of doing any such thing. What she had got, she was going to keep. Or thought she was. Larry had other ideas.

48

Tuesday was another of those long interminable days. Cara spent much of it reviewing the altercation between Lytton and Rochelle and had to fight against the temptation to go out, hunt the girl down and confront her. Not yet, she told herself. If the two of them were in cahoots, Rochelle was only going to tip him off about her suspicions. Her first priority was the meeting with Neil. Once that was over, she'd reassess the situation.

It seemed to take for ever for five o'clock to come around. By then Cara had changed into black trousers, black polo neck sweater, a black woollen hat and an old black bomber jacket. The jacket was lightweight, offering little protection against the November cold, but it was better than nothing. The dark clothing would, with luck, enable her to get off the estate without being seen.

Deciding to leave her bag at home – it would only get in the way – she took out her purse, removed a couple of quid, folded up the notes and slid them into her trouser pocket. She thought longingly about the knife in the kitchen drawer, but neither her jacket nor trousers had deep enough pockets. She considered alternatives – down a sock, in her trainers – but decided there was nowhere safe to hide it without running the danger of inadvertently stabbing herself. Anyway, if she was jumped, her attacker would be prepared this time. No one made the same mistake twice.

With no way of knowing whether her tails had returned to duty she wasn't going to risk leaving through the gates. She'd already planned out an alternative route and after locking up the flat she took the lift down to the basement. The wisdom of this decision felt debatable as she stepped out into the dimly lit car park. Its quietness was eerie. She quickly looked around. The numerous concrete pillars, all covered in graffiti, offered easy hiding places for anyone with bad intentions. Shadows haunted the corners. It wouldn't be difficult for someone to take her by surprise, and down here there would be no witnesses, no one to hear her cries. Her fingers curled around the keys . . .

Before she could become immobilised by fear, Cara strode rapidly across the diameter of the car park towards the exit ramp that would eventually bring her out around the back of Carlton. Her ears were pricked for the slightest sound, her eyes alert to any movement. She skirted around the cars, most of them old and battered, and some permanently abandoned. The air, musty and damp, was overlain by the stink of petrol.

By the time she reached the other side, Cara had almost broken into a jog. Was this what it was going to be like from now on – always on edge, always waiting for the worst to happen? She sped up the ramp and burst through the door into the outside world. From here it was only a short walk to the tunnel that linked Haslow to Carlton. Although the prospect of another enclosed space hardly filled her with joy, it was still preferable to being out in the open where anyone might spot her.

After another furtive look round, she took a few deep breaths and set off again. The tunnel was busier than usual, with people back from work using it as a short cut home and a shelter from the rain. The estate was like a rabbit warren with its numerous tunnels and passageways. By physically linking the two towers the idea had probably been to promote a sense of unity and community, but all the designers had actually achieved was a fertile hunting ground for muggers. The dealers took advantage too, hawking their wares away from prying eyes.

Cara pulled the front of her hat down over her eyebrows and walked at a brisk pace from one end of the tunnel to the other. She glanced over her shoulder more than once, prepared to leg it if anyone dubious came into view. Nobody did. The place was relatively low risk at this time of day, but she wouldn't like to repeat the experience late at night. Lonely places were dangerous places.

When she reached Carlton House, she scooted across the busy foyer and out through the back door to where the bins were kept. It was quiet here and dark, the only light coming from the streetlamps on the other side of the wall. The wall itself was around six foot tall but not too difficult to scale, she reckoned, if you were young, keen and relatively fit.

Cara didn't hang about. She did a short run-up, jumped, grabbed the top of the wall and tried to get some purchase with her feet. But the brick was wet and slippery, and the soles of her trainers couldn't get a grip. She struggled, swearing softly, hanging with her elbows bent, her feet scrabbling for a foothold before eventually managing to haul herself over. As she dropped down on the other side, she felt positively mortified. What kind of cat burglar struggled with a six-foot wall? An out-of-practice one, apparently.

After brushing herself down, Cara had a good look in all

directions and then hurried along Peter Street, past the shops and the terraced houses. The rain was slight but persistent, a relentless drizzle. She could feel it seeping through her clothes. At the end of the street, she took a right and then, using the smaller roads, circled round until she hit Station Road about a hundred metres up from the Fox. By now she was as certain as she could be that there was no one on her tail.

Don't screw this up, she said to herself as she quickly advanced on the pub. She was only going to get one chance and she knew it.

49

Cara did a quick check on the car park – no black BMW, no vans – before removing her woollen hat, stuffing it into her jacket pocket and ducking into the Fox. Neil was already there with a pint in front of him. She was prepared this time to see that other version of Jimmy, but as she joined him at the bar and he turned his face to her, she still felt an inner jolt.

'Cara,' he said. 'How are you doing? Let me get you a drink.'

Cara thanked him and asked for half a bitter. Neil caught the attention of the barmaid, who was busy flirting with two blokes at the other end of the bar – Holly, that was her name – and put the order in. She could tell he was nervous and on edge even though he did his best to hide it. They made small talk until her drink arrived and then, at her suggestion, moved to a table away from the other customers.

'So, I'm intrigued,' Neil said with forced levity. 'What was it you wanted to see me about?'

'It's about last Monday.'

'Oh?' Neil said, trying to keep his voice casual, but not

making much of a job of it. His face tightened a little. 'What about it?'

'I suppose I'm just confused.'

Neil took a gulp of his pint and put the glass down on the table. He frowned. 'Confused?'

Cara had prepared herself for this. She was about to take a gamble, a big one, and was praying that it would pay off. 'You see, Jimmy came to visit the day before I was released and told me that he *had* met up with you. It just seems kind of strange, you know, you saying one thing and him saying another.'

A tic jumped in the corner of Neil's eye, but he soldiered on. 'Heavens, I don't know why he'd say something like that.'

'No, nor do I. That's why I wanted to talk to you.' She left a short pause. 'One of you wasn't telling the truth, and I don't see why Jimmy would lie about it.'

'Why would *I* lie about it?' Neil countered defensively.

'Exactly. Why would you?'

Neil's gaze slid away, and he glanced around the pub as if trying to decide how to play this. 'Well, you know what he was like.'

Cara decided to take a harder line. 'Oh, for God's sake, Neil, will you stop it? This isn't a game. Jimmy's dead and the reason he's dead probably has something to do with what he told you. He did tell you something, didn't he? Let's cut through the bullshit and just be straight with each other.'

Playing for time, Neil briefly attacked his pint again. He was shaken, that much was clear, but he still couldn't decide what to do. Stick to his guns or come clean? She could almost see him weighing it up in his mind.

Cara piled on the pressure. 'I won't stop asking. And I'll go to the law if I have to and tell them that you lied. I mean it. Either you tell me the truth or I'm going straight down Cowan Road.'

If Neil had known her better, he'd have realised it was a bluff, but the threat was enough to scare him. He leaned forward and said almost angrily: 'I don't want anything to do with it. Why do you have to drag me into all this? I told Jimmy I wasn't interested. He was the one who got himself into the mess. I told him he was asking the wrong person.'

Cara tried not to look triumphant. Finally, she was getting somewhere. 'Please don't imagine I know what the hell you're talking about because I don't. What mess? What do you mean?'

'You said he'd come to see you.'

'He did,' Cara lied. 'And I knew he was hiding something, but he wouldn't tell me what. So now it's down to you. Come on, Neil, just spit it out.'

'It's not that easy. Jesus, if Jennifer's father . . . I can't afford any scandal. Do you understand? I'm talking about my future here, my job, my marriage, everything. If it comes out that I even *talked* about it with Jimmy, I'll be done for. I'll be dragged into this whole murder inquiry, and everyone will think . . . Well, I'm not going to come out of it smelling of roses, am I?'

'But if you haven't done anything wrong, what's there to worry about? You just said you told Jimmy you weren't interested.'

'I did. But the police are still going to hang me out to dry. Withholding information and whatever else they can throw at me. I lied to them, for God's sake. How's that going to look?'

Cara was losing patience. 'Hey, whatever it is, I need to know. I'm not going to tell anyone that the information came from you. Especially the law. Okay?'

'You say that now but what if—'

'There are no what ifs. You haven't got any choice. Either you trust me or you're on your own. I'm not kidding, Neil. I'll kick up enough fuss to make your life hell. I'll go to the law, I'll call

Jennifer, I'll find witnesses. I'll go to the Princess Louise if I have to and show Jimmy's photo to the bar staff. It's only a week ago; I'm sure they'll remember him – and who he was with.'

A long silence followed. Cara held her breath, waiting. Neil glared at her. She glared right back, dreading that he might stand up and walk out. Then where would she be? But just as she was giving up hope, he suddenly came good.

'Antwerp,' he blurted out. 'Jimmy asked me to go to Antwerp with him.'

'What for?'

'He said he was in trouble, that he had to sell something quickly. I didn't ask what. I didn't want to know. It had to be stolen, didn't it?'

Cara didn't dispute this. She was thinking of her conversation with Douglas. She was thinking diamonds again. That's what Antwerp was famous for, the Diamond Quarter near the Centraal station. She'd heard her dad talk about it, and Jimmy had probably heard too. 'Why you, though? Why did he ask you to go with him?'

'He wanted someone who could speak the language. I think he was worried about getting ripped off.'

Cara had a vague idea that Antwerp was in Belgium's Flemish region. 'Do you speak . . . Dutch, is it?'

'A little. Enough to get by. I've got some German too. But I told him I wouldn't do it. I mean, Christ, it was ridiculous. Not to mention illegal. We were both going to end up getting arrested. You can't expect to walk in somewhere, flog your iffy valuables and just walk out again. People aren't stupid. They'd have realised what was going on.'

Cara wondered if Jimmy might have wanted Neil for more than his language skills, perhaps for his appearance too. With his classy clothes and expensive watch, he could have passed for the type of man who might be rich enough to own legitimate diamonds. 'I suppose you'd have to know who to approach.'

'I had no intention of spending the next ten years in a Belgian jail.'

'Yeah, I can see how that wouldn't be appealing.'

Neil scowled. 'Of course it wasn't bloody appealing. I told him he was mad.'

Cara drank her bitter while she thought some more. If Jimmy had planned on going to Antwerp to flog the diamonds, it meant they were too hot to handle over here. Too hot because Gerald Myers had been murdered in the course of nicking them? It made a kind of sense. 'I still don't get why you lied to the law about seeing him. You didn't have to mention any of the Antwerp business.'

'I don't know. I just . . . Steadman would have asked what we talked about and . . . I hadn't intended to lie, but then I panicked and thought it was easier to say he hadn't turned up.'

'Even though you'd told Jennifer the very opposite?'

'Yes, well, I've explained that to her. I mean, not the Antwerp stuff, only that I wanted to keep the family name out of it.'

Although Cara was grateful that he'd finally come clean, she also felt a rush of resentment. The family name – the *Hopcroft* name – was apparently more important than passing on information that might help to catch Jimmy's killer. But then she could talk. She hadn't exactly been honest with the law herself.

Neil was clearly doing some thinking of his own. 'Last week, when we came to see you, why did you ask when I'd last seen him when you already knew?'

'I was just making small talk.'

Neil gave her a look, the kind of look that suggested he was starting to realise that he may have been manipulated into

278

saying much more than he'd ever intended. But it was too late now to do anything about it.

'Do you think he went to Antwerp?' Cara asked.

'I've no idea.'

If he'd flown, Jimmy could have got there and back in a day, but she didn't reckon he would have taken the risk of going on his own. He must have been desperate, though, to offload those diamonds. And desperate too to ask Neil to help him. A last resort.

'So what now?' Neil asked.

Cara shrugged. 'I'm not sure. I need to do some more digging.'

'But you'll keep me out of it?'

'I said I would, didn't I?'

'Only I can't afford to get caught up in all this. I can't—'

'Yeah, I heard you the first time. You don't need to say it again.'

Neil's lips tightened into a straight line. He sat in silence for a moment and then said, 'Right, I take it we're done here?'

'We're done.'

Neil rose to his feet and then stood there like he didn't know what to do next. She had the feeling that he didn't entirely trust her, that he'd have preferred her to have written out her promise in blood. Eventually he gave an abrupt nod, turned and walked out of the pub. She wasn't sorry to see him go.

50

Cara slowly sipped her beer, making it last. She didn't want to leave too soon in case she bumped into Neil again. He'd probably take a cab to Waterloo, but if the station rank was empty, he would have to try and hail one off the street. Anyway, she wasn't in a hurry. She wanted to think about what he'd told her and here was as good a place as any.

Now that Neil had gone, all the questions she should have asked came to her, like what state Jimmy had been in, whether he'd said anything about what he was going to do next, if he'd seemed afraid. Although perhaps she was better off not knowing the answers. She wondered why Jimmy hadn't come to her. She could have helped. There were phone numbers in her dad's address book, numbers for men in Calais and Paris who'd have been more than happy to take the goods off his hands.

Why hadn't Jimmy said anything to her? Pride, perhaps. Not wanting her to know that he'd screwed up, or that he couldn't deal with the situation himself. And then there was all that loose talk right here in the Fox, about how she'd be a rich woman and how no one knew the half of it. And Terry Street. And the Russians. And Rochelle and Lytton. And that dangerous silver box . . .

Cara could feel her head getting crowded. The more she brooded on it all, the less clear it became. There was an abandoned copy of the *Evening Standard* on the next table, and she reached across to retrieve it. While she flicked through the pages, grabbing nothing more than the headlines, she tried to clarify her thoughts and work out where to go from here. She was still doing this when she became aware of someone approaching her. She looked up to see the barmaid, Holly, holding a drink in her hand.

'Here,' Holly said, putting a glass down in front of her with what appeared to be a double whisky in it.

'I didn't order anything.'

'I know. It's on the house. You look like you need it.'

'You didn't have to do that,' Cara said. 'Thanks.'

'We'll all miss Jimmy. The Fox won't be the same without him. Are you all right, hon? You seemed . . . well, kind of upset while you were talking to that bloke.'

'That was Jimmy's brother.'

'Yeah, I thought there was a similarity. Not more bad news, I hope?'

Cara wondered what could be worse than Jimmy being dead, but she knew the girl was only trying to be nice so she shook her head and managed to raise the flicker of a smile. 'We were just . . . going over it all. It's still sinking in. None of it seems . . . it still doesn't seem quite real.'

'No, it'll take a while, I suppose. Jimmy never mentioned that he had a brother.'

'You were friendly, then?' Cara asked a little sharply, suspicion suddenly rising in her. Perhaps Holly had been serving him more than drinks while she'd been away. The thought of it made her stomach shift. It was bad enough knowing that he'd slept with Rochelle without having to make small talk with another of his conquests.

'Not really. Just the usual chat, but you get to know people after a while.' Then, as if the true purpose of the question had suddenly come to her, Holly gave a light laugh. 'Oh, no, nothing like that. Not me and Jimmy. He wasn't my type.' She had a quick look round, lowered her voice, grinned and said, 'To be honest, you're more my type than he was, if you get my drift.'

Cara did get her drift. She'd never have guessed, although there was no reason why she should have. Holly had a distinctly heterosexual vibe to her, a vibe that had been reinforced by the blatant flirting she had witnessed earlier.

Holly winked. 'Keep quiet about it, though. I've got my tips to think about.'

'Of course I will.'

'You're not shocked, are you?'

'No, I'm not shocked. I've just spent eighteen months in Leaside, remember?'

Cara took a sip of whisky and felt the warmth spread through her. Seeing as Holly showed no inclination to leave – the pub was quiet and a barman was dealing with the few customers there were – she decided to take advantage of the situation. 'I don't suppose you know a girl called Rochelle, do you? She used to drink in here with Jimmy.'

'The redhead, yeah?'

'That's the one.'

'Sure, I've seen her in here.' Holly tapped the side of her head. 'She's got a screw loose, that one. I think she had a thing about Jimmy, but he wasn't interested.'

Cara wondered if Holly didn't know about the fling they'd

282

had, or if she was just trying to spare her feelings. The latter, she suspected. 'Have you ever seen her in here with anyone else – a bloke in his early thirties, slim, light brown hair? He's called Will Lytton.'

Holly thought about it, but then shook her head. 'It doesn't ring any bells. Is it important?'

'No, I shouldn't think so.'

'She was in here on Saturday night, though, blind drunk. She was talking to that Tierney.'

Cara didn't like the sound of this. 'Why was she talking to *him*?'

'Thought she was on to a good thing, didn't she? Until she discovered he was a cop.' Holly laughed. 'Mind you, she'd still have been barking up the wrong tree even if he hadn't been.'

'What?'

'Let's just say it's not girls he's interested in.' Holly swept back her long brown hair and gave Cara a knowing look. 'It's a gay old world, hon,' she said softly, but not without glee. 'I could tell you I've got remarkable gaydar, but it wouldn't be true. I just notice things. He tries to play the straight man, but it's not the women he stares at when he thinks no one's watching.'

'I shouldn't think that would go down too well at Cowan Road.'

'They'd hang him out to dry, poor guy.'

Cara wondered why Holly was telling her all this. It felt like more than idle gossip, as if she was trying to forge a connection or some kind of friendship. In a way, Holly was giving her ammunition, should she choose to use it, against a cop who couldn't afford to have his private life made public. There was something off about it, something distasteful. Then, realising they'd digressed somewhat, she said, 'Do you have any idea what they were talking about?'

'About Jimmy, I think, but it wasn't for long. A couple of minutes, that's all, then Rochelle made herself scarce.'

Cara reached for the whisky glass again and her gaze fell on the open newspaper. It was a photograph that caught her attention, a small unsmiling passport photo of a man found dead at the weekend in Soho. But even that might not have held her interest if the name beneath it hadn't jumped out, sending a sliver of ice straight down her spine. *Pavel Kuzmin*. Christ, that was the bastard who'd tried to abduct her . . .

Cara felt panic rising inside her, a sudden and nauseating horror. Had she inadvertently killed the man? Stabbed him in an artery? Or had it been blood poisoning, perhaps? That knife, stuffed into her pocket, could have picked up all sorts of germs. Maybe he had died in the van. Maybe the others had driven him back to the West End and dumped his body there.

'What's the matter?' Holly asked.

Cara jabbed a finger at the photograph. Had she not been in a state of shock, she might have been more cautious, but the words spilled out before she could stop them. 'Him. That man. Wasn't he the one who was here on Saturday, the one you said was watching me?'

Holly bent down to look more closely at the photo. 'Could have been,' she said. 'It's hard to tell with pictures like these. People never look quite like they do in real life.'

Cara's chest felt tight, and she was not entirely sure that her heart hadn't stopped beating. She hadn't meant to kill him, only to fend him off. To take someone else's life was a dreadful thing, no matter what the circumstances. There was no going back on murder, no second chances, no possible way to make it right. God, what had she done? Her hands dropped limply into her lap. She stared hard at the copy beneath the photo, but the words swam before her, blurry and unreadable.

Holly was still leaning over her. 'It says here he was shot. Someone must have had it in for him.'

Cara was abruptly wrenched out of her despair. Her voice sounded hoarse and unnaturally hopeful. 'Shot? Are you sure?'

'On Saturday night, they reckon. They found his body in an alleyway.'

A wave of relief rolled over Cara, cool and calming, closely followed by a rush of thankfulness. It hadn't been her. She hadn't killed him. She felt like a condemned woman suddenly given a reprieve.

'Are you going to tell the law?' Holly asked.

Cara's first thought was of Steadman and his cold, calculating eyes. 'Erm ... I don't know. I don't think so. I mean, it might not be the same bloke. I didn't really get a good look at him.'

Holly stood up straight again and nodded. 'Yeah, I couldn't swear to it, either. There's probably no point, is there?'

'Not if we can't be certain.'

Cara exchanged what felt like an almost conspiratorial look with the girl. Neither of them wanted to get the police involved. She knew what her reasons were but couldn't speak for Holly. Perhaps she just didn't want the hassle. After knocking back what remained of the whisky, Cara reached forward and closed the paper. 'Okay, well, I'd better be going. Thanks again for the drink.'

'You're welcome, hon.'

As Holly returned to the bar, Cara rose to her feet on legs that were not entirely steady. She picked up the paper, folded it and put it under her arm. She had dodged a bullet, so to speak, but Pavel hadn't been so lucky.

51

Cara was as sure as she could be that she didn't have a tail. No one suspicious had followed her into the Fox. Now, as she left the pub, her intention was to get home as fast as possible. A couple of cabs were waiting outside the station and she decided to damn the expense – not that it would cost *that* much – and avoid the risk of walking on her own.

As she was heading towards the rank, she glanced across the road and saw that the light in Glen Douglas's office was still on. She stopped, thinking. Perhaps it would be an even better idea to get him up to speed with the latest developments. He might not have seen the *Evening Standard*, and he certainly didn't know about what Neil had told her. She could call when she got home, but he might have gone by then, and anyway she wouldn't be able to talk openly if Lytton was around.

Cara only dithered for a second before making up her mind. She waited for a gap in the traffic and quickly crossed the road. After glancing over her shoulder – there was no one behind her – she hurried to the building and tried the front door. Locked. She pressed the button for Douglas's office and waited.

Eventually, just as she was starting to wonder if he'd left without turning the light off, a gruff voice came over the intercom. 'Yeah?'

'It's Cara.'

The buzzer went and she pushed open the door, closing it carefully behind her before ascending the stairs. The carpet was as threadbare as the last time she'd been here, the banister as worn. She walked along the landing and found the door to the office was ajar. She went into the empty waiting room and called out, 'Hello?'

Douglas emerged from the inner room with a raincoat over his arm and an A4 brown envelope in his hand. 'Everything all right?'

'Yes, but I've just met up with Jimmy's brother and—'

'Sorry,' he asked, waving the envelope at her. 'Can it wait? I have to deliver this and I'm already late. You can hang on here if you like or I can call by the flat. It's up to you. I shouldn't be too long – an hour or so?'

Cara, who'd been eager to share her news, felt instantly deflated. She didn't want him in the flat, not when Lytton was present, so she said, 'Okay, I'll wait.'

'Help yourself to coffee.'

'Thanks.'

Douglas briefly retreated to his office, came out with a small bunch of keys and threw them to her. 'These are the spares. It's the middle one you need. Lock the door after I've gone. The downstairs locks automatically. Don't let anyone in, yeah? Don't even answer the buzzer if it goes.'

'I won't.'

And then he was gone.

Cara had locked the door before he'd even started down the stairs. This precautionary measure, along with his other warnings, reminded her of the danger she was in. Already her anxiety levels had racked up a notch. But she was as safe here as anywhere, she thought: there was no reason to believe that anyone apart from Douglas knew where she was.

Just to make sure, she went over to the window, stood to one side, and cautiously looked down on the street. People were still emerging from the station, although the worst of the rush hour was over. She scanned the pavements but noticed no loiterers. Douglas appeared and walked off at a brisk pace towards wherever his car was parked. She had not considered that he had other work, other jobs, and it irked her slightly, as if her forty quid should have been enough to secure his undivided attention.

Cara moved away and went in search of coffee. The kitchenette was off the waiting room, a tiny galley with a sink, a few cupboards, a fridge and just enough of a counter to hold a kettle and some mugs. The walls were a dull magnolia, the lino floor an indeterminate shade of beige. Nothing was very clean. She switched on the kettle and while she waited for it to boil, rinsed out a mug under the hot water.

When the coffee was made, she went back into the waiting room and sat down in one of the plastic chairs. She picked up the paper she had left on the low table and flicked to the page with the report of the murder. It was only a small piece and there wasn't much in the way of solid information, but at least the most basic facts were there in black and white: Pavel Kuzmin had been shot (no mention of any knife wounds) and he'd died in Soho some time on Saturday night. Police were still investigating. She read it several times just to be sure that she was completely in the clear as regards to his death.

Cara gave a fresh sigh of relief, closed the paper and put it down. She glanced at her watch – six-fifteen – and wondered what to do with the next hour. The pile of magazines didn't look inviting. The date on the top one, a tedious publication about cars, was dated 1981. Three years old. That was probably the last time the office had been cleaned. A layer of dust lay over everything. If any prospective client did happen to wander in off the street, their first inclination, just as hers had been, would be to turn around and walk straight out.

With little else to do, Cara went into the kitchen and checked out the cupboard under the sink. Here, amidst a jumble of ill-assorted items, she found a few old cloths, a bucket and a bottle of bleach. She half-filled the bucket with hot water, added a cupful of bleach, went back to the waiting room and set to work.

Within twenty minutes she had washed down the door, the window ledges, the coffee table and the chairs, removing layers of grime and revealing colours that hadn't seen the light of day in years. She looked around the room, pleased by the result. It might not make it on to the front page of *Good Housekeeping*, but at least it was presentable.

She moved on to the kitchen. Although the scrubbing and the wiping didn't entirely take her mind off Jimmy's murder, it enabled her to think about it less head on. She let it swirl about in the back of her thoughts while she concentrated on the job in hand. Sometimes, by not directly searching for an answer, it would find a way to creep up on you. She scraped something sticky off the lino and hoped to be enlightened soon.

It was an hour and ten minutes before Douglas returned. By then she had made an assault on the small bathroom too, scouring out the basin and pouring what remained of the bleach down the loo. She had just gone back into the waiting room when she heard a heavy tread on the landing floor. For a moment she held her breath – was it him or had someone else discovered her whereabouts? – but then the key turned in the lock and she was able to exhale again.

Douglas came in and asked, 'Everything okay? No problems?'

'No problems.'

'Good.' He stopped and sniffed. 'What's that smell?'

'Bleach,' she said. 'I thought I might as well make myself useful while I was waiting.'

Some people would have taken offence at the presumption of an almost stranger taking it upon themselves to clean their place of work, but Douglas had no such qualms. He merely raised his eyebrows and said: 'I should have stayed out longer. You could have given the place a lick of paint, too.'

'Just say the word. I'm very handy with a paintbrush.'

'An unnecessary expense,' he said.

'First impressions,' she countered. 'And my rates are excellent.'

'I could tell you I'll consider it, but I won't. Shall we get down to business?'

More coffee was made, and they retired to the office. Cara hadn't touched this room – it could have looked like she was snooping – other than to give the poor plant a much-needed drink of water. She sat down opposite him at the desk and passed over the *Evening Standard*, open at the right page. 'Have you seen this?'

Douglas quickly read the report. 'Ah, so our Mr Kuzmin has come to a sticky end.'

'Are you going to tell the law?'

'Tell them what?'

'That you've been following him. That he was probably the one who attacked me on Saturday.'

'Do you want me to?'

Cara thought of Steadman and shook her head. 'Not unless you feel you have to.'

'We'll leave it, then. It wouldn't appear to have any bearing on his murder and might only serve to confuse the boys in blue.'

Cara sat back, relieved. 'Good. That's what I think too.'

'I imagine Mr Kuzmin was involved in all sorts of unpleasant activities before he went to meet his maker.'

'You still don't have any idea who he was working for?'

'No one specific. There are several Russian firms in London, all after a slice of the pie, and prepared to go to any lengths to get it. I'd say this killing has the whiff of gangland.' Douglas closed the paper and put it to one side. 'You wanted to tell me about Jimmy's brother.'

Cara proceeded to tell him what she'd learnt from Neil. She kept it short, sticking to the facts, and when she'd finished, she paused and then added, 'I promised him I wouldn't tell anyone.'

'You've just told me.'

'Yes, well, you're not just anyone, and when it comes to finding Jimmy's killer or keeping Neil's confidence, there isn't really any competition. I'd like to keep his name out of it if I can, but if I can't . . .' Cara shrugged. 'That's just how it is. I'm not going to lose any sleep over it.'

'I don't entirely understand,' Douglas said, picking up a pencil and tapping the end of it against his chin. 'Why would he deliberately withhold information that could help find his brother's killer?'

'Because of how he thinks it will look to other people, especially the police and his family. He knows what they're all going to ask themselves: why would Jimmy approach him in the first place unless he thought there was a chance he might say yes? Which would rather call into question Neil's integrity and his possible willingness to break the law. No smoke without fire

291

and all that. There'd be a kind of guilt through association, I suppose, and he's afraid of any scandal.' Cara huffed out a breath as she felt her resentment towards Neil rise up to the surface again. 'He didn't say all of this, not in so many words. I'm just drawing my own conclusions.'

'Why would Jimmy even ask if there wasn't any chance of him agreeing?'

'He wouldn't have ordinarily, not unless he was desperate. But maybe he thought that just this once ... blood being thicker than water, perhaps? I don't know.'

Douglas stared for a while at the black oblong of the window and then returned his gaze to her. 'Antwerp,' he repeated thoughtfully. 'So we're probably back to diamonds again.'

'It seems that way.' Cara was reassured by the fact he had made the connection. 'He could have gone on his own, of course, but if he did and he managed to sell them, then what did he do with the money?' She gave a tiny shake of her head. 'No, I don't reckon he went. It would have been too risky on his own.'

'I've checked out the insurance claim made by Fiona Myers,' Douglas said.

'Oh, is that sort of information open to anyone?'

'No, not to anyone, but there's nothing you can't find out for a price.'

Cara, thinking of the bill, wondered how high that price had been, but then realised that she didn't care. 'And?'

'The bulk of the claim was for gold bars – about four hundred thousand quid's worth – and the rest was made up of various items of jewellery and a couple of small paintings. The gold wouldn't have been a problem for the thief; they come with serial numbers, but he could have easily had them melted down or sold them on to someone who'd deal with the messier side of the business. There was a diamond necklace and earrings – both of which could have fitted neatly into our box – but they were only worth about thirty grand. I say only, but you get what I mean: not enough, I suspect, to murder Jimmy for.'

'I imagine people have killed for a lot less.' But she did understand what he meant. 'So the diamonds we're talking about either didn't come from the Myers house or they weren't declared on the insurance.'

'That's about the sum of it. I'm inclined towards the latter. What do you know about Gerald Myers?'

'Not much, other than what I read in the papers at the time. He seemed to be one of those rich businessman socialite types.'

'He made his money from high-end property sales, mainly in the West End, Mayfair and the like. And here's an interesting thing – it's rumoured that some of his best clients were wealthy Russians, looking to invest their ill-gotten gains.'

'A rumour or a fact?'

Douglas smiled briefly. 'Let's call it a well-informed rumour. The Soviet Union is, apparently, on its last legs and certain Russians want to get their money out before it's too late. Anyway, it's possible that Myers wasn't always paid for his services in the conventional way, thus avoiding unnecessary contributions to the coffers of the taxman. It would explain why the diamonds weren't insured.'

'If Fiona Myers knows all this then she isn't exactly innocent herself.' Cara felt an instant spasm of remorse for voicing this thought which had only entered her head because she still felt aggrieved by the judgement of the older woman. 'Oh, I probably shouldn't have said that.'

'Why not? You could be right. And she could have asked these Russians – former clients or friends of her husband, whatever they are – to help her out.'

'She can hardly need the money.'

'People always need money, Cara, especially when they're used to having it. It's worth exploring every avenue.'

'But how do we find out if these avenues lead anywhere?'

'Through thorough and painstaking investigation,' he said drily.

'And if that doesn't work?'

Douglas sat back and laid his hands on his ample stomach. 'Then we may have to put the cat among the pigeons.'

52

Ray Tierney was on his way home, driving along Station Road and stifling a yawn, when the traffic lights turned to red and he was caught in a short queue of cars near the Fox. With his fingers he tapped out a beat on the steering wheel, more restless than impatient, knowing it would be a few minutes before he could move off again.

On the other side of the road a door to one of the houses opened and two people stepped out, a man and a woman. He wouldn't have thought anything of it if the couple hadn't briefly stopped under a lamppost, their faces illuminated by the orangey light. It was then that he recognised her – Cara Kendall – with her slim figure and cropped fair hair. She was dressed all in black, the uniform of the burglar or the grieving, and he wondered what was going on.

Ray watched as they set off again in the opposite direction to where he was headed. The conversation between them appeared animated but amicable. He didn't know who the older man was. Not her father – he was dead – but maybe another relative. Or an associate of a different kind. Like a fence, for instance. Despite Cara's protestations that she had no idea what the 'it' was, referred to in the note, he was not entirely certain she was telling the truth. He grinned. Well, of course he couldn't be certain. She was, after all, the sort of girl who broke into rich people's houses and relieved them of their valuables.

Although Ray didn't share Steadman's dislike of her and didn't believe that she'd had anything to do with Jimmy Lovell's death, he was still curious. He followed their progress until they turned down a side street and disappeared from view. By now the traffic was starting to move again. He made a quick decision. Instead of driving straight on as he'd intended, he switched on his left indicator light and slid into the Fox car park. He killed the engine and sat in the dark for five minutes until he was as sure as he could be that Cara and her companion had left the area.

Ray got out of the car, crossed the road and made his way to the building he'd seen them coming out of. A lot of the houses along this stretch were B&Bs, but not this one. Even as he approached, he could see the row of metal nameplates to the side of the door, an indicator that this particular house had been divided into business premises.

It was gloomy in the doorway, but light enough for him to read the names. He started from the top, looking for a likely candidate for Cara's companion: Maurice Longthorne, Surveyor (unlikely, he thought); J. Henderson & Co., Chartered Accountants (possible, if she had some kind of tax problem); Glen Douglas, Private Investigator (now that was more like it). His gaze lingered on the name, and he was sure that this was the one. For the sake of thoroughness, however, he continued down to the fourth and final plate: James H.

Robbins, Dental Surgeon. This gave him momentary pause for thought and temporarily rocked his conviction until he wondered why a dentist would be working this late and decided, on balance, that he probably wouldn't be. Mr Robbins could be dismissed on these grounds and on the grounds that no one voluntarily stayed in the company of their dentist for any longer than they had to.

Ray quickly moved away from the building, crossed back over the road and returned to his car. He didn't set off for home straight away, but instead took some time to consider what he'd learnt. He'd never heard of Glen Douglas before, but that wasn't so surprising. He hadn't been at Cowan Road long enough to know every cowboy in the district. With a reputation for going their own way, regardless of the law, private investigators were not held in much esteem by the police.

He lit a cigarette, wound down the window and wondered what Cara Kendall wanted from an investigator. Someone to track down the 'it' that had gone missing? Or someone to help clear her name as regards the Gerald Myers murder? Or perhaps, God forbid, someone to try and track down Jimmy's killer. The latter would be bad news. They didn't need some amateur scaring off any potential witnesses or, even worse, trampling over any evidence he might be lucky enough to come across.

'What are you playing at, Cara?' he murmured.

He wondered where she'd got the money to pay Douglas. She'd only just come out of jail and most ex-cons didn't have a pot to piss in.

Ray looked towards the pub and thought about going in for a pint. If Holly was there . . . but even if she was, it wouldn't be safe to speak to her, at least nothing beyond the usual small talk and banter. He wouldn't be able to ask about Cara. The

Fox was full of spies, lowlifes who wouldn't think twice about relaying a tale to Terry Street about the barmaid and the cop. No, he couldn't afford to take any chances. Holly was the best nark he'd ever had and he intended to keep hold of her.

53

Cara had too much stuffed inside her head: Russian business-men, Antwerp, diamonds, dodgy deals, gangsters, widows, brothers and, of course, the most grievous thing of all, Jimmy's murder. She wasn't sure what to do with any of it. It lay entangled in her mind like cooked spaghetti. Six days had passed since she'd discovered Jimmy's body – her lower lip trembled – and the law, so far as she was aware, weren't even close to making an arrest.

She went over last night's conversation with Glen Douglas. Theories were all very well, but they still had to be proved. Could Fiona Myers really be behind the attempted abduction on her? How long before the Russians had another go? What about Terry Street? And there was Steadman to think about too. God, yes, she couldn't forget about him.

One thing at a time, she told herself. While Douglas was working on the Myers/Russian connection, she was going to see Rochelle, not for a confrontation – that was too risky – but to try and subtly wheedle some information out of her.

Cara had avoided Lytton this morning, waiting until he'd left for college before emerging from her bedroom. Had things been slightly strained last night after she'd asked him about Rochelle? She wasn't sure if they had been – not on his part, at least – but his story about the girl begging him for money hadn't quite rung true. It could just be her paranoia. Was it? Trusting anyone was hard when you knew someone was out to get you.

Of course, one way to solve the problem was simply to kick him out. One less thing to worry about. And yet there was no solid evidence that he was plotting against her. She knew that she was looking for reasons to believe in his innocence but wasn't entirely sure why. Perhaps it was because she had let her guard down with him and didn't want to admit that this had been a big mistake.

Cara was sitting at the table by the window, keeping watch on the estate from above. She ought to have asked Murch for Rochelle's flat number and then she could have just gone round. Instead, she was stuck with what could prove to be a long and boring vigil. It was unlikely the girl had left home yet – it was only eight-twenty – but she was bound to show her face eventually. Patience. That was what was needed.

Beneath her the workers, the residents lucky enough to have jobs, were spilling out of the towers and heading for the bus stops and the railway station. They were people whose thoughts, she presumed, were less chaotic than her own: what to have for dinner tonight, what to do at the weekend, whether they could afford to pay the electricity bill. She doubted if murder was on anyone else's mind, or if it was, only somewhere on the periphery, a fleeting thought about a man who'd been killed on the Mansfield, a man whose name they were already beginning to forget.

Gradually the workers were replaced by the kids going to school, and these in turn gave way to the shoppers, and these to the unemployed men and women en route to the Job Centre or the Record Shack, and eventually those starting later shifts at shops and supermarkets and the local hospital. It was after twelve before the first dealer took up his post near one of the passageways at Carlton House.

By now Cara's patience was starting to wear thin and she was wondering whether Rochelle was staying home for the day or if she'd left by the other exit on the far side of the estate. Frustration gnawed at her. She'd spent the last few hours planning what to say, and how to say it, and now it all felt like an almighty waste of time.

She was on the verge of calling it a day when Rochelle finally put in an appearance, tottering on high heels down the main path from Temple with her hands in her pockets. The same puffa jacket as yesterday and probably the same miniskirt too. Her legs were pale, her head bent against the wind, her hair a ruffled blaze of red.

Cara leapt up, grabbed her keys, whisked her jacket off the peg in the hall and ran for the lift. It seemed to take for ever to descend to the ground floor, and, while she waited, she danced impatiently from one foot to the other. What if she missed her? At this rate, Rochelle would be out of the gates and gone. It would probably have been quicker to use the stairs.

In the event, she needn't have worried. Even as she dashed across the foyer, Cara could see that Rochelle hadn't gone far, but had come to a stop at the low wall by the gates and was sitting smoking a fag. Cara braced herself against the cold as she pushed open the door. An icy wind was blowing across the estate, the kind of wind that stung your face and brought tears to your eyes.

She scanned the surrounding area for possible threats, looking behind her, to the left and right, up and down Mansfield Road. She was, perhaps, a complete fool for returning so openly to the scene of the crime, to the place where she had so nearly been snatched, but was counting on her enemies still being absent. Would they really try the same thing in the same place twice? The odds seemed against it, but she couldn't afford to take anything for granted.

Cara slowed her pace as she approached, wanting it to appear casual, a chance encounter. Rochelle had her back to her and was smoking the cigarette in a fast, jerky fashion, as though she feared someone might come along and snatch it away. Cara passed through the gates, turned left and stopped as if she was surprised to see the girl. 'Oh,' she said. 'Hey.'

Rochelle glanced up, looking surly, probably hungover. 'Where are you going?'

'Nowhere in particular. Just for a walk.' Cara paused for effect. 'Come along if you want.'

'What for?'

As Rochelle showed no inclination to stand, Cara sat down beside her. 'It's bloody freezing here.'

'No one's asking you to hang about. Just fuck off if you don't like it.'

Cara didn't like it. She didn't like Rochelle much, either, but it was hard not to feel a small amount of pity for her. There was something lost and brittle about the girl, as if she'd found herself on a path from which there was no turning back. 'I've had the law round again, that Tierney. Do you know him?'

'No.'

'Yeah, you do. The young bloke, the DC who works with Steadman.'

Rochelle hunched her shoulders and buried her chin in the

collar of her jacket. A silence followed. Then Rochelle suddenly turned her face, her eyes flashing with anger. 'You were the one who told him about me, weren't you? You said you wouldn't, but you did.'

'I didn't, I swear. Why would I?'

'To get your own back, 'cause of me and Jimmy. How else could he have known who I was? The shithead tried to talk to me in the Fox, bought me a drink and everything. Thought I was a fuckin' pushover.'

'For Christ's sake, Rochelle, loads of people must have seen you in the Fox with Jimmy. Any one of them could have told Tierney. Why are you blaming me? And anyway, what does it matter if the law knows that you and Jimmy were mates? It's hardly a crime.'

'It's none of their fuckin' business.'

'Yeah, well, Jimmy's dead, so I suppose it is their fuckin' business now.'

Rochelle chucked the fag end on the ground and stamped on it with her heel. 'If it weren't you, who told him? Who told Tierney?'

Cara thought she was like a dog with a bone, refusing to let go.

'You can't trust no one round here,' Rochelle spat out, throwing Cara the kind of look that suggested she wasn't just included in the comment but top of the list when it came to suspects.

'Think what you like about me. It won't make it true.'

Rochelle wasn't even listening. 'No one. Fuckin' no one. This place is a pisshole.'

Cara could feel the cold seeping into her bones. She had come out with the intention of using guile and cunning to slowly bring the conversation around to Lytton but could see that she'd be wasting her breath. Instead, she went for a more direct approach. 'Did Jimmy ever talk to you about renting out my flat while I was inside?'

The change of subject caught Rochelle off guard. She looked down, pretending to study the small heap of litter that had gathered in the gutter. 'No.'

'Are you sure?'

'I just said, didn't I?'

'A bloke called Lytton, Will Lytton.'

'Never heard of him.'

'That's odd,' Cara said, 'only I saw you talking to him on Monday.'

Rochelle shrugged, as if the suggested oddness was neither here nor there to her. 'Talking where?'

Despite Rochelle's attempt at nonchalance Cara was sure she'd seen a flash of panic cross her face. 'Here. On the path. Not far from Haslow.'

'I don't remember any bloke.'

'It was about three o'clock, maybe a bit after. You were angry with him.'

'Why would I be angry with him?'

'I don't know. You tell me.'

Rochelle gave a rasping laugh that sounded false and strained. 'Can't tell you what I don't know. I've no idea what you're talking about.'

Cara was already tired of the exchange. She'd had enough. She wanted to be back inside, in the warm and away from any potential danger. Her eyes darted left and right again. Her nerves were rattling. One last try and then she was off. Time to stir the pot, she decided, to make some waves. What did she have to lose? 'That's funny because he says he knows you, says he knows you pretty well, in fact.' She smiled thinly and left a pause for dramatic effect. 'He's told me everything, in case you're wondering.'

The colour drained from Rochelle's face. Suddenly all the pretence was gone. She leapt up and glared down at Cara, her body visibly shaking. 'Whatever that bastard told you, he's a fuckin' liar!'

Adrenaline had started to surge through Cara. She tried to keep her own voice calm. 'So why don't you give me your side of things?'

'Go to hell,' Rochelle hissed. And with that she stomped off down Mansfield Road, leaving in her wake a disturbing combination of sweet perfume, tobacco and the rotten odour of something having been unearthed.

Cara stood up too, trying to decide whether to go after her. The trying didn't last long. Rochelle, she suspected, had said as much as she was going to today. She turned, stepped over the low wall and strode back towards Haslow. Her heart was thumping. *Lytton and Rochelle knew each other.* There was no doubt about it now. But why the lies from Lytton, the denial? And why the angry row between him and Rochelle on Monday? Thieves falling out, perhaps. She shivered, and not just from the cold. It was time to face an unwelcome truth: at least one of her enemies was sleeping under the same roof as her.

54

Terry Street was in a good mood, the type of mood that sprang from a job well done and no incriminating evidence left behind. The elimination of Kuzman had been necessary, a warning to Azarov that he couldn't do what he liked, where he liked, without there being repercussions. To try and snatch Cara Kendall off the street like that had been a step too far. Even in the underworld there were codes to be observed and boundaries that should not be crossed.

He whistled softly while he waited, a tune he had heard on the radio. Azarov wouldn't be happy with the hit, but he knew better than to go to war over it. Or did he? Who knew what went on in the heads of those commies? Terry stopped whistling. Some men let their pride get the better of good sense. But there was too much at stake for the Russian to hold a permanent grudge: if he wanted the goods back, he would have to play by Terry's rules. A deal had been made and there was no going back on it.

Glancing in the rear-view mirror, he saw Holly approaching

and watched her swinging hips with the usual combination of lust and admiration. The girl had style. He liked a woman with confidence and nerve, a woman who knew her own mind and knew what she wanted. There was no shortage of birds who'd happily go to bed with him – a state of affairs that he frequently took advantage of – but sometimes he fancied a bit of a challenge.

Holly climbed into the car, bringing with her a blast of cold November air and the scent of a perfume that was by now familiar to him.

'Hi, hon,' she said, settling into the passenger seat and crossing her long legs. 'I've got some news on Cara Kendall.'

Terry listened as she told him about Cara asking after a girl called Rochelle and a bloke called Will Lytton. She went on to describe Cara's meeting with Jimmy Lovell's brother in the Fox, a meeting that had not gone well, although she hadn't, as yet, been able to find out why. 'She said they were just upset, but I reckon there was more to it. He had a face like bloody thunder when he left.'

And then there had been the business of the picture in the *Evening Standard*. 'That shook her up good and proper,' Holly continued. 'She went white as a sheet, asked me if I recognised him, if he was the same guy who'd been watching her on Saturday. It was, of course, but I told her I wasn't sure, that it was hard to tell from the photo. I asked if she was going to go to the law, but she didn't seem keen. I told her she was probably right, that it could be more trouble than it was worth, or words to that effect. I said I'd keep quiet about it, too. Did I do the right thing, Terry?'

Terry, who was careful never to give anything more away than he had to, gave a nod. 'Yeah, you did good. I don't know nothin' about this geezer, but it never pays to go running to the law. What about the others – this Will Lytton and Rochelle?'

'I've never heard of him,' Holly said. 'But I know Rochelle. She's one of Jimmy's exes, the type who could never take the hint and was always hanging round him like a bad smell. You've probably seen her in the Fox. A redhead, young – twenty or so – always dressed like something the cat dragged in. Always off her head, too. She's lucky she hasn't been chucked out, the liberties she takes.'

Terry thought he might have seen her around but couldn't put a clear face to the name. 'Cara say anything else about this Lytton?'

'She gave me a description – early thirties, light brown hair – but that could apply to half the customers who come into the Fox.'

'She tell you why she wanted to know about him?'

'No.'

'You could have asked her.'

Holly raised her eyebrows. 'I could have,' she agreed, 'if I'd wanted to come across as someone who was overly interested in her business.'

Terry grinned. 'Okay, I get your point, but don't go too bleedin' easy or you'll still be at it by Christmas.'

'Leave it with me.'

Terry peeled off the customary number of notes from the wad he kept in his pocket. 'See you soon, sweetheart.'

'Ta, hon.' Holly stashed the payment in her bag and flashed a smile. 'Anything you want me to tell Tierney?'

'Not for now.'

Holly looked up and down the empty street, half opened the door, hesitated and turned back to Terry again. 'Is Cara in big trouble?'

'Depends how you look at it.'

'What does that mean?'

'It means if she's sensible, she ain't got nothin' to worry about.'

Holly inclined her head a little. 'Has Cara Kendall ever been sensible?'

'There's a first time for everything.'

Holly smiled again, got out of the car, closed the door and walked away.

Terry narrowed his eyes and a coldness came into them. He hoped she wasn't going soft on him. You couldn't rely on women when it came to the sharp end of business. There was something about the way she'd ... But almost immediately he dismissed the idea. Holly didn't care about Cara's welfare. Why would she? No, there was nothing to worry about on that score. He knew Holly's type: she only cared about one person and that was herself.

He thought about the Russian flunky, dead in a Soho alley-way, and let the satisfaction roll over him. But now wasn't the moment for gloating or for sitting back. There was work to be done. Cara Kendall might have got the better of Kuzmin and his mates, but he was a different prospect altogether. It was time for a face to face, time to put the screws on.

55

Ray Tierney didn't share his boss's conviction but didn't go so far as to vocalise his doubts. Sometimes it was better to keep your mouth shut. Steadman had been in a sullen mood for the past few days, brooding and snappy, but the news about Cara Kendall and the private investigator had finally put a smile on his face.

'What did I tell you?' Steadman said smugly. 'That girl's in it up to her neck. Why else would she have hired Douglas? She's looking for her missing pal from the Hampstead job. Find the murdering bastard, find the money. I always knew she was lying.'

Ray reckoned there could be other reasons why she'd gone to the P.I. – the threatening note, the assault on Saturday – but wasn't about to pour cold water on the inspector's theory. He kept his eyes on the road as he drove down the high street. 'Do we know much about him, this Glen Douglas bloke?'

'Small time. A one-man band, by all accounts. Deals mainly with insurance cases, spying on all those lying fuckers who claim they can't walk any more after they slipped on a wet patch in the supermarket aisle.'

'Sounds challenging.'

'He won't give us any trouble. His sort never does. Too worried about losing his licence to get on the wrong side of the law. All we need is a name and then we're one step closer to nailing her *and* the killer of Gerald Myers.'

'And Lovell?' Ray asked. 'You reckon our mystery man could have killed him too?'

Steadman shrugged. 'It's not impossible.'

Ray had the impression, and it wasn't a new one, that Steadman was only interested in Lovell's murder in so far as it connected to Cara Kendall. He suspected that the actual killing itself, and the arrest of the perpetrator, wasn't as high on the inspector's list of priorities as it should have been. 'Our man could still be in the area, then.'

'Could be. Which is all the more reason to put a stop to Mr Douglas's activities. There's nothing worse than some bloody amateur trampling all over an investigation.'

Ray swung a left at the lights, went into Station Road, drove as far as the pub, indicated right and slid the Ford into the Fox car park. They got out and crossed the road. 'This is it,' he said, stopping outside the building he had visited last night.

Steadman stared at the nameplates for a moment and then pushed the door. It opened and they climbed the stairs in silence. Ray was immediately aware of the shabbiness of the place, of the threadbare carpet and general air of neglect. Mr Douglas was either at the lower end of the earnings scale or the premises were a clever cover for a multi-million-pound operation that preferred to keep a low profile. He knew which one his money was on.

They stopped at the first landing and located Mr Douglas's

office. Steadman turned the door handle and they both went inside. A bell tinged an alert as they crossed the threshold. A man's voice called out, 'I'll be right with you.'

Ray's gaze swept the waiting room, the magnolia walls and plastic chairs. It was a dreary space, but surprisingly neat and clean. A vague smell of bleach drifted in the air. The owner of the voice emerged from the inner office, without jacket or tie, his white shirt crumpled.

'Mr Douglas?' Steadman asked.

'That's me. What can I do for you, gentlemen?'

Steadman made the introductions, flashing his ID. Ray reached into the inside pocket of his jacket and produced his card too, relieved that this was the same individual he'd seen last night.

Glen Douglas, middle-aged and overweight, had the look of a man who had a bad diet, drank too much coffee and hadn't had much sleep recently. However, his small eyes were shrewd and he gazed at the warrant cards with no visible signs of anxiety.

'We're investigating the murder of a man called Jimmy Lovell,' Steadman said.

'I heard about that. Not sure how I can help you, though.'

'I believe you've been hired by his former girlfriend, Cara Kendall.'

Douglas neither confirmed nor denied the statement. He raised and dropped his shoulders in a silent and perhaps somewhat scornful version of 'No comment'.

Steadman's face hardened. 'Please don't mess us about, Mr Douglas. We know you're working for her, and we know she's looking for someone. All we need is a name and then we'll leave you in peace.'

'I'm sorry, I don't have any names for you.'

'Are you saying you're not prepared to cooperate?'

'It's not a matter of cooperation, inspector. I can't tell you what I don't know. End of story.'

'But you have been hired by Cara Kendall?'

'Not in relation to finding anybody.'

Steadman was growing increasingly frustrated. 'So why *has* she hired you?'

'I'm not at liberty to tell you that, I'm afraid. Client confidentiality.'

'You do know it's an offence to obstruct the police?'

Douglas held his ground, unperturbed. 'I'm not obstructing your investigation, inspector. My business with Cara Kendall, as I've already said, isn't in connection to a search for anyone. Nor am I looking into the circumstances of Jimmy Lovell's unfortunate death. As such, I don't see how anything I could tell you would aid your investigation in any way. Now if there's nothing else I can help you with, I really have to be getting on.'

Steadman glared at him, his body stiff with fury. 'If you're lying, there will be consequences. You do understand that, don't you?'

'Why would I lie to you? A man's dead and I have no desire to impede your attempts to bring the murderer to justice. So unless Cara Kendall is a suspect ... But I believe she was in jail when the murder took place, wasn't she?'

'Licences can be revoked, Mr Douglas.' Steadman spoke softly, but with vehemence. 'If I was you, I'd think very carefully about your position here.'

Glen Douglas assumed the weary expression of a man who was used to those in authority trying to impose their will on him. 'I'll be sure to do that, inspector.'

Steadman, aware that his threat had fallen on deaf ears, made a show of looking round the waiting room. A sneer curled his upper lip. 'Nice place you've got here. I suppose it's hard to refuse any kind of business in your situation.'

Douglas let the insult wash over him. He smiled, walked past them to the door and held it open. 'Good afternoon, officers.'

They were out on the street before Steadman spoke again. 'That man's lying through his bloody teeth. There's only one good reason why Cara Kendall would be paying out money to the likes of him. She's given him a name. I'd stake my life on it.'

Ray didn't know if he was right or not. However, he had the feeling that Douglas might have been more obliging if Steadman hadn't been so officious. More courtesy and less intimidation could have achieved better results. Not that he was about to share these thoughts. Instead, he nodded, made an ill-defined sort of noise and kept his opinion to himself.

56

The first thing Cara did on returning to the flat was to search Lytton's room again. It seemed obvious, now that she was doing it for the second time, that it wasn't so much what was there as what wasn't. The absence of a passport, of any of the usual paperwork and paraphernalia that accumulated through a person's life, was clearly suspicious. She couldn't ask him why he kept so little in the flat, not without revealing she'd been snooping, but could imagine the answers he'd come up with: that the rest of his belongings were in storage or at his parents' place or piled in some mate's garage. And who was to say that wasn't true? They were all perfectly feasible answers.

The problem was that when you caught a person out in a lie, there was no saying what else they were lying about. She thought about everything she'd told him and regretted the sharing of confidences. She had let her guard down and that had been stupid. Thankfully there were things she hadn't divulged – the silver box Murch had passed on to her, hiring Douglas, her conversation with Neil in the Fox. All of this she had kept to herself and was glad of it.

Why had Lytton lied about knowing Rochelle? She couldn't see any reason, other than the probability that they both had something to hide. She should have interrogated Murch when she had the chance, but she'd had her mind on other things. He knew Rochelle, perhaps knew Lytton too. They could all be working together. She could feel the weight of a conspiracy bearing down on her, but still couldn't make the connections.

She gave up on the search and returned to the living room. Anger rippled through her. She paced and stopped, paced and stopped. She should have chucked Lytton out when she'd had the chance. What was wrong with her? It had been the shock of Jimmy's death, the horror of it all. She hadn't been thinking straight. She had needed someone on her side and he had seemed the best candidate. Or maybe just the only candidate.

While she waited for Lytton to return, Cara had the opportunity to go over their conversations, to dissect them sentence by sentence, the questions asked and the answers given, trying to prise something from them, anything that she might have missed first time around. But nothing other than a mild evasiveness presented itself. He was playing the long game, perhaps, wheedling his way into her trust while he tried to discover where the diamonds were.

That was what all this was about, wasn't it? The diamonds that Jimmy had somehow acquired, the diamonds that the Russians and Terry Street both wanted, the diamonds that someone had been prepared to kill for. Rochelle must have found out about them, told Lytton, and together they had hatched a plan to have them for themselves.

Cara gave a hollow laugh. Everyone thought she knew where they were hidden, that all they had to do was send her threatening notes, bundle her into the back of a van or lend a sympathetic ear and dole out curry and beer, and eventually she'd cave in and reveal their whereabouts. Except that was never going to happen. Jimmy had gone to his maker without revealing the secret, and the diamonds, if he'd hidden them well enough, might never be found. If it wasn't all so tragic, so bloody frightening, it might almost be funny.

She wished Jimmy had given them up – nothing, no matter how valuable, was worth sacrificing your life for. Easy come, easy go, had always been his mantra, so why on earth had he been so stubborn this time? She pondered on what he'd said, about how she'd be a rich woman when she came out of a jail, and a shudder ran through her. If Douglas was right about a deal having been made with Myers's murderer, then maybe Jimmy had refused to hand them over because he believed them to be rightly hers. God, she hoped that wasn't true. She didn't want it to be. The thought of it was unbearable.

It was three-forty before she saw Lytton walking up the main path. She rose to her feet, took a few deep breaths and braced herself for confrontation.

57

Cara listened as Lytton came in through the front door, heard him stop to take off his jacket in the hall, felt her heart start to hammer. She stood by the window, her right hand clutching her left arm. *Keep calm.* But she had no idea how he'd react. Was it really such a smart idea to confront him here, away from any witnesses? It would be better, surely, to go somewhere more public and ask her questions there. What if he . . .

But it was too late. As soon as he walked into the room and saw her face, he knew that something was amiss. 'What is it? What's happened?'

'We need to talk,' she said as firmly as she could. Even as the words came out, they seemed wrong, too much of a cliché.

Lytton's eyebrows went up. 'That sounds ominous.'

Cara pulled out a chair and sat down at the table, deciding that having a piece of furniture between them was better than nothing. That mild-mannered façade could quickly slip away. She waited until he'd taken a seat too. She thought about what she would say next, tried to keep the fear at bay. To some extent she had come to trust him, and the shattering of that trust was hard to take.

'What is it?' he said again.

Cara's mouth felt dry. She ran her tongue over her lips. *Get on with it*, a voice in her head insisted. The longer she delayed, the harder it would be. She cleared her throat. 'I saw Rochelle today. She told me about you, told me everything.'

If she'd expected shock, even surprise, she was disappointed. His face remained impassive. He didn't deny it, but instead said coolly, 'And what do you mean by everything?'

The liar's ploy, she thought, trying to suss out how much she actually knew. She countered his question with one of her own. 'Why did you lie to me? Why did you tell me you didn't know her?'

Lytton held her gaze and was silent for a moment. 'She didn't tell you anything,' he said with infuriating calmness.

And suddenly something inside Cara snapped. She leaned forward with anger in her eyes. 'For God's sake, will you stop it? Jimmy's dead, I've got the local hoods threatening me, probably the bloody Russian mafia too, and I've got the law on my back. Please don't make everything worse than it already is.'

'Rochelle doesn't have anything to do with all that.'

'So what does she have to do with?'

Lytton's face twisted slightly, a sigh escaping from the back of his throat. He hesitated for what felt like a long time but was probably only seconds. 'She's my sister.'

'Your sister?' Cara spluttered. 'What?'

'I should have told you, but—'

'But you didn't,' Cara interrupted, still struggling to absorb what he'd said. 'You didn't say a word. Why would you keep quiet about something like that? Why? What's the point? What's the big secret?'

'No big secret, not really. I don't know why I lied about it.' Lytton laid his hands on the table and grimaced. 'No, I do know. It just seemed easier than having to explain it all. I'm sorry.'

'I'm all ears,' she said.

Lytton shrugged and sighed again. 'Rochelle's always been . . . how shall I put it? Troubled, I suppose. She disappeared over a year ago and eventually I tracked her down to the Mansfield. She refused to go home, and I couldn't make her. She was eighteen then, old enough to do what she liked. Unfortunately, what she likes will probably end up killing her. So, I made the decision that if she was going to stay on the estate then so was I.' He gave a rueful smile. 'She hates me being here. Thinks I'm spying on her, which I suppose I am to some degree. But at least I can watch out for her, be here if she ever needs me.'

'So how did you end up here? In this flat, I mean.'

'Rochelle was hanging out a lot with Jimmy. She was all right to me when I first arrived – didn't think I'd be staying for long, I guess – and she introduced us. It was obvious that she had a real thing about him. They'd gone out for a while, but only for a month or two. I don't think Jimmy could cope with all the intensity. For him it had just been a fling, but it meant more to her: she was convinced he was the only person who understood her.' Lytton's hands separated, moved across the table and came back together again. 'Anyway, when I told Jimmy I was looking for somewhere local to rent, he suggested this place. I think he quite liked the idea of having me around. Perhaps he was hoping I'd take her off his hands.'

'What did Rochelle think about you living here?'

'She wasn't happy, as you can imagine. I wanted her to move in with me, but she wouldn't. I thought if we were sharing a place that I might eventually persuade her to go home.'

'And where is home?'

'St John's Wood,' he said. 'That's where Mum lives, but the two of them have a pretty fraught relationship. Rochelle's been in trouble with the police – nothing serious, drunk and disorderly and the like – and Mum finds it hard to cope with her. She wouldn't turn her away, though.'

Cara didn't know how much to believe. Was this the truth or some fall-back story he'd concocted in case she discovered they knew each other? 'You don't even look alike.'

'No,' he agreed. 'But that's not unknown.'

Which was true, of course. It didn't prove anything, one way or another. 'And you speak completely differently.'

'Rochelle just puts it on, the whole local accent thing. To try and fit in, I suppose. She doesn't normally talk like that.'

'You're much older than her.'

'She was a late addition to the family. I was thirteen when she was born, away at school. I only ever saw her in the holidays.'

Cara hadn't realised that he'd been packed away too – something they had in common – but then immediately wondered if this was just another part of the story. 'I still don't understand the secrecy. Why didn't you just tell me that she was your sister?'

'I should have done. It was stupid. But after you came back and told me about Jimmy being dead, I knew Rochelle would take it badly. Truth is, I didn't want you to chuck me out. Not right then. I was scared she'd go well and truly off the rails. I needed to be here, keeping an eye on her.'

'So why not just tell me that?'

Lytton briefly looked away, looked back at her. 'I would have done, but I wasn't sure how much you knew about her and Jimmy. If you were aware of it, I couldn't see you'd be overjoyed at the prospect of sharing a flat with her brother. So . . . so I just kept my mouth shut and hoped for the best.'

'That worked out well.'

'There's something else you should know. Jimmy rang me a couple of weeks ago and said I had to get out of the flat, that you were coming home earlier than expected. We argued about it, but he wouldn't budge. Said he'd give me back what was owed, but I might have to wait a while. I was pissed off, to be honest, and decided to stay put until I saw the colour of his money. Anyway, that was the last I heard from him. I thought he'd be in touch again, but he wasn't.'

Cara felt there was a ring of truth about this at least. It was just like Jimmy to remember at the last minute that she was getting out and wouldn't be best pleased to find a stranger in the flat – and not surprising either that Lytton would object to being told to leave. 'So why was Rochelle having a go at you on Monday?'

'The usual. She just wants me to go away, to leave her alone. But how am I supposed to do that?' Lytton pulled a face and ran his fingers through his hair. 'She's like a bomb waiting to go off. That's if she doesn't drink herself to death first.'

Cara could see the concern on his face, the worry. Unless he was an excellent actor. 'She has a flat in Temple, doesn't she?'

'Who told you that?'

'She did. Well, she said that was where she was living.'

'She was, for a while. In some squalid little squat with no running water or electricity. That's why I thought she might be prepared to move in with me. The lure of heat and hot water.' He gave a wry smile. 'Turned out she preferred it where she was.'

'And now? You said was. Where's she living now?'

'I believe she's sleeping on Murch's sofa.'

'He didn't say anything to me about that.'

Lytton shrugged. 'Better there than out on the street. Murch is all right. Well, compared to some.'

Cara was about to say that Murch didn't even like Rochelle

but held her tongue. What did she know? She supposed the two of them, if nothing else, had Jimmy in common. Perhaps that was why Murch was letting her stay there. Or perhaps, if she was going to be cynical about it, he was hoping that Rochelle might repay the favour in other ways.

'There's something I still don't understand,' she said. 'Why did Rochelle lose her rag when I told her I knew about the two of you? If she wants you gone, then getting you out of this flat would be a pretty good first step.'

'Because I asked her to keep quiet about it. And before you ask why she'd agree to that, it was for the same reason she agrees to anything – money. She was probably worried that once you knew who I was, the bank of big brother would immediately dry up.'

Cara wasn't sure if this was an entirely adequate explanation. It might be true. It might not. Dusk was creeping through the windows, casting a grey shadow over the room. Even if Rochelle was his sister, it didn't mean they weren't conspiring against her. And yet she knew it was unlikely: Rochelle was too crazy, too unpredictable, to trust with anything important.

'I should have been straight with you,' Lytton said. 'I'm sorry.'

Cara didn't know where they went from here. Did she chuck him out or accept his apology? She couldn't decide. She needed time to think about it, and space. Quickly she got to her feet.

'Are you all right? Where are you going?'

'Out,' she said.

58

Cara felt the cold hit her as she left Haslow House and set off towards Temple. She hunched her shoulders against the wind, fastened her jacket and put her hands in her pockets. Was it a good idea to be roaming around on her own? Probably not, but she'd needed to get away from the flat, away from Lytton. In the scheme of things, she supposed his lie wasn't such a big deal, simply a means to an end, but she wished he'd been honest with her. Did she believe him? God, she didn't know what to believe any more.

The estate was moderately busy, busy enough at least for her to feel confident that no one would launch an open attack on her. Not that it had stopped them on Saturday. But the Russians, she hoped, had other things to occupy them at the moment. She glanced over her shoulder – something that was becoming a habit now – and quickly scanned the faces. Nobody caught her attention. Nobody made her think twice.

She stopped when she got to Temple, not sure now that she was here whether to proceed or not. Her intention had been to go to Murch's flat and see if Rochelle was there. But what was the point? Whether the girl admitted or denied being Lytton's sister wouldn't change anything, and she wasn't in the mood for another run-in with her. It might be better to speak to Murch instead. She looked at her watch. It would be another hour or so before he got home from work.

Cara turned around and retraced her steps. She paid extra attention as she approached the gates that led out to Mansfield Road, but the coast was clear. Within a couple of minutes, she was on the high street, mingling with the shoppers and the early-finish commuters making their way home from the station. The traffic was building up, moving at a snail's pace, and she was able to cross the road without any trouble.

As she walked alongside the green, a scruffy oblong of land with a few spindly trees and bushes, she could smell the wet earth. There was an empty bench close enough to the road to make it seem relatively safe, and on impulse she went over and sat down on it. It wasn't really sitting-down weather, but she wanted to be still, to try and get her thoughts in order.

A kid, small and skinny with an almost feral appearance, was idly kicking a football against the post of a sign that said no ball games. From the Mansfield, she guessed. All the kids from there had that same untamed look about them. He threw her a glance as if to say, 'Go on, then. I dare you.' But Cara didn't care about rules and regulations. If he was after a fight, he was going to be disappointed.

She sat back, the chill wind blowing against her face. The wooden bench was wet from the rain, and she felt the damp seeping through her jeans. Lytton was stuck in her head. She couldn't blame him, she thought, for wanting to watch out for Rochelle, but the deceit still rankled. He could have told her. She wasn't so petty that she would have thrown him out. Why was she letting him get under her skin? She had more pressing things to worry about, like finding out who'd killed Jimmy. So far as she could tell, neither Lytton nor Rochelle was in the running for that.

Cara's mind was still on the murder when she heard the light tread of footsteps on the grass. She barely had time to turn before the man had skirted round the side of the bench and sat down beside her. Even in the failing light she didn't have any trouble recognising him. Terry Street. Christ! She went to leap up, but instantly his hand snaked out and tightly encircled her wrist.

'Don't be like that, love,' he said softly. 'I only want a little chat.'

Panic was streaming through her. She tried to snatch her arm away, but his grip only tightened. 'Let go of me or I'll scream.'

Terry shook his head as if dealing with an exasperating child. His voice was calm and quiet. 'And what's that going to achieve? Just a load of fuss and bother. And then we'll both spend the next two hours down the nick, you telling your side of the story and me telling mine. A waste of everyone's time. Come on, love, five minutes, that's all I'm after. You can spare me that, can't you?'

Cara glanced quickly towards the high street, but no one was taking any notice of them. Even the kid had picked up his football and cleared off, streetwise enough to know when he wasn't wanted. Her pulse was racing, her heart drumming in her chest. 'Let go of me,' she said again.

'Only if you promise not to do a runner.' Terry grinned. 'I'm too old to be chasing after girls. A chat, that's all I want. Just you and me. Where's the harm?' He gestured towards the street. 'Nothing's going to happen. We're in plain view of all these lovely people.'

'Okay,' she said. 'I promise.'

Terry finally released her wrist, and in that split second she had to make a decision as to whether she stayed or bolted. Her first instinct was the latter – she reckoned if she made a dash for it, he probably wouldn't even try and catch her – but then what? She might get away today, but she couldn't run for ever. Eventually, whatever her fears, she was going to have to have this conversation.

Cara rubbed her wrist and stared at him. 'What do you want?'

'We need to talk about Jimmy.'

'Jimmy's dead,' she said bluntly, shifting back against the arm of the bench to try and put more distance between them.

'Yeah, it's a shame. He was a decent sort.'

'For all the good it did him.'

'It was nothing to do with me in case you're wondering. The last person I'd have wanted dead was Jimmy.'

Cara stared at him. On the surface there was nothing overtly scary about Terry Street. He was a good-looking man in his mid-thirties with a strong angular face, brown eyes, dark hair and a ready smile. But she knew his reputation. You didn't get to run the East End by being Mr Nice Guy. Sensing that he'd take advantage of any sign of weakness, she held eye contact and attempted to keep any tremor from her voice. 'And why was that?'

'You know why,' he said.

But Cara didn't know, at least not for sure. She had theories, possibilities, but not anything that could be nailed down. 'To be honest, I'm a bit short on the detail.'

'A bit short on detail, huh?'

'I haven't seen much of Jimmy over the last eighteen months. I don't know what he was up to.'

Terry gave a sigh. 'Let's not play games, love. We both know what I'm talking about. Me and Jimmy had a deal. He was in over his head, and he knew it. I offered him a way out and he grabbed it with both hands. That deal still stands.'

'I don't know anything about a deal.'

Terry's tone took on a harder edge. 'Don't mess me about, sweetheart. You can try and sell them, but you won't get far. You won't find a fence anywhere in London, anywhere in the country, who'll do business with you. The minute you try, alarm bells are going to go off. The word's out, you see, has been for quite a while. No one's going to buy something that's going to land them in the shit.'

Cara could have told him the truth, could have told him that she didn't have a clue where the diamonds were, but Terry Street was never going to believe her. And the longer she denied knowing their whereabouts, the angrier he was going to get. Instead, she played for time. 'So what's in it for me?'

'You give me the goods, I give them back to their rightful owner, they hand over the reward and everybody's happy. Fifty-fifty is what I agreed with Jimmy.'

'And how much does that come to?'

'Ten grand each. And yeah, I know that's only a fraction of what they're worth, but this way you won't have to spend the rest of your life looking over your shoulder. You were lucky on Saturday. Our Russian friends won't be so careless next time. You can do it the easy way or the hard, but in the end, they'll get what they want.'

'Why should I trust you?'

'Because you don't have a choice,' he said. 'What else are you going to do? You can't sell them, that's for sure. Try and cut me out, take the full reward for yourself? You could do that, but they won't let you walk away. It's a matter of commie pride, you see. Those reds don't like it when they're crossed. They'll make you pay . . . just like they made Jimmy pay.'

Cara shuddered, ice running down her spine. 'Did they kill Jimmy?'

'I don't reckon they meant to – not much use to them dead, was he? – but they screwed up, went too far and . . . well, now you're the only one left who can give them what they want. Let me do the deal and I'll make sure they leave you alone. Otherwise, you're on your own.'

'Do you know who it was? Do you have a name?'

'You don't have to worry about that. It's been dealt with.' A smile slid on to Terry's lips. 'Mr Kuzmin won't be bothering anyone again.'

Cara felt a rush of emotions, a tumultuous mix of shock, horror, disgust and relief. But above all she was glad, glad Kuzmin was dead, glad he had been made to pay the ultimate price for murdering Jimmy. No sooner had she acknowledged this than she was ashamed of it and looked away, trying to hide her confusion.

'He got what he deserved,' Terry said. 'You can be sure Jimmy wasn't the first, and he wouldn't have been the last, either.'

Cara nodded, accepting that this was probably true. She still felt queasy though, off balance, as if she had mined the deepest part of her soul and found something dark and disturbing there. She suspected that Terry hadn't avenged Jimmy's death because he'd cared about him, but for reasons of his own, reasons that were more to do with territory and respect and imposing his own will. Did that matter? The end result was the same. An eye for an eye and all that.

'So do we have a deal?' Terry asked.

Cara looked back at him. There were questions she wanted answers to, like how Jimmy had got hold of the diamonds in the first place, how the deal had come about, who the Russians were working for, but to ask was to admit to ignorance and she

329

couldn't afford to do that right now. 'I haven't got much choice, have I? But I'll need some time.'

'How much time?'

'A week,' she said. 'Ten days, perhaps.' Even as she was speaking, Cara wondered what the hell she was doing, but she had no other option than to play along. At least this way she would get everyone off her back for a while. 'There are things to . . . organise.'

'What sort of things?'

'Well, he didn't keep them under the bed, did he?'

'A week. I can hold them off for a week, but not any longer.'

'And no tail,' she said. 'You or them. If I catch anyone following me, the deal's off. I mean it. I'll throw the damn things in the Thames if I have to.'

Terry laughed, his mood lighter now that he'd got what he wanted. 'That would be a dreadful waste.'

'Take it or leave it,' she said, with more courage than she felt.

Terry nodded and stood up. 'I'll pass the message on. A week, then.' He took a slip of paper from his pocket and handed it to her. 'Call me on this number as soon as you have them.'

'How do I know you'll stick to your side of the deal?'

'Honour amongst thieves?' he said, looking down at her and grinning again.

Cara would have snorted if she'd dared.

Terry started to walk away but then stopped and glanced back. 'And the box as well, if it's not too much trouble. Sentimental value, apparently.'

59

'You did what?' Glen Douglas said, staring at Cara with what could only be described as incredulity. He was sitting at his desk with his arms folded across his chest.

'What choice did I have? Tell him that I didn't have a clue where the diamonds were? He wasn't going to believe that, not for a second. At least this way I get a week's reprieve.'

'And then what?'

Cara was pacing from one side of the office to the other, from the wall to the window and back again. 'I don't know. Maybe I'll have figured out where Jimmy hid the damn things by then.'

'Just sit down, will you? You're jangling my nerves pacing around like that. Perhaps you should think about going to the police. He was here this morning, Steadman and his constable.'

This startled Cara. 'Christ, how did he find out about you?'

'I've no idea.'

'What did you say to him?'

'Nothing he wanted to hear. The inspector seems to have got

it into his head that I've been hired to find a missing person. Your accomplice, I imagine, on the Hampstead job.'

'You see what I mean about that man? It's Jimmy's murder he should be investigating, not me.'

'But with this latest development, are you sure you shouldn't be talking to them?'

'And tell them what? That Terry Street confessed to killing Kuzmin, or at least to having had him killed? He's only going to deny it, and he'll know I told them and then I'll be in even deeper shit.' Cara pulled out a chair and perched on the edge of it. 'No, I can't get the law involved. I need Terry on side. I need him to keep those bloody Russians away from me. Have you managed to find any link between them and Fiona Myers yet?'

Douglas shook his head. 'I've found out who Kuzmin was working for, though: a piece of work called Ivan Azarov, a Russian émigré with his finger in a lot of pies. Prostitution, gambling, drugs – you name it, he's in it. He owns a couple of clubs in the West End, and a fair amount of property too. Not a pleasant character, from what I can gather.'

'You don't say.'

'I'm still looking for the connection between him and Fiona Myers. Could be he was simply a business associate of her husband's.'

'I wonder how he found out about Jimmy. How did he even know he had the diamonds?'

'Well, we've established that Jimmy told Terry Street about them, probably in a moment of drunken male machismo. At a guess, and that's all it is, I'd say that Street knew Azarov had been hired to look for them and saw a chance to make some money with minimal effort. He must have persuaded Jimmy that doing a deal – with himself as the middle man – was a better option than trying to sell the stones himself. How Azarov discovered Jimmy's identity – who knows? Perhaps by putting Street under surveillance. Or perhaps Fiona pointed him in the right direction. I presume she knew that Jimmy was your boyfriend?'

'She'd have seen him at the trial, I suppose. But if a deal was in place why would Azarov renege on it?'

Douglas shrugged. 'Perhaps he got wind that Jimmy wasn't playing ball and decided to take matters into his own hands.'

'And Jimmy wasn't playing ball, was he? Not if he was planning on going to Antwerp.'

'It would appear not.'

'Jesus,' she said. 'What did he think he was doing? You don't make deals with the likes of that lot and then do the dirty on them.'

'Not unless you think you can get away with it. Perhaps he wasn't planning on coming back.'

Cara considered this but couldn't really see Jimmy making a new life for himself in Europe. But perhaps she was wrong. After all, what was there to keep him here? A grotty flat on a grotty estate with nothing better to look forward to. Why settle for ten grand when he could have ten or twenty times that? He might have thought it was a risk worth taking, his best chance of escape from a future that was all too predictable.

She half rose to her feet again, saw Douglas frown and sat back down. 'I don't get what's so special about these diamonds. I mean a diamond's a diamond, isn't it? Why should these be any more difficult to shift than any other?'

'Because there's something unusual about them, something distinctive. Bigger, clearer, more valuable? I don't know. I'm no expert. But if they're prepared to pay twenty grand to get them back, they must be worth a damn sight more.'

Cara glanced towards the window. It was dark outside, and

the wind rattled the pane. Every time the glass shuddered, she flinched. Seven days, she thought, and the clock had already started ticking. Anxiety streamed through her. She knew she had to stay calm, mustn't panic, had to keep a clear head, but it was easier said than done.

Douglas leaned forward. 'Have you had any more thoughts on where Jimmy could have hidden them?'

'No. I mean, they could be anywhere, couldn't they? He wouldn't have kept them in his flat or his van or even my place – too obvious – but as to where he *would* have stashed them . . .'

'Bank vault, garage, someone else's house? What about the guy who gave you the box?'

'Murch. No, I don't think so.'

'You have to put yourself in Jimmy's shoes, think like he'd think. You probably knew him better than anyone. Where would you have chosen if you were him?'

Cara racked her brains, but nothing came to her.

'Somewhere local, probably,' Douglas said. 'I doubt he'd have hidden them too far away in case he needed to get hold of them in a hurry.'

'Just the whole of Kellston to search, then. Shouldn't take too long.'

'You got a plan B in case you can't find them?'

'Do a runner?' she suggested, only half joking. 'Get as far away from here as possible.'

60

What Larry Steadman was feeling was aggravation: aggravation that a two-bit private investigator wouldn't cooperate, that he'd been made to look a fool in front of Tierney, that Cara Kendall was running rings round him. No one could accuse him of not putting in the hours, but hard work apparently didn't guarantee results.

He twisted a paper clip, straightening out the curved edges. The sounds of the police station – voices, ringing phones, the clatter of typewriters – flowed over and around him, barely heard. He was growing to hate Kellston more by the day, despising the borough and everyone who lived in it: liars, thieves, dealers, whores and murderers, the lot of them. If he had his way, he'd raze the bloody place to the ground and start again. Or maybe not even bother starting again. What would be the point? It would only return to what it had always been, a crime-ridden dump devoid of any moral backbone or conscience.

Larry snarled into his coffee. He thought about hauling Cara back into the station, of going through her statement again, line by line. Would she break? Not a chance. But it would inconvenience her at least, maybe eventually propel her into making one small mistake. That's all he needed. One inconsistency, one proven lie and he might begin to prise the lid off this whole sordid business.

He wondered where she'd got the money from to hire Glen Douglas. Investigators didn't come cheap, even the ones as far down the ladder as Douglas. She must have taken him on to track down her accomplice on the Hampstead job so she could claim her share of what she saw as rightly hers. She had kept her mouth shut at the trial, kept his identity a secret, and now she was owed.

If she didn't know exactly where the man was then that put Will Lytton out of the picture, and Murchison too. The chances of finding the mystery man seemed slight to Larry, but perhaps Cara had an idea of where he'd be. Sunning himself on some foreign beach, no doubt, enjoying his spoils from Hampstead and laughing at the whole bloody lot of them. Half a million quid was the estimated worth, although he'd get a good deal less from a fence. Enough to keep him in champagne, though. Enough to live a life of luxury until the money ran out.

Larry's fingers curled in frustration. They had been over Jimmy Lovell's flat and van with a fine toothcomb and found nothing but unpaid bills and receipts for petrol, beer and takeaways. All the receipts had been local, giving no indication that he had travelled further afield. But he'd been in it up to his neck, Larry was sure of it. And someone else had been sure of it too; Jimmy hadn't received that beating for nothing.

The Hampstead file, perused so many times, was beginning to take on a slightly tattered appearance. He laid his palms down on the papers and took several deep breaths. His head was full of all the frustrations he had felt back then, and all the longings. A dull ache throbbed in his temples. He had always considered himself a decent man, honourable, hard-working, but in the middle of the night, while his wife slept beside him, he fantasised about making Cara Kendall submit. And it was more than a confession he was after. He wanted to take her, possess her, *force* her to his will. Larry had become, he thought, the kind of man prepared to do anything to get what he wanted.

61

Ray Tierney was parked at the Fox, watching Douglas's office. He had seen the lights go on and off on the various floors, seen the people leave, until the only light left was on the first floor. It was an unofficial surveillance – he was off duty – and just something to pass the time until the pub opened, but now Cara Kendall had turned up and it had all got more interesting.

Ray sat in darkness, his gaze flicking between the windows and the door. What he wouldn't give to be a fly on the wall, to be able to overhear what the two of them were saying. Something must be happening. What if Douglas was planning to jump on a plane tonight in his quest to track down Cara's accomplice on the Hampstead job? That would mean a long and tedious drive to the airport but would be worth the bother if he found out where Douglas was going.

Until recently the favoured destination for London villains wanting to escape the law had been Spain. Now, with a new extradition treaty in place, they were having to look for fresh pastures, different destinations like North Cyprus or Brazil.

But for those that were already settled, who had their villas and their fancy cars, who were living it up on the Costa del Sol, the decision was a tough one. Did they move on or run the risk of staying?

Ray gazed out at the bleak November evening, thinking that he wouldn't mind a spot of sunshine himself. Perhaps, if luck ran their way, he and Steadman could be flying out to Malaga or Marbella to bring back a murderer. What were the odds? Slim, he thought. Unlike his boss, he was yet to be convinced that Cara had had anything to do with the death of Gerald Myers. Or Jimmy Lovell's death, either, come to that. But she *had* hired a private investigator and you didn't invest that kind of money unless you were sure of a return.

It was fifteen minutes before Cara Kendall left the building, turned right and headed for the high street. He watched until she disappeared round the corner. Going back to the Mansfield, he presumed. If he'd been closer, he might have been able to read her expression, but all he had to go on were her hunched shoulders and speed of pace, both of which could have been down to the cold as much as anything else. He lit a fag and waited to see what would happen next.

Another half-hour passed before Glen Douglas finally emerged. He crossed the road and went into the Fox. Ray was in two minds as to what to do next. Douglas could just be going for a quick pint, in which case he was better off staying put, or he could be there for the duration. He settled on a compromise: he would give it ten minutes, and if Douglas didn't reappear, he'd join him in the pub.

The Fox hadn't been open for long, but a slow and steady trickle of customers were already arriving for a well-deserved drink after a hard day at the office, or what might be, perhaps, an even harder evening at home with a disagreeable spouse or a ready meal for one in front of the TV. He was in no great hurry to get home himself. He might as well be here as anywhere else, keeping watch on a middle-aged man of doubtful integrity, and chasing after phantoms.

When the ten minutes were up, Ray got out of the car, locked up and strolled to the pub. Inside was pleasantly warm with a fire blazing in the hearth. He went over to the bar where his target was leaning against the counter with an almost empty pint glass in front of him. Douglas clocked him straight away, caught his eye and gave him a nod.

'Oh, hello,' Ray said, putting on a surprised look, as if it was sheer coincidence that the two of them had happened to meet again. He gestured towards the man's glass and asked, 'Would you like another?'

'What's the catch?' Douglas asked drily.

'No catch. Just doing my bit for community relations.'

'If I was the suspicious sort, I might think you were here to pick my brains about Cara Kendall.'

'Strictly off duty,' Ray said. 'I promise I won't even mention her name. Do you want that pint or not?'

Douglas considered it and then nodded again. 'All right, I'll have a drink with you.'

As if he was doing him a favour, Ray thought, even though it was the other way round. Perhaps he reckoned that a lowly DC didn't pose much of a threat when it came to wheedling information out of him. The barman came over – no Holly tonight – and Ray put in the order.

For a while they made the usual small talk: the weather, the state of the economy and whether West Ham were likely to win the league that year. Once these subjects had been exhausted, Ray moved on to the more interesting material.

'So what got you into the detecting business, Mr Douglas?'

'Insurance. I used to work in the investigations unit of Sullivans until they began "outsourcing" the cases.' He gave a rum shake of his head, as if outsourcing was the devil's work. 'So on the basis of if you can't beat 'em, join 'em, I decided I may as well be the one they outsourced it to. I make a living, not a *great* living, but I get by.'

'Your own boss, at least,' Ray said. 'There's a lot to be said for it.'

'I imagine *your* boss isn't the easiest to work for.'

'No comment,' Ray said.

'A man with a bee in his bonnet.'

Ray shrugged. He couldn't dispute the fact but wasn't about to badmouth Steadman in public. 'A man who doesn't like loose ends.'

'That's one way of putting it.'

The pub was filling up now and they moved a little further round the bar to make room for other customers. Ray allowed a few seconds to pass before saying, 'And what else do you investigate, apart from insurance claims?'

'Anything that comes my way: cheating husbands, cheating wives, thieving employees, lost dogs. Every day's a new adventure.'

'Missing persons?'

'Occasionally,' Douglas said with a sly smile on his face, knowing exactly what Ray was getting at.

'Must be like looking for a needle in a haystack sometimes.'

'It's not that easy to disappear completely, not unless you're living on the streets. You should know that. People usually leave some kind of trail.'

'Unless they're rich enough to cover their tracks.'

'Even then,' Douglas said. 'It's not as easy as it sounds. New place, new identity, always looking over your shoulder, always

341

thinking, perhaps, about the family and friends you've left behind.' He drank some of his pint and put the glass down on the bar. 'If it helps, I'm not looking for the man who killed Gerald Myers. I have no idea who that was, and Cara Kendall doesn't either.'

'I thought we weren't talking about Cara?' But then, because Cara was exactly the person he *did* want to talk about, Ray quickly added, 'But seeing as we're on the subject ... what makes you so sure?'

'Have you ever considered that she could be the victim in all this?'

'She was hardly a victim when she climbed into the Myerses' house and tried to nick their valuables.'

'That was then, this is now. She's paid for that. She's done her time, hasn't she? DI Steadman seems determined to make her pay twice.'

'It's the murder of Jimmy Lovell we're investigating.'

Douglas raised his eyebrows. '*You* might be, but I think your boss is more interested in past history.'

'You don't reckon the two murders could be connected?'

'Could be. On the other hand ...'

Ray had a quick glance around the bar before his gaze came to rest on Douglas again. 'Shouldn't we be on the same side? I mean, if Cara does know anything, anything useful, then surely we're better pooling our resources, working together rather than against each other.'

'It's a fine idea, but I think she may have lost faith in the boys in blue.'

'If she isn't straight with us, it's hard to help her.'

'Do you want to help her?'

'We're not the enemy, Mr Douglas.'

'I'll take your word for it.'

Ray wasn't surprised by the attitude. Steadman's overbearing approach that morning had done little to encourage either cooperation or trust.

Glen Douglas drained what was left of his beer. 'Thanks for the pint. I owe you one.'

'You off home?'

'Bradshaw Street,' Douglas said, 'to save you the bother of following me. Have a pleasant evening, Mr Tierney.'

Ray didn't respond to the dig about the tail. 'No parting words of wisdom?'

Douglas smoothed down his tie while he thought about it. 'I'll give you this for nothing. You don't strike me as a happy man. Perhaps you should do something about that.'

It wasn't what Ray had been expecting. As he tried to think of a suitable reply, Douglas was already walking away. After he'd gone, Ray gazed at his reflection in the mirror behind the bar. Was that the face of an unhappy man? He thought, on balance, that it probably was.

62

Cara could see Murch's van parked in front of Temple as she strode up the main path of the estate. Good, he was home. She wasn't looking forward to what would probably be another less than pleasant conversation with Rochelle, but the sooner she got it over with, the better. And maybe Rochelle wouldn't even be there. She might get the chance to talk to Murch on his own, to ask if the girl was in fact Lytton's sister and, once it was confirmed, put the whole thing to rest.

After her recent encounter with Terry Street, she wondered if the Lytton/Rochelle thing even mattered. She knew who was after her now, and why. Lytton's lies, although disheartening, weren't relevant to the major crisis unfolding around her. Still, it never did any harm to tie up loose ends.

She thought of Terry Street again and shuddered. Would she have been better off denying everything? But that way she'd have had him, and the Russians, permanently on her back. She wouldn't have been able to go anywhere or do anything without them watching her. And maybe worse than just watching. Not that she had a clue when it came to where to go or what to do: all that was still firmly resting in the realm of the great unknown. Would Murch have any idea where Jimmy had hidden the diamonds? Did he even know about the diamonds?

She reached Temple, took the lift to the seventh floor, walked along the corridor and knocked on Murch's door. Music was coming from the other side, a heavy metal beat. When no one answered, she knocked again, harder this time. Eventually there was the sound of the door being unlocked.

Murch looked neither surprised nor pleased to see her. 'Oh, hey, you all right?'

'Can I come in?'

Murch shrugged, turned away and walked back into the living room, leaving Cara to close the door behind her. The music was much louder inside, harsh and insistent, the kind of noise that stopped you being able to think. She followed him through, wanting to put her fingers in her ears.

Rochelle was lying on the sofa, smoking a joint. It was warm in the flat and the smell of dope lay heavily on the air. She looked at Cara and scowled. 'Jesus. What do *you* want?'

Cara got straight to the point. 'Why didn't you tell me Will Lytton was your brother?'

'You never asked.'

'I don't see what the big secret is. Why didn't you want me to know?'

Even under the influence of cannabis, Rochelle was about as chilled out as an angry cobra. 'What business is it of yours?' she hissed. 'Why can't you keep your fuckin' nose out of it?'

'It is my business when he's living in my flat.'

'So get rid of him. You think I want him hanging around? Kick him out, see if I care.'

Cara looked at Murch. 'Did you know about this?'

345

Murch gave a dismissive shrug as if he not only considered the whole matter irrelevant, but also had no desire to get involved. 'You want a beer?'

'No, thanks. Look, can we have a word in private? Just the two of us.'

'Is this about Will because—'

'No, it's nothing to do with him.'

Murch considered the request, probably trying to think of a reason to refuse, couldn't come up with one, sighed and said, 'Make yourself scarce, Rochelle.'

'Huh?'

'You heard.'

Rochelle sat up, glaring at him. 'And go where?'

'Anywhere. Just get the fuck out for five minutes.'

'It's freezing out there.'

'So take a coat. Or wait on the landing.'

Rochelle, realising this was an argument she wasn't going to win, got to her feet, threw Cara a filthy look and exited the flat, taking the joint with her. Cara waited until the front door had closed before saying, 'Could you turn the music down a bit?'

Murch went over to the stereo and reduced the volume to a level that was more tolerable. 'So what is it? What do you want?'

Cara sat down on the sofa, giving her ears a moment to adjust. Although her main reason for coming had been to check out the Lytton story, she was desperate enough to probe him again about the silver box. 'That box Jimmy gave you. Was there anything in it?'

Murch remained standing, as if to press home the point that this conversation wasn't going to last too long. 'I already told you. It was empty.'

'Yeah, well, people say all sorts of things.'

'You calling me a liar?'

'I'm just asking, that's all.'

'And I'm telling you. There was nothing in the box. End of story, okay?'

Cara stared at him, wondering where it had started, this enmity between the two of them. A strained politeness was about the best they'd ever managed to achieve in the five years she'd been with Jimmy. She suspected Murch of resenting her for taking his best mate away, and she knew that she'd often resented the amount of time the two friends had spent together. She and Murch had been like jealous kids, each one vying for the most attention. 'Okay, I get it.'

'Good. So, is that it? Are we done here?'

Cara heard relief in his voice and saw him visibly relax. As if he'd got away with whatever he was trying to hide. And he *was* hiding something. She was sure of it. Murch wasn't a good liar, not even a passable one. She took a shot in the dark. 'What else did he give you to keep, apart from the box?'

'Jesus, I've just said that—'

'That there was nothing in the box. Yeah, I heard you. But he gave you something else. I know he did. You need to hand them over, Murch. You hang on to them, and you're going to be in even bigger trouble than I am. Terry Street collared me an hour ago and he's not a happy man.'

Murch paled at the mention of Terry Street. 'What?'

'They're no use to you,' Cara went on. 'It's not like you can sell them. You try and you'll be a dead man. Terry Street will see to that.'

Murch's eyes widened. He shifted from one foot to the other, his gaze sliding around the room, his eyes resting anywhere but on her face. He didn't protest, didn't claim he didn't know what she was talking about. Cara said nothing, letting him think about it, letting it sink in. Suddenly he caved. 'Jimmy brought

347

them round on Wednesday evening. It was about ten o'clock. He said he didn't want them in his flat, that he'd pick them up early in the morning before I went to work, but he didn't show. I called him but . . .'

Relief streamed through Cara. She hadn't expected it to be this easy, hadn't even dreamed that Murch might actually have the diamonds in his possession. Now she knew that he had, it was an end to all her problems. She could collect the box from Douglas, put the stones back inside, pass the box to Terry and he could give it to the Russian. End of story. Everyone happy. Well, as happy as they could be in the circumstances. She tried not to look too pleased, too triumphant.

'Is that where he went on Wednesday evening, to pick them up?'

'Dunno. I guess.'

'Do you know who gave them to him?'

'He didn't say. He didn't tell me nothin'. Just asked me to take care of them until the morning.'

Cara didn't believe that Murch wouldn't have asked. Your best mate gives you a load of flashy diamonds to take care of and you're likely to have a few questions. But she wasn't going to push him. What did any of that matter now? It was enough to know that they were here, safe and that the nightmare would shortly be over. Impatiently she asked, 'So, can I have them?'

Murch stopped his restless shifting and put his hands in his pockets. For one awful moment she feared he was going to refuse, maybe even try to negotiate a deal and squeeze some cash out of her, but if the thought crossed his mind, it must have exited again at speed. Clearly, he was as scared of Terry Street as she was.

'They're in the bedroom. I'll go and get them.'

'Thank you.'

Murch stopped by the door and said, 'I told him to stay away from Terry.'

'Shame he didn't listen.'

Murch mumbled something she couldn't hear above the music.

Cara waited, relieved beyond measure. She could feel the quick beating of her heart in anticipation of what she was about to see. Thank God, she thought.

It was less than a minute before Murch came back holding a large brown envelope. 'Here,' he said, throwing it into her lap.

As soon as Cara felt the contents, she frowned: not lumpy like a stash of diamonds should be, but a couple of slim hard oblongs. Now she was getting anxious. Quickly she tore open the envelope and delved inside. What she pulled out caused her heart to sink. Instead of a pile of glittering gemstones, she had two British passports in her hand.

'I don't understand,' she said, looking up at Murch. 'Is this it? Is this all he gave you?'

'What were you expecting?'

Cara almost blurted it out but bit her lip at the last moment. She didn't think Murch was holding out on her and perhaps the less he knew about the diamonds, the better. 'It doesn't matter.'

She flipped open the first of the passports and saw an unsmiling photo of Jimmy along with the name Jack Marshall. A fake, obviously, but a good one, and certainly good enough to pass muster at a bustling ferry port. The second contained her own picture – a copy of her legitimate passport photo – and the name Ella Marshall. Confusion swept over her. Why would he have got her a fake passport too? But the answer was obvious: Jimmy had been planning on doing a runner with the diamonds and had expected her or wanted her to leave with him.

'Why didn't you tell me about these?' she asked, looking up at Murch.

'Why should I?' he retorted, sounding as petulant as Rochelle. 'They're not much use to you now.'

'Did Jimmy tell you he was leaving?'

'He said he was in trouble, had to make himself scarce for a while.'

Cara nodded. She wondered why Murch would think Terry Street had the hump over a couple of forged passports, but maybe he thought they hadn't been paid for yet or that Terry wanted them back for some other reason. She stuffed the passports into the envelope, put the envelope in her bag and pulled the zipper across.

'Anything else I should know about?'

'Like what?' Murch said.

'You tell me.'

'You've got what you came for,' Murch said sullenly.

Cara stood up, at a loss as to what to do next. She suspected that Murch had kept the passports out of spite, resentful perhaps that Jimmy had been planning on leaving with her. She could have told him that she hadn't had a clue about it, about any of Jimmy's plans, but she wasn't going to waste her breath. Crushing disappointment bore down on her. Fear crept back into her head. Just for a while she had imagined everything was going to be all right, and now she was back to square one.

63

There was no sign of Lytton when Cara got back to the flat. It crossed her mind that he could have packed his bags and left, but when she checked his room, his belongings were still there. Just keeping out of the way then. Probably a wise move in the circumstances.

She sat down, took the envelope out of her bag, slid the passports on to the table, opened them both and laid them side by side. Jack and Ella Marshall. A fake marriage as well as fake identities. She felt a spurt of resentment at Jimmy's presumption. Why *would* she have wanted to leave with him? They'd been over, finished, an ex-couple when he'd decided to plan her future for her. He'd had no right. Although, if she looked at it another way, it could also mean that he'd finally realised that *she* was the one he wanted to be with. Had he simply intended to give her the choice? *Come with me if you want to. It's up to you.*

She wondered where he had got the passports from, although it wasn't hard in a place like Kellston to find someone willing to point you in the right direction. If you had money almost anything was available. Perhaps Terry had given him some cash up front, a down payment on what would eventually be coming to him.

If nothing else Jimmy's intentions for last Thursday morning were clearer to her now: pick up the diamonds (from wherever they were hidden), collect the passports from Murch, meet her outside the jail and make her an offer she couldn't refuse. She tried to imagine how that offer would have gone: 'How do you fancy spending the rest of your life on the run with me?' A proposal no right-minded girl could possibly resist. 'I'm in a spot of bother, you see. I've got a stash of diamonds, but Terry Street and some Russian bastards want them back. We can go anywhere you fancy so long as it's out of the country.'

Cara thought about where she would have liked to go: Paris, Florence, a Greek island with sandy beaches and bustling tavernas. Would she have turned him down, knowing that she would probably never see him again? Or would she have taken the ultimate gamble? In truth, she couldn't put her hand on her heart and swear she wouldn't have been tempted.

Perhaps Jimmy would have packed a bag for her on that Thursday morning, come to the flat when Lytton wasn't around and taken some clothes, a few bits of jewellery, the photograph of her dad. Maybe, if he'd had the nous to think of it, even her dad's old address book with its useful list of contact numbers.

'What have you got to keep you in Kellston?' he might have said. And the answer would have been 'nothing'. She had no family here now, no close friends. Or perhaps he would have taken a different approach, told her she wouldn't be safe staying in London or that he loved her and needed her with him or that . . .

Cara gazed down at the passports. All she had was her imagination. Jimmy's reasoning, whatever it may have been, had died with him. Why Ella, she wondered. Why had he chosen that name? Why Jack? But perhaps he hadn't had a choice. The passports could have been stolen and the photographs replaced with new ones.

She understood now why Jimmy had never got back to Lytton about vacating the flat. It hadn't mattered any more, not if she was going away with him. And if she'd said no? Well, he wouldn't have been around to face the music when she found she had an unexpected flatmate. He'd have taken off by then, driving down to Dover or Folkestone to catch the first ferry out of the country, to start a new life with his dreams and his diamonds.

Cara closed the passports and placed them back in the envelope. She wasn't sure what to do with them. Her first thought was Glen Douglas. But then she reconsidered. Steadman knew that he was working for her. If the inspector managed to get a search warrant for the office, he would demand that the safe be opened. The silver box wouldn't be a problem – it was doubtful that anyone had reported it as stolen – but the fake passports would be tricky to explain. No, she couldn't put Douglas in that position. Even if he agreed, it wasn't fair on him.

Until she could think of somewhere better, she'd have to keep the passports in the flat. Her usual hiding place, in the base of the wardrobe, would do. If Steadman decided to search here, they might be found or might not depending on how smart the officers were. There was another option, of course, and that was to get rid of them. She could burn them in the kitchen sink, reduce them to ashes. The only reason she dismissed this idea was the disturbing thought that she might be needing one of them in the not-too-distant future.

64

By Saturday Cara was tearing her hair out. She had searched high and low, everywhere she could think of. When all else failed she had even checked out the other cisterns in the Fox. If Murch had concealed the box there, maybe Jimmy had done the same with the diamonds. This had been tricky when it came to the gents, but she'd got to the pub straight after opening time, praying that no male customer would be so inconsiderate as to want to open his bowels before she'd completed the check. All she'd got for her trouble, however, was wet hands and a suspicion of having caught something from which she might never recover.

Cara blew her nose, threw the tissue in the wastepaper bin and tried to get her brain in gear. She had a fog in her head and an ache in her temples. None of it was helped by a rising sense of panic. Was it possible that the stones were still in Jimmy's flat, hidden somewhere she hadn't thought of? But this didn't tally with the other precautions he'd taken, like leaving the passports with Murch or asking him to get rid of the box. No, he would have stashed the diamonds somewhere else, just in case he had any uninvited visitors. But where?

Trying to get into Jimmy's mind, like Douglas had suggested, was proving an impossibility. Half the places she thought of, she almost instantly dismissed as being too public or too difficult to get to in a hurry. There was no paperwork for anything official like a safety deposit box. Could he have hidden them, or buried them, on the green? But that would have been too risky. They could have been discovered by a dog or a kid or one of the council gardeners who put in an appearance from time to time. What about the lifts, here or at Temple? The panels on the ceilings must lift off. She considered it but then dismissed this idea too. The damn lifts were always breaking down and the engineers being called out.

She heard Lytton moving around, heard him go into the bathroom and the door close behind him. He'd been avoiding her for the past couple of days, leaving early and coming back late. The whole Rochelle business felt irrelevant now, unimportant compared to what could be described as the life and death situation that was currently playing out. And she wasn't even being melodramatic. If she failed to produce the diamonds, certain people were going to get very, very angry. And she was the one they were going to vent their fury on . . .

Cara shivered and blew her nose again. The harder she tried to think, the greater her headache. She gazed out of the window at the iron-coloured sky. She felt more trapped than when she'd been in prison, even less in control of her own destiny. Unless she could find the stones, she'd had it.

It was another five minutes before Lytton came into the living room. He was wearing jeans and a sweater and the sort of hangdog expression that suggested he was expecting more recriminations. But she was past all that. There were more important things to worry about. In case he started trying to explain again, to apologise again, she quickly said, 'Where would you hide something round here? I don't mean in the flat, just locally.'

'How big a something?' he said, relieved perhaps that they had moved on from the subject of his sister.

'Small,' she said. 'Smallish, at least.' Cara lifted her left hand from the table and curled her fingers. 'Small enough to fit in my palm, I should think.'

'Are we talking about the "Give it back" note here?'

'Yes, that's exactly what we're talking about.'

Lytton didn't ask what she thought the something was but instead walked past her towards the kitchen. 'I'll need a coffee before I put my mind to that. You want one?'

'Thanks,' she said, reaching for the tissues again.

While the kettle was boiling, Lytton leaned against the doorjamb and said, 'You got a cold?'

'You'd better keep your distance if you don't want to catch it too.'

'Too late for that,' he said. 'I've been sniffling since I got up.'

Cara reckoned he deserved it, a just reward for his deceit. 'If you don't want to hide it where you live or in your car or at a mate's place, what are the alternatives?'

'At work?'

'Jimmy worked out of the van,' she said. 'If anything had been there, the law would have found it. He did some jobs for Murch's dad, but he doesn't have an office either.' She wondered if Jimmy could have hidden the diamonds at Mr and Mrs Murchison's house but thought it unlikely.

Lytton made the coffee, came back into the living room and put the two mugs on the table. 'What about a lockup?'

Cara considered this. Lockups were where most villains stored their dodgy gear until they could sell it on. There was a long row of them at the Arches, underneath the railway station, the size of their padlocks probably in proportion to the value of the stolen goods stored inside. 'Then where's the key gone? So far as I know the law didn't find it at Jimmy's flat or in the van. I think they'd have asked me if they'd come across one that couldn't be accounted for.'

'But a key's easy to hide, much smaller probably than what you're looking for.'

Cara's heart sank as she acknowledged the truth in this. 'Wouldn't there be paperwork, a contract, if you wanted to rent out somewhere like that?'

'I should imagine a lot of these agreements are cash in hand. Or Jimmy could have got rid of any contract if he wanted to make sure there wasn't a paper trail.'

'Now you're depressing me.' Cara thought of all the places a key could be hidden, all the crevices and gaps, all the spaces tiny enough to conceal a small piece of metal. You could put it behind a loose brick, under a stone, push it into the soil of a plant pot, sew it into the hem of a jacket or make a slim cut in a mattress. You could drop it into a coffee jar or maybe, if it was small enough, even hide it inside an electrical plug. The possibilities were endless.

'Would he have used a lockup, though?' Lytton said, his brow furrowing. 'It might have felt too risky. What if someone had broken into it? What if he was seen there? If it was me, I'm not sure, on balance, if I'd have taken the chance.'

Cara perked up, praying he was right. It was true that anyone could have come along and taken a pair of bolt cutters to the door. And Terry Street probably knew the identity of everyone who used the lockups at the Arches. If Jimmy had rented one, Terry would have heard about it by now. She drank her coffee, trying to be positive.

Lytton gazed into the middle distance for a moment, his mug poised halfway to his mouth. Then, as if an idea had suddenly come to him, he put the mug back down on the table. 'Wouldn't he have hidden this thing somewhere familiar, somewhere you'd have been able to figure out? You know, a favourite haunt or somewhere special to just the two of you. He'd have wanted you to have it if anything happened to him, wouldn't he, to be able to work out where it was?'

'But I can't. I can't think of *anywhere*.' Cara rubbed her face and sighed. 'The Fox is where we went to most and I've looked there. Well, in the only places it was likely to be. I mean, we did the usual stuff – the cinema, theatre, days out, holidays – but I can't think of a place that was more special to him than any other.'

'Special to you, then. Isn't there anywhere he was sure you'd eventually look?'

And that's when it came to her. In a blinding flash, she realised exactly where the diamonds were. How could she have been so stupid? What an imbecile! The one place Jimmy was sure she'd go to when she got out of jail.

'Have you thought of something?'

'No,' Cara lied, trying to keep her voice steady. 'Not yet. I need some fresh air. I can't think straight. I need to get out of here for a while.'

'Want some company?'

'No, I won't be long. I'm only going round the block. I just want to clear my head.'

'Are you sure it's safe?'

'I think they've given up for now,' she said. 'Don't worry, I'll be fine.'

As she headed for the door, Cara felt the excitement rising inside her. She had it. She knew where they were. With

Lytton's help she'd finally figured it out. What better place to hide a stash of sparkling white gemstones than in the middle of a pile of quartz? The diamonds, she was certain, were on her dad's grave.

65

On her way to the cemetery Cara crossed the high street twice, carefully choosing the moment to abruptly dart between the cars and buses, trying to flush out anyone who might be on her tail. Then she walked at a leisurely pace, stopping and starting, gazing in shop windows and checking out the reflections of the people behind her. She had to be certain that she wasn't being followed. Did she trust Terry Street to stay away? Not in the slightest. And she didn't trust the Russians either.

So far as she could tell, she was alone. But maybe they were using more people this time, men and women who could merge unnoticed into the crowd of Saturday shoppers. She went into the chemist, browsed for a while and bought a small pack of tissues. As she came out, she glanced quickly to her left and right, hoping to catch anyone who might have stopped to wait for her. No one. But still she couldn't relax. She was excited, desperate to get to the grave, but it wasn't worth taking any chances.

One last precaution. When she reached the station, Cara went in, checked out the times of the trains and bought the cheapest ticket she could. She went down the steps to the platform and walked to the far end. She took a tissue from the pack, blew her nose and surreptitiously looked around again. There were about ten other people waiting. A couple more came down the steps, two women with carrier bags in their hands, followed by a youngish man and then a group of lads. None of them looked at her, but that didn't mean anything.

It felt like a long five minutes before the train finally pulled into the station. Cara got into the last carriage on her own and stood watching as the other passengers got on and off. Then, just as the beeps went to indicate that the doors were closing, she quickly stepped back on to the platform. As the train pulled out, she had the satisfaction of knowing that if she had had a tail, they were now on their way to Liverpool Street.

She walked rapidly to the steps, took them two at a time, and hurried out of the station. It was quite possible that the entire manoeuvre had been unnecessary, but she felt less anxious having done it. Now she could get on with the business of retrieving the diamonds.

Cara took the fastest route to the cemetery and strode up the main path. It was busier than the last time she'd been here, with half a dozen cars parked by the gates. She wasn't sure if this made it safer or less safe: more witnesses if anyone went for her, but also more people to keep an eye on. Hopefully she no longer had to worry about being followed, but that worry was hard to shake off completely.

She veered off the path on to a narrower one and was glad to see that there was no one in the immediate vicinity. Her pulse was racing as she knelt by her dad's grave. 'It's only me,' she said, touching the smooth white marble of the headstone.

The flowers she had placed in front of it had begun to wilt and she wished she had brought some more with her. She had a final good look round before starting to gently shift the quartz chips aside in the oblong kerb.

Jimmy would have made sure the diamonds were well hidden, buried down at the bottom. She carefully burrowed towards the base, shifting the layers, poking and prodding, but it soon became apparent that if they were here, they weren't in any kind of package.

Cara sat back on her heels and sighed. They must have been split up and scattered more haphazardly. Being loose would make them harder to spot, but she wasn't discouraged. They were here somewhere, and she was going to find them.

For the next ten minutes she worked quickly but methodically, picking up handfuls of the quartz chips, examining them and putting them to one side on the grass. While she went through this procedure, she thought about what she would do next: get the silver box back from Douglas, arrange to meet Terry Street and hand over the accursed diamonds that had been the cause of so much misery. And then it would be over. No more threats, no more fear, no more looking over her shoulder.

But the longer her search went on, the more her confidence began to drain away. One handful after another was discarded until eventually the kerb was empty. She stared down at it, distraught and disbelieving. Not a damn diamond in sight.

'Where are you?' she muttered in frustration.

Cara picked up several of the chips and held them to the light. Was she missing something? No, she knew the difference between a quartz chip and a diamond. Slowly, carefully, she reversed the procedure, returning the quartz to the kerb after re-examining each small handful. The result remained the same. When the job was done, she could have wept. Nothing. Racked with dismay and disappointment, she covered her face with her hands. She'd been so sure, but she'd been wrong. Wherever Jimmy had put them, it wasn't here.

66

Larry Steadman had that familiar feeling of distaste as he walked across the Mansfield, taking in the three high-rise towers, the litter and graffiti. A concrete monstrosity. The buildings, probably once white, had taken on a uniform greyness, their exterior walls stained by the weather and exhaust fumes. Endless rows of windows were like blind eyes staring out. A pall hung over the place, a depressing shroud of hopelessness.

He always thought the estate had an odd smell, something he couldn't quite put his finger on, something more than the lingering stink of dope and urine that lingered in the air of the foyers. He lifted his head and sniffed. Perhaps it was simply desperation. As he made his way to Haslow House he noticed how no one was prepared to acknowledge him, how every gaze slid away. Even the innocent didn't want to know. For the residents the law was like an unpleasant disease, something to stay away from, to be avoided at all costs.

Larry had better things to do on a Saturday morning, or should have, but he couldn't get Cara Kendall out of his head.

He could have called and asked her to come to the station, but he wanted to see her at home. It was an idea he had that he might learn more from talking to her in her own surroundings. Or was he just curious to see where she lived again? It was over eighteen months since he'd last been in the flat, after the murder of Gerald Myers, when they'd done a search to see if there was any other stolen property there – or any clues to the identity of her accomplice.

Larry pushed through the door into the foyer, took the lift up to the tenth floor, found the right flat and rang the bell. The man who answered was in his early thirties, dressed in jeans and a sweater. Larry flashed his badge. 'DI Steadman. Is Cara Kendall here?'

'Sorry, she's not in. Do you want to leave a message?'

'Do you know how long she'll be?'

'No idea, I'm afraid.'

'You must be Will Lytton.'

'That's me,' the man said.

'Perhaps I could come in and wait.'

'If you like, but she could be gone all day.'

Larry stepped forward anyway, forcing Lytton to retreat. 'Did she say where she was going?'

'No. She isn't answerable to me, inspector. We just share a flat.'

Larry looked around the living room. It was a clean, tidy space with a good view over the city. There were books on the shelves, magazines in a rack and a large print of a woman and child standing in front of a hill. A photograph of Richard Kendall had pride of place on the cabinet, his smiling face gazing out from a gilt frame. It was all vaguely familiar to him and yet five minutes ago he couldn't have described it.

'Would you like tea or coffee while you wait?'

'Tea, please,' Larry said. 'One sugar.'

While Lytton went off to the kitchen, Larry sat down on the sofa. He tried to imagine Cara here, moving around or standing by the window. Would she be long? When she came through the door, she would not be pleased to see him and the thought of this sent a small ripple of pleasure down his spine. In the meantime, he would make the most of the opportunity to interrogate Lytton.

There was the sound of the kettle boiling and then switching off. A few minutes later Lytton appeared with two mugs. He placed them on the coffee table, sat down in the easy chair and asked, 'Do you have news about Jimmy?'

'Did you know him well?' Larry asked, deflecting the question with another.

'Hardly at all. We got talking in the Fox one night and I told him I was looking for somewhere to live. Jimmy said this place was free for six months so . . .' Lytton raised and dropped his hands. 'Here I am. After that I didn't see much of him. We'd bump into each other occasionally, but that was about the sum of it.'

'He rented it out to you?'

'That's right.'

'And Cara? How well do you know her?'

'About as well as anyone can when they've been sharing a flat for five minutes.'

'You've not met before, then?'

'No, never,' Lytton said.

'And now you're stuck in the middle of all this.'

Lytton frowned and leaned forward a little. 'I can't say I really view myself as being in the middle of it, inspector. I do feel sorry for her, though. It's shocking what happened, truly awful, especially with her finding him like that. It's enough to knock anyone for six.'

'She'll get over it,' Larry said. 'She's tougher than she looks.'

'But I gather they were close once. A couple, weren't they? That's what she told me. I think she's taken it pretty hard. Christ, why would anyone want to kill Jimmy?'

'For the usual reasons, I expect: profit, revenge, love, hate. Take your pick. Do you have any ideas, Mr Lytton?'

Lytton looked startled. 'Me? God no! Like I said, I hardly knew him.'

Larry was watching him closely, alert to any sign he might be lying. Nothing was immediately obvious, no nervous or defensive gestures, no avoidance of eye contact or excessive blinking. Larry drank some tea. He let a silence fall over the room. People were often discomfited by this, wanting to fill the emptiness with any kind of blather, but Lytton said nothing.

'I understand you're a student,' Larry said eventually.

If Lytton was unnerved by the police knowing his business, he didn't show it. 'That's right. History. I'm at Kellston Poly.'

'A bit old for that, aren't you?'

'Never too old to learn. Isn't that what they say?' Lytton gave a thin smile. 'Am I being interviewed, inspector?'

'Just trying to solve a murder, Mr Lytton. You don't mind helping with enquiries, do you?'

'Of course not, although I'm not entirely sure how I *can* help.'

'Has Cara had any visitors since Jimmy Lovell's death?'

'Only Jimmy's brother – Neil, is it? – and his wife. I don't remember her name. They came the day after, Friday. Other than that . . .' Lytton gave a shrug. 'I'm out all day so I wouldn't know. She hasn't mentioned anyone else.'

'And phone calls?'

'No, well, not unless you count the heavy breather. I believe she told you about him or told the constable. And the threatening note.'

'But you weren't actually here when she got the call or received the note?'

'What exactly are you implying, inspector?'

'Just trying to establish the facts.' What Larry was also trying to work out was if Lytton was Cara Kendall's type, but as he only had Jimmy to go on it was hard to tell. The two men certainly appeared very different. Jimmy, with his obvious good looks, had always been a man's man, a bit of a lad, a charmer with an eye for the ladies. A small-time villain too. Not stupid, but not overly smart either, unless he'd had hidden depths. Will Lytton, on the other hand, was a different kettle of fish altogether. He was the quieter, more thoughtful type, although that might just have been the impression he was trying to give.

Larry finished his tea and glanced at his watch. 'Would you mind if I had a look round?'

'Why?' Lytton looked faintly amused. 'Do you think Cara might be hiding from you?'

Larry wouldn't have put it past her. He rose to his feet, struck by a sudden desire to see where it was that she slept, where she laid her guilty head at night. 'If you've got no objections ...'

'Don't you need a search warrant for this kind of thing?'

'I don't wish to search the place, Mr Lytton. Just a quick look will suffice.'

Lytton hesitated but then stood up too. 'All right, I'll show you.'

All the flats in the blocks were similar, laid out to the same plan. The only difference was the colour of the walls, the carpets and the furniture. Larry had been in lots of them, but this was the only one he had ever really looked at. His eyes took in every detail as Lytton led him out of the living room and along the hallway towards the rest of the accommodation.

'My room,' Lytton said, pushing open the door and standing aside.

Larry poked his head in, his gaze quickly absorbing what little there was to see. The room was very masculine, simply furnished without any frills. There was a T-shirt lying on the bed and a few books piled up on one of the bedside tables. He presumed this had once been Richard Kendall's bedroom, but if he had ever stamped his personality on it there was no evidence of it now.

The bathroom was next. Towels folded. Toilet and sink clean. Taps gleaming. Larry glanced inside and moved on. There was only one room he really wanted to see and his pulse quickened as they approached it.

'And this is Cara's room,' Lytton said unnecessarily. Perhaps there was a hint of mockery in his tone.

Larry stepped inside. The walls were white, the curtains and carpet light green. A double bed, neatly made, was covered with a patterned bedspread. On the dressing table was a comb, deodorant, a bottle of perfume and some cosmetics. A suitcase lay on top of the wardrobe. On the wall directly opposite the bed was a large, framed print of a lonely stretch of beach merging into a sea-blue horizon. There was an emptiness about the scene, something that disturbed him slightly. He looked away, looked back, as if with a fresh pair of eyes he could see what she saw. He was searching for the essence of her, but it still eluded him.

Lytton stuck close, concerned perhaps that he might try and plant something incriminating. No one on the Mansfield trusted a cop. Larry continued to examine the room, deliberately taking his time. There was no sign of any cohabiting, no cross mingling of clothes or shoes, of dressing gowns or slippers. No, he couldn't see the two of them together, at least not in a sexual way.

'I'll tell Cara that you dropped by,' Lytton said. 'Would you like to leave a message?'

Larry turned to him, his expression affable, his voice less so. 'When she gets back tell her to come to the station. I need her to go through her statement again.'

67

Cara traipsed along the landing to the flat, cold and miserable and weighed down by disappointment. What was she going to do now? The cemetery had been her last roll of the dice, the only place she could think of where Jimmy would have stashed the diamonds. He hadn't just left her with a puzzle she couldn't solve, but a whole heap of trouble too. The thought that she hadn't known him quite as well as she'd imagined filled her with gloom. Five years they'd been together, and she clearly didn't have a clue.

Things didn't improve once she was inside.

'You just missed DI Steadman,' Lytton said, looking up from the book he was reading.

'God, what did *he* want?'

'To go over your statement, apparently. He said to call by the station when you got back. I told him I didn't know when that would be.'

'Good. Thanks. He can wait until tomorrow then.'

'Any more ideas about the Jimmy thing?'

'No,' she said, unwilling to share her recent failure. Or to share the only idea that was left in her head: she had to leave Kellston before it was too late. Terry Street would expect her to hand over the diamonds next week and she'd exhausted all the possibilities of where they could be. She could sit around and wait for inspiration, or she could get the hell out while she still had the opportunity.

Cara's thoughts were shifting quickly now. Where would she go? How would she pay for it? What would she need? The bare essentials, that was all. And one of those was right in front of her. She picked up the photo of her dad and said casually, 'You know, I think I'll put this in my own room.'

'You don't need to move it on my account.'

'No, I'd prefer it in there.'

Lytton put down his book. 'Steadman insisted on looking round while he was here.'

'What did he want to do that for?'

'I don't know. To check that you weren't hiding under the bed, perhaps. Don't worry, I kept an eye on him. I made sure he didn't touch anything. He seemed very interested in your room, though – just stood there staring at everything.'

'Probably trying to think of a way to stitch me up.'

'He asked if you'd had any visitors. I told him about Neil and his wife. That was okay, wasn't it? I figured he might know anyway.'

'Sure, that's not a problem. Anything else?'

'Only about the note and the phone calls. Whether I was here or not when you received them.'

Cara rolled her eyes. 'No prizes for guessing what he thinks about them, then. Jesus, that man never stops. He'd arrest me for Jimmy's murder if he could.'

'Yeah, well, you've got a cast-iron alibi for that. I could be wrong, but I got the impression he might have suspected there was something going on between the two of us, that we were more than just flatmates. He was interested in how I came to be living here.'

'Now he really is clutching at straws.'

Lytton's eyebrows went up. 'I'll try not to take that too personally.'

'You know what I mean. I wasn't . . .'

Lytton grinned. 'It's all right. I won't take it to heart. I think you could have a point about him, though: he strikes me as a man on a mission. You should watch your back.'

If Cara had retained any doubts about leaving, they were rapidly slipping away. Steadman was up to something. If she hung around, she could find herself in a cell by this time tomorrow on a trumped-up charge of accessory to murder or the like. 'Today's just getting better and better,' she said, before retreating from the room with the photograph.

In her bedroom Cara put the photo on the dressing table and then took down the suitcase from the top of the wardrobe. She laid it on the bed, unzipped it, pulled out the backpack that was stored inside and put the empty suitcase back where it had been. A plan was already forming in her head. She had to get out of Kellston, and fast. If Steadman didn't get her, Terry Street or the Russian would.

France seemed like the smartest option – a bus to Victoria, a train to Dover and then the ferry to Calais. It would help if she had a timetable, but she'd just have to hope that there would be some crossings tonight. November, well out of the tourist season, was hardly the best month to travel. Still, if the worst came to the worst, she could find a cheap B&B until she could get across the Channel.

Cara packed carefully, choosing only what was strictly

necessary. She wrapped her dad's photo in a sweater and slid it between the clothes. From the bathroom she took shampoo, her toothbrush and toothpaste. Travelling light was the best way to get around. This time tomorrow, if all went well, she'd be a hundred miles from here.

Once the packing was done, she cleared out the shoes in the bottom of the wardrobe, unscrewed the base and retrieved the one hundred and fifty pounds that was left of her stash. What about the fake passports? She couldn't leave them here. Her own might be useful, but she would have to destroy Jimmy's. She chucked them both on the bed, re-screwed the base into place and put the shoes back in their straight tidy lines.

Cara went to the living room where Lytton was still sitting on the sofa with his head in a book. She walked over to the cabinet and, taking care to block his view, removed a pad of writing paper, some envelopes, stamps and her dad's old address book. From a cubbyhole she dug out a handful of French francs, coins left there by her father after one of his Calais trips. Probably only enough for a cup of coffee or two, but every little helped.

Back in the bedroom, she perched on the edge of the bed and wrote a letter to her mother, telling her not to worry but that she needed to get away, was going to Edinburgh for a couple of weeks to stay with an old schoolfriend and that she'd be in touch again before Christmas. Whether Shelagh Kendall would have worried on not hearing from her was debatable, but at least this way Cara's conscience was clear.

Next, she wrote a short note to Glen Douglas, thanking him for all he'd done and explaining that she felt she had no other choice but to get away from Kellston. She paused at this point, pen poised over the sheet of Basildon Bond. Douglas had worked hard for her, put in the hours and been a sympathetic ear when she'd desperately needed someone to talk to. Now she was rewarding him by clearing off with the balance of her bill unpaid. Her ingratitude, apparently, knew no bounds. Feeling guilty, she quickly added a line saying that once she was settled, she would send the rest of the money owed. It was doubtful he'd believe this, but she intended to surprise him.

Cara put the notes in envelopes, addressed them and added stamps. If she posted them this afternoon, they should arrive on Monday or Tuesday, by which time, with luck, she'd be a long way away.

Two down, one to go. Now for Will Lytton. Should she tell him she was going or not? She thought about it and decided it would be better to leave him in the dark. That way he wouldn't have to lie for her or feign surprise when her disappearance was discovered. Once this was decided, she immediately had doubts. He might panic when she didn't come back tonight, might worry that she'd fallen victim to the Russians again and share those fears with the law. No, that wouldn't do. She would need a good excuse for her absence, a plausible explanation. Well, she would think of something later.

In the meantime, she had an even trickier problem to consider: money. She still had what was left of her stash, but it wouldn't be enough. There would be train and ferry tickets to buy, food and accommodation to pay for until she could find a regular source of income. She could speak enough French to get by – that expensive schooling hadn't gone entirely to waste – and come spring she would easily get a job in a bar or café, but the winter months would be more problematic.

There was a solution, but it was risky. She thought of the grand, imposing house she had seen in Weld Road just over a week ago. She thought about its high walls, its sturdy drainpipe and the dark red Mercedes parked in the drive. The idea grew and blossomed. She wouldn't need to take much, just a few carefully chosen items she could sell on to her dad's contact in Calais. If it all went according to plan, she could be in and out in a matter of minutes. And if she got caught? No, she couldn't afford to think like that. She'd been unlucky last time, that's all. This time she'd get it right.

68

By a quarter past four the light was fading fast. For Cara the wait had felt like an eternity. She took one last look round her room, padded softly to the hallway, put on her jacket, quietly opened the door and placed the backpack outside. Then she went into the living room.

'I'm off out,' she said. 'I'm going over to Mile End to meet one of Jimmy's old mates and his wife. You never know, they might have some bright ideas about where he could have stashed something.'

'Good luck,' he said.

'It's a long shot, but I may as well give it a go.' Cara's gaze roamed involuntarily around the four walls – to think she would never see this place again – before coming back to settle on Lytton. 'Um, look, I may stay over if it gets late so . . . Just so you don't think anything bad has happened.'

'Okay.'

'I'll see you later then, or tomorrow.'

'Are you all right?'

Cara, concerned that Lytton might have picked up on her deceit, quickly forced a smile. 'I'd just rather be doing something than sitting here going mad.'

'Yeah, I can understand that.'

Cara nodded, said goodbye and withdrew. Shortly after, she was out of the front door and heading for the lift with the backpack flung over her shoulder. Had he believed her story? It didn't really matter. So long as he didn't alert the law tonight, she stood a reasonable chance of getting away.

In the lift, she pressed the button for the ground floor. While it descended, she thought about how she'd never be returning. This was it. The end. And there was nothing to cry over – the Mansfield was a dump, and no sane person would be sorry to see the back of it – but she *would* miss the flat, not because it was anything special, but because of the memories. When she'd come to live here, it was the first time she had felt like she had a proper home.

And then there was Jimmy, of course. Kellston was where she'd met him, fallen in love with him, shared a life with him despite all their ups and downs until . . . The image of Jimmy lying dead on the kitchen floor rose into her mind. She shrank from the memory, unable to cope with it. She had to look to the future. Now that he was gone, that her dad was gone, there was nothing to keep her here.

Cara kept an eye out as she walked up the path towards the gates. She was hoping that Terry Street would be sticking to his side of the deal and keeping his distance, but nothing was certain when it came to men like him. All she could do was pray that he'd think she was too afraid to even consider a double cross.

She walked at speed along Mansfield Road and on to the high street. Although it was still early, the November evening was starting to gather around her. She glanced over her shoulder, checking for company. When she came to the chippy she stopped, pulled a small plastic bag out of her pocket and pushed it down into the bin between the greasy wrappers and the discarded food. Inside were the cut-up remnants of Jimmy's fake passport, mixed in with some potato peelings. A waste, but she couldn't think what else to do with it.

Cara carried on until she reached the junction near the railway station where she crossed over and began to wend her way towards Weld Road. Her thoughts travelled back to Hampstead, to the last time, the disastrous last time, she had committed a break-in. That had all come about as a result of a casual conversation with Murch. He was the one who'd told her and Jimmy about the top floor of the house not being alarmed. 'That can't be true. No one would be that stupid,' Jimmy had said. But Murch had insisted it was, that a mate of his had installed the alarm a year ago. 'Straight up. A bloke called Myers lives there.'

That was all it had taken. A few more questions and they'd got all the information they needed to check the place out, to make plans, to organise the job. And then when Jimmy had dropped out, when he'd had his 'bad feeling', she'd gone ahead with it anyway. If she hadn't, he might still be alive today.

Cara shook her head, knowing that these thoughts were only going to plunge her into a downward spiral of regret and despair. She couldn't change the past no matter how much she wanted to. She had to concentrate on the present. There was still time to change her mind, she didn't have to go through with it, but she knew she wouldn't back out now. She was in a corner and there were no more choices.

If she failed, Steadman would throw the book at her. So, she had to make sure she didn't. If she was careful, if she only took a few choice items, the householder might not even notice they were missing for several days. All she needed was twenty-four hours and she could be clear of Kellston for ever.

Ten minutes later, as she approached the house, her pulse was starting to race. She didn't pause but walked straight on past, a quick glance taking in the open gates, the car parked in the drive and the lit ground-floor window with its curtains pulled across. Someone was in. On the one hand this made it more likely she could be caught, on the other that the alarm was likely to be switched off.

At the end of the road, she turned right and began to circle round, taking the opportunity to go over the mental picture she now had of the dark upper windows, the sturdy drainpipe and the large square of front garden with its well-established shrubs and bushes. She had to focus. She visualised what she would do: the grasping of the metal pipe, one hand over another, the bend and stretch of her thighs as she ascended. Already the adrenaline was coursing through her veins.

She was almost at the house again. Her eyes took in the adjoining properties and the ones opposite, most of them with their lights on and their curtains drawn. Was she being watched? She didn't think so.

Cara had a final look round – no one in front, no one behind – before slipping through the open gateway. She skirted round the Mercedes and sidled to the left, across the square of lawn and away from the front door. No security lights came on. Good. She removed the small jemmy from the backpack, attached it to her belt and then deposited the backpack behind a large hydrangea bush where it couldn't be seen by anyone passing on the road.

She waited for a while, making sure that her trespass hadn't been noticed, before slowly moving forward towards the house. Hopefully, the TV would be on inside, or there'd be music playing, sounds that would mask any noise she made as she broke in. She looked up at the drainpipe, put her hands around it and tested its stability. The last thing she needed was for it to break away from the wall when she was halfway up. It felt solid and safe. A whispery sigh of relief escaped from her lips.

Cara checked the surrounding area. There were a few empty terracotta flowerpots to the right of the pipe, along with a garden fork propped against the wall. She made a mental note to avoid them when she came back down again. Was she ready? Her heart was beating furiously. It was now or never. *Don't lose your nerve.* Although it was eighteen months since she'd last done anything like this, she had to believe in herself. Shifting her hands further up, she took off from the ground and began to climb. But she had hardly started the ascent when the very worst happened. There was a dull, ominous thud of running footsteps on the grass, and she barely had time to look down before a hand snaked around her ankle and held it tight.

69

The shock ran through Cara. If her heart had been beating hard before, now it was almost jumping out of her chest. Nabbed before she'd even properly begun. Panic swept over her. She had no idea who it was – the police, the householder, a passing do-gooder – but it didn't really matter. All she could think about was getting away. Instinctively she kicked out with her other foot, but to no avail. Desperate, she twisted and turned, but there was no escape.

'Get down!' the man ordered.

Cara felt sick and trapped and terrified. She could see her life flashing before her, not the past but the future, and it was only iron bars and a small, cramped cell. Sweat formed on her forehead. Horror coiled inside her. And then, through the fear, the voice suddenly registered. She peered down through the darkness, her eyes widening in disbelief. It was Lytton, bloody Lytton. 'What the hell are you doing?' she hissed.

'What the hell are *you* doing?'

'Get off me!'

But all Lytton did was hold on even tighter, yanking at her ankle. She wasn't strong enough to resist and gradually her hands slid down the pipe. She kicked out again, caught him a glancing blow on his upper arm, and he dodged to the right where he collided with the fork and sent it clattering to the ground.

At this point Lytton finally let go and Cara slid back down to earth. Just as she had her feet on the ground, a light came on in the hall, the front door opened, and a bloke came striding out. He was tall, over six foot, muscled and ready for trouble. He cut across the grass, his face furious as he approached. 'What the fuck's going on here? What are you doing on my property?'

It was Lytton who had the presence of mind to give a sharp whistle and then call out, 'Molly? Molly, where are you?' Then he turned to the man and said, 'I'm so sorry. I think our dog ran in here. I opened the car door and before I could put her lead on, she saw a cat and she was off.'

Cara thought the ploy was dubious but with little other choice she pretended to look around, staring into the shadows as if the imaginary Molly might suddenly materialise.

'She's only young,' Lytton went on. He raised his voice. 'Molly? Molly? Here girl!' Then he turned his attention to the man again. 'She's a whippet, fawn-coloured. Fast on her feet, that's the trouble. I do apologise. We didn't mean to disturb you.'

The man seemed partially mollified although, unsurprisingly, still suspicious. 'There's no dog here,' he said.

Cara knew that she couldn't look more like a burglar if she'd tried – dark clothes, black woollen hat pulled down over her forehead – but fortunately the man wasn't paying her much attention. He had, perhaps, the somewhat sexist view that males were more of a danger to his property than females, and as such was focusing his attention on Lytton.

'Could she have got round the back?' Lytton persisted. 'Can you get round the back from here?'

'No.'

'Oh, okay. Maybe I was wrong. I was sure this is where she came but—'

'I told you to put her lead on before you opened the door,' Cara snapped. 'Why don't you ever listen to me?'

'It's not my fault she ran off.'

'So whose fault is it then?'

'All I'm saying is—'

'And it's not like it's the first time. You should be more careful. How often have I told you? God, it's like talking to a brick wall.'

The man glanced from Lytton to Cara and back to Lytton again, somewhat nonplussed at suddenly finding himself in the middle of a domestic. 'Yeah, well, it doesn't look like she's here.'

'No,' Lytton said. 'She must be down the road somewhere.'

'She'd better be,' Cara said. 'Or you can explain to Mum why her dog's gone AWOL. She won't be happy.'

'She's never happy.'

'Well, come on,' Cara said sharply, starting to edge away. 'What are you waiting for? We're not going to find her standing here, are we?'

Lytton rolled his eyes at the bloke. 'Sorry, mate.'

The man nodded and said, 'Good luck,' like he wasn't just referring to the dog.

As they walked towards the gate, Cara noticed that Lytton had her backpack flung over his shoulder. He must have picked it up on his way in. In fact, he must have seen her hide it behind the hydrangea. She couldn't believe he'd managed to follow her without her realising, but now wasn't the time to be dwelling on that. Although the man seemed to have accepted their story, he was still standing there with his hands on his hips, watching them closely and wondering, perhaps, if there was something more to this than a bickering couple and a missing whippet.

As soon as they were on the pavement, Lytton started calling out again – 'Molly! Molly!' – and kept it up until they reached the end of the road. Side by side they turned the corner and only then did Cara begin to relax. Her fear was rapidly being replaced with anger. She glared at Lytton and said, 'For God's sake, what's the matter with you? You could have got us both arrested.'

'What, for looking for a dog?'

'You know what I mean.'

'And you don't think breaking into someone else's house *isn't* going to get you arrested?'

'I didn't intend to get caught.'

'I'm sure you didn't intend to get caught last time, either.'

Cara tensed. 'How do you know about that?'

'Rochelle told me. Some house in Hampstead, wasn't it? Jimmy mentioned it to her, said you'd broken in and stumbled on a corpse.'

'Since when did you and Rochelle get so chatty? I thought you two were barely on speaking terms.'

'When it suits her,' he said. 'Anyway, it's not exactly a secret, is it? The case was all over the papers.'

Cara marched on, heading for the high street as she couldn't think of where else to go. 'You had no right to follow me. It's none of your bloody business what I do.'

'Even if you end up inside again?'

'And how is that any concern of yours?'

Lytton shrugged. 'Did you see the size of that bloke? I wouldn't have fancied your chances if he'd caught you red-handed.'

'You still haven't answered the question. How is it any of your business if I end up back inside or not?'

'I owe you one for letting me stay in the flat.'

Cara gave a snort. 'And this is your way of repaying me? Jesus, you've ruined everything. I could have been out of here tonight, halfway to France, if you hadn't stuck your interfering nose in.'

'You'll thank me for it one day.'

'You think? You can remind yourself of that when I'm six feet under or being stitched up by Steadman again. You've got no idea what you've done.'

'Running away never solved anything.'

Cara stopped and turned her face to glare at him again. 'Christ, you're a patronising bastard! You don't know the half of it. You haven't got a bloody clue.'

'So tell me,' he said.

70

Cara had reached the point where she was beyond frustration, beyond all hope. Even her anger was ebbing away. What was the point? She could rant and rave, but it wasn't going to change anything. It was done now and couldn't be undone. Because of Lytton her plans had come to nothing; she was back to square one. Dismay and disappointment swept over her. The thought of what would happen next filled her with a cold dread.

'Talk to me,' he said.

Cara spoke through gritted teeth. 'I needed the money, all right? I needed it to get away from here.'

'Why didn't you ask me?'

'Why on earth would I do that?'

'Why not? It seems a slightly better option than breaking into someone's house.'

They were on the high street now, back with the traffic and the people and the bright streetlamps. 'You're a student. Last time I checked, students weren't exactly rolling in it.'

'I've got some savings. I used to work, remember? I could have helped you out.'

'I'm not your responsibility.'

'God, you're weird. You should do something about that pride of yours.'

Cara stared at him. 'I'm weird? You're the one who follows people. That's hardly normal behaviour.'

'And what you were just doing is? Anyway, you've been skulking around all afternoon. I knew you were up to something.'

'I wasn't skulking.'

'Acting suspiciously, then. And that story about going to see Jimmy's friends didn't ring true.'

'Well pardon me for being such a crap liar.'

'You didn't even leave a note.'

'If I'd done that, you'd have either had to show it to Steadman or lie to him. I was saving you the bother of having to make that decision.'

'You could have just told me you were going.'

'I could have but I didn't, so what's the point of going on about it?'

Lytton produced a noise in the back of his throat, a sound that could have been annoyance or exasperation, but held back from saying anything else. They continued in silence until they reached the estate. Cara could hardly believe she was back here again. A black cloud of depression settled over her. A few more days and she'd be for it. Terry Street wouldn't take kindly to her failure to deliver.

Up in the flat, Lytton dropped the backpack in the hall, went through to the living room and headed for the kitchen. 'I'll put the kettle on,' he said, as if a nice cup of tea would solve everything.

Cara slumped down at the table. 'I don't want a brew.'

'I'm not making one.'

'Or a coffee.'

'I'm not making that, either.'

Cara gave up, blew her nose and gazed disconsolately out of the window. What next? She felt drained of energy, drained of hope. Her one last chance of escape had been snatched away and she couldn't see any way forward.

A few minutes later Lytton placed a steaming mug in front of her. 'Whisky, hot water, honey and lemon. Purely medicinal. Drink it: you'll feel better.'

Cara doubted that, but she drank it anyway. While she sipped the hot concoction, she began to fill in the gaps of what Lytton knew. Caution no longer seemed important to her. What difference did it make now? The tale was all a bit rambling – Terry Street, the missing diamonds, Hampstead, Azarov, the murder of Kuzmin, Glen Douglas – but she ploughed on until it was all out in the open.

Lytton was quiet for a moment and then he said, 'Yeah, it's a bit of a mess, isn't it?' He paused and frowned. 'Although I still don't really understand why you think the diamonds have anything to do with Hampstead.'

'Where else could they have come from?'

'Couldn't Jimmy have nicked them from this Russian geezer?'

Cara shook her head. 'No, it all goes back to Hampstead. It must do. Jimmy was shooting his mouth off in the Fox about how no one knew the half of it and that I'd be a rich woman when I came out. Why would he be saying that if it had nothing to do with me? I mean, we weren't even together any more.'

'I suppose. But if this bloke, the one who killed Myers, *did* approach Jimmy, why didn't Jimmy tell you about it?'

'I don't know.' She drank some more of the hot whisky, feeling the warmth spread through her. 'Yes, I do know. Well,

I've got an idea. He'd have guessed I wouldn't like it, wouldn't have wanted to profit from something like that. You might find it hard to believe but I do have *some* morals. It wouldn't have been right, would it, accepting those diamonds? Even though I didn't see anything, couldn't have identified the bloke in a million years, it would still have felt like I was conspiring with a murderer.'

'Shame Jimmy didn't share your scruples.'

'I think he'd have just seen it as taking advantage of the situation. Nothing was going to bring Myers back so . . .' Cara shrugged, a part of her still wanting to defend Jimmy even if she didn't approve of what he'd done. 'He probably thought that after eighteen months inside, I wouldn't be too fussy about where a windfall came from, so he'd just wait and tell me when I got out. And I reckon he felt guilty about not coming with me that night. In his own way, he was just trying to put things right.'

'Okay, but what about this Russian? Azarov, is it? How does he tie in with Myers's widow?'

'Douglas thinks he could have been a business associate of her husband.'

'What sort of business?'

'Property, probably. Myers could have been helping him to launder money. Do you think I should go and see Fiona Myers, tell her the truth, tell her I don't have a clue where the diamonds are?'

'Not if she's hand in hand with this Azarov.'

'No, Douglas doesn't think it's a good idea, either.' Cara reached for the tissues, blew her nose again and sighed. 'She's not going to believe me, is she? Terry Street isn't going to, either. That's why I wanted to get away.'

'Why France?'

390

'Because my dad had a contact in Calais, a fence. He used to go there sometimes when what he had was a bit too hot to shift over here. I could have sold the stuff from Weld Road and then moved on: Nice or Cannes, perhaps. There are always jobs where there are tourists.'

Lytton turned his head and gazed out of the window at the dark sky and the distant lights. Then he looked back at her again. 'I can give you some money, but it won't be until Monday when the bank opens. How much do you need?'

'I don't want your money.'

'Borrow it, then. You can pay me back when you're on your feet again.'

Cara didn't say yes or no. Now wasn't the time to be burning all her bridges. Borrowing off Lytton was a last resort, but she was running out of options. 'I was sure those diamonds were on Dad's grave. I thought about what you said, about how he'd have chosen somewhere that meant something and it just seemed the perfect place.'

'Not that original, though.'

'It took me a while to think of it.'

'And how long do you think it would have taken Terry Street or Azarov? It's not unknown for thieves to hide their loot in cemeteries. Not that I'm calling Jimmy a thief. I just mean ...'

'I know what you mean.'

'They'd have checked out the grave, wouldn't they? Terry would have known about your dad dying, and it wouldn't have been too hard for the Russian to find out. If Jimmy didn't have any family buried in Kellston, yours would have been next on the list.'

When he put it like that, Cara could see that he was probably right. And Jimmy hadn't been stupid: he'd have realised the grave was somewhere they'd look. She was revolted by the thought of them rooting around, their filthy fingers probing into the white quartz chips. The only upside was the crushing disappointment they'd have felt when they realised the diamonds weren't there.

'I can't think of anywhere else,' she said.

By now the whisky was starting to take effect. She hadn't eaten anything today and the alcohol was surging through her bloodstream, softening the edges of her fear and making her thoughts drift in unexpected directions. She remembered the last time she'd seen Jimmy alive, sitting across from her in the visiting hall, grinning like he always did when he was pleased with himself. She went over their conversation, taking it apart, searching for clues. But she was still sure he hadn't said anything of significance.

'You look miles away,' Lytton said.

'I wish I was. No offence.'

'Sorry I screwed it up for you.'

Cara shook her head. The past was rolling in on her, an avalanche of memories. She fought her way through it all until she was back in that pub, fourteen again, waiting for her dad, seeing Jimmy for the first time. She could feel the sun on her face and taste the Coke in her mouth. Her heart skipped a beat. Jimmy was standing there, talking to his mates, smiling, laughing. She couldn't take her eyes off him. The man she was meant to be with. Not now but eventually. She had felt it in her bones. Later, when they'd been together a while, she had told him about that afternoon, skipping the love at first sight business – his ego was big enough – but just that she remembered him and that it was the day she'd discovered exactly what her father did for a living. And then it came to her. It was so simple, so obvious. Suddenly she knew exactly where the diamonds were.

71

It was half past seven when Cara woke on Sunday morning, and she knew she wouldn't be able to go back to sleep. Excitement was skimming her nerves, but she refused to acknowledge it. Expectation was a dangerous thing. What if she was wrong again? She wasn't going to get her hopes up.

She took a quick shower, got dressed, went to the kitchen and made tea and toast. Her cold was just as bad today, worse maybe, her nose streaming and an irritating cough tickling the back of her throat. She was trying hard not to acknowledge this, either. She couldn't afford to be sick.

Cara ate her breakfast at the living-room table with her eyes fixed firmly on the first floor of Temple. She was waiting for a light to go on while she wondered what a respectable time to call round would be. Old people didn't sleep much. They rose early, but you still couldn't go knocking on their door before the sun was even up. That sort of thing could scare the living daylights out of them, send them into the kind of panic that could induce a heart attack. Not that Alma seemed especially nervous, but she had lived on the Mansfield long enough to know that out-of-hours callers were rarely good news.

She would have phoned her last night if she could have found a number, only a search of the directory had drawn a blank. There were plenty of Todds in the area, a whole list of them, but no A. Todd living in Temple. Perhaps Alma was ex-directory or didn't even have a phone. For many people living on the estate, it was too big an expense. She could have walked across and talked to her face to face, but it had been dark by then and she'd had the same reservations as she had now.

While she ate, Cara went through her own reasoning again, looking for flaws, worried that she was clutching at straws. She wasn't sure what she'd do if Alma told her exactly what she didn't want to hear. Take Lytton up on his offer, perhaps. Take the money and run. She hadn't emptied her backpack yet: it was sitting in her bedroom, ready for action.

It was another twenty minutes before she saw Alma's light go on. Still too early to go round, but at least she knew the old lady was up and about. She fidgeted, fighting against the impulse to get to her feet and pace. Dawn was lurking on the horizon. She hated these long dark November mornings when everything felt like it was on hold until the sun deigned to rise. Her impatience was growing by the second.

Lytton came into the living room, looked at her and said: 'Morning. You okay?'

Cara didn't answer directly. Instead, although she already knew the answer, she asked, 'What's a reasonable time for me to go and see Alma?'

'Not before nine,' he said. 'Do you still think—'

'Yes. I don't know. I think so. It makes sense, doesn't it?'

'It's possible. You knew Jimmy a lot better than I did.'

Cara sensed caution in his reply, but perhaps he was just

394

trying to rein in her hopes. If she was right about her idea, then Lytton had done her a favour yesterday, removing the need for her to run away. But if she was wrong . . . She frowned, not wanting to face the prospect of being right back where she'd started.

'What's wrong?'

'Nothing. I'm just on edge. Don't answer the door if anyone rings the bell.' She had suddenly remembered Steadman and his request for her to drop by the station. 'I can do without the inspector this morning.'

'He can't have anything on you, nothing new at least.'

'That won't stop him. He'll keep me down Cowan Road for as long as he can. All day if he feels like it.'

The thought of Steadman made Cara even more jumpy. It would be just like him to show up at the most inopportune moment, to haul her back to the station, to make her go over her statement about finding Jimmy again and again until she could no longer think straight. And by then the place she needed to go to would be closed and she'd have to wait until tomorrow.

Cara spent the next hour standing by the window wishing time away. She drummed her fingertips on the window ledge and split her scrutiny between Temple and the gates to the Mansfield. Eventually the magic hour of nine o'clock came round. It was light now but still grey. The sky was the colour of wet slate.

'Right, I'm off,' she said. 'Wish me luck.'

Lytton rose from the sofa. 'I'll come with you. I'll wait downstairs while you go and see Alma.'

'You don't have to come,' she said, even though she wanted him to. If she did find the diamonds, she'd feel safer if there were two of them to escort those valuable items home. And it would mean another pair of eyes to watch out for any uninvited company. Did this mean she trusted him? She supposed it did.

Cara left Lytton in the foyer of Haslow House and strode over to Temple. She took the stairs up to the first floor and went over what she would say as she approached the door. She rang the bell. There was a short wait, during which she was sure she was being studied through the spyhole, but then she heard the chain being taken off and the bolt sliding back.

'Hello, dear,' Alma said, smiling brightly. 'What a nice surprise.'

'I'm sorry to come by so early. I hope I'm not disturbing you. I was just wondering if you could help me with something.'

72

Cara jogged down the stairs and hurried back along the path to Haslow. Alma's information had come at a price, a promise to come for a cup of tea later in the week, and she intended to honour it so long as she was still in Kellston. If the old lady had been surprised by the question, she hadn't shown it; perhaps nothing surprised her any more. An answer had been given and directions provided.

Lytton was leaning against the wall just outside the foyer. She was smiling as she approached. 'Good news?' he said.

Cara nodded. 'He's there.'

'Let's go, then.'

It was quiet on the high street with most of the shops shut. Only the newsagent had a steady flow of customers, people buying their Sunday newspaper, their fags or a carton of milk. Cara glanced over her shoulder, watching for a tail. She made a note of the cars that went by. If she was right and the diamonds were where she thought they were, she wasn't going to let them slip through her fingers at this late stage.

Cara was too nervous, too on edge to talk. She was painfully afraid of the possibility of being wrong and tried to prepare herself for disappointment. Except disappointment was too small a word. Despair, desolation? This was her last chance. She was relying on the fact that, for once, Jimmy had been listening to her, that the memory she'd shared had stuck in his head and that he'd chosen this place because only *she* would understand the connection.

They crossed the road at the lights and soon they were at the cemetery. Several cars were already parked beyond the black wrought-iron gates, and she could see people at the graves, tidying up and preparing fresh flowers. Sunday was a popular day for visitors. As they walked down the main thoroughfare, Cara's eyes darted everywhere. How could you tell a genuine mourner from a fake one? She glanced over her shoulder again and again. No one had followed them in.

Not far now. Less than twenty feet. Her heart was in her mouth. She'd been afraid that Albert North had been cremated and his ashes scattered, but Alma had put her straight. The old lady knew where all the old faces were buried. Her words echoed in Cara's ears: 'Straight down the main path. Then take the third turning on your left. You can't miss it, it's just by the holly bush.'

Albert's name had come into her head last night while the whisky had been rippling through her veins. The man her father had once worked with. The man who had, in a roundabout way, brought her and Jimmy together. Jimmy would have been pleased by his own cleverness, although not quite so pleased that it had taken her so long to figure it out. And she was supposed to be the sentimental one.

'Here,' Cara said, taking the instructed turn. She could already see the bright red berries of the holly. Her legs had begun to shake, and she might have grabbed on to Lytton's arm if she hadn't been afraid of showing weakness. Instead, she took a few deep breaths and silently prayed.

The headstone was grey marble, the gilt inscription a little worn by a decade of British weather. Beneath Albert's name was that of his wife, Louisa Elizabeth, who had died less than a year after him. It was clear that nobody attended the grave – perhaps there had been no children, or they lived far away – as there were no flowers in the urn, not even dead ones, and weeds were poking through the layer of cream-coloured stones in the oblong kerb.

She and Lytton stood and stared. Eventually, when she didn't move, he said, 'Would you like me to look?'

Cara shook her head. 'No. You keep watch. Let me know if anyone comes near.'

She dropped to her knees and began to quickly rummage, pulling out the weeds and bits of twig, her hands trembling as she searched. It was odd to think of Jimmy having been here, of having knelt perhaps in this very same spot. Where would he have placed the diamonds? Deep, she thought, as close to the base of the kerb as possible.

'Sorry about this, Alfred,' she murmured, feeling it was faintly sacrilegious to be disturbing his grave in this way.

It was less than a minute before she made her first discovery. The prize was right down in the centre, about four centimetres in length and a different shape and hue to the other stones. She held it up to the light and gazed at it. The colour was a greenish-blue, distinctive, not like anything she'd ever seen before. She squinted at it, frowning, before passing it to Lytton.

He held it in his palm and his eyebrows went up. 'That's the strangest diamond I've ever seen. What is it, an emerald?'

'I don't know.' Cara's exhilaration was mixed with confusion.

'It could be. I've never come across one quite that shade, though.' As she went back to work, she wondered if there had been a mixture of gemstones in the silver box. Maybe diamonds and whatever this was. Her fingers were moving even faster now, and it wasn't long before she came up with a second, similar-looking stone. She brushed off the dust and gave it to Lytton.

'Do you know how many there are supposed to be?' he asked.

'No. But Terry Street definitely said "them".'

'And did he definitely say the word diamonds?'

Cara thought about it. 'No. That's just what we presumed – me and Douglas – because whatever was in the box had to be valuable. And small.'

'How much would emeralds this size be worth?'

'I've no idea. Not as much as diamonds, though.'

A further five minutes' rooting didn't reveal anything more, and so, afraid of having missed something, she did what she had done at her dad's grave and started removing the loose stones by the handful, examining them and laying them on the grass. Once she'd established that there was nothing left to find, she piled everything back into the kerb, smoothed out the surface and stood up.

'That's it,' she said, holding out her palm to take the two mystery gems from Lytton. She stared at them, looked around, returned her gaze and stared some more. 'You wouldn't think they'd be worth killing for.'

Lytton shrugged. 'What now?'

'Let's get out of here.'

73

Cara placed the two gemstones in the breast pocket of her jacket and pulled the zip across. It felt unreal to finally have them in her possession. Now all she wanted was to be rid of the cursed things as soon as possible, get them returned to their owner and make all the bad stuff go away. Afraid of mislaying them, her hand repeatedly rose to her pocket.

'You should stop doing that,' Lytton said as they walked out through the cemetery gates.

'I keep thinking they might disappear.'

Dark thundery clouds had gathered overhead, and it was starting to rain. Cara, still paranoid, scanned the road in both directions. It would be just her luck for something to go wrong at this late stage. To lighten her mood and steady her nerves, she said, 'I hope Fiona Myers appreciates the effort we've had to go to.' She saw the look Lytton gave her and raised her eyebrows. 'Well, she didn't have to set the Russian dogs on me.'

'Did I say anything?'

'You looked disapproving.'

'Only of the Russian dogs,' he said.

For a moment Cara was back in the house in Hampstead, creeping down the stairs, her curiosity getting the better of her judgement. She shivered, wishing she could blank out the memory of what she'd seen that night. All the bad things that had happened since stemmed from that one irreversible decision to break in. If only she had listened to Jimmy.

'Where are we going?' Lytton said.

At the junction Cara had veered right instead of going down the high street. 'To see if Douglas is in the office. I want to pick up that box.'

'Does he work on Sundays?'

'We'll soon find out.'

They crossed the road and Cara pressed the bell. While she waited, she stamped her feet impatiently. If he wasn't there she would have to hold on to the stones until tomorrow, and that meant twenty-four more hours of angst and worry. What if Steadman did a search of the flat and found them? What if the Russians came calling? She quickly pressed the bell again.

This time a gruff voice came over the intercom. 'Yes?'

'It's Cara.'

The buzzer went and Cara pushed open the door. When she realised Lytton wasn't following her in, she glanced over her shoulder and said, 'Come on.'

'You go. I'll hang on here and make sure we haven't got a tail.'

'You'll get soaked,' she said, glancing up at the sky. 'It's about to throw it down.'

'Try not to take too long, then.'

Cara went inside and hurried up the stairs. The door to the waiting room was open and she walked straight in. Douglas was standing by the window looking down on the street. 'Good morning,' she said, suddenly feeling more cheerful now that everything was coming together. 'I wasn't sure if you'd be here or not.'

Douglas turned to face her. 'Just catching up on some paperwork. It's usually quiet on a Sunday.'

'I only called by for the box. I've got good news.'

'You've found the diamonds?'

'Well, I've found something. They're not diamonds, but they're some kind of gemstone. Anyway, I want to get rid of them as soon as I can, put them in the box and hand them over to Terry Street. Today, hopefully.' She would have taken the stones out to show him if he hadn't chosen that moment to look down on to the street again.

'Do you know there's a man loitering outside?'

'Oh, that's just Lytton, Will Lytton. He's my flatmate.'

'I didn't know you had one.'

'A legacy from Jimmy. It's a long story. But he's all right. You don't have to worry about him.'

Douglas frowned. 'Lytton,' he repeated. 'Why does that name ring a bell?' He frowned some more, shook his head and said: 'Never mind. It'll come back to me. Let me get the box.'

Cara waited while he went into his office and opened the safe. She saw a flash of lightning cut across the sky and heard a distant rumble of thunder. Storms always made her uneasy. There were things you could control and things you couldn't. The rain was starting to fall harder now, slanting against the window panes.

Douglas came back with the silver box and handed it to her. 'So where did you find the stones in the end?'

'On a grave,' she said.

Douglas chuckled. 'On a grave, eh? Well, I suppose it's as good a place as any to hide them. Do you want me to come with you when you go to see Street?'

403

'No, it's okay. It's better if I do it alone. He might get antsy if I turn up with someone else. I'll be careful, though. I'll meet him somewhere public.'

'The offer's open if you change your mind. You got any plans for when all this is done and dusted?'

Cara slid the box into the roomy side pocket of her jacket. She was finding it hard to grasp, hard to believe, that the whole nightmare might almost be over. 'Get through Jimmy's funeral and then ... God knows. Sort myself out, get a job, try not to do anything stupid?'

'I've heard worse plans.'

'I guess this is it. Thanks for everything you've done. I appreciate it.'

'No thanks needed. It's made a change, to be honest, from chasing after fraudsters.'

Cara shook his hand, glad that she hadn't posted the note she had written and that he'd never be aware of her plans to disappear without paying what she owed. 'Let me know about the bill.'

'Take care of yourself, Cara.'

'You too.'

As Cara went down the stairs, a loud clap of thunder made her flinch. The storm was coming closer. She could feel it gathering, sense the heaviness in the air. There was something ominous about it. And suddenly it seemed like a warning, an omen, a sign that she shouldn't take anything for granted.

74

Unsurprisingly, Lytton wasn't standing outside. Cara looked around, saw him sheltering in the entrance to the station and dashed across the road to join him. While she ran, she kept her right hand firmly in her pocket, clutching the silver box in case it fell out.

'You get it?' he said.

Cara nodded. 'Let's take a cab. I don't fancy walking back in this.'

There was a rank by the station, with a single cab waiting. As they got in Cara glanced up at the office window and saw Douglas gazing down on them. She raised a hand to wave, but already he had turned away.

They were silent on the short journey home. The only thing to talk about was what they didn't dare talk about, not within hearing distance of the cabbie. The thunder shook the sky and the rain pounded down. Cara stared out of the window, thinking about Jimmy and Albert North and how things came together in the strangest of ways . . . and how they could so easily fall apart, too.

It only took a few minutes to get to Haslow House. Cara leaned forward and paid the driver. 'Keep the change,' she said, feeling generous now that her future looked a little brighter. Once they were out of the cab, she and Lytton ran for the foyer.

In the lift Cara pressed the button for the eleventh floor.

'Why eleven?' Lytton said.

'We can walk down a floor. I want to make sure Steadman isn't hanging around.' It would be just her luck, she thought, to be hauled down Cowan Road Station before she had the chance to get rid of the gemstones. 'Or anyone else, for that matter.'

The lift made its usual slow ascent, jolting and groaning like some weary donkey being forced to carry them up a mountain.

'Thanks for coming with me to the cemetery,' she said.

'It's the least I could do.'

'That's true.'

Cara went first down the stairs, walking as quietly as she could, keeping her ears pinned back for any sound coming from the tenth floor. She peered cautiously around the corner, checking that the corridor was clear before advancing. By the time she got to the door she had the key in her hand. A couple of seconds later they were both safely inside.

The first thing she did, even before taking off her damp jacket, was to dig out Terry Street's number and grab the phone. It rang half a dozen times before a woman finally picked up.

'Hello?'

'Is Mr Street there, please?'

'Who is it?'

'Cara Kendall.'

There was a short pause as if the woman was about to ask her something else before Cara heard the dull thud of the receiver being placed on a hard surface. While she waited, she could hear voices and the thin wail of a baby crying. She had never

406

really thought of Terry as a family man, although she supposed even gangsters did domestic bliss. Eventually the phone was picked up again.

'Yeah? What is it?' a man asked brusquely, in a voice that could have belonged to any London male.

'Is that Mr Street?'

'Who's this?'

'Cara Kendall.'

'He's not here. I'll tell him you called.'

'I need to talk to him this morning.'

The man sighed down the line as if she was being deliberately difficult. 'So, I'll get him to call you back.'

'And when would that be?'

'How the fuck would I know? When he feels like it, I should think.'

Cara bristled at the man's rudeness. 'Tell him it's urgent,' she said and hung up without saying goodbye. It was only as she replaced the receiver that she realised she hadn't left her number. Should she ring back? No, Terry probably already had it – she remembered the call from the heavy breather – and if he didn't, he was smart enough to find a way of getting it.

'No joy?' Lytton said.

Cara shook her head. 'Some moron, but hopefully he'll pass the message on.' She should have known that Terry wouldn't have given her his private number; he was too savvy, too wary of the law, to connect his number directly to hers. She would have to try and be patient, but all she felt was frustration.

Cara took the silver box and the stones out of her pockets and laid them side by side on the table. Then she shrugged off her jacket and hung it over the back of the chair. She went to the shelf and found her dad's book on gemstones. While she was waiting, she might as well make good use of the time.

She sat down and checked the contents page, turned to the section on emeralds and compared the pictures with the stones they'd recovered from the grave. She wasn't convinced, but then she was hardly an expert. Could they be green diamonds, green sapphires? It wasn't beyond the realms of possibility. She carried on flicking through the book, sighing repeatedly when she couldn't find an exact match.

'Does it matter what they are?' Lytton said.

'I'd just like to know what I'm handing over.'

Cara was about to admit defeat when she came across something interesting. She quickly read through the copy, stared at the pictures, stared at the stones, and then looked at Lytton. 'I may have something. While you're on your feet can you close the curtains?'

'What?'

'Humour me,' she said. 'I've got a hunch.'

Lytton walked to the window and pulled across the curtains, probably wondering if she'd lost her marbles. The curtains were old but heavy and they blocked out most of the outside light. Cara leaned forward, switched on the lamp and moved the stones underneath it.

'Look!' she said triumphantly.

Lytton came back to stand beside her. 'They've changed colour. That's bizarre. I've never seen anything like that before.'

Like magic, the two stones were now a rich ruby red.

'Alexandrites,' Cara said. 'They're very rare, more expensive even than diamonds. One colour in natural light, another in artificial. Something to do with chromium traces.' She glanced at the book again. 'It says here they're found in the Ural mountains. That's Russia, isn't it?'

'Yes.'

Cara picked one up and shifted it from side to side, making

it glint. 'We could go to South America and sell them there. They must be worth a fortune.' She heard Lytton nervously clear his throat. 'Don't worry, I'm only kidding. Although it is tempting, don't you think? Running away to Buenos Aires or Brasilia. No more crappy British weather. A brand new life in a brand new country.'

'If you don't mind looking over your shoulder for the rest of that life.'

'I don't reckon Terry's empire reaches quite as far as South America.'

'The same might not be said for your Russian friend.' Lytton reached down and picked up the other alexandrite. 'You really think they're worth that much?'

Cara looked at the book again. '*Very* rare, it says here. And they're not tiny, are they? Four or five carats, maybe. They were probably smuggled in by Azarov or one of his flunkies. Mr Myers must have done something extremely useful to be given these.'

Lytton opened his mouth, but whatever he had to say was interrupted by the ringing of the phone.

Cara started, prayed it wasn't Steadman and snatched up the receiver. 'Hello?' For a moment there was nothing and then the pips began, a rapid beeping heralding a call from a phone box. Then, as a coin was inserted, the line suddenly cleared. 'Hello?' she said again.

'It's Terry. Do you have them?'

75

Cara paid, climbed out of the cab and walked into the Fox. It was only five past twelve – she was ten minutes early – and the first customers of the day were being served. Terry hadn't been overly keen to come to the pub, but she had insisted. She didn't want him at the flat and she certainly wasn't going to meet him anywhere unfamiliar to her. A public place, somewhere she felt relatively safe, had seemed like the best option.

Cara looked around but there was no sign of him yet. She went over to the bar and ordered an orange juice. Holly gave her a wide smile and asked how she was, and she said she was fine, thank you, and how was *she*, and the general chit-chat continued while the drink was being poured. Fortunately, someone else was waiting so she could move away without any further small talk.

Cara walked through to the very back of the pub. There was no one else there and she sat down on a bench seat from where she could see the door. Once she was sure that no one was taking any notice, she slipped the wrapped package out of her pocket and laid it down beside her. One silver box, two alexandrites and a whole pile of relief. Soon it would all be over.

She blew her nose, balled up the tissue and put it in her pocket. She wondered what it would be like to go out without always being worried that some goon or some Russian psycho was on her tail. 'Happy days,' she murmured to herself. One simple transaction and she would get her life back.

But as she waited, all kinds of fresh fears began to worm their way into her head: what if there had been more than two alexandrites? What if Jimmy had split them and put the others somewhere else? What if Terry didn't show up? What if Azarov wouldn't be content at just getting the gemstones back? She thought of what Kuzmin had done to Jimmy and her stomach turned over.

Cara had reached the point where fleeing to South America didn't seem such a bad idea after all, when the door to the Fox opened and Terry Street strolled in. He gazed along the length of the pub, saw her, but gave no sign of acknowledgement. Instead, he went straight to the bar and ordered a drink. She guessed what he was doing – sussing out the situation, making sure that she was alone, and that he wasn't about to walk into some kind of set-up where the law would arrest him the moment he had the gemstones in his possession. Men like Terry were always cautious.

Tapping her foot impatiently against the floor, she continued to wait. It was warm in the room. She took off her jacket, laying it over the package. She drank some more orange juice. A minute passed by. She saw him say something to Holly, and Holly say something back. Then, finally, he left the bar and walked casually down the length of the pub.

Terry nodded, moved a chair from another table and sat down at right angles to her. If he'd sat down opposite, he would have had his back to the room – something he'd never do – and sitting right next to her would have looked odd. His voice was soft when he spoke. 'I wasn't expecting to hear from you so soon.'

Cara inclined her head towards the jacket. 'They're under there. Take them.'

Terry didn't. Not right away. 'You've got the box as well?'

'Yes. Is this it now? Are we done? No more hassle from Azarov or anyone?'

'A deal's a deal,' he said. 'You've made the right decision.'

'I don't remember having much choice.'

Terry swirled the contents of his glass, making the ice cubes chink. 'Sometimes it's smarter to cut your losses.'

'I'll take your word for it.'

He looked at her through cold, dark eyes, scrutinising her face. And then looked away. His gaze swept over the other customers as the pub began to fill up. 'You know the law drink in here?'

'What's wrong? Don't you trust me?'

'I don't trust no one, love. It's easier that way.'

And lonelier, Cara could have added, but she didn't. He was unlikely to appreciate her girlish pearls of wisdom. 'Shall we just get on with it?'

Terry reached under her jacket, slid out the package and slipped it into his overcoat pocket. 'Five minutes,' he said, as he stood up. 'Wait for me here.'

Cara watched as he walked out of the Fox. His unfinished whisky was still on the table. A ruse perhaps to make her believe he was coming back. Not that she would care if he didn't. Never having to speak to Terry Street again would be a major bonus once this was all over.

But she was anxious now, stressed that what he had taken

away to examine in private, would prove to be inadequate, that some stones would be missing, that he would return hissing out fury like a fire-breathing dragon. And then what would she do? Her head had started to ache. Her nerves were frazzled. She chewed on her fingernails.

Five minutes passed and nothing. Her anxiety levels shifted up a notch. She tried to concentrate on something else, but her thoughts only ran as far as Jimmy and the deal he had made and how that deal had gone so badly wrong. None of which made her feel any better. She closed her eyes for a moment, listening to the sounds around her, the rise and fall of voices, a sudden burst of laughter. She had to be positive. The fingers of her right hand curled into a fist.

When Terry came back, nearly ten minutes later, he was smiling. He swaggered through the pub and sat down on the same chair. 'Azarov will be a happy man.'

Relief flooded through Cara, but she was determined not to show it. Instead, she said drily, 'I can't tell you how much that means to me.'

Terry laughed. 'You're a funny one.' He had a good look round, took a folded-over plastic bag from his pocket and slid it under her jacket. 'Ten K as agreed.'

'I don't want it,' she said.

Perhaps Terry thought she was joking, because he laughed again. Then he said: 'Don't worry, it's all legit. No dodgy notes.'

'I mean it.' A part of her wondered what she was doing throwing away ten K, but the other part, the stronger part, had already made the decision. 'He can keep his lousy money. Jimmy made a deal that I knew nothing about – you can believe that or not, it really doesn't matter to me – and he's dead so ... It's like blood money, isn't it?'

Terry frowned, unable to understand. Scruples were probably a novelty to him.

'And you know what the irony is,' she continued, 'I didn't see anyone's face that night. All I heard was footsteps. I couldn't have picked that murderer out in a line-up of two. I'm sure Jimmy thought he was doing the right thing, but if he'd asked me, I'd have told him to have nothing to do with it.'

Terry stared blankly back at her. 'Huh?'

'He shouldn't have got you involved.'

'He needed a fence,' Terry said. 'Someone discreet who could handle valuable stuff. I mean, we're not talking about a couple of gold chains here.'

'And you were happy to help him out.' Cara drank her orange juice, wishing it was something stronger. She knew that she should keep her mouth shut, that having a go at Terry Street wasn't a good idea, but everything was bubbling up inside her. 'Except you didn't, did you? You went off and made a deal with Azarov instead.'

If Terry was offended by the accusation, he didn't show it. Perhaps he didn't care about her opinion now that he had the alexandrites in his possession. His lips curled into a slow smile. 'I did him a favour. The moment he'd tried to flog those stones, he'd have been dead meat. Azarov had put the word out. He wanted them back, whatever it took. Nobody would have bought them off Jimmy: they wouldn't have dared.'

'But he ended up dead anyway.'

'Only because he changed his mind and decided to go back on the deal. He got greedy, love. Ten K wasn't enough for him. Azarov wasn't best pleased.'

And Cara knew what form his displeasure had taken: a beating from Kuzmin, a beating that had proved fatal. The image of Jimmy lying dead on the kitchen floor leapt into her head again. She moved her jacket and pushed the carrier bag towards him. 'I don't want the money. You can give it back to Azarov or keep it. I don't care.'

'Don't be hasty, love. Your old man would have wanted you to have it.'

Cara stared at him, confused, frowning. 'What's my dad got to do with anything?'

And Terry frowned back. He left a long pause as if he was trying to figure out what to make of the question. He lit a cigarette and pondered. Eventually he spoke again. 'Where do you think those stones came from?'

'Hampstead, of course,' she said, wondering if Terry had lost the plot. Why was he even asking? 'The Myers house. They were taken on the night I broke in. They were taken by the bloke who . . .' But slowly something was starting to stir in the back of her mind, a dawning realisation. She and Douglas had compiled a story, a perfectly reasonable one based on the evidence, but that didn't mean it was true. She swallowed hard. *Her old man*. A chill ran through her bones, and she shuddered. 'What are you saying?'

Terry smoked his cigarette, watching her. 'Jimmy must have told you.'

'Jimmy didn't,' she snapped. 'But please feel free to enlighten me.'

'He was there on the night it happened, the night your old man fell off Azarov's roof.'

Cara flinched, pulled in a breath, felt her heart start to hammer. 'No, he couldn't have been.' It was her first instinct to deny it because it didn't make any sense. Firstly, her father would never have done a job with Jimmy – he didn't work with amateurs – and secondly, and even more importantly, Jimmy wouldn't have kept something like that from her, not for two long years. Yet there was no reason for Terry to invent such a tale. That didn't make sense, either. And suddenly, with a gut-wrenching certainty, she knew that it was true. 'He couldn't have been,' she repeated dully.

Terry shrugged, unmoved by the shock that must have been written all over her face. 'Azarov thought the stones were gone for good. They weren't found on your old man by the law. Well, nothing was found according to *them*.' His upper lip curled a little. 'Although you can't always rely on what the law say. It was possible that some bent cop had pocketed them, or that they'd been dropped during the fall and picked up by a passing tea leaf. Either way, it didn't look like Azarov was ever going to see them again.'

Cara was still struggling to understand it all, to grasp with one half of her mind what Jimmy had withheld from her, while the other half was preoccupied with the house in Mayfair, Azarov's house, the icy, slippery roof and the spiked iron railings that had pierced her father's body and brought his life to an end. 'Until Jimmy started shooting his mouth off in here.'

'He had a lot of patience, your Jimmy, hanging on to the stones for all that time.'

Or a lot of guilt, Cara thought. Rochelle hadn't been wrong about him having secrets. He must have watched her dad fall, maybe even watched him die, and yet he'd never said a word about it. Why would he keep that from her? Had he thought that she'd blame him, resent him? But blame him for what? She had questions, lots of them, but they weren't the sort of questions that Terry could answer.

Cara's face had grown hot, and her hands were clammy. Bile rose into her throat. Quickly she rose to her feet. 'I think we're done here,' she said. 'I need the ladies. Please take the money with you when you go.'

The toilets in the Fox were clean and smelled of lemon air freshener. Cara turned on the tap, splashed cold water on her face and stared at her reflection in the mirror. Her hands gripped the edges of the white basin. She felt like she was looking at a stranger, at someone she had never seen before, a girl who had once thought she knew it all but who actually knew nothing. She went for a pee and sat there for ten minutes, too bewildered to leave the sanctity of the cubicle.

When she got back to the table, both the money and Terry Street were gone. She grabbed her jacket and left.

76

Cara could not have described her walk back to the Mansfield in any detail. She had been in a daze, simply putting one foot in front of the other while Terry's revelations spun around the inside of her head. The rain must have been pouring down. Cars must have swept past her. People must have passed within feet of her. She had been oblivious to it all.

It was just after one when she got to Temple, took the lift, made her way to Murch's flat and rang the bell. He opened the door and gave an audible groan. Today he was dressed in what was, for him, a relatively subdued shell suit, his Sunday suit perhaps, black with a single tangerine stripe down the arms and legs. 'What is it now?' he said, as if she made it her life's mission to inconvenience him at every given opportunity.

'I need to talk to you about Jimmy.'

'You're wet,' he said.

Cara skimmed a hand through her rain-soaked hair. 'Can I come in?'

'If you want,' he said, with more resignation than enthusiasm.

418

Cara followed him into the living room where Rochelle was laid out on the sofa watching TV, with a cigarette in one hand and a glass of what might have been water but was more probably vodka in the other. The girl was still in her dressing gown, a flimsy silken affair that didn't leave much to the imagination. The pungent smell of her perfume dominated the air.

'Well, look who it is,' Rochelle said, narrowing her eyes. 'What a lovely surprise.'

This time Cara didn't ask to speak to Murch in private. She suspected Rochelle might know as much as he did, maybe even more, about what Jimmy had done. After sitting down in the armchair, she immediately leaned forward. She had a curious feeling of detachment, as if she was watching herself from a distance, as if she was observing a different Cara Kendall.

'Shift yourself,' Murch said to Rochelle, shoving her legs out of the way as he slumped down beside her.

Cara's eyes slid towards the TV where an old Hollywood western was playing out that much repeated tale of male machismo and the triumph of good over evil. She gazed at it for a moment before rallying her thoughts and returning her focus to Murch. 'Why didn't you tell me Jimmy was with my dad on the night he died?'

Murch showed only mild surprise at this information coming to light. He hesitated and then shrugged. 'That was up to Jimmy.'

'All right, let me put it another way: why didn't *Jimmy* tell me he was there?' This question had been revolving in her mind, caught in a loop, for the past half hour. 'Why would he keep something like that from me?'

'Jimmy's secret,' Rochelle said, smirking.

'Not that much of a secret if the two of you knew about it.'

Murch threw Rochelle a hard look, a warning to keep her

mouth shut. 'He was going to tell you when you got out of the slammer.'

'He had six months to tell me before I went in.'

'Yeah,' Murch said. 'He meant to, he wanted to, but . . .'

'But what, for God's sake?' Cara could feel the anger rising in her, cutting through that feeling of remoteness. Her voice rose in volume. Her fingers gripped the arms of the chair. 'I mean, it's not normal behaviour, is it? You don't lie to your girlfriend about something like that.'

'Didn't want to upset you, I suppose,' Murch said. 'You had enough on your plate.'

'Not upset me?' Cara repeated. 'You're not making any sense.' Fear was mingling with her anger now, a deep swirling sickening fear. She had to know what happened but dreaded knowing it. She could tell that Murch was only going to volunteer the very minimum, that she would have to prise the truth from him one small piece at a time. 'What were they even doing together?'

'Just hanging out. Jimmy bumped into your dad by the station, and they decided to go up West and have a few bevvies.' Murch shifted on the sofa, his eyes refusing to meet hers. 'You were working that night, so . . .'

'And then?'

'And then later, on their way home, they were walking through Mayfair and there was this row of houses, those tall fancy ones where the rich buggers live. There was a skylight open on one of them and your dad said that was just asking for trouble.'

'And?' Cara prompted again as Murch fell into silence.

'You know what happened next.'

'I don't know how it went from that to him actually breaking in. It was cold. It was icy. Dad wasn't stupid. Why would he take a risk like that?'

420

'He was pissed. They both were. He told Jimmy it was easy, that there was a fire escape beside the end house and all you had to do was climb up to the top floor, get on to the roof, crawl across and ...' Murch shrugged again. 'He said he could do it with his eyes shut.'

Cara could imagine the two of them, full of beer and stupidity, staring up at the skylight as if it was an open invitation. 'Jesus,' she muttered.

'And then somehow it got real. Jimmy was to act as lookout, to whistle if he saw the law.'

Rochelle's mouth pursed. 'It wasn't like that,' she said. 'You're missing out the important bit.'

Murch turned his head to glare at her. 'Shut the fuck up!'

'You shut the fuck up! It don't matter to Jimmy no more. She may as well know what really happened.'

'And what's the important bit?' Cara said, even though she knew she was going to regret the question. She was under no illusion that the girl was doing her any favours: what Rochelle had to say was going to hurt and that's why she wanted to say it.

Rochelle bent her head, examining her toes. She knew something Cara didn't and was revelling in the advantage it gave her.

'Are you going to tell or not?'

Slowly Rochelle lifted her head, a sly smile playing on her lips. 'It's a secret.'

Cara was rapidly losing patience. She had to resist the urge to jump up, grab Rochelle by the hair and shake the truth out of her. 'Don't push your luck,' she said softly but with menace. 'This isn't a game. You can tell me or you can tell the law. You've got five seconds. Either you spit it out or ...'

At the mention of the law, Rochelle's face drained of what little colour there was in it. 'Jimmy dared your dad to go ahead.

It was all his idea. He said, "Go on, prove it, then." That's why he felt bad. That's why he didn't tell you he was there.'

Cara looked to Murch for confirmation, but he wouldn't meet her gaze. Which pretty much told her all she needed to know. And now, at last, she understood Jimmy's silence. Guilt. A stupid dare. A drunken challenge that had got out of hand. But even as this was sinking in, she knew that there was more. Her mouth went dry. She had to force the words out. 'So how did Jimmy end up with the box?'

Murch finally looked at her again. 'Your dad was only in the house for a few minutes. When he crawled back on to the roof, he held up something and waved it. Jimmy was standing across the road. It was dark and he couldn't see what it was. When—'

'He took it,' Rochelle interrupted, almost gleefully. 'The box was in your dad's pocket, and Jimmy took it after he fell.'

It took a moment for this to sink into Cara's head. Her dad slipping and sliding down the icy roof, falling into open space and then . . . She briefly closed her eyes, unable to complete the sequence. It was too grotesque, too brutal. She couldn't bear to see the end even in her imagination.

'He was dead,' Murch said. 'There was nothing Jimmy could do for him.'

Anger flared up in Cara again. 'Except put his hand in his pocket and nick the silver box.'

'It wasn't like that,' Murch said. 'He just panicked. It was late and there was no one else around. He couldn't think straight. He was drunk and in shock. He thought . . . he thought . . .'

'What did he think?'

'That your dad would have wanted you to have it. The box, I mean – and what was in it.'

Cara's laugh was hollow. 'Sure, because there's nothing like a nicked silver box and a couple of gemstones to bring you consolation when your father has just managed to kill himself.'

'I didn't say it made any sense. It didn't make any sense to *him* when he'd sobered up. That's why he didn't tell you about it.'

'He didn't tell me because it was all his bloody fault,' she said fiercely. Even as she was saying it, she knew it wasn't strictly true. Her dad had been a grown man and had made his own insane choices, but she still wanted someone else to blame. And Jimmy had been there, been there when it happened, a witness and an instigator.

'He didn't want you to hate him.'

Cara remembered Jimmy comforting her after her dad's death. She hadn't picked up on anything odd, anything that might have rung alarm bells, but then she'd been too wrapped up in her own grief to notice anyone else's emotions.

Rochelle shifted on the sofa, put her thumb in her mouth and took it out again. 'Jimmy knew you wouldn't understand.'

Cara glared at her. 'What's it got to do with you? Why don't you just keep out of it?'

Rochelle smirked again. 'I told him my secret and he told me his.'

'For all the good it did you.'

'At least he told me stuff. He told you fuck all.'

Murch dug an elbow into Rochelle's knee. 'Knock it off,' he said.

'Tell her to knock it off.'

Cara stood up. She'd heard enough, more than enough. It was time to get out of the flat before she said or did something she'd regret. On the TV the cowboys were squaring up to each other, squint-eyed in the sun, hands poised over their holsters. She left before any more shots could be fired.

423

77

Cara hung her wet jacket on the hook in the hall, went through to the living room and said, 'Is there any of that whisky left?'

'That bad?' Lytton said.

'Bad enough.'

'It's in the cupboard, the one beside the sink.'

In the kitchen, Cara grabbed the bottle and a couple of glasses. Back in the living room she sat down at the table, poured herself a stiff drink and knocked it back in a single gulp. Then she poured two more, one for him and one for herself.

'You going to tell me what happened?'

Cara held up his glass and said: 'Only if you have one too. I don't feel like talking to sober people right now.'

Lytton got up off the sofa and joined her at the table. 'It didn't go too well with Terry Street, then?'

'Depends how you look at it. I gave him back the box and the gemstones, and he tried to give me ten grand. I told him to keep his bloody money.' Cara drank some more whisky, knowing it was going straight to her head. She didn't care. Drunk was what she wanted to be, the drunker the better. 'You know what he told me? That Jimmy was with my dad on the night he died, that the house that was broken into was Azarov's. That's where the alexandrites came from, not Hampstead.'

Lytton played with the glass, listening, not drinking anything.

'Jimmy was there when my dad fell, but he never had the guts to tell me. He cleared off and left him there on his own. I know he was dead but . . .' Cara shook her head. 'He took the box, though. He went through my dad's pockets and took the bloody box. How could he have done that? How could he even have been thinking of that after what had just happened? It's sickening.'

'I don't suppose he *was* thinking.'

'Now you're sounding like Murch. Oh, yes, he knew all about it. I've just been to see him. And Rochelle. They *both* knew.' Cara stopped and gave Lytton a searching look. 'Did you know too? Did Rochelle tell you?'

'Since when did Rochelle tell me anything? No, I didn't have a clue. I swear.'

'They thought it was okay to keep me in the dark, to keep their precious secret. If it hadn't been for Terry, I'd never have found out. Why aren't you drinking?'

Lytton lifted the glass to his mouth and took a small sip of whisky. 'At least you know the truth now.'

'Why would he have even told Rochelle?'

'Some people aren't good at keeping secrets. It's too much of a burden for them.'

'He'd already told Murch. Wasn't that enough? He didn't have to tell her too. Do you think he'd have ever confessed to me?' Cara was aware that Lytton couldn't give an answer to this – he'd barely known Jimmy – but she was talking to herself as much as him. 'I don't think he would. I think he'd have just kept quiet about it.'

'You should eat,' Lytton said. 'I could make pasta.'

Cara scowled at him. He had a habit of trying to save her from herself. Now he wanted to feed her, to line her stomach, to stop her from getting so drunk she'd spend the rest of the afternoon with her head down the toilet. 'I'm not hungry.'

'At least put something in that,' Lytton said, nodding towards her glass. He stood up, went into the kitchen and came back with a jug of water.

Cara slopped some into the whisky, but only because it would make it last longer, long enough she hoped for her to finally reach unconsciousness. What she craved was oblivion, a deep dreamless sleep where she didn't have to think about anything any more. In the meantime, all she had was reality. 'Still, it explains why he didn't want to go ahead with the Hampstead job. It was all a bit unnecessary, wasn't it, when he had thousands of pounds' worth of alexandrites stashed away?'

Lytton glanced towards the shelf and the book on gemstones. 'I wonder when he realised what he'd actually got.'

'God knows. But when he did ... well, he should have had the sense to keep his mouth shut. But that was Jimmy for you. He saw a chance to impress Terry Street and couldn't resist. If he hadn't been showing off, he'd still be alive today.'

'I suppose Terry realised the stones must have been the ones stolen from Azarov.'

'It wouldn't have taken a genius. They're rare, aren't they? It's not like there'd be hundreds of them knocking around London. I reckon Jimmy kept them here for a while, in my room. Then, when it all kicked off with Azarov, he had to find somewhere safer.'

Lytton lifted his glass, gazed into it and put it down again.

'Would you have gone away with Jimmy if he'd asked? I mean, if he'd turned up at the jail, told you he was in trouble and had to get out of London?'

'I'm not stupid,' she said. 'It would never have worked out.' But she knew she was only practising that familiar art of self-deception. She would have refused at first, dug her heels in, asked what he didn't understand about their relationship being over, but eventually he'd have worn her down. Eventually she'd have given in. One last chance, she'd have told herself, and then she was done.

Lytton gave a half smile, as if he believed her about as much as she believed herself.

That smile got under her skin. 'You're judging me.'

'No, I'm not. I promise.'

Cara narrowed her eyes. The whisky was starting to harden the edges of some thoughts and to blur the edges of others. 'You must have been in love at some point in your life. It's not simple or straightforward. It's not all hearts and flowers. There's the madness too, the fear of rejection, the hate and resentment, the longing for something that probably doesn't even exist.'

Perhaps there was a fierceness in her voice because he said with deliberate calmness: 'We've all been there. I'm not arguing with you.'

'You're not giving much away, either. You know half my life story and I hardly know anything about yours.'

'You've had the highlights. Believe me, it doesn't get any more interesting than that.'

Cara, seeing that he wasn't about to be drawn, tried a different tack. 'Tell me about Rochelle, then.'

'What's to tell? It's just the usual story of teenage angst.'

'So what's the plan? Wait around until she grows out of it? You could have a long wait.'

Lytton lifted his shoulders in a half shrug. 'I haven't really got as far as an actual plan.'

'How come you're always looking out for other people all the time? Maybe you're some kind of control freak.' Cara knew she was doing that transference thing, shifting the anger and frustration she felt towards Jimmy on to someone who didn't deserve it, but she couldn't stop herself. Her emotions were all churned up inside her like a volcano about to erupt. She wanted to prod and provoke, to try and break through his composure.

'Rochelle's my sister.'

'But I'm not. I'm not your anything. But you can't stop interfering in my business, either.'

Lytton gave her the kind of look that parents reserve for tiresome children. 'I'll try to stop doing that.'

'Do you have to be so bloody reasonable?'

'Do you have to be so bloody *un*reasonable?'

Cara was still thinking up a suitable retort to this when the phone starting ringing. Her first inclination was to ignore it, but then, thinking it could be Steadman, she decided she was just in the mood to tell him where to shove his endless questions. Quickly she snatched up the receiver.

'Yes?'

'It's Glen Douglas. I've just remembered.'

'Remembered what?'

'Where I know the name Lytton from.'

Cara pressed the phone against her ear. As she listened to what Douglas had to say, fear wrapped around her. Sweat prickled her forehead. She could feel her chest tightening as her heart began to thump.

78

Cara put the phone down. The shock had produced a degree of sobriety, as if a bucket of cold water had been thrown over her. But it had paralysed her too. Her instinct was to jump up and get away from Lytton, to put some distance between them, but her body felt frozen. It was like one of those bad dreams where she wanted to run but her legs were heavy as lead and her feet rooted to the ground. She sat in the chair and couldn't move.

'Shall I come round?' Douglas had said.

'No, don't do that. I'll deal with it.'

Cara's gaze slid over to Lytton. Suddenly her face was burning hot, her hands clammy. She didn't seem to be doing much dealing. She wasn't even sure if she could speak. Tentatively she cleared her throat. It had to be done. She had to do it now. Her voice was hoarse and trembling. 'When were you going to tell me?'

She saw Lytton's face change, like a shadow had passed over it, but almost instantly his expression regained its usual composure. 'Tell you what?'

Cara had to force the words out of her mouth. She had no way of knowing how he'd react, if he'd lash out or worse, and she tried to brace herself. 'That you're Fiona Myers's son.'

'Ah.'

Cara stared at him, wide-eyed and incredulous. 'Ah? Is this all you've got to say?'

'What would you like me to say? There doesn't seem much point in denying it.' Lytton put his elbows on the table, briefly raised his hands to his face and sighed. 'Yes, I'm her son.'

'Jesus,' Cara said. 'That's why you're really here, isn't it? To find out if I killed your father.' Her mind, despite her whisky-addled brain cells, was working quickly now, putting the pieces together. 'All that stuff about Rochelle was just a blind so I wouldn't realise what you were actually up to. The two of you started with Jimmy and then when that didn't get you anywhere you decided to hang around until I came out of jail. What did you think I was going to do? Fall on my knees and confess?'

'Strictly speaking, Gerald was my stepfather, but that's neither here nor there. And I never thought that you killed him, only that you might have known who did.'

'Well, I didn't. I didn't see a damn thing that night. So it's all been a waste of time for you and your slutty sister.'

Lytton's face hardened. 'Don't talk about her like that.'

'Why not? It's the truth. She wasn't exactly slow in jumping into bed with Jimmy. After some useful pillow talk, was she?'

'It wasn't like that.'

'So what was it like?'

Lytton took a while to answer, as if he was inwardly debating how much to tell her. 'Look, I'm not denying that she came to the Mansfield to find Jimmy. She was convinced that he knew something, that *you* knew something. But that isn't why she stayed. She grew to like him, love him even. She reckoned he understood her. Her father was murdered, Cara, shot dead in his own home. That's a bloody awful thing. Her head was all over the place. You know how it feels to lose your dad.'

'Don't bring my dad into this.'

'Why not? Tell me you wouldn't have done exactly the same thing if it had been the other way round? You'd have done anything you could to find out the truth, played as dirty as you had to.'

Cara reached for her glass, and although she knew she should be trying to keep a clear head, she still took a gulp of whisky. 'You've lied from the moment I met you.'

'And you've been completely honest? Come on, we've both been economical with the truth.'

Cara could hardly deny this, but his lies still felt worse than hers. Her courage had returned now, and the fear was subsiding. Lytton wasn't a threat, at least not in any physical sense. But he might be a danger in another way. An ugly thought occurred to her. 'Have you been working with the law?'

'What? No, shit, of course not.'

'But Steadman's been here. He's talked to you. Why didn't he realise who you were?'

'Because we've never met before. On the night Gerald was shot, I was with Rochelle at my flat. By the time we heard about what had happened and got over to Hampstead, Steadman had already left. Some PC took a statement from us both and that was it. We weren't under suspicion and so no one ever spoke to us again.'

'No, Steadman was too busy putting the thumbscrews on me.'

'Unsurprisingly. You *were* found with the body.'

'He never believed I'd had nothing to do with it.' Cara paused, wanting to reach for the whisky again but forcing herself to resist. 'Just like you.'

'I had no way of knowing, did I? Not for sure. Not back then. And once Rochelle took it into her head to come here, I couldn't leave her on her own.'

'She wasn't on her own, not for long. It didn't take her five minutes to get her claws into Jimmy.'

'Takes two to tango,' Lytton said.

Cara glared at him. 'Jimmy must have told her I was innocent.'

'He wasn't going to say anything else, was he? He was always going to protect you, no matter what.'

Cara felt tears spring into her eyes and quickly tried to blink them away. Thinking about Jimmy was too hard, too painful. 'Douglas said Lytton was your real dad's surname. I'm surprised Steadman didn't make the connection.'

'I don't suppose he was ever interested in the distant past. My father died a long time ago. Why would he be bothered about my mother's first husband?'

'And what about Rochelle? Is that her real name?'

'Amanda,' he said.

'Amanda,' she repeated, finding it hard to match the name to the girl. 'She told Jimmy who she really was, didn't she?'

Lytton shook his head. 'She'd never have done that.'

'Well, Jimmy told her about what happened with my dad. One secret in exchange for another. That's what she said to me earlier, that he'd told her a secret and she'd told him one back.'

'No, she'd never have taken the risk. Jimmy wouldn't have been too pleased, would he? She'd have been out of the door before her feet touched the ground. She was probably just trying to wind you up.'

'She doesn't have to try to do that.' After a short silence Cara said: 'So have you come to a conclusion yet? Am I guilty or not guilty? What do you reckon? Or maybe you're still on the fence. That's why you stopped me from going yesterday, wasn't it? You were worried I'd just disappear, that you'd never get the answers you want.'

Lytton shook his head again. 'I came after you because I thought you were making a mistake. What's the point of going on the run if you don't need to?'

'What's so great about staying here? I could have been in Paris by now, miles away from you and your sister and Terry Street and any other bastard who wants to make my life a misery.'

'And always looking over your shoulder, wondering when your enemies are going to catch up with you.'

'I'd take the trade,' she said. 'Anything's better than sitting here listening to a grade A liar.'

'Don't get all holier-than-thou, Cara. You're hardly an angel yourself.'

Cara stared at his face, wondering how she'd ever come to trust him. He was like a stranger to her now, someone she didn't know at all. 'At least I'm not . . .'

But she didn't get the chance to finish the insult. The bell went, two long rings, closely followed by a hammering on the door. Steadman, she thought, as she reluctantly got to her feet. Cops never did have any patience.

79

But it wasn't the inspector. Cara opened the door to find Murch and Rochelle on her doorstep. The girl, dressed now, didn't wait to be invited in, but just pushed past like some red-haired fury with a fire up her arse, leaving in her wake the combined aromas of cannabis, booze and perfume.

'Sorry,' Murch said. 'I couldn't stop her. She wanted to talk to Will.'

Rochelle stormed into the living room, took in the scene – the table, the bottle of whisky, the two glasses – and stared daggers at Lytton. 'This is cosy. Been having a heart to heart, have you?'

'A drink,' Lytton said coolly. 'But not as much as you, from the looks of it. What are you doing here?'

'You see?' Rochelle said, turning to Murch. 'I told you. They're up to something. Plotting, that's what they're doing.'

'They're just having a few bevvies, babe. What's wrong with that? Don't be so bleedin' paranoid.'

The colour was high in Rochelle's face. 'Don't call me paranoid,' she screeched. 'Who the fuck do you think you are?'

Lytton stood up. 'For God's sake, calm down. What's wrong? Why are you so upset?'

'Why do you think? *Her*. You and that tart. Don't think I don't know what's going on. You've told her, haven't you?'

'Everything,' Cara said, coming in from the hall. 'I know everything, the whole bloody lot. The cat's out of the bag, Rochelle ... or should that be *Amanda*?'

At the mention of her real name, Rochelle blanched. The shock pulled her up short. She flinched, placing a hand on her stomach, as if she'd been punched. 'You bastard!' she hissed at Lytton. 'You swore. You said you'd never—'

'I didn't. She found out. Don't go off on one, all right? It's not a problem.'

But Rochelle wasn't listening to him. Her legs seemed to be giving way beneath her. She staggered to the sofa and slumped down. For a moment her eyes flashed with anger, but then the fire went out. Her face crumpled. 'He deserved it,' she said. 'He only got what was coming to him.'

'Shut up,' Lytton said. 'Just stop talking, for Christ's sake.'

'Why should I? What does it matter now? He's dead and I killed him.'

At first Cara thought Rochelle was talking about Jimmy, but that hardly squared with what Terry had told her. Or the girl's alleged love for him. No, Kuzmin had murdered Jimmy. She glanced at Murch, who seemed as much in the dark as she was.

'You didn't kill anyone,' Lytton insisted. 'Nobody's saying that.'

Nobody except Rochelle, Cara thought. 'What does she mean? Who did she kill?'

Lytton's voice rose, his usually calm demeanour splintering before her very eyes. 'She doesn't mean anything. Don't listen to her. She's pissed, stoned, off her head.'

Cara glanced from him to Rochelle, the truth gradually dawning. The girl's face was pale now, her upper lip drawn back to reveal a row of small white teeth. Her jaw was set, her freckled hands clenched. She had the look of a cornered animal.

'She's not in her right mind,' Lytton persisted.

But it was too late for his protestations, too late for a cover-up. Like a bloated corpse the truth had finally bobbed to the surface. 'Gerald Myers,' Cara whispered. 'Her father. She killed him, didn't she?'

80

Cara knew that things must have been said, further words exchanged, but she had no memory of them. Her own announcement was the last thing she clearly recalled before there was a gap in time during which she was only faintly aware of other voices, of movement, and of walking over to the chair and sitting down again. She had that odd, disconnected feeling like she'd had in the Fox, as if she was watching herself from a distance. It was the shock, of course, the shock of finding out who had really killed Gerald Myers. Even now it hadn't quite sunk in.

Lytton was telling Murch to take Rochelle back to Temple and she was leaving without protest, rising from the sofa like an obedient child. He walked them to the door, making reassuring noises, saying that he'd be over soon, not to worry, everything would be all right. There was an authority in his voice that Cara hadn't heard before.

When Lytton came back into the living room his expression

was grim. He sat down at the table, reached for the bottle, and poured an inch of whisky into his glass. Only then did he speak to her. 'You have no idea what that man was like.'

'Start from the beginning,' Cara said.

Lytton stared into his glass for a while, as if trying to decide where the beginning was. Or perhaps he was just collecting his thoughts. 'Rochelle . . . Amanda . . . was born a year after my mother married Gerald. By then he'd already packed me off to boarding school. He did it under the pretext of giving me a "good education", but the truth was he just couldn't stand having another bloke's child living under his roof.'

Cara nodded, watching him closely. His face was taut, his shoulders hunched. He looked like a man who'd been carrying a heavy burden for a long time and was simultaneously afraid and relieved to finally be getting rid of it.

'He was a bully, a controller, but clever too. In public he was never less than charming, the perfect husband, the perfect father, but it was different behind closed doors. He wasn't physically violent – he was too smart for that – but he chipped away at my mother's confidence, making her question herself as a wife, a mother, until all that was left was an empty shell. Gradually he scraped all the joy out of her. I was only a kid, and I wasn't there much, but I could still see the changes in her every time I went home.'

Lytton paused, his brow furrowing. 'Anyway, to get to the point, Amanda showed up on my doorstep about eighteen months ago saying she'd had a row with Gerald and asking if she could stay. That was at my flat in Swiss Cottage. She wouldn't tell me exactly why they'd fallen out, but I got the idea it was the usual teenage stuff: drinking, smoking, mixing with the wrong crowd. To be honest, I didn't know my sister that well – I hadn't spent much time with her – but I wasn't

438

about to turn her away. I presumed that whatever it was would all blow over once everyone had calmed down.'

Lytton stopped again. His hands curled around the glass. He glanced at Cara but then focused back down on the table, as if it was easier to talk to that inanimate square of wood than directly to her. She heard him take a deep breath. 'Amanda wanted to pick up some things from Hampstead. This was a few days later. She didn't want to go when Gerald and Mum were around, didn't want another row, and so we settled on an evening when we knew they'd both be out. I drove past the house, made sure there weren't any lights on and found a parking space down the road.'

Cara lifted her glass to her mouth and took a swig of whisky. She had the feeling she was going to need it. She could see where all this was going and wanted to urge him on, to get it over and done with, but knew she had to let him tell it in his own time.

'She was inside for . . . I'm not sure exactly, but it wasn't more than ten or fifteen minutes. When she got back, when she got into the car, she was shaking. It was dark and I didn't see the blood on her at first. She started to garble all this stuff about Gerald, weird stuff, half sentences, nothing that made any sense. She was crying and I couldn't understand what she was going on about. It took a while before . . . before something clicked and I finally realised what she was trying to tell me.'

Lytton took another breath, let it slip from his mouth in a sigh. 'It was all jumbled up, but then it got clearer, some of it at least: what Gerald had done to her when she was a kid, what he'd made her do, how he'd said it was their secret and if she ever told anyone she wouldn't be believed. He told her she'd be sent away and locked up in a home for bad girls who lied.'

'Jesus,' Cara said, because she didn't know what else to say. It was all too big, too monstrous, to process properly. She had to let it sink in slowly.

'And then she just came out with it. "I killed him," she said. "I put a bullet in his chest."'

A silence fell over the room.

When Lytton started talking again his voice was a dull monotone, as if the only way he could continue was to block out the emotion and keep it matter of fact. 'She was in the study, going through his desk looking for her passport when she found the gun. Then suddenly Gerald was there, standing at the door. I wonder now if he knew she'd be coming, that he guessed she'd choose a time when she thought they'd both be out. She was alone with him and she was scared. She pointed the gun and said she wanted her passport. He said it was in the safe. She told him to open it, and he did. What happened next? I'm not sure if even Amanda knows. There was some taunting, mocking, threats. He knew all the right buttons to push. He'd had years of practice. Maybe he lunged at her, maybe he just said the wrong thing, but she pulled the trigger and that was that.'

'You went into the house to check,' Cara said, understanding now who it was she had heard that night.

Lytton nodded. 'I told her to stay in the car. I thought he might not be dead, that she'd only wounded him, but as soon as I got there, I could see that he was gone. I know what I should have done then – called the cops, waited with Amanda, reassured her that all she had to do was tell the truth and everything would be all right. But I didn't do any of that. I didn't do it because I didn't believe that everything would be all right. I saw how she could easily go down for murder. Who could back up her story about what he'd done to her in the past? Nobody. And even if the police did believe it, they still wouldn't see it as justification for what she'd done.'

'The law are hardly renowned for their sensitivity,' Cara said. 'You panicked. That's understandable.'

'I decided I could make it look like a robbery. The safe was already open so I went to the kitchen, found a sturdy carrier bag, went back and piled as much as I could into it. The gun was lying on the floor, and I took that too. Then I thought about Mum coming home and finding Gerald's body. I couldn't do that to her, so I made a 999 call from the study, muffling my voice. Then I cleared out of there as fast as I could.'

'I heard the phone ting as you put it down.'

'You must have got there shortly after me,' Lytton said. 'You were quiet. I didn't hear you.'

Cara shrugged. She could have made a quip about it being her job *not* to be heard, but this wasn't the time for wisecracks. Instead, she said, 'You had other things on your mind.'

'I drove Amanda back to my place, got her in the shower and put all her clothes in the washing machine. There was a girl who lived across the landing from me. She was away on holiday, but we had spare keys to each other's flats. I dumped the bag there, in the back of her wardrobe. Then I made Amanda get dressed and gave her a brandy. I think she'd gone into deep shock by that point. I went over the story again and again with her, how we'd stayed in all night, how I'd been working and she'd been listening to music. I wasn't sure how much, if anything, she was taking in.'

Lytton's glass was empty. Cara picked up the bottle and poured him another. He made a vague movement with his hand that could have meant he didn't want any more or that he was grateful for the top up. 'Go on,' she said.

'The longer we waited, the worse it got. I realised it had been a mistake to call from the house, to call at all, probably. I mean, what kind of murderer tips off the cops after he's pulled the trigger? That was going to set alarm bells ringing. By the time the police turned up, I pretty much thought we'd be top of the list of suspects.'

'But you weren't,' Cara said. 'Far from it. So far as Steadman was concerned, he'd already got the guilty party – or at least one of them – safely behind bars. You were in the clear.'

'Yes,' Lytton said. 'That came as something of a surprise.'

'And I don't suppose anyone was suspicious of how Amanda was behaving, either. Why wouldn't she be in a state after her father had been murdered? Yes, I must have been the answer to all your prayers. Steadman was so convinced of my guilt he didn't bother looking anywhere else.' Cara stared at Lytton, her eyes fixed on his. 'Just out of interest, what would you have done if he had managed to pin an accessory to murder charge on me? Or a perverting the course of justice charge, or anything else that would have earned me another ten years in the slammer?'

Lytton must have heard the coolness in her tone because he withdrew a little, leaning back in his chair. 'I wouldn't have let that happen.'

'And how would you have stopped it? You weren't about to throw Amanda to the wolves.'

'I'd have thought of something.' Lytton took another drink while he tried to think of what that something might be. 'Anyway, it didn't come to that. I knew it wouldn't. Steadman was never going to get the evidence he needed because it didn't exist.' Then, perhaps a touch defensively, he added: 'Don't ask me to feel guilty for the time you spent inside. You *did* break in. That wasn't my fault.'

'I'm not saying it was. I'd have served a damn sight less time, though, if there hadn't been a body in the study.'

There wasn't much Lytton could say to that and so he didn't even try.

81

Cara drank for a while, gazed at the ceiling for a while. Mulled things over. Then eventually she said: 'I still don't understand why Amanda came to Kellston. Why bother if you were both in the clear?'

'She had this idea, even after you were convicted, that you were playing some sort of game, that you'd seen one of us in the house, or both, and that one day you'd tell. I'm not claiming it makes any sense – it doesn't – but her head was all over the place. She wasn't eating, wasn't sleeping. She started hanging around the estate, got in with some local girls and it wasn't long before she heard about Jimmy.'

'And not long before she and Jimmy were ...' Cara stopped, hearing the bitterness in her own voice, and not liking it. 'You must have been worried about that, worried that she'd let something slip.'

'Why do you think I came here? And when she wouldn't come home, I decided the best thing was to move here too.' Lytton leaned forward and stared at her intently. 'Look, Amanda won't last five minutes if you go to the police.'

'Why the hell would I do that?'

'To clear your name. To get Steadman off your back.'

'So why tell me all this, then?'

'Because it's better you know the full story. That man abused her for years. I know you don't like her much, but the person she is is the person he made her.'

Cara sighed. 'I get that. And I'm not about to go running to the law. Does your mother know what happened?'

'Which part of it?'

'Any. All.'

Frown lines appeared on Lytton's forehead. 'Somewhere, perhaps, in the back of her mind. A little niggling suspicion. Nothing she wants to examine too closely. She and Amanda never had much of a bond; Gerald made sure of that.'

Cara remembered Fiona Myers sitting in the courtroom, her upright pose and steely gaze. 'You didn't come to the trial.'

'No.'

'Your mother thought I was guilty. At least she thought I knew who'd killed her husband.'

'It was what she wanted to believe. Better a stranger than someone closer to home.'

Cara nodded. 'You were lucky none of the neighbours saw your car or heard the shot.'

'All those houses are detached, set well apart from each other. Well, you already know that. Nice high walls or nice high hedges. The rich like their privacy. But what stops the riffraff from looking in also stops the residents from looking out. One of them did hear a noise but just thought it was a car backfiring.'

'What did you do with the gun?'

'Cleaned off the fingerprints and chucked it in the Thames.'

'And the rest of the stuff?'

'It's in a safety deposit box at the bank.'

Cara raised her eyebrows. 'You're a rich man, then.'

'Hardly. It's not as though I can do anything with it. Or even want to. I just couldn't think where else to put it. If I dumped it and it was found, then that was going to look pretty odd, maybe odd enough for the police to take another look at the case. What kind of burglar dumps his loot in the Thames? I figured I'd just hide it away until I could think of something better to do with it.'

'I take it your mother claimed on the insurance?'

'Yes.'

'So use it to get Amanda away from here. Go abroad. If she stays, she's going to self-destruct.'

'I can't sell it. The police will have circulated all the details.' Lytton's hands did a dance on the table. His mouth turned down at the corners. 'And anyway, I don't want anything to do with that bastard's money.'

'Perhaps you should be looking at it in a different way.'

'Meaning?'

'Meaning you can use that money to do some good, to get her a fresh start somewhere else. She deserves that, doesn't she? She's owed that much.'

Lytton thought about it, but then shook his head. 'It's impossible. The minute I try and sell anything, I'll end up getting arrested.'

'There are ways round that. Remember that fence I told you about, the one in Calais? I could call him, vouch for you. He'd take the stuff off your hands, no questions asked. You won't get the true value, nothing like, but it'll be enough to keep you in suncream and tequila for the next few years.'

'Or confined to a cell for the next ten.'

'Maybe it's a risk worth taking.'

Lytton considered this. He was quiet for a while. 'But what about Murch? He knows now, doesn't he?'

'You don't have to worry about him. He won't say anything. He can't stand the law.'

Silence fell again. The rain pattered against the window. A distant gull glided across the sky, a white dot on the horizon.

'You could come with us,' Lytton said softly. 'Why not? There's nothing to keep you here.'

There was one of those moments where their eyes met, and Cara was almost tempted. She felt a bond, a connection to this man that might one day be worth exploring. But she wasn't ready to take the leap yet. She shook her head and said, 'That's just the whisky talking.'

EPILOGUE

Six months later

It was a warm May afternoon. Cara sat outside a café in Covent Garden, feeling the sun on her face as she watched the people go by. To say she was happy would be an overstatement, but the raw edges of her grief had softened into something almost bearable. She was coping. She was getting her life back together again. Gradually, she was coming to terms with everything that had happened. She looked across the table and said, 'The last time we met up was at Jimmy's funeral.'

Her mother drank her cappuccino and sighed. 'Yes, poor old Jimmy.'

Cara rolled her eyes, but said placidly: 'Come on. You didn't even like him.'

'That's not true. I *did* like him. I just didn't like him going out with you. He could be very charming when he put his mind to it. But he was too old for you, darling.'

'Dad was ten years older than you.'

'Exactly. And look how that turned out.'

Cara had not told her the true sequence of events that had led

449

to Jimmy's death, and never would. Some secrets were best kept safely hidden away. 'You must have loved Dad once.'

For a moment her mother looked wistful, her eyes filling with regret. 'The people we love most aren't always the people who are good for us.' Then, because it was not in her nature to be sentimental, she patted her hair, took another sip of coffee and quickly changed the subject. 'Whatever happened to that nice young man you were sharing a flat with?'

'He went away.'

'That's a shame.'

'You only met him for five minutes.'

'Well, he seemed like the reliable sort. Decent. Not the kind to go getting into trouble. You could do a lot worse.'

Cara smiled, wondering what she'd think if she knew the truth about Will Lytton. She reached out her hand and briefly placed it over her mother's. They were never going to have a perfect relationship, but life was too short to bear grudges. Anyway, you couldn't choose your family, you just had to make the best of what you'd got.

As Holly Abbott sashayed across the foyer of the West Berlin hotel, she checked out her reflection in the long mirrors and liked what she saw. A smart young woman with cash in her pocket and the world at her feet. This was a city she could relax in, a city where she could be herself. Nobody here cared if you were gay or straight or anything in between. Kellston was a distant memory. She had taken a chance and got away with it.

It had been an unexpected windfall. As Terry had left the Fox that Sunday, he had asked her to keep an eye on Cara's jacket. 'I've got to go, love. Make sure some tea leaf doesn't make off with it.' And because Holly had wanted to keep Terry sweet, she had gone over to the table to do exactly that. It was pure curiosity that had made her check out the lump under the jacket and discover the carrier bag. After a speedy glance round, she'd eased it open. Her eyes had popped. Money. Lots of it.

After several minutes when Cara still hadn't come back and Holly had been needed behind the bar, she'd made the decision to take the bag with her. If somebody did nick it, she'd be in big trouble with Terry. This way she could keep it safe until Cara put in an appearance. Except Cara hadn't. By the time Holly had cleared the queue of waiting customers there was still no sign of her, and when she'd checked the table, she'd found that the jacket had gone.

Holly had never intended to keep the money. It was only a matter of time, she'd been sure, before Cara or Terry Street came looking for it. But neither of them had. Not that day and not the day after or the day after that. Ten thousand quid and nobody seemed to care that it was missing. She could have found out where Cara lived, taken the bag round to her, but she hadn't. Some opportunities only came by once in a lifetime. She had liked Cara, but she liked money more. So, she had packed her bags, bought a plane ticket and said goodbye to Kellston for ever.

Terry Street didn't feel any guilt about letting Cara Kendall think that Kuzmin had murdered Jimmy. Shifting the blame was second nature to him. This way Boyle got away with it, everyone who mattered was happy and the status quo was re-established. Azarov might have lost one of his lackies, but he'd got his precious gemstones back and it didn't take a genius to know which one he valued more.

When Terry thought about Cara, which wasn't often, he mainly thought about that moment in the Fox when she had refused to take the money. But he'd known she'd change her mind. When it came to a battle between conscience and cash, there was only one side that was going to win out in the end. That was human nature, wasn't it? All he'd had to do was leave it for her and let temptation do the rest.

Larry Steadman got out of his car, leaned against the iron railing and gazed out to sea. When he sniffed the air, it smelled of salt instead of diesel, sharp and clean instead of foul. But it didn't make him feel any better. He could put a hundred miles between himself and Kellston but he couldn't escape what he'd done.

That night, the one before Cara got out of jail, still haunted his dreams. It was frustration that had led him to Jimmy Lovell's door, his determination to have one last try at prising the truth out of him about Hampstead. But he hadn't been Jimmy's only visitor that evening. Someone had got there first. Someone had given him a beating and he was still unsteady on his feet.

If Jimmy hadn't laughed in his face, hadn't goaded him about his obsession with Cara, he would never have lashed out. One punch was all it had taken. He could still hear that crack as Jimmy's head hit the side of the sink. Larry winced. He was not a murderer. He told himself this a hundred times a day. It was true that he shouldn't have lost his temper, but Jimmy, he was sure, would have died anyway from the injuries that had been inflicted on him.

Larry was almost certain that no one had seen him leave the flat. He'd taken every precaution, waited for over an hour and slipped out as softly as a cat. But nothing was ever a hundred per cent. It was the only time he'd ever been grateful for the tight-lipped non-cooperation of the Mansfield residents. If anyone had noticed anything they'd kept their mouths shut about it.

His decision to transfer again had been an easy one. It had

been something to do with that final interview, with the way Cara had looked at him – as if she knew something, as if she suspected – that had made him realise he'd have to let go before everything collapsed in on him. He could have a fresh start here in this seaside town. He could concentrate on his marriage and watch his children grow. No one need ever find out what had happened. All he had to fear was his own guilty conscience.

After her mother had left, Cara ordered another cappuccino. She was so busy these days she rarely had time to relax. Although she had not entirely ceased to be at war with the world, she was currently confining her efforts to the realms of the fraudulent and the unfaithful. It had been a surprise when Glen Douglas had offered her a job – office duties and the chance to train up as his assistant so long as she promised that her cat-burgling days were over.

Glen was teaching her the ropes: how to stay out of sight, how to take decent photographs, but above all the art of patience. She was still working on the latter. Patience didn't come naturally to her. That he trusted her, however, meant a lot, and she was determined not to betray that trust.

She was not the only new member of the business. It had been a shock when she'd walked into the office to find Ray Tierney there. She had thought at first that he was following in DI Steadman's footsteps, intending only to hassle and harass her, but it had turned out he was looking for new horizons too. Now there were adverts for the business in the local papers and the phone rang with ever-increasing frequency. She was not sure what had prompted Glen to forego his solitary status – perhaps he had just grown tired of his own company – but for her it had been a godsend.

Sometimes she wondered about the money she'd told Terry

Street to keep. Ten thousand pounds was no mean amount. Was she sorry? No, it would have been like making a deal with the devil. Occasionally she would see him in the Fox and their eyes would meet and he would give her a nod. She had never spoken to him since that Sunday and, with luck, would never need to do so again.

Cara found it faintly amusing that her limited circle of friends now consisted of a private detective, an ex-cop and an old lady. Alma Todd talked about the past, about the old East End and what it had been like. She talked about Jimmy too. Once she had said that she'd seen a man leave the building on the night of his death, a man acting furtively, a man who had hurried away as if he had something to hide. Alma had mentioned it to the law but didn't think they had taken her seriously. Cara had told her not to worry, that she'd heard that the man who'd killed Jimmy was dead now too.

Sometimes, even after all these months, Cara would walk into the flat expecting Will Lytton to be there. He sent her postcards, from Italy, from Portugal, the latest from New York. She lined them up on the shelf in front of the books. They were like soft whispers from across the ocean, like delicate threads still connecting the two of them.

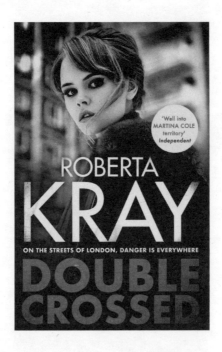

Double Crossed: gripping, gritty and unputdownable –
no one knows crime like Kray

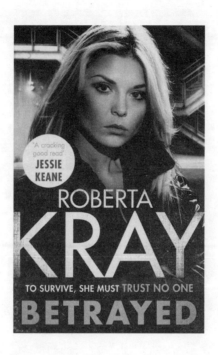

'Action, intrigue and a character-driven plot . . . sure to please any crime fiction fans' *Woman*